The Christmas Eve Promise

Book 4

A Time Travel Romance Novel by

Elyse Douglas

COPYRIGHT

ISBN: 9798671702989

BROADBACK BOOKS USA

"Whatever our souls are made of,
his and mine are the same."
—Emily Bronte

"The past is not history, but a much vaster region of the
dead, gone, unknowable, or forgotten."
—Joseph Ellis

"All journeys have secret destinations of which the
traveler is unaware."
—Martin Buber

To our readers. Thank you for time traveling with us.

The Christmas Eve Letter - Book 1

The Christmas Eve Daughter - Book 2

The Christmas Eve Secret - Book 3

The Christmas Eve Promise - Book 4

THE CHRISTMAS
EVE PROMISE

CHAPTER 1
Christmas Eve 2019

"What should we toast to?" Patrick asked.

Eve gave him a measured look, one calculated to challenge. With her lips parted and head tilted to one side, it was part flirtatious and part undecided. They stood in their New York City brownstone apartment before the gleaming fireplace, champagne flutes filled, raised and about to touch.

Eve's right arm was in a blue support arm sling, the result of a gunshot wound from her time travel journey to 1884 New York.

Colleen lay in her crib nearby, asleep, cozy under a quilt. Near the bay windows, a magnificent eight-foot Christmas tree stood in glorious splendor, adorned with colored lights and Victorian ornaments. Bing Crosby sang *White Christmas* and, as if ordered from Hollywood, snow drifted by the windows. It was the perfect Christmas card scene.

Patrick lifted an eyebrow. "I'm not sure I trust that look, Eve. There's some mischief behind it, I think."

Eve grinned, still in love with his bit-of-an-Irish accent. "Well, of course there's mischief behind it, Detective Sergeant Patrick Gantly," she said, calling him by the name she'd called him during her first time travel journey to 1885. "What fun would it be without mischief? You'd get bored with me, steal the time travel lantern and send yourself back to 1885."

Patrick frowned. "Don't even joke about that. I'd no more send myself back into the past than I'd try to fly out that window. We're finished with the lantern."

Eve reached a finger and touched his lips. "Yes, my darling, we're finished with the lantern... But, then again, it did bring us together, didn't it? If I hadn't time traveled to 1885, I never would have met you, we wouldn't have Colleen and, may I say it and risk being gauche? We wouldn't have almost two million dollars in the bank."

Patrick stayed silent.

"So it's been a good thing, hasn't it?" Eve said. "I mean, for the most part."

Patrick grew thoughtful. "Yes, Eve, like most things in life, it's been a good thing and a bad thing. It nearly separated us for all eternity."

Eve touched his thick, curly, black hair, staring into his steady blue eyes. She never grew tired of looking at him: the broad chest, muscular neck and wide shoulders.

"What is it, Patrick? Why the long face?"

"I'm thinking of our little baby son, Eve. The son you were carrying. The baby that the lantern took from us when we tossed the cursed thing into the Hudson River and everything in our lives was suddenly wiped clean. If you hadn't time traveled back to 1884 and found me... Well, where would we be today?"

Eve lowered her gaze. "... I think about that too. Yes, I'm sad we lost our baby, but we have Colleen, and I'm sure that someday we'll have another baby boy. For now, Colleen is a blessing and a wonderful Christmas gift."

Eve smiled, tenderly. "It's Christmas Eve, Patrick, and we have a lot to be thankful for, so let's forget about the past and toast to our love, to Colleen and to the future."

Patrick nodded, his eyes clearing of past grief. "Yes, my love. You are right. We do have much to be thankful for." He glanced at his watch. "And our new dog will be here any minute."

They chimed a toast and sipped.

Eve held Patrick's gaze, his glass still poised. "Patrick, before the new puppy comes crashing into our lives, I want us to toast to something else."

"Now, there's that mischievous gleam in your eyes again, Mrs. Eve Gantly, even though we're not technically married after our last time travel journey."

"But we will be married in January... again."

"Indeed we will. Now what are we about to toast to? This is becoming a very long and drawn-out Christmas toast."

Eve worked to find the right words. "Okay, here it is. Do you believe in soulmates?"

"Soulmates?" he asked, testing the word. "Yes, you have used that word before. I know of it, but I haven't thought about it. I assume you are about to educate me?" He sighed, playfully. "Thus, the second Christmas toast must wait."

"I've done some research," Eve said. "The term 'soulmate' first appeared in the English language in

1822, in a letter written by the English poet, Samuel Taylor Coleridge."

"I haven't read much poetry, Eve."

"It doesn't matter. Anyway, some psychologists believe that it's an unrealistic expectation to think that a soulmate exists specifically for another person."

"What are your thoughts?" Patrick asked, shifting his feet. "And, can we step away from the fireplace? I feel like I'm being roasted as a Christmas goose."

Eve drifted over to check on Colleen, her mind at work. Patrick moved to the couch but didn't sit. He was intrigued by Eve's obvious interest in soulmates.

"So continue with your interesting discourse," Patrick said.

Eve turned to him. "According to an esoteric religious movement called Theosophy, God created androgynous souls—equally male and female. A little later, there were theories that the souls split into separate genders, perhaps because of karma. Anyway, over a number of reincarnations, each half soul seeks the other soul. And then, after all the karmic debts are purged, the two fuse back together as one. They are connected by a kind of invisible thread."

Patrick scratched his head and took another drink from his glass. "Eve, my love, I know nothing about soulmates, reincarnation or karma. I only believe in time travel because it has happened to me, against my will, I might add. But had it not happened to me, I would never, ever, under any circumstances, have believed in it. Maybe what you say is true, I don't know, but it seems rather airy, the stuff of dreams and fertile imaginations."

There was a long gap in the conversation as Eve wandered the room, finally returning to Patrick, who watched her with keen interest.

"Patrick... I met you because I time traveled. We have both time traveled back and forth several times. We could have easily lost each other or never found each other."

Patrick nodded.

"But we found each other every time. We fell in love at first sight, didn't we?"

He leaned and kissed her wet, champagne lips and felt the same electric charge he always felt when he kissed her. That first-time burst-of-love and desire for her.

"Yes, Eve. I fell in love with you at first sight as I followed you along the 1885 New York City streets. I fell in love with you when we were across the street from Zarcone's Tea & Coffee House and when you boldly walked up to me and said, 'Have you been following me?'"

Eve held up her glass and touched his. "Yes! And I fell head-over-heels in love with you—and it scared me how fast and how much I fell in love with you. But that love seemed timeless, didn't it? As if love had been just waiting for us to come together on that street corner in 1885? As if I'd known you before and you'd known me before. As if we were soulmates just waiting to come together again, to merge again. Didn't you feel that, Patrick? Don't you feel that now?"

Patrick narrowed his eyes on her. "You are quite the romantic, aren't you?"

"I wasn't a romantic before I met you. I was married to a man for a little over two years, and I never felt the love I felt for you that very first time I looked into your face."

Patrick kissed her again. "Yes, I'll admit it. You seemed remarkably familiar the first time I stared into your lovely eyes."

Eve smiled knowingly. "And that's what I propose in this toast."

She raised her glass to his. "I want both of us to promise that no matter what happens to us; no matter if we're separated; no matter what time or place we find ourselves in; no matter what obstacles we face, we will always find each other, help each other and love each other, for all time. Will you make this Christmas Eve promise, Patrick?"

He gave her a warm smile. "All right, Eve. Yes, I promise. But I pray to the saints in heaven that we are not separated. I've had enough of that."

They touched glasses.

Colleen cried out and a burst of wind rattled the windows, making the room suddenly chilly.

CHAPTER 2
One Year Later
December 16, 2020

Eve and Patrick stood by the front door to their apartment, Eve anxious to start her trip and Patrick uneasy to see her and Colleen go.

"Are we masked up?" Eve asked, touching her KN95 protective face mask.

"Check," Patrick said, tapping his.

"Do you have everything?" Patrick asked, clutching the black baby bag in one hand and gripping the handle of Eve's roller wheel suitcase in the other.

"I think so," Eve said. "Do you have the baby bag?"

Patrick held it up. "Right here."

He was proud that he'd found the new baby bag online; becoming a clever online shopper. It was encased in cloud-like waterproof nylon and featured a roomy interior with plenty of exterior pockets for diapers, wipes, bottles, a change of clothes and toys.

Colleen was tucked securely in Eve's arms, all bundled up for the winter day and wrapped in a pink blanket.

Eve looked around. "If I've left something, you can bring it when you come." Then she sighed. "I'm beyond thrilled that we're not stuck in this apartment like we were during the first months of the Covid-19 pandemic. What a nightmare."

"And, like I've said, a hundred times, I'm deliriously happy that you didn't come down with it, working as a nurse all those weeks."

"So let's get out of the City for a while and enjoy ourselves in a completely different environment. It's been a long year."

Outside, they climbed into the Uber SUV and started for the airport. As they traveled across West 125th Street, Patrick glanced over.

"I'll miss you."

She lowered her mask and smiled into his eyes. "Me too. It won't be long. Finish your exams and come as fast as you can." She grimaced. "Well, as fast as Amtrak can bring you."

Patrick lowered his mask as well. "I'm still a nineteenth-century man, Eve. I don't like being up in those things. It seems unnatural. I told you when we flew back from Canada that I would never ride in an airplane again. It scared the dickens out of me."

Eve flicked a hand. "Okay, whatever. I just wouldn't have the patience for it," she said, gently rocking Colleen, whose sleepy eyes fluttered open and then closed.

"That's the difference between nineteenth-century time and twenty-first century time, Eve. I don't think that twenty-six hours on a train is all that long."

"But that's if you don't break down someplace, and nobody gets sick, and you're not delayed by freight trains. Then it could be a lot longer."

"I'll be in no hurry. I'll catch up on my sleep. And anyway, I'll be riding the Silver Star. I think that sounds rather adventurous and romantic."

Eve gave a little laugh. "Okay, Mr. Gantly. I'll be in need of some of that Silver Star romance when you reach Florida."

She leaned toward him, lowering her voice to an intimate whisper. "Last night was sooo good. You're always surprising me, sir."

Patrick grinned. "And you can do things with those feet of yours that constantly amaze me."

Eve laughed again. "I took dancing lessons when I was a little girl, you know."

"No, really? Now that's something about you I didn't know."

"My dancing teacher called me Sugar Toes."

"Why Sugar Toes?"

"Because of Tim."

"Tim?"

"Yeah, Tim Carson was the only boy in class and he had a big crush on me. Sometimes during a dance, for no reason at all, he'd drop to the floor and start kissing my little pink ballet slippers."

Patrick laughed. "And what did you do while he was kissing your slippers?"

"I was trying to dance, of course, and it wasn't easy. Sometimes I had to kick him away. Mom said it was very funny. He even did it during one of our performances, and most of the audience thought it was part of the dance. At the end, Tim was singled out and he got a standing ovation."

"And what ever happened to Tim Carson?" Patrick asked.

"I don't know. We moved away a year later."

"You should look him up on *Facebook*," Patrick said. "I'll bet he's a pastry chef or…"

Eve cut him off. "… or a shoe salesman."

"Or a choreographer," Patrick added.

They kept the joke going for a time, while outside, the morning traffic was heavy and slow. The shops and stores were festively decorated for Christmas, and the sky was overcast with the promise of snow.

As they approached LaGuardia, Patrick stroked his daughter's head. "I'm going to miss you, little lass. Ask your mother why she wants to leave beautiful New York at Christmas time to travel to Ohio and then to that hot place, Florida."

Eve modulated her voice to sound like a little girl. "Because, Daddy, my Mommy's parents want to spend time with me. They've only seen me twice, and that was here, in New York. Like Mommy has told you, about fifty times, I've never met any of my Ohio relatives and they want to see me. That's why we're going there first. Then we're taking my grandfather's nice airplane and flying to Florida. I think it will be fun. I will like being hot for a change."

Just then, Colleen flashed a dimpled smile.

Like all parents, Eve and Patrick thought Colleen's smile was the cutest and the most unique smile anyone had ever seen.

Eve looked on with new love, her eyes bright with it. "Isn't she beautiful, Patrick? The most beautiful little beauty you've ever seen?"

"She is that, Eve. She is a little darling and our own little lass. And it's a good thing no one can hear us. They would think us sugary sweet and a bit over-the-moon."

Eve touched Colleen's nose with a finger. "And so we are over-the-moon, aren't we, Colleen?"

With their protective masks in place, Eve and Patrick walked to the security entrance. Patrick kissed Eve with his mask on her mask, then touched Colleen's forehead.

"Text me when you arrive in Cincinnati, Eve."

"Of course I will."

Patrick stood stiffly, his hands stuffed into his pockets. "I don't like being separated for these five days. Since we got back from 1884, we haven't been apart."

Eve exhaled a soft breath. "I know, but hey, everybody says that absence makes the heart grow fonder."

"Well everybody is a fool... Daft fools. Are you sure your father is good at piloting that airplane of his?"

Eve shook her head. "Patrick, stop worrying. I've told you a thousand times. Dad was in the Air Force before he joined the FBI. He's flown airplanes most of his life, since he was sixteen. I've flown with him at least ten times. It's an easy flight from Cincinnati to Atlanta. The plane will be refueled and then we'll fly to West Palm. It's a good plane and Dad's an excellent pilot. Okay? So relax. We've got to go."

She lifted on tiptoes and gave him a final kiss. "I love you. Get A's on all your tests, especially the one on Commitment Readiness. I'm not so convinced you're all that committed to our relationship and marriage," she said, with a playful wink.

Patrick placed his hands on his hips and grinned. "You, Mrs. Gantly, are still a mystery to be solved, and a woman to love… and I do… yes, I do love you. Go on now with Colleen, and go with God. I'll be in touch."

CHAPTER 3

Patrick spent the next two days studying for his exams and taking their dog, Colin, out for walks. Colin was similar to Eve's former dog, Georgy Boy, except that he was mostly springer spaniel, with black spots on his white coat, his paws, and the left side of his face.

Colin was a spirited dog, whose first love was sprinting after squirrels in Riverside Park, and whose second was splashing through any puddle he could find. He was fiercely protective of Colleen, sleeping close by her, and he was faithfully attached to Eve. Although he and Patrick were good buddies, he was Eve's dog, and that was fine with Patrick.

While Patrick studied on the living room couch, Colin paced the house from the front door to the bedroom waiting for her, his brown eyes searching, his ears pricked, his nose working.

"It's okay, Colin. Take a rest. She'll be back in a week or so. In the meantime, we're all going to have a vacation."

Dr. Simon Wallister, a doctor friend of Eve's and Patrick's, had agreed to take Colin in while they were away, promising to spoil him with doggy treats, romps in the country, long walks in Central Park, and gourmet dog food. It would be the first time Colin would be away from them since Patrick had gifted him to Eve on Christmas Eve, almost a year ago.

Though Patrick's train wasn't until the next evening, they'd agreed that Simon would pick Colin up late Friday afternoon, since he and his wife, Edith, were leaving that evening to spend the weekend at their house in upstate New York. He arrived just as Patrick was making coffee. As soon as he entered, Patrick handed him a mug.

Dr. Wallister had been a colleague and friend, first to Eve, and then to Patrick. After Eve and Patrick had returned from their time travel journey to 1884, Dr. Wallister had been instrumental in saving Eve's life and deflecting the police away from Patrick.

The couple hadn't fully explained their time travel adventures to Simon, even though he'd pressed them often. Simon knew they were involved in something bizarre. When Eve finally explained that her father was a special agent with the FBI, without embellishing, Simon had reluctantly stopped his many questions, assuming that, by association, they must have been involved in government work.

Simon Wallister entered the apartment wearing a mask, jeans, an old sweatshirt, a parka and sneakers. He was a fit, middle-aged man of average height, with short salt-and-pepper-hair, a military erect posture and alert, intelligent eyes. The black-rimmed glasses added to his professional bearing.

Colin swam his legs as he moved to the center of the room.

"Hey there, Colin. You and me are going to have fun while papa and momma are gone."

Simon slipped off his mask, sipped the hot coffee and grimaced. "Wow, Patrick. Your coffee is as strong as espresso. If I drink a cup of this stuff, I'll be able to run a mile in three minutes, forty-five seconds, and then I'll need to be hooked up to a ventilator."

"It's an old recipe," Patrick said, grinning. "My old Da liked his coffee as strong as his whiskey."

Simon saw Patrick's 28-inch suitcase parked by the front door. "So, you're all ready to go?"

"No... I just took the suitcase out to remind me to think about packing. I've never been to Florida."

"You'll like it. Palm trees, beautiful beaches, and the best sunsets. Don't forget to pack plenty of sunscreen."

"Eve did."

"Have you heard from her?"

"Yes. She's having fun showing off Colleen to all her Ohio friends and relatives. She said to thank you again for taking Colin."

Simon stooped to stroke Colin's head, and Colin lifted his nose, sniffed, then sneezed.

"He knows something's up," Simon said. "They always know. Animals have more brains and intuition than we give them credit for."

"Eve prepared a bag of Colin paraphernalia," Patrick said, gesturing toward a shopping bag filled with treats, dog food, an extra leash and one of his favorite blankets.

"Are you taking an Uber down to Penn Station tomorrow?"

"No, I'll just catch a yellow. I want to help keep those guys in business."

Patrick's phone "dinged" and he reached into his pocket and drew it out. He logged on and viewed the text. "It's from Eve. She's excited about flying to West Palm tomorrow. Says it's cold in Cincinnati." He glanced up, shaking his head. "I don't like those things."

"Which things?" Simon asked.

"Those flying things… airplanes."

"Obviously," Simon said. "Otherwise you'd fly to Florida and be there in three and a half hours. I could never take a slow train to Florida."

"At least I'll see some of the countryside," Patrick said. "It'll be educational."

A few hours after Simon had left with Colin, Patrick was propped up on the couch, watching the flickering flames in the fireplace, listening to country music. His last exam had been that afternoon, and for the first time in weeks, he had nothing to do. He didn't even have to take Colin for a late-night walk.

His phone rang. He was happy to see Eve's name appear.

"So how are my guys?" she asked.

"Good as gold. I'm on the couch, listening to Johnny Cash, and Colin is on his way to Kingston, New York with Simon and Edith. How are you and Colleen?"

"Colleen is the life of every party; she hardly cries. But she misses her father."

"And how do you know she misses her father?"

"She points in different directions and says 'Da-da oooohhh.'"

"And Da-da oooohhh translates as 'Where's Daddy?'"

16

"Of course. Don't you understand your own daughter's language? She does the same thing at home when you're not around. I know this girl, Patrick. She misses you, and I miss you."

"And so that makes four of us. But I'll board the train at seven tomorrow evening and be in Florida with you and Colleen before we know it. Are all of you still planning to fly out tomorrow morning?"

"Yes, at nine o'clock. I'll text you when we leave. Have you packed yet?" Eve asked.

"No. I'm sipping a Belgium ale, having just toasted myself for completing my last exam."

"And how did you do?"

"I think I did quite well. Let me ask you one of the questions and see which answer you give. Ready?"

"Yeah, ready, Professor Gantly. Let me have it."

"Okay, here goes. When in a new situation, you make a judgment by processing new information and comparing it to your experiences. What type of judgment are you most likely to make? Monotype? Reflexive? Stereotype? Or fundamental attribution error? Choose one."

"What the heck is fundamental attribution error?"

"No explanations, just choose one."

"Okay... I choose stereotype."

"Well, aren't you the smart one?"

"I had psych in college. And I've often thought about that one when I time traveled. But it didn't always work."

"I should write my term paper on your time travel psychology."

"Yeah, right. Your teacher would kick you out of his class."

"Her class," Patrick tossed back.

"Her?" Eve's voice grew suspicious. "Is she pretty?"

"Very… A full-figured, shapely brunette, rather like a nineteenth-century woman."

Eve's voice turned low and threatening. "And have you flirted with her? Has she flirted with you?"

"No and yes."

"Which is 'no' and which is 'yes'?"

"I have not flirted with her. She asked me to join her for a cup of coffee the other day."

"She what? That's unethical. What did you say?"

"I said, I don't drink coffee. How about a good Irish whiskey?"

Eve shouted. "You what!?"

Patrick yanked the phone from his ear, laughing. "Calm down. I was just teasing. It's a joke, Eve."

"So did she, or did she not, ask you out for coffee?"

"She did, and I politely thanked her for her kind invitation, adding, in my best gentlemanly voice, 'Madam, I am a married man with a daughter and a dog.'"

"What did she say?"

She shrugged and said, "Ditto that… except I have a son and a cat."

Eve's voice turned husky with anger. "That flirtatious bitc…"

Patrick cut in, "… Now Eve, be careful. Don't let Colleen hear you."

"She's in the other room, asleep."

"Mrs. Gantly, have no worries. I bowed to the good woman and said my goodbyes, thanking her once more for her invitation. My only fear now is that she'll fail me, for spite."

"If she does, she and I will have one of your good old-fashioned donnybrooks."

Patrick laughed. "I left her with a good old Irish verse…"

"Oh, no… Not one of those. What was it?"

"A successful marriage requires falling in love many times, but always with the same person."

Eve's voice softened. "Ahhh, aren't you the charmer, Mr. Gantly?"

"But let us not forget that handsome doctor who flirted with you and asked you to meet him in a quiet tavern, to sit in a shadowy corner."

"Yeah, and I told him if he didn't leave me alone, I'd sic Colin on him," Eve said.

Patrick laughed again. "Well, he has good taste, I must admit that. Didn't he say you were the prettiest nurse he'd ever met?"

"Patrick, how did you leave it with your professor?" she asked, ignoring his last comment.

"Professor Carol Blakely gave me a bit of a smirk, and then she left me standing in the hallway next to a poster entitled *Signs You Need a Mental Health Day*."

"Get on that train and hurry back to me, Patrick. I miss you."

"And you have a good flight. Tell your father to drive carefully."

That night, Patrick slept fitfully, visions of the past sliding in and out of his mind. He saw images of dark, rain-washed, cobblestone streets under amber lamplight, revealing shadowy figures with top hats and sneering faces turning toward him. He heard the echo of children playing, a train rumbling by and the whine of a violin.

He saw himself wandering a fog-heavy street as if searching for someone. He heard Eve's voice in the distance, calling his name in a pleading voice. Alarmed, he responded, but he couldn't tell from which direction she was calling or if she could hear him.

Patrick jerked awake, damp with sweat. Morning light leaked in from beneath the bedroom curtains. He sat up, his eyes sleepy, his heart racing. Blinking, he tried to erase the urgent, unpleasant dream.

Looking to his right, at the empty space where Eve slept, he felt a chill. Although he tried to dismiss it, worry pushed its way through, gnawing at his gut. One of the joys of his life was waking up with Eve, seeing her sleepy face, watching her yawn and reach for him. Was he excessively attached to her? Yes, and he would make no excuse for it. Eve was the love of his life. The only and forever love of his life and he didn't like them being separated.

Patrick glanced at the clock to see it was after 9 a.m. He'd slept longer than usual, probably because Colin wasn't pawing at the door, whining.

CHAPTER 4

Eve sat behind her father in the backseat of the single engine, four-seat Bonanza, traveling at 142 knots, or about 160 mph, at six-thousand feet. She pulled Colleen close, staring anxiously out her window at the mass of gray and white clouds boiling around them.

Eve's mother, Kay, was noticeably nervous, shooting worried glances to her husband. "Why is it so bumpy up here today, Chet? You said it would be smooth."

Eve's father, Chester Sharland, switched the computer screen to check weather and air traffic. "I don't know. It looks like microbursts."

Eve leaned forward. "What's that?"

"Short-lived downdrafts, after storms. They can create wind shear. Must be a storm nearby. We'll be out of it soon enough."

The airplane had a state-of-the-art glass panel and a Garmin G1000, an avionics device that makes flight information easier to scan and process. On the moving map screen, Chet saw red splotches crawling across it, indicating small bursts of storms.

Just then the airplane was punched by a fist of wind. The plane dipped and shook. Eve felt that pit-of-the-stomach sensation of freefall as the plane plunged and rose, straining against the updrafts and downdrafts.

Colleen started to cry.

Eve caught her breath and yelled. "Maybe we should land somewhere, Dad? It's really scary up here."

Another wall of wind struck the plane so hard it jarred Eve's eyeballs. The engine sputtered and coughed, while Chet wrestled with the controls.

Kay cursed, something she rarely did. "All right, Chet, I'm really scared. Find an airport and get us on the ground."

Chet's eyes jumped from the computer screen to outside, and back to the computer again. If he was scared, he didn't show it. His was a lean, angular face with sharp features and keen, steady eyes. He was not an impulsive man or a fearful one.

"It's okay," Chet said, reassuringly. "We'll be out of this soup in a minute. We probably just hit a small-scale column of air that was sinking toward the ground. Rain usually comes right after, but we'll fly out of it."

Eve stared out into the surging, gray sky as it lowered to meet them.

"Where are we, Dad?" Eve asked.

"About a hundred miles from Atlanta."

A sharp feeling of dread filled her gut, and she unrolled Colleen's tight fingers from their fists as she wailed. Eve held her close, gently rocking her.

"It's okay, Colleen. It's okay, baby. It's just the wind."

Chet eyed the control panel, his expression turning grim. "Damn."

"What?" Kay snapped, her eyes wide with fear.

"Looks like another squall is coming at us." He raised his voice. "Hang on, I'm going to try to fly around it."

Eve shut her eyes and saw Patrick's handsome and calm face. She whispered a little prayer, and then she said to herself, *No matter what happens, Patrick, you'll find me. I know you'll always find me.*

Since Patrick didn't have to leave for Penn Station until 5:30, he decided to do some last-minute Christmas shopping in midtown. He wanted to see the tree at Rockefeller Center one last time before he left New York, and he also planned to buy Eve a special Christmas present at Saks Fifth Avenue. If he had time afterwards, he'd stop by F.A.O. Schwarz to find a special stuffed animal for Colleen.

With his mask on, Patrick was roaming the lingerie section of Saks when he felt his phone vibrate. He retrieved it from his jean's pocket and glanced at the screen. He didn't recognize the number, so he let it go to voicemail.

Minutes later, Patrick was paying for a lemon-colored silk nightie when his phone vibrated again. It was the same unknown number, not on his contact list. He pondered, waited, and again he let it drop into voicemail.

He left Saks and walked through Rockefeller Center, staring for long minutes at the majestic Christmas tree, wishing Eve and Colleen were with him. He took his phone out to snap a selfie and grew curious as to who might have called him. Patrick found a seat on one of the concrete benches just north of the tree and dialed his voicemail. Holding the phone to his ear, he heard a weepy, frantic voice.

"Patrick, it's Denise, Eve's cousin from Ohio. Please call me. Call me when you get this."

Patrick's heart jolted. He listened to the next voicemail. Denise was crying, her voice cracking between the words, between the sobs.

"Patrick, call me… Call me… I've got to talk to you. Call me when you get this… please call me."

Patrick glanced up, his expression grim, eyes moving, blinking, hot fear shooting through his veins. People around him were taking photos, laughing and shouting to each other. He shot up, forgetting his gloves and his Saks package, searching for a quiet place to call Denise.

He darted into the lobby of 75 Rockefeller Plaza, the Art Deco building behind the tree. Frantic to get away from the tourists and office workers, he moved his way quickly to a less crowded hallway. Leaning a shoulder against a wall, his breath staggered, he pulled down his mask so he could breathe, touched the number and brought the phone to his ear. It rang twice before Denise's shaky voice answered.

"It's Patrick, Denise. What's happened?"

"Oh, God, Patrick… I'm so devastated. It's about Eve and Colleen…"

"What's happened to Eve and Colleen," he asked sharply. "Tell me!"

Patrick steadied himself.

"Patrick… their plane went down in a storm. A little boy flying a kite saw it go down. He saw the plane crash to the ground."

Denise's words didn't translate. They were too unthinkable—too terrible. "Just tell me how they are. Where are they? What town? What hospital?"

Denise sobbed into the phone.

"Denise... Tell me!"

"Patrick... they're all dead. All of them. Dead."

Patrick dropped his phone and staggered. He bent over, as if he'd been punched in the gut. A knifing pain sent him to his knees, as tears stung his eyes.

Someone came to help, but Patrick couldn't lift his head. He couldn't think. He couldn't speak. He couldn't move.

"Should I call 911?" a concerned male voice said.

A woman said, "Has he had a heart attack?"

Still another voice. "A security guard's coming."

Patrick heard the guard say, "Sir, can you talk? Can you stand? Are you in any pain?"

Patrick tried to lift his head, but it was too heavy, his agony too great; the brutality of Denise's words too awful.

Patrick heard the guard call EMS. Struggling to speak, Patrick forced out some words. "No... I've got to go. I've got to..."

He felt the guard's hand under his arm, working to help him stand.

"Come on, buddy, let me help you to your feet. Can you get up? You've got to help me. You're a big man and..." the guard's voice died away as he braced himself for the lift.

Through blurring tears, Patrick managed to raise his head and speak. "Yes... Please help me up."

"Sir, have you been drinking?" the guard asked.

Patrick shook his head. "No... I've got to go."

"Go where? Is there someone you want me to call? Is that your phone over there?"

Patrick nodded. "Yes... my phone. I've got to go. No ambulance. No..."

With a straining effort, the guard finally boosted Patrick to his feet. He was shaky, but standing, his vision returning, his pulse racing. He saw somber faces looking back at him. The guard handed Patrick his phone, but Patrick stared at it as if it were an enemy. Finally, he accepted it.

A cop approached. "Are you sick, sir?"

"I called EMS," the guard said to the cop.

"Cancel...," Patrick said, in a hoarse whisper. "Cancel it. I'm okay. I'm going home."

"Where is home, sir?" the young cop said, his eyes shifting, his hand resting on the butt of his 9mm holstered handgun.

"I'm okay. I'll be okay. I live here. In New York. I need to get home now," Patrick said, looking around for an exit sign, disoriented. "Where can I get a cab?"

The guard pointed. "Your best bet is on Fifty-First Street. Are you sure you can make it? I can go with you."

"Cancel the ambulance," Patrick said, his breathing heavy and staggered. "I'll go alone. I'm okay."

Concerned onlookers whispered speculation as they watched Patrick stagger down the hallway.

The cop looked at the guard and shook his head. "There's something bad wrong with that guy. From the looks of him, he'll drop dead before he gets home."

CHAPTER 5

Patrick sat slumped on the couch, alone in the dark, a glass of Irish whiskey in one hand, the half-drunk bottle on the floor beside him. He didn't know what time it was, and he didn't care.

His cell phone, on the couch beside him, had buzzed repeatedly, but he hadn't glanced at it or reached for it. Patrick hated it. At that moment, he hated all things modern: the cars, the noise, the bright lights, the relentless news cycle spewing out bad news 24/7, and the airplanes. He especially hated airplanes.

While he sat there drinking, feeling the sharp booze slide down his throat and warm his chest, he felt a brewing rage, a dark rebellion against all things twenty-first century. In his near-drunken state, he reached back to his time—to the nineteenth century. He was a nineteenth-century man, after all, and he'd never felt comfortable or synced to this time.

Often he'd had to work hard to adjust, seek balance and soldier on. Of course, loving Eve and Colleen had erased much of the strain and confusion; living with them had washed away most of the longing to return to his own time. But now that he had been emotionally stabbed and beaten by fate—punished by fate—he felt the pull to return, to vanish, to escape. He felt more himself; more a man who lived and breathed 1885 air.

So to hell with the miracle pills and the feel-good therapy and the New Age crap that spoke of healing and forgiveness. None of it was as good as a good old bottle of Irish whiskey, and it had been too long since he'd been drunk. Good and drunk, like a man ought to be when his guts have been kicked out.

He lifted the glass and took down the whiskey in one gulp, wincing, grinning, angry and cursing. On an impulse, he shot up and flung the glass into the dark fireplace. It exploded into shards.

Patrick stood there, shaking, empty and lost. He hardly recalled getting back home from Rockefeller Plaza. His agony was all consuming; battering him, bullying him. His thoughts had stalled and everything he saw or thought was a blur; out of focus and confused.

Standing in the living room, dulled and buzzed by the whiskey, Patrick knew he had to act or he would go out of his mind. He was already mostly out of his mind, and he had been ever since he'd heard Denise's voicemail. Something inside had snapped and broken, and he knew he'd never be the same. Without Eve and Colleen, he would never be the same. With them, he'd been saved. Without them, he was a dead man.

Patrick heard Eve's words in his head and he wanted to scream. "Things happen and then we get to deal with them, Patrick. That's just the way life is."

He dropped heavily onto the couch and put his head in his hands. A wave of despair engulfed him, and he teetered over and passed out.

In his dream, Patrick heard a hammering. It was a blacksmith, hammering a hot piece of iron, just inside a carriage house. Eve stood by, dressed in a maroon riding suit, holding the leather reins of a lovely chestnut horse. She was all smiles when she looked at him. They were separated by a three-rung wooden fence.

"It's a beautiful day for a ride, Patrick. Will you ride with me?"

And then she said something else, but Patrick couldn't hear her because that damned blacksmith kept hammering.

Patrick hitched a leg to climb over the fence, but the fence began to shake. It pitched him back. He tried again and again, but each time the fence shook and fought him.

"Come on, Patrick," Eve called, waving at him. "Hurry. It's going to rain. See the clouds over there?"

Still, the blacksmith hammered.

Patrick reached out for Eve, but she pulled herself up and onto the horse and then galloped away without looking back.

Patrick shook awake, that damned hammering still in his ears.

"Patrick! Patrick. It's Simon. Patrick."

Dazed and blunted by the booze, Patrick sat up, his head pounding like Simon's fist pounding the door.

In his inner mind, Patrick watched in misery as Eve rode off into the misty distance toward those low-hanging, dark clouds.

"Patrick!? Are you in there?"

Patrick's throat burned and screamed for water. "Yes..." he said, hoarsely. "Stop that infernal pounding!"

"Open the door, Patrick. It's Simon Wallister."

With effort and moans of complaint, Patrick pushed up and staggered to the door. He released the lock and opened the door a foot.

"What do you want?"

Simon studied him, and then he spoke quietly. "Let me in, Patrick."

"Go away."

"Patrick. Please... Please let me in."

Patrick opened the door fully and backed away, his bloodshot eyes squinting into the hall light. Simon entered and closed the door behind him, finding the light switch. Patrick shielded his eyes and grimaced. "Damned light."

The two men were silent, only their breathing and a distant siren filling the space.

"What time is it?" Patrick asked.

"After eleven... night, if you haven't noticed."

"I'm thirsty," Patrick said, and then he wandered off toward the kitchen.

When Simon entered the kitchen, Patrick had tipped back a bottle of water and was drinking it down, the refrigerator door open, and the light spilling out from it.

Simon closed it and turned on the overhead light. "We're all worried about you," Simon said.

Patrick finished gulping down the water, refusing to look at him. Finally, he tossed the empty water bottle into the recycling can and wiped his mouth with the back of his hand.

"Worried about me?"

"Yes... You didn't answer your phone. Nobody knew where you were... what had happened to you."

Patrick inhaled and blew the air out in a huff. "Well, it doesn't really matter what happens to me now, Doctor. Without Eve and Colleen, I'm an intruder walking around in someone else's story. I have no life. I have no home and no reason to be in this place."

"I want you to come and stay with Edith and me. I think it's best if you get out of here for a while until you have time to..." His voice dropped.

"Until I have time to do what, Doctor? Time," Patrick said, spitting out the word. "I'm sick of that word. Time. Time mocks me." Patrick's voice grew louder. "Every TIME I turn around, time slaps me in the face and says, 'you silly, daft fool!' To hell with time!"

Simon let Patrick's voice fall away. When he spoke, Simon's was soft. "You need time to get over all this. I can prescribe some medication..."

"I don't want your cursed medication, Simon!" Patrick snapped. "I don't want anything this time has to offer. It's been nothing but a damnable curse, filled with confusion, doubt and loss. Don't let anyone tell you that traveling through time is a good and fun thing to do. My life has been as wild as the wind, and I have been a shadow searching for the light that gives me life. That light was Eve, and that light was Colleen, and now there is no light. Time, Doctor, has given love to me, and time has taken it all away. So I curse time."

Simon gave Patrick a quizzical look. "I don't understand what you're saying, Patrick. You don't look well."

Patrick laughed darkly. "Well? I have been drunk, Doctor, and I intend to stay drunk for the foreseeable future. No pills, no kind and soothing words, and no companionship. A date with my Irish whiskey girl is my only needed and wanted prescription, and she'll do just fine."

Simon pocketed his hands, hunching his shoulders. "Patrick... Eve's family couldn't reach you. There are legal issues... they've started planning a memorial service in Ohio."

Patrick exploded. "To hell with that! My Eve and Colleen are not dead! No, sir! They are not dead and they never shall be dead."

Simon was startled by Patrick's outburst. He took a step back, seeing the tears spring into Patrick's eyes.

Patrick turned away. "Go, Simon. Go away and leave me alone. I'm not fit company, nor do I want to be fit company."

Simon lowered his voice. "Patrick... please come with me. Edith and I came back into the City as soon as we heard the news. You shouldn't be alone now. It's the worst thing."

"The worst thing? No, I don't think so. No, I do not believe that my sorry, despicable state is the worst thing, Doctor. Not by a long shot."

"You know what I mean. Don't twist my words," Simon said, firmly. "You know how much I loved and admired Eve. I am hurting, too, Patrick. All of her friends and family are hurting. You're not the only one. It's a tragedy that affects all of us."

Patrick's shoulders sagged. He stared at nothing, his eyes unfocused as he breathed, lowering his head in defeat. When he spoke, his voice was calmer and resigned. "I'm sorry, Simon. Yes, I am sorry. I have been selfish... thoughtless. Of course you and they are suffering."

"It's an awful thing, Patrick. Just... awful. Edith and I, and many from the hospital, are going to the memorial service."

Patrick's eyes twitched. He tried to speak, failed, then tried again. "When is it?" he asked at a whisper, not lifting his head.

"Wednesday, the twenty-third... The family is concerned about you. They want you to attend... and they need your input right away. Please call them."

Patrick wiped his eyes, looking away. "They're good people. Fine and good people. Her parents were good to me... They welcomed me and helped me. I will call... I will..." and then Patrick's voice fell into a sigh.

"Come home with me, Patrick. Edith is waiting. She wants to see you. Friends and family should be together at times like these. We must support each other now."

Patrick raised his head, fixing his swollen and red-rimmed eyes on Simon. "Thank you... You are right, of course. I should call them. I should go to the memorial service. I should go with you."

Patrick didn't move. "But..." he continued. "I have to be alone now. I have to think. I have to... well, plan."

"Plan? Plan what, Patrick?"

Patrick slowly turned toward the bedroom—toward Eve's walk-in closet where the time travel lantern sat, locked away in a carpeted, three-and-a-half-foot safe, illuminated by an LED light. It was accessed by a six-digit PIN—Eve's mother's birthday. Patrick had written it down and tacked it to the wall inside his closet.

"Yes, Simon. I have to think, and I have to plan."

CHAPTER 6

O n Christmas Day, two days after Colleen's, Eve's and her parents' memorial service in Ohio, Patrick walked the streets of New York City in the quiet, early morning. He wandered through midtown and Times Square, eventually finding himself at the Central Park running track, a 1.58-mile loop around the Reservoir that provided magnificent panoramic views of the city's skyline.

He took in the skyscrapers—rising in the distance, reflecting the morning light from thousands of glass windows, and he whispered a prayer for Eve and Colleen. With all his heart, he prayed that at the moment of their deaths, their souls had been blessed and welcomed by the light of everlasting life.

A flock of birds flew out of the trees in a thunderous flapping of wings, and Patrick watched them sail over the water to the far side and disappear.

In the early afternoon, Patrick sat alone on a park bench in Riverside Park, not far from their apartment. The morning sun had fled, and the sky had turned overcast, with a chilly wind and a scattering of snow flurries.

Patrick tilted back his head and watched two squirrels in a game of chase, skittering along the branches of tall trees, leaping, clinging like acrobats. One false step and they'd plunge to the ground. But they didn't fall. They were skilled, fast, and daring.

He turned his collar up against the blowing wind, noticing that he was the only person in sight, sitting on a park bench as if it were a beautiful spring day.

A dog walker came into view, a tall woman, wearing a long winter coat, boots and a red ski hat. Her pet was one of those little waddling dogs, with fluffy white hair, a panting tongue and a springy step. To Patrick, he looked like a wobbling snowball.

As she was passing him, she glanced over. "Merry Christmas."

Patrick nodded. "Yes... Merry Christmas."

The woman paused, her dog sniffing at the air. Patrick thought she looked about his own age, somewhere in her thirties, and she was attractive, with a friendly face. She looked him over.

"So, are you escaping from the family for a while? I am."

Patrick lowered his eyes. "No..."

She lifted a hand, catching snowflakes. "We're getting a white Christmas. How nice. I can't remember the last time."

Patrick thought he should say something, so he nodded. "Yes, can't remember."

"You're sitting on my grandfather's bench."

Patrick sat up, gently startled. "Pardon me?"

"No… It's okay. It's just that we dedicated that bench to my grandfather. See the little bronze plaque on the back?"

Patrick stood up, turning to face the bench. Sure enough, there was a small plaque screwed into the upper back rail, and he stooped to read it.

The woman said, "It says, *To Amos Lewis, a Lover of Parks*."

Patrick straightened and looked at her. "Yes, I've seen these inscriptions. Very nice."

"He used to sit there and smoke a cigar. Smoking is prohibited in the park, but he did it anyway. He was old school."

Patrick nodded wistfully. "Old school. I can appreciate that. The plaque is a good way to remember someone."

"Are you Irish?" she asked, taking a step closer.

"No, not really. I was born in New York. My father was from Limerick; my mother from a village in County Clare," Patrick said, again turning toward the plaque. "How did you arrange to get the plaque?" he asked.

"You can go online, to the Riverside Park website."

He nodded. "Well, that's a lovely thing, isn't it?"

"Please sit down," the woman said. "I'm sorry if I interrupted you. I often pass by and look at the bench."

Patrick kept his eyes on the plaque.

"Is there someone…" The woman said, then hesitated. "Are you thinking of someone you'd like to dedicate a plaque to?"

Patrick turned, folding his arms across his chest. "Perhaps."

The woman didn't move, but her dog was itching to go. He looked up at her and whined.

Patrick didn't meet the woman's eyes. "I guess he has squirrels to chase," he said.

The woman lowered her chin. "Yes. Well, yes, I should go. Enjoy the bench. By the way, do you smoke cigars?"

"Not in a while... I used to, but that was a long time ago. Centuries ago."

She smiled sweetly. "Perhaps you should have one someday while you join my grandfather on the bench."

"Perhaps... Yes. Perhaps I will."

And then she started off. "Merry Christmas."

Patrick gave her a little head bow. "And Merry Christmas to you and to your family."

He eased back down on the bench, his low mood falling deeper into darkness. Death seemed all about him, even on the damned bench he was sitting on. He shot up. No, he wouldn't order a bench plaque for Eve and Colleen. No, he wouldn't accept their deaths. No way. Not until he lit the time travel lantern.

Why had he put off the inevitable? Why had he refused to enter Eve's bedroom closet, kneel by the safe, open it and remove the lantern? Yesterday, in a drunken stupor, he'd almost summoned the courage, but he'd stopped in the doorway, stopped cold.

Eve's perfume still lingered, wounding him. The bed mocked him with sexy, loving memories; her clothes hung in that closet, and Colleen's baby clothes lay folded on the side chair near the bed, where Eve had left them.

All those things had been barriers, blocking the closet and the lantern. And yet, he knew it was his only chance— their only chance. He'd have to scale the barriers, open the safe, remove the lantern and light it.

Back inside the apartment, Patrick paced the living room, making a detour into the kitchen to splash cold water onto his face. He stood, towel in hand, water dripping from his chin, but he did not wipe his face. Lost in thought, he flung the towel away and returned to pacing.

When he did finally get around to lighting the lantern, there was no guarantee his wish would be granted. There was no sure way of knowing where the thing would take him, or even if it would take him. It was Eve's lantern, wasn't it? She had found it.

Would he end up in the past, back in 1885? And if he did, would Eve be there? Would he land in 1900, or earlier, or later, or a few days or hours before Eve's plane crashed? Of course, that was his wish. Even a few hours before her plane went down would be enough time to save Eve, Colleen and Eve's parents.

But the lantern, with its light and unpredictable power, was a complete and total unknown. He'd be tossing the dice, as it were, leaving his life and his past and his future all up to fate… or to Nikola Tesla, the creator of the time travel lantern.

Patrick and Eve had never been able to agree on whether the lantern had any intelligence of its own or if it simply fed off the thoughts and emotions of the people who lit it, thus transporting them in time to a place that would personally affect them.

When he and Eve were living in 1884, Nikola Tesla had been no help. At best, he had been vague and non-committal about the lantern he'd created. He'd been passive and seemingly bored, as if he didn't care one way or the other what happened once his "toy time travel lanterns" were lighted. He had given them birth and then, like Christmas toys, he had tossed them out into the ocean of time.

In 2016, Eve had found one of those lanterns in the Time Past Antique Shop in Pennsylvania, and after she lighted it, she was hurled back to 1885. That's how it all began. That's when Patrick had met Eve and fallen in love with her.

In the living room, Patrick drew back the curtains and gazed out the bay windows, down onto the street. Two inches of snow covered the ground. How Eve would have loved it! She loved snow. She would have taken Colleen to the park, and they would have danced and laughed and sung *Jingle Bells*.

He pivoted and started for the bedroom, pausing at the threshold. He still had one problem to solve. After he lit the lantern, who would take possession of it? The lantern did not time travel with the person who lit it. It remained in the present, and that meant somebody had to be there to take it.

But whom could Patrick trust? He had run through a list of people in his head, family, friends, even neighbors. Only one name kept bobbing up to the surface: Dr. Simon Wallister.

Simon was still in Ohio. He and his wife had attended the memorial service and then stayed in Cincinnati a couple nights to visit with friends. They would return tomorrow, December 26. Patrick had spent hours straining to come up with the right words to explain the lantern's origin and power, but he always returned to the same intractable spot. Would Simon Wallister believe it? Of course he wouldn't believe it. Patrick hadn't believed it either until he'd experienced its power for himself and crashed into the twenty-first century.

No, Simon would never believe such a tall tale. He was a scientist, a doctor and a pragmatist. But Patrick couldn't leave the lantern, just sitting there on a bench in Central Park. It had too much power and potential to be used for evil.

Patrick would have to find somebody, and he'd have to find them fast. One way or the other, Patrick was going to light the lantern and throw his fate to the wind. What else could he do? He couldn't live without Eve and Colleen.

Patrick stepped into the bedroom and, heart racing, he crept to the closet where the time travel lantern lay waiting.

CHAPTER 7

"Central Park? Why? What's going on in Central Park?" Simon Wallister asked.

It was Sunday, December 27, and Patrick was outside on his cell phone, walking the carriage path in Riverside Park, under a heavy gray sky.

"Simon…" Patrick said, struggling for words. "Simon… I need a friend right now. I need your friendship and I need you to trust me. I'm asking you to meet me in Central Park at The Poet's Walk, at the southern end of The Mall. You know where it is. There are four statues of well-known writers there, Fitz-Greene Halleck, Robert Burns, Sir Walter Scott and William Shakespeare, and not too…"

Simon cut in. "Patrick…, you really sound stressed. You don't sound like yourself."

"I'm not myself, Simon, and I'm definitely nervous and stressed, and I'm asking, as a friend, if you'll meet me there tomorrow at ten in the morning. It won't take long. I'll explain as much as I can then. Will you meet me? Please."

Simon sighed heavily into the phone, making a hissing sound. "Damn it, Patrick. You should have been at the memorial service."

"I can't talk about that now. What I should have done or could have done does not matter now. All that matters is that you meet me at ten tomorrow in Central Park. Will you, Simon? Will you please meet me? I don't trust anyone else to do this."

"You and Eve always had some mystery about you that I could never grab hold of. Okay, I'll meet you. I'll cancel my morning patients, but it won't be easy."

Patrick sighed out relief. "Thank you, Simon."

"Patrick, listen to me. I know a good grief counselor. You'll like her. She's experienced and sensitive. Why don't you give her a chance?"

"No, thanks."

"Are you off the booze?"

"Yes… I'm off the booze. No more self-pity. By the way, how's Colin?"

"He's fine. Confused a bit, but he's eating better now. He'll be fine. He and Edith are becoming good friends, but I know he misses his home."

"Thanks again for looking after him."

"What are your plans?" Simon asked. "Are you going to stay in New York?"

"That depends on what happens tomorrow."

"You certainly have me intrigued. All right, Edith's calling. Dinner's ready."

"Simon," Patrick said, quickly. "How was everyone? I mean, how was Eve's family?"

"Just what you'd expect. Devastated. It was the worse Christmas Eve of my life."

"See you tomorrow, Simon."

For the rest of the day and well into the night, Patrick wandered the streets, past restaurants where he and Eve had eaten, past Eve's favorite wine shop and bakery. He browsed a bookstore, a candy shop, and a lingerie boutique, where he had once bought her a silk nightgown. He ended up at a local diner they often patronized for weekend brunch.

Patrick had a reason for his wanderings. He had no idea where he'd be tomorrow, whether he'd be hurled into the past—perhaps his old past—or dropped into another time and place, or simply tossed out into the blackness of infinity and death. There was one flicker of hope—that somehow he'd find Eve and Colleen. Where or when he had no idea.

His worst thought was of lighting the lantern and traveling nowhere, finding himself sitting on the bench staring at Simon, who would stare back at him, worried, concerned and ready to call the men in the white coats.

If the lighted lantern was faulty or lifeless and he remained in 2020, what would he do? He had no idea, but he couldn't, and wouldn't, comprehend a life without Eve and Colleen.

Patrick slept little that night, the couch cramped and uncomfortable. He had been unable to sleep in his and Eve's bed since her death. At first light, he was up, tense and anxious. He showered and moved stoically through the apartment, like a man about to be sentenced for a crime.

The black pants and off-white shirt he wore were nondescript. He hoped they would blend in with whatever time he found himself. His boots were a glossy black, his wool greatcoat was warm.

At the hall mirror, he examined his hair and face. He broke into a mournful grimace. There was no denying his eyes were bloodshot and tired. He was pale and his face thin. He ran his hand along the line of his jaw, feeling the smooth chin after his early morning shave.

The haircut he should have had would have given him more of a clean-cut look, but did it matter? His thick, black hair was long, wavy and over his ears, and he messed with it, trying to tame some of the wildness, and then he gave up. He'd have to go with the long-haired, windblown look. Eve had liked that look. He recalled a conversation they'd had only a few days before.

"Don't get a haircut. Keep your hair long. It softens you and makes you look less pugnacious."

"And pray tell, Mrs. Gantly, what does pugnacious mean?"

She shrugged a shoulder. "You know, aggressive, defiant."

He had laughed. "I thought you liked me aggressive and defiant."

Eve had pulled him into a kiss. "I do... at certain times, like when you get all worked up about how much better things were back in the good old days, in the nineteenth century. But I also like to play with your long hair in the dark... when you're almost asleep."

In the cab traveling down Fifth Avenue, Patrick again examined the newly purchased gold rings on the fourth fingers of both hands. No matter what time he traveled to, gold would provide a quick bankroll. He'd learned this from Eve, who had always packed jewelry when she time traveled.

He sighed when he thought about his wedding ring, tucked away in Eve's jewelry box. He didn't want to sell that or take a chance it would get lost.

The lantern lay next to him, packed inside a black leather travel bag, along with a box of kitchen matches. The day was gray and cold, the clouds low and moving. He wasn't about to run out of matches on this blustery December morning.

At the curb of East 66th Street, Patrick paid the driver and stepped outside, taking the leather bag with him. He entered Central Park and walked west in a quick, snappy breeze, his greatcoat open, his stride long and determined. To say he was nervous was an understatement. His thoughts were fidgety, his grip on the leather bag so tight that his hand began to hurt.

Couples strolled hand in hand, tourists took selfies, and a policeman on horseback trotted along a winding path, smoky vapor puffing from the horse's nostrils.

Patrick took the walkway, the same walkway Eve had described to him when she'd first used the lantern to time travel. It led to the Central Park Mall that runs through the middle of the Park from 66th to 72nd Streets, ending at Bethesda Terrace.

Minutes later, Patrick arrived at his destination, The Poet's Walk, at the southern end of The Mall. He glanced about, looking for Simon, feeling highly charged from anxiety and adrenaline. A man was seated on a park bench, gazing into his cell phone. It was Simon. Patrick started toward him.

Simon flipped his eyes up to Patrick and gave him a few seconds of evaluation. "Good morning, Patrick. What's in the bag?"

Patrick hesitated. "A lantern."

Simon stared. "Okay… A lantern."

Simon put his cell phone away and rose, facing Patrick, who was easily three inches taller. He spread his hands. "So what happens now? Are you going to tell me what this is all about?"

Patrick's eyes were cool, direct and intense. "If everything goes as I hope it will, you'll see for yourself. I won't have to tell you. I'm going to sit on that bench, remove the lantern from my bag, set it down beside me and, with a match, I'm going to light the lantern."

Simon waited for more. "And then…?"

"And then, I hope to vanish before your eyes. When I am gone, please take the lantern and keep it in a safe place. One day, I hope to return and ask for it."

Simon examined Patrick's face. "We need to talk about this, Patrick. I'm going to be honest with you. I think you've had a serious breakdown and need help. Please… let's go. Let me call some people. Let's get you the help you need."

Patrick didn't move. "Simon, if I do not vanish after I light this lantern, then I promise, I will go with you and see whoever you want me to see."

Simon pressed his lips tightly together and shook his head. "Patrick…" But his voice faltered, and he was unable to express the weight of concern and sympathy he felt. "All right then, light the damned thing and then let's get out of here. It's cold."

Patrick stepped to the bench and set the leather bag down. He unzipped it, reached in, and withdrew the old time lantern. Lifting it by the wire handle, he gently set it down on the bench.

Simon moved toward it, studying the old antique. It was twelve-inches high and made of iron, with a tarnished green/brown patina. It had four glass windowpanes, with wire guards and a painted anchor design on each side of the roof, one anchor painted a faded red and the other a faded blue. Simon stooped toward it, staring at it in a strange way. "Where did you get this thing?"

"It was a gift from an old friend."

Simon slanted up a look. "How old?"

"1884."

Simon felt a chill, but not from the cold. Something he saw in Patrick's eyes unnerved him. There was nothing in those eyes to suggest Patrick was mentally unbalanced. On the contrary, his eyes were clear and full of purpose. Ever since they'd known each other, Patrick had impressed him with his cool, keen and practical intelligence.

The wind blew rough and strong. People passing flipped up the collars of their coats and yanked up their hoods.

Simon straightened, growing irritable. "Okay, light the thing. Let's finish this."

With the box of matches in hand, Patrick sat next to the lantern. Dread, excitement and nerves beat away at him as he reached and opened the glass panel door. The unlighted wick awaited.

He thought of Eve and Colleen as he stared at the lantern with cold speculation. "Take me to them," Patrick whispered.

Simon didn't hear the words.

Patrick hooded his eyes as he reached for a match. He struck it along the match box striker and watched the flame burst to life. He cupped the trembling flame in his hand, but before he could lead it inside to the wick, a burst of wind blew it out.

Soon another match was at the ready. Patrick swiped it against the striker, his hand cupped and ready.

Simon watched, enthralled, as Patrick guided the trembling match flame through the panel door to the wick. In an instant, the wick came alive and the flame danced. Patrick shut the panel door and tossed the match, staring eagerly at the light; a soft golden light.

Simon moved in to get a closer look.

"Get back!" Patrick warned. "Get back at least fifteen feet."

Startled, Simon obeyed, but he kept his entranced eyes on the trembling light. Gawking with an astonished wonder, Simon witnessed Patrick's form fade in and out, like a swimmer rising to the surface, then sinking down into rippling currents.

Simon witnessed the swelling light expand into a rich, scintillating radiance, accompanied by a weird, purring hum that seemed to hover in the air. It plunged him into a soft, hypnotic trance.

It might have been minutes, or an hour, before Simon was aware that the lantern's light had been extinguished and Patrick was gone. Dizzy and disoriented, Simon staggered toward the bench, searching the area for Patrick, certain his mind had played a trick on him. Surely, it was a joke. Patrick had performed some magic trick. He'd run off. He was hiding somewhere.

The lantern sat dark, still and quiet. Simon backed away from it, feeling as though the thing were somehow alive and watching him. It seemed to have consciousness and intelligence.

Simon stood shivering, troubled and shaken. A minute later, he found his voice. He called out into the breathing, sharp wind that rattled the bare branches of trees.

"Patrick… Patrick… Where are you?"

CHAPTER 8

Patrick was tossed and tumbled through blue waves, hurled into the sky like a rag, sailing with fleeing birds and boiling, black storm clouds. When he broke through the clouds, a buttery full moon flashed by, so close he could almost reach out and touch it. All he could do was let go. He was an arrow that had been shot randomly into the air, and God only knew where he'd land.

As he sucked in air and fought for balance, he was flung downward, falling like a stone toward a vast, craggy mountain range. Sure he'd plunge into the earth, he prepared to die.

He slowly descended to solid ground, but he was engulfed in a dense, smoky fog, a rowdy wind whipping his hair, face and clothes. He staggered about like a drunken man, arms out, hands reaching, searching, not knowing where to turn or where to go.

A distant voice stopped him, and he straightened, alert, chest heaving, an ear cocked, straining to hear. The voice seemed to be riding the wind; it was everywhere and nowhere; an ethereal, whispering voice, an urgent voice.

It was Eve! It was Eve's voice. "Patrick... remember? Promise... we'll always find each other. Promise... No matter what time or place, we'll find each other... Promise..."

Patrick darted off into the thick fog, searching for the source of the voice that flew over him, around him, and past him. He searched for Eve. "Eve! Where are you? Eve! I'm coming... Keep talking. I'll find you. Keep talking."

He stumbled ahead, waving his hands through the swirling clouds, as Eve's voice faded away into a distant echo.

In a near panic, Patrick turned in a circle, lost. "Eve, where are you?"

He ran blindly in a mad panic, shouting for her. And then the ground fell away and he sank, falling, arms flailing.

It was cold. He was lying on his side. The bench was hard. His eyes were half opened, his vision blurry. Patrick tried to sit up but failed. His mind was spinning. He lay there, his entire body aching, his muscles cramped.

A low, scraping woman's voice floated down to him. "Hey, Buster Boy. What's the matter with you? Are you on a toot? Are you all boozed up?"

Patrick tried to lift his head, but it weighed a ton. "What?"

"Old John Barleycorn came a visitin', did he? Oh well, look at you. You're a big one, aren't you? So you and your pretty old lady must have had a good fist-swingin' argument, huh? She gave you a toss, did she? The old heave-ho out the back door?"

The woman laughed, but it was more of a cackle. "No kissy, huggy-roll in the feather bed for you tonight, Buster Boy. Just the good and hard park bench and the fist of the wind for you. Well, you picked the wrong bench. This is my bench, so scram. Hit the road."

Patrick wished the voice would go away. It sounded like a squeaky wagon wheel.

"Get up, Buster Boy. The coppers will be along and they'll have you in the wagon, and then you'll be spending a good night or two in the caboose."

"Caboose?" Patrick managed to force out, between his dry lips and parched throat.

"The jailhouse, Buster Boy."

Patrick cleared his throat and forced open an eye. "Stop calling me Buster Boy."

The woman laughed and then fell into a deep, hacking cough. "You got some Irish in you, huh, Buster Boy?" she said, bringing an old rag of a hankie to her mouth. "I can hear it in your words. Well, I got some Irish in me, too. So get up, Buster Boy."

Her taunting angered him. He pushed up to a seated position, his head whirling and pounding. He touched it with a shaky hand, feeling as though he had one of the worst hangovers of his life. He squinted a look at the woman. It was night, and in the lamplight and with his fuzzy vision, she slowly came into focus.

There was no other way to say it. She was a dumpy old hag, dressed in a long, shabby gown, her rounded shoulders wrapped in a frayed shawl, with a kind of makeshift turban swathed about her head. Hers was an old, wrinkled, dumpling face, with beady, mischievous eyes and a sardonic twist of a mouth, showing gaps of dark teeth. She was a witch right out of a kid's storybook. All she needed was a cauldron and a book of spells.

She cackled, just like a witch, coughed some more, then stopped, abruptly. She pointed a sure finger at him and her eyes widened in sudden, wild surprise.

"By the Lord above, and in all his mercy, you favor my second son, Joseph, God bless him. He fell in 1917 in France. Dead as he is, for a minute there, I thought he'd come back to haunt his old Mum."

Her mood swiftly changed from surprise to distaste, and then to accusation. "Now, who the hell are you and why were you spread out on my bench like a corpse?"

Patrick took a quick breath to steady himself. It took a few deep breaths before the ringing in his ears stopped and some of the dizziness cleared. "Your bench?"

She pounded a fist against her chest, and that made her cough, bringing the hankie again to her mouth. "Yeah, Buster Boy, my bench."

Some of the fog in his mind had cleared just enough for him to focus on something she'd said. "Did you say 1917?"

"What do you mean, 1917? Barleycorn's got you, Buster Boy, and that's a good and hard fact."

"You said your son fell in France in 1917?"

She softened again, her face falling into grief. "He was a good boy, Joseph was. He was good to his Mum. Sent me money and a few knick-knacks now and then. He sent me a straw hat, too. I had it for two years until the coppers snatched me from my home. But I fought them, I did. I fought them, kicking and fighting with my teeth and my fists. I got some good licks in, but that's when I lost my hat, and that was the last thing Joseph ever sent me before he fell in France."

"What year is it?" Patrick blurted out. "What's the date?"

The woman was lost in her own dark memories, wandering in a sad place. She hadn't heard him.

Patrick softened, waiting for her, as his limbs tingled and slowly awakened, as his brain sharpened and his memory returned. He nearly leapt to his feet, remembering the lantern. Simon. Time travel.

"Eve!" he called out.

That snapped the woman from her old, bad dreams. "Eve?" she asked. "Who's Eve? Is that your woman?"

Patrick looked at her. "Yes... My woman."

"It's a Bible name. It's good to have a Bible name."

Patrick stared at her. "What's your name?"

Her eyes cleared. "Name? My name?"

"Yes, what is your name?"

"My name is Sarah Finn. Named after my mother, God rest her soul. She said Sarah was a good name. It's also a Bible name, you know."

Patrick swallowed hard. "Sarah, what year is this? What's the month and the year?"

She scrutinized him anew. "Have you gone all balmy, Buster Boy?"

"No, Sarah, please. What is the month and year?"

She slowly rolled her shoulders, showing a slight fear of him. "When your old lady tossed you out of the house, did you fall on your handsome head, Buster Boy?"

She dropped the bundle she'd been holding to her feet, put fists to her hips and looked him up and down. "Are you tellin' me you don't know the year? What's the matter with you?"

"Sarah, please, just tell me... what is the month and year?"

She took a step back and lowered her wary eyes on him. The raspy cough returned.

Patrick looked at her with concern. "Are you sick, Sarah?"

"No, I'm not sick. I'm as healthy as a work horse. Don't you worry about Sarah none, Buster Boy."

"Sarah... What's the month? The day?"

She coughed and put a hand to her mouth. She had to swallow twice before she could speak. "It's October. October... I don't know what day. I never know the day. What's it matter what day it is?"

"What year?" Patrick asked, sitting on the edge of the bench.

"Okay, Buster Boy, this old rag woman is gonna set you straight and put your mind at ease. It's 1925. October something, 1925."

Sluggishly, suddenly feeling sick, Patrick bent forward, closed his eyes and cupped his forehead in a hand. "1925... How can it be 1925? Why 1925?"

"Hey... what's the matter with you?" Sarah asked, dropping her voice into sympathy. "It ain't that bad, is it? With your manly, good looks, your woman will take you back. Hell, if she don't, you just come on back here and share Sarah Finn's bench. That'll show her."

Sarah let out a deep, weary sigh. "Now I'm as tired as a poor old dog."

She sat down heavily on the bench next to him, picked up her bundle and placed it snuggly against her. "I've got to rest these old bunions now," she said, reaching down to massage an ankle.

"Do you have anywhere else to go?" Sarah asked.

Patrick slowly lifted his head, staring into the night. "No, I don't. I have nowhere to go."

Sarah snaked a hand into her bundle and pulled out a half-eaten loaf of bread. She held it up to him. "Are you hungry? I'll break you off a piece. I stole it from Frankel's Deli. He's got the best bread around. It's rye."

Patrick looked at her, unsure. During the 2020 pandemic, he would have never taken bread from this woman, but it was 1925, and the bread looked good. "I am hungry," he said.

He watched as Sarah's chubby hands went to work. She yanked off a piece and offered it to him. He took it with a grateful nod. "Thank you, Sarah."

Patrick was ravenous. He pulled off a bite and chewed. "It's good. Fresh."

"You bet it's fresh. I only get the freshest bread, Buster Boy."

"Will you please call me Patrick, Sarah?"

Sarah's bushy eyebrows lifted and then she coughed into her hand. "Sure, I can call you Patrick. Patrick's the name of a saint, ain't it? It's a good name."

They ate in silence as the night deepened and grew cold. After Patrick finished eating, he turned up the collar of his coat, glancing skyward, gazing at the swirl of stars. He thought, *Why am I here?*

Sarah brushed the crumbs off her lap and glanced over. "You gonna spend the night with me, Buster Boy?"

"Don't you have a place of shelter, Sarah?"

She brought the tattered hankie to her mouth and coughed into it. "The good old sky above, with its mass of twinkling diamonds, and all the trees around are good enough for old Sarah. That mission over on Second

Avenue ain't so safe. There was a woman who got her throat cut the other night. No, this park bench will do just fine for these old bones."

She leaned toward him, lowering her voice. "You just have to watch out for the coppers. They make one pass and then it's okay. That big coat of yours will keep you warm enough. You just sit back and relax, Buster Boy, and spend a cozy night with old Sarah Finn."

CHAPTER 9

Patrick's eyes flickered open at dawn. They widened and searched. He was sitting on a park bench, slumped over to one side. Where was he? Images of Eve stuck to his eyes. He remembered dreaming about her, but the dream had fled as soon as he'd awakened. He was chilled to the bone, dazed and confused. People passed, staring at him suspiciously, some with compassion. He must have looked a mess, a mess from another time, and, of course, he was. Yes, he was now living in 1925 and he had no idea why the lantern had dropped him here.

The electric park lights glowed violet in the silvery morning light and misty fog. Surrounding him was an autumn haze of green and gold and the echoing cry of scattering birds, and the faraway murmur of traffic. He sat up and kinked his neck, gently working his stiff, aching shoulders. Looking to his left, he saw that Sarah was gone, as was her bundle and any evidence that she'd spent the night. Had he dreamed her, that strange character from some old novel? No, he didn't think so, though his head felt stuffed with Styrofoam, and reality seemed half movie and half imagination.

Fortunately for them both, the cops hadn't come by and it hadn't rained or snowed; the wind had been calm. Still, he wasn't about to spend another night on a cold park bench. It was a good way to catch pneumonia. Normally, sleep would have never come, but he was exhausted from the time travel and, surprisingly, he'd slept through the chilly night.

But now he was hungry and cold. It was time to set out and explore, hock one of his gold rings, get a good breakfast and find a place to live. Then he could get some rest, steady his thoughts and formulate a plan.

He rose on stiff legs, stretched and put the back of a hand to a yawn, turning one last time toward the bench. Where had poor Sarah gone, and how long would she survive sleeping outside on a Central Park bench? From the sound of her cough, she probably had bronchitis, maybe even pneumonia. He rubbed his temples, hoping he hadn't caught some kind of disease from those few bites of bread.

Patrick started off along a meandering path that, in 2020, would have led to Fifth Avenue. He soon found the source of the traffic sounds, the honking horns and grumbling motors. Fifth Avenue loomed ahead, and he plodded along, shaking off his sleepy state as the walkway ended, and he stopped to take the famous avenue in.

It wasn't dramatically different from 2020, except that the buildings appeared newer, the traffic less dense. Interestingly, the cars appeared like rattling new antiques, many with their tailpipes spewing out puffs of foul exhaust. There was a tarnished, dingy haze of dampness and smoke in the air that he'd never experienced, not in the mid-1880s and not in the twenty-first century. Was this the beginning of air pollution?

As he started across Fifth Avenue, dodging traffic, Patrick observed three attractive women strolling the sidewalks, their hips swaying, their talk animated, hands moving. They sported trim winter coats; two wore close-fitting cloche hats, and one was hatless, with a short, bobbed hairstyle.

A black limousine drew up to an impressive art deco style building that rose up into a tower. It had a golden door, a gold-trimmed burgundy awning and a gold-trimmed blue-uniformed doorman, who presented a proper, pompous attitude.

She emerged from the limousine, a woman dressed in an emerald, pleated turban hat with a crystal brooch placed dead center. Patrick was amused by the T-strap golden heels and the cocoon of a lavish fur coat. In her mid-forties, hers was a lonely glamor, as she ambled toward the doorman, looking weary and slightly tipsy. The door opened, and she passed the doorman a lopsided smile that seemed to say, "to hell with it all." He touched two fingers to his hat.

On Lexington Avenue, Patrick stopped in front of a clothing boutique for women. The window mannequins wore below-the-knee, drop-waist dresses with a loose, straight fit, something he'd never seen before. The clothes seemed bold and strange to him, and he wondered what Eve would have thought of the styles.

It soon became apparent that he was an oddity, a standout, not dressed in the proper uniform among the well-dressed men of this time, in their stylish suits, rich overcoats and fedoras. The curious, disapproving stares that latched onto him were all the evidence he needed that a 1925 wardrobe was an absolute necessity, if he was to fit in. And he had to fit in, if he was going to learn the mystery of why the lantern had brought him here.

Patrick's stomach growled from hunger. He craved breakfast and a cup of coffee, but he'd have to wait until a pawnshop opened on Lexington and 65th Street so he could hock a ring and get some cash.

Of course, Patrick had no idea what the prices of anything were in 1925, so he'd have to use a bit of arrogance and intimidation on the pawnbroker, and hope the man would offer a good price for the gold ring.

At 9 a.m., he entered a narrow and dimly lit pawnshop that held all the usual items: watches, jewelry, and tie pins. There were two ukuleles displayed on the wall, side-by-side, and a curious glass case exhibiting silver flasks and gold cigarette cases.

The proprietor was a balding man with a waxed graying mustache, who possessed the upright sternness and the martial eyes of a Prussian officer. His left eye gripped a monocle; his black suit, stiff white shirt and black tie seemed to be forcing him to stand at attention.

"Vhat can vee do for you, sir?" he asked in a thick, German accent.

Patrick straightened to his full height, a full five inches taller than the man. He removed the gold ring from a finger and placed it on the glass counter before the German.

The proprietor peered at Patrick through his monocle. He was not impressed by Patrick's attire, nor by his shadow of beard and weary eyes, and when the German's nose twitched, ever so slightly, it searched for signs of whiskey breath.

The German plucked the monocle from his eye and it fell, bouncing on a leather string that was connected inside his coat. He reached for a loupe, wiggled it into his left eye, picked up the ring and began his careful, skeptical examination.

Patrick took the opportunity to ask the man a few questions. "Sir, I've been traveling and I'm new in town. Can you recommend a good place to live... A neighborhood that is pleasant, and perhaps a furnished apartment or a boarding house that is reasonable?"

The German didn't pull his eyes from the ring. "Humm," he hummed. "Gold is good. It is eighteen-karat. Yes, fine gold."

"What can you offer?" Patrick asked, placidly, not wanting to show how hungry, bewildered and lost he felt.

The German popped out the loupe, raised his eyebrow and fit the monocle back in place into his right eye socket. He scrutinized Patrick anew.

"Ver you in dah vhar, sir?"

"The war?"

The German nodded.

Patrick knew the man could only be speaking about World War 1. "No, sir, I was not."

"I saw dees kind of rings from families after dah vhar. Terrible it was, you know. I was here, in New York. My son fought with dah doughboys," he said, proudly. "Yah, he was a good soldier."

Patrick saw sudden pain rise in the man's eyes, and some of the hard edges in his face softened.

"I hope your son is well, sir," Patrick said, earnestly.

The German scratched his cheek as he looked down and away. He cleared his throat, as if to push away emotion. "I vill give you one-hundred seventy dollars for dis ring. It is a fair price. Vill you come back for it in future?"

"No, sir. I won't."

After Patrick had received the cash and placed the bills in several different pockets, the man came out from behind the counter, his hands clasped behind him. He did not look at Patrick directly.

"How long vill you be in New York?"

"I'm not sure. Maybe a month. Maybe longer."

The German pointed to his right. "Not far from here are good apartments and they are not so expensive. Dis here is a fine neighborhood."

Patrick wondered what he'd said that had saddened the man. It must have had something to do with the gold ring.

"Thank you, sir. I hope whoever purchases the ring will make good use of it."

The German finally met Patrick's eyes with his somber ones. "My son vas to be married with such a ring. Yes, a ring like that. He was perished… that is to say he died in the vhar, and you will please excuse me for my sadness. He was a good son to me and to my good wife."

Patrick lowered his head. "I'm sorry you lost him, sir."

The German surprised Patrick. "I also zee sadness in you, sir. Sadness shows through the eyes."

Patrick didn't have the strength to talk about it. "Yes… I wish you well."

Outside, a light mist fell and Patrick felt a sinking emptiness as he thought about Eve and Colleen. The big world was a great mystery, even if one didn't time travel using an antique lantern. The mysteries expanded when time travel sent you willy-nilly into the unknown.

Patrick walked briskly, needing food and a place to live. Once he had achieved those, he would begin his explorations and try to learn why he was here in 1925. Was Eve somehow tied to it? He prayed that she was.

CHAPTER 10

Patrick sat at a table in Child's Restaurant eating eggs, toast and ham. The coffee was hot and bold and never tasted so good. His young, perky waitress had red puckered lips, frizzy curls and waves, and she wore a yellow uniform with white trim.

With the breakfast rush nearly over, she wandered over to Patrick, obviously intrigued by his odd clothes and good looks.

"Are you from New York?" she asked, in a soft, high, girlish voice.

"Yes," Patrick said.

She stood picking her teeth, one white-stockinged ankle crossed over the other and resting on its toe. "I noticed you weren't wearing a hat."

"No... Should I?"

She shrugged a shoulder. "Most men do. I don't know any man who doesn't wear a hat."

"I guess I'll have to get one, then."

"What part of New York are you from?"

"I grew up on the Lower East Side."

"They have a lot of bully punks down there."

"That they do."

Patrick decided to ask some of his own questions. "What day is this?" he asked casually.

She arched an eyebrow. "You mean what day of the month?"

"Yes, I kind of lost track. I've been traveling."

"It's Wednesday, October twenty-first."

Patrick had left 2020 in late December. This was yet another mystery. Why October?

"Is business good?" Patrick asked, draining the last of his coffee, trying to make conversation.

"You know, it's okay. The Child's on Fifty-Seventh Street is better."

"Better tips?"

"Yeah. Here, the tips ain't so good... Anywhere from five cents to a half dollar. Women tip nickels, but then women always tip nickels, don't they?"

"Do you know a good men's store close by? I need some new clothes."

She looked him over again, her exploring blue/gray eyes resting on his face. Her face was filled with street-wisdom and cunning. "There's a men's shop on Sixty-Second Street called the Cosmopolitan. They have sharp clothes. A lot of jazz musicians buy their clothes there."

"Jazz musicians?"

"Yeah, you know, the guys who play at the juice joints and gin mills downtown and up in Harlem. They've got to be spiffy to get the good jobs, at least that's what one guy told me. He eats here a lot."

She lowered her lids and leveled her eyes on Patrick. "Do you ever go to gin mills to dance to jazz?"

Patrick thought of Lucy Rose, the young woman who only last year had time traveled with her low-life boyfriend from 1925 to 2019. The boyfriend had stolen Eve's lantern to return to 1925, but Lucy had remained, for many reasons. Patrick recalled her reasons, hearing Lucy's voice in his head. "I was tired of dancing in that night club for peanuts," she'd said. "I was tired of being called 'doll face' and 'my dancin' rag doll' and 'come here, baby toes, let me kiss away some of that lipstick,' because that's what the mugs in nightclubs shout out when you're on stage dancing under those hot spotlights. Well, I had had it up to my eyeballs with all that, see?"

Patrick lowered his eyes and slumped a little. That seemed like years ago, like lifetimes ago. Anyway, everything had changed since then.

"Did I say something wrong?" the waitress asked, noticing his sudden change of mood.

Patrick shook his head as he pulled a dollar bill from his pocket. "No. I have to be going. How much?"

Patrick's primary plan for the rest of the day was to take care of the basics, buy clothes and get an apartment. He easily found the Cosmopolitan Menswear Shop. There was a shoe store nearby, so he stopped there first and bought a good pair of black boots for four dollars, along with six pairs of socks.

At the Cosmopolitan, he purchased two three-piece suits for a little over twenty dollars each. A stylish, double-breasted overcoat was twenty-eight dollars, a dark fedora hat, six dollars, and the five dress shirts were two dollars each, with two detachable collars tossed in for another eighty cents.

It was the thin, effusive salesman who reminded Patrick that he needed neckties. Patrick bought four at four dollars each, as well as six pairs of underwear.

Although Patrick was pleased with the price and quality of his purchases, he realized he'd already spent more than half his money. He would soon have to sell the second ring in order to pay for rent and food. Assuming he got another $170 for that ring, he should have enough money to last for several months, if he was careful.

As he was about to leave the shop, he mentioned to the salesman that he was looking for a furnished room or apartment. With enthusiasm, the man clapped his hands together and declared, "I know the perfect place for you, sir."

He led Patrick outside and pointed. "Up the street two blocks and directly across the street. That's where I live. Only this morning I saw a sign in the window, advertising a room. It's off Third, at 58th Street."

By the time Patrick inquired about the room, it had already been taken. Fortunately, the kind landlord directed Patrick to another building close by.

Toting his bags of clothes and shoes, Patrick finally landed a place on Third Avenue, near 57th Street. The landlady was a heavy woman, who puffed out straining breaths after every two or three steps and held her hip as if she were in pain.

In the narrow lobby, where wooden mail slots filled one wall, the landlady pointed up into the shadows of the steep, wooden stairs. She wheezed out a breath, handed him a key and said, "Fourth floor, apartment 42. You look, I'll wait here with your bags."

Patrick reluctantly mounted the stairs, feeling his legs grow heavier with each flight. At the top, he paused, wheezing, gulping in air, cursing time travel for weakening him. Normally, he could have taken the stairs two at a time. He crossed the threadbare carpet to the room on the far right.

It was a long "railroad apartment" near a furrier's store, and even though it smelled slightly of wet cats, it was clean. Patrick found the stiff, Victorian furniture and burgundy draperies a bonus, as they made him feel somewhat at home, reminding him of his life in the 1880s.

The place had a small, private bathroom with a bathtub, and a narrow bedroom with two windows looking out onto rooftops, where clotheslines were strung, and sheets and towels flapped in the wind. Pigeons wheeled against the gray sky and settled on chimneys or rooftops, strutting, pecking for scattered seeds. It was a forlorn view, with the hazy distance of factories and tapering smokestacks, black, curling smoke rising into the dark sky.

He turned back to the place. Another drawback was the gas heating. The rooms were warm, but the living room smelled fetid. The fireplace obviously didn't work. Patrick lifted a window a few inches and that helped clear the stale air.

Downstairs, Patrick paid the old, grunting woman for a month, forty-seven dollars. She squeezed the bills tightly into her fat fist and stared up at him, warily, as if to ensure that he was a man of sound mind.

Patrick took the place because he was too tired and too dispirited to look any further, and then there was something about being on the fourth floor that he liked.

But not the stairs. As he climbed those imposing stairs once more, bags in hand, fatigue filled him up like a drug.

The eccentric rooms would be his home, at least in the short term, until something was revealed to him as to why the lantern had dropped him here.

After his clothes were unpacked and placed neatly in cedar drawers and the closet, he left the building to search for a drugstore. Finding one close by, he purchased toiletries, took a quick stroll through the neighborhood and then returned to his apartment.

Back upstairs, Patrick sank wearily onto the edge of the bed, folded his hands, and let out a long breath. He thought of Sarah Finn and wondered if she would return to her park bench that night, a stolen loaf of fresh bread tucked in her bundle. Why he felt compassion for the old, pitiful woman, he didn't know. Perhaps because she'd shared her meager dinner with him, as well as her only perceived possession, her park bench.

He vowed to return to the park and bring her some real food and, if she'd let him, he'd try to find her a safe place to live.

But his head felt heavy, his body weak. He closed his eyes as waves of exhaustion washed over him. Within minutes, he teetered over and dropped into a deep, black sleep.

CHAPTER 11

Patrick awoke to a sun-bright morning, wishing he had his cell phone to check the weather, the time and the date. He sat up, frowning when he saw he was still wearing his clothes from the day before, his 2020 clothes. Standing, he did a full body stretch, yawned, and stepped to the window, squinting out into a deep blue, autumn sky.

He came to full consciousness slowly, reluctantly, and with dread, like a man facing a possible death sentence. The pain of losing Eve and Colleen never left him; it beat in his veins, made him restless and agitated. They lived, and they breathed in him. He often heard the whisper of Eve's words, felt her hand clasped in his, and smelled the scented magic of her.

When he'd lighted the lantern, he'd prayed to be sent back in time a few days—just a few days—to prevent Eve, Colleen and her parents from climbing aboard that death trap of a flying machine, that airplane.

Patrick left the window, staring ahead, pushing a hand through his tousled hair. Now, with hours of sleep to fortify him, and most of his brain restored, it was time to strike out into this world of the Roaring Twenties, as it was called in the history books. It was time to find the connections between past and present.

After a bath and a shave, Patrick put on a white shirt, a gray suit, and a royal blue tie. He tugged on his boots, stepped to the tarnished mirror and examined himself.

"Who are you, sir?" he said to himself, nosing toward the mirror. "You know where you must go first, don't you? Perhaps she will have some answers. Perhaps Joni will have all the answers and, most certainly, she will have the lantern from 1884."

At the cafeteria where he'd just eaten breakfast, Patrick slipped into a public phone booth, sat down, closed the door and tugged the phonebook from the lower shelf, placing it on his knees. He opened it, flipping through the thin pages until he came to the Fs. Running his index finger down the page, he searched for Foster. When he found Darius Compton Foster, he smiled. "Hello, Darius. Won't you be surprised to see me again, you old man?"

With excitement and anticipation, he dropped five cents into the slot, heard the "ding" and, using the slow rotary, he dialed the number.

Tapping a finger on the phonebook, he heard a long, fluttering ring. Finally, an affected male voice answered, sounding polite and polished. "This is the Foster residence. I am Charles. May I help you?"

Patrick licked his lips. "Hello, is the lady of the house in? That is, is Mrs. Joan Katherine Foster available?"

The man's voice lowered to a bass baritone. "No, sir. The Fosters are in Europe and they will not return until the end of next month."

"Next month. Do you mean, November?"

"Yes, sir."

Patrick's shoulders sagged. He swiftly recalled Joni's daughter and son. They would both be in their 30s. "Is Lavinia available, or William?"

The voice lowered further, to a rich authority. "No, sir, Mrs. Lavinia Vanderbilt and Mr. William Foster do not reside here."

Patrick fought to keep his voice even. "I am an old friend of the family. Could you please tell me how I can get in touch with either Mrs. Vanderbilt or William Foster?"

Silence.

"Are you there, sir?" Patrick asked.

"Unfortunately, sir, I cannot give out that information. I'm sure you understand. Good day."

There was a final click as the man, probably the butler, hung the phone up. Leaning back with disappointment, Patrick decided to look for William Foster first. The name Vanderbilt was intimidating, and there would most likely be many layers of butlers, maids, secretaries, and maybe even a husband before Patrick would be able to speak directly with Lavinia.

He consulted the phonebook and, unfortunately, there were many William Fosters.

A tap on the glass startled Patrick, and he swung around to see a stout, middle-aged woman wearing a fur collar coat and a flat brim hat, decorated with a blue ribbon and a rose-colored bow. She stared at him with tight lips and scolding eyes, pointing at her watch to inform him that his time was up.

With a strained smile, he nodded politely, then returned to the phonebook. There were eight William

Fosters, and Patrick couldn't remember what William's middle name was. Before his time travel, he hadn't thought to reread Joni's 2019 Christmas Eve Letter, in which she'd mentioned her two children. Patrick decided to take a chance and call a few.

He dropped another nickel into the coin slot and dialed the first. There was no answer.

He dialed the next. A woman answered. She was gruff and spoke in a cockney accent. "Bill's mother died when he was just a li'al tyke. Bill's father didn't like her none. She was hard at the gin, she was. I 'eard 'im say so many a time."

When Patrick hung up, the woman rapped on the glass again with more force. Patrick turned, and she glared at him. She pointed aggressively at her watch and mouthed the words. "Your time is up."

He looked at her, but his thoughts were elsewhere. When he finally found William, of course Patrick couldn't tell him about the lantern or time travel. Had Joni ever told them? What had that letter said? He wasn't sure.

But perhaps William would give Patrick a phone number or address where the Fosters could be reached. He could then ask Joni where the lantern was. With luck, he'd retrieve it, light the thing and return to 2020.

Patrick stared at the fuming woman, and while he did, his thoughts shifted. But what if the lantern simply hurled him back to where he'd started, to Central Park, with no time change and nothing gained? What if Eve and Colleen had still perished in an airplane crash?

He lowered his head, as two people joined the line behind the infuriated woman. Patrick replaced the phonebook, pushed the door open, rose from the wooden booth stool and stepped out.

"You are rude and selfish, and I find you offensive," the woman said, flushed with outrage.

Patrick removed his fedora and bowed. "Madam, as my old Da used to say, 'Accept that some days you are the pigeon, and some days you are the monument.' Good day to you."

Outside, Patrick searched for another phone booth, acknowledging that he missed many conveniences of the twenty-first century, namely his cell phone and the internet where people, places and things could be found with the simple touch of a finger.

He'd long forgotten about his days as the nineteenth century New York City detective flatfooting it all over the City.

Sliding into a corner phone booth, he continued calling the remaining William Fosters, finally achieving success with the sixth name in the phonebook.

"Yes, sir, Mr. William Foster, Esquire is the son of Mr. and Mrs. Darius Compton Foster."

It was a housekeeper at the Foster residence, a soft voice with the pleasant tone of an older woman.

"As I said, I am an old friend of the family, only in town for a short time. Are you comfortable providing me with William Foster's place of business? I would like to contact him right away."

She did so, and Patrick scribbled it down using a pen and pad he'd purchased at a stationery store that morning. He thanked her, hung up the phone and stepped out onto the street, studying the address. The New York Merchant's Bank was located on Broadway and 36th Street. William's private office was on the 4th floor.

On Lexington Avenue and 66th Street, Patrick glanced about, searching for the nearest subway station, moving to the corner to ask a well-dressed man for directions. At that moment, the traffic light changed from green to red and a line of cars came to a stop.

The man pulled a cigarette from the side of his mouth and pointed with it. "Two blocks up on 68th. Take the Six down to Forty-Second. It's an easy walk from there."

When Patrick saw her, his breath caught. She was sitting leisurely in the backseat of a yellow and green Checker Cab, plainly visible through the large windows. He couldn't believe his eyes. She was wearing a forest green winter coat and held a green, stylish hat on her lap. Her blonde hair was neatly arranged around the base of her neck, pulled into a twist at the back.

Patrick was jolted by hot adrenaline. His eyes focused, then widened. She turned her head slowly, and he got a clear look at her. Her lips were a ruby red, her expression somber, her eyes sad. For an instant, their eyes met, but there was no recognition in hers.

Patrick's heart kicked in his chest. Were his eyes playing tricks on him? He rubbed them. He blinked. It *was* Eve! Sitting there in that taxi in the flesh. There was no doubt about it! It was his wife, Eve!

The light changed and, just as Patrick darted off for it, the car lurched ahead and changed lanes, edging into heavy traffic. Patrick raced after it, horns blaring, cars swerving around him; angry drivers cursing, yelling at him to get out of the street.

The taxi retreated, sunlight glinting off its back windows, the glare blinding him. She swiveled around to look at him, or was she looking at something else? He called her name, but his voice was swallowed up in the cacophony of motors, horns and shouts. Still he ran, dodging, weaving, car bumpers bouncing to a stop, nearly colliding. And then, to his horror, the taxi turned right off Lexington Avenue, the driver boosted the engine, and the taxi sped away. She was gone.

Patrick staggered across the chaotic street to the sidewalk, drained and devastated. He leaned heavily against a streetlamp and bent over, winded. When he lifted his head, a uniformed cop stood five feet away, his cold eyes clamped to him.

"Are you drunk?"

Patrick lifted his head, his suffering eyes trying to focus. "No. I'm not drunk."

"You can't be running down the middle of the street like that," the policeman said, with a touch of an Irish accent. "You'll be getting yourself or somebody else killed that way. What's the matter with you?"

Patrick dropped his eyes. "I'm sorry, officer. I'm not feeling so well right now."

"Well then, go see a doctor. And for the love of Mike, stay out of the flow of traffic."

Patrick lifted his head and there was a wildness in his eyes. He stared at the cop, but he didn't see him. "I think I've just seen a ghost," he whispered.

The cop glared at him, shook his head, turned and walked away.

CHAPTER 12

As the subway went thundering down the tracks, Patrick sat in a heavy helplessness. How would he ever find her? The woman in the taxi? Eve in the taxi or, at the very least, Eve's twin, her doppelganger. The detective in him hated these kinds of things—a chance sighting; a random, nebulous event.

Was fate toying with him? Why had he seen the woman? For what purpose, if he couldn't meet her, talk to her and solve the mystery? It unnerved him. It was maddening, and yet it held promise.

The lantern had tossed him haphazardly into a world he knew nothing about, and all he could do was keep going, putting one foot before the other, following his instincts.

The New York Merchant's Bank was impressive on the outside, with its colossal Greek limestone columns and broad staircase leading up to two massive oak doors that opened into hushed, impressive luxury. Curved above the entrance, in gold letters, were words to warm any banker's heart:

You Can Have No Friend More Faithful Than the Money You Have Saved

Inside, the expansive oval lobby was trimmed in gold leaf, with white marble floors and a golden dome 48-feet high, further proof that this temple of commerce was built to honor the glory of the rich and the fortunate.

At the lobby desk, two stern men in dark suits and ties anticipated Patrick's approach, their eyes watchful, sizing him up.

Patrick removed his hat and smiled formally. "Good morning, gentlemen, my name is Patrick Gantly. I am here to see Mr. William Foster."

The taller of the two men did not move a muscle. "Is he expecting you, sir?"

Patrick was ready with his answer. "He will want to see me when you mention that I am personally acquainted with his father, Dr. Darius Compton Foster, and his mother, Mrs. Joan Foster. Tell him it is about a bracelet and a trust that his mother set up for a very good friend of hers, Eve Gantly."

Patrick was referring to the bracelet that Eve and Joni had time traveled with from 2019 to 1884, with the intention to pawn it. They never did.

During the subway ride downtown, Patrick had worked to recall most of a letter Joni had written to them on Christmas Eve 1943, when she was eighty-nine years old. She'd entrusted the letter and the old lantern to a law firm that had delivered both items to Eve and Patrick in 2019, after they had returned from their time travel journey from 1884. Joni's letter had read,

"Remember we pawned the necklace, but we never did pawn the bracelet? Well, guess what? Years ago,

*Darius had it appraised. We sold it for a good price, and
I told him I wanted the money to go into a trust fund for
you. You should have seen his eyes.*

*Anyway, he said he had a broker friend who could
invest the money, and I agreed. Years later, my son,
William, took over management of the money. He is
quite gifted at making money."*

The two desk men exchanged a glance. The tall man
had a pencil-thin mustache and small, skeptical eyes.
"One moment sir," he said, reaching for a black
telephone. Lifting the receiver, he mumbled into it.
Patrick assumed an operator somewhere in the building
connected the call to William's office.

Minutes later, William Herbert Foster exited a golden
elevator from a bank of golden elevators. He came
striding into the lobby with the drawn expression of a
mourner. As he approached Patrick, his face wasn't
comfortable or friendly.

Patrick swiftly sized him up. In his mid-30s, William
was shorter and broader than his father, with a square
face and dark hair combed precisely back, parted neatly
on the left. His bearing was erect, his manner mildly
arrogant, like his father's. He had Joni's sharp nose and
prominent chin, but none of his mother's playful
mischief in his blue/gray eyes.

He drew up to Patrick and, being several inches
shorter, he lifted his chin slightly. He did not offer to
shake Patrick's hand, so Patrick did not extend his.

Since he had not been invited upstairs, Patrick figured
either William was a cautious man, or he was abiding by
bank policy.

"I am William Foster," he said, crisply.

"Patrick Gantly."

William was unimpressed. "Is your claim about being acquainted with my parents an accurate one?"

"Yes... I know them, and I would love to see them again."

"And you are who you say you are? That is, you are Mr. Patrick Gantly?"

"Yes."

William's jaw tightened. "I see."

Patrick said, "I would like to contact your parents."

"That is quite impossible," William said curtly. "They are away in Europe."

"So I have learned."

"Over the telephone, I was told you mentioned something about the trust fund for Mrs. Evelyn Gantly. Are you a relation?"

"Yes, I'm her husband."

William's mouth twitched. "I see. And is your wife with you?"

Patrick ignored the question, going on the offensive. William had purposely thrown up a protective wall between them, and Patrick wondered why.

Patrick said, "Mr. Foster, did your mother ever mention Evelyn to you? Did she mention me?"

William ignored Patrick's question. "If you have come seeking to draw funds from the trust, I can say, emphatically, that it will be impossible."

Something was wrong. William was being antagonistic. Patrick didn't care for this man, Joni's son. He had neither the refined manners of his father nor the sense of fun and grace of his mother. He was stiff, condescending and cold. Why?

"Has your father spoken to you about me, Mr. Foster?"

William's eyes were cool and direct. "I do not know for certain if you are who you say you are, Mr. Gantly, but if you are, then we have little to discuss, other than this. Some years back my father did speak to me about a Patrick Gantly. He was rather vague about the man, and he deflected all my questions. He said a Patrick Gantly, or his wife Eve, might show up some day and, if they did, I was to ignore their entreaties and send them on their way."

Patrick appraised William carefully, mildly stung by the implication. "Your father told you that?"

"Yes, sir. Now, I am a busy man and I must return to my business."

Patrick had believed that he and Darius Foster had been friends. Why would he paint such a negative picture of him and Eve to his son? But then Patrick recalled another part of Joni's letter. "*After you and Patrick vanished, I took the lantern and hid it. That lantern scared Darius to death, and he wanted no part of it.*"

So it seemed obvious that Darius wanted nothing more to do with the lantern or with Eve and Patrick. Although Darius surely never confided to his children that Eve and Patrick had time traveled using a lantern, he'd instructed them to ignore the Gantlys if they ever appeared, as indeed, Patrick had just appeared.

No doubt, Darius had accomplished this in private, swearing his children to secrecy, never sharing those conversations with his wife.

Patrick stood there, his thoughts circling. It made sense. Darius did not want Joni to leave him by time traveling to the twenty-first century, and he certainly didn't want Eve or Patrick to return and rupture his good and stable life with his wife and kids.

Patrick looked at William in a new way. William believed Patrick to be a threat, and now it all made sense. Although Patrick believed his reason for coming had been upended, he decided to try anyway.

"Mr. Foster... I do not need or want any funds. I came here to meet you because I would like to contact Mr. and Mrs. Foster. I truly believe your mother would like to know I am here. We were good friends. Would you please give me the name of a hotel where I can reach them?"

William's frosty manner didn't thaw. "I think you know the answer to that, Mr. Gantly. I will not."

"All right, sir, then would you tell me when they plan to return to New York?"

"They are traveling throughout Europe and the Mediterranean, and they made it quite clear when they left on their voyage that they will return only when they are good and ready to return. This is, as my mother said, their first real honeymoon."

Patrick's hopes faded. The lantern was so close, and yet, so far. Only Joni knew where it was, and Patrick had no way of knowing when he'd be able to contact her.

William lowered his voice. "Let me say this to you, sir. I believe my father thought you a scoundrel and a threat. If you ever try to contact me or my sister, Lavinia, again, I will have you arrested and put in jail."

Patrick narrowed his eyes on the man, trying to find some of Joni's generous spark in him. "You are Joni's son, are you not?"

William took offense, but Patrick was past caring.

"I beg your pardon?"

"William, your mother is a kind, fun and lovely woman, with a good heart and a generous nature. Your father is a good man, if a bit arrogant at times. But your father and I became good friends. I see none of their generosity of spirit in you. Go back to your money, sir, and may the good Lord above grant you the wisdom to see the truth of a person from your own eyes, and not through the words and the fearful lens of another. Good day, sir."

Patrick turned, put on his hat and strode aggressively across the marble floor, his footfalls echoing in the silence.

William called after him. "And don't contact my sister. I will have you jailed."

Patrick didn't look back as he exited the building.

William seethed, his face flushed with insult. When he turned to face the lobby desk, the two clerks glanced away, busying themselves.

"Don't you ever let that man in this building again! Do you hear me? Never."

CHAPTER 13

Patrick wandered aimlessly, pausing to take in construction in a city that, no matter what the year or the century, was always in motion and transition. He ambled through neighborhoods and passed new row houses that, in the twenty-first century, would be old neighborhoods, if they hadn't been knocked down years before and replaced by high-rises.

In an open boulevard, he passed young trees, playgrounds, and newly paved roads. He saw the façades of apartment houses laced with fire escapes, with front lawn signs announcing all apartments had been newly wired with electricity. Further downtown, carriage houses he'd recalled from the 1880s had been replaced by car garages and automobile stores.

At Columbus Circle, he stared up at a series of large billboard signs that advertised New York hotels and theaters, underclothes, candy and shaving soaps.

On the West Side, the landscape bristled with chimneys and cranes along the railroad tracks. Here and there were human habitations: feeble-looking houses, unpainted and gray, next to a rough mountain range of coal cinders. Many poor families were struggling to scratch out a living, just like families had in the 1880s and were still doing in 2020.

Being a time traveler had greatly expanded Patrick's world view, his thinking and his emotions. Eve had once said, "Patrick, we've seen and lived more history than anyone else on this planet. Has it made us any wiser?"

He had shrugged. "Wiser? I don't know. Certainly, it has allowed me to experience more of the mystery of life and the human condition: our struggle to survive, to love, and to understand loss and death."

"You're too philosophical for me, Patrick," Eve had said. "I see life as a thing that never stops. Evolution never stops. It's relentless. So, when I look at you and I feel love for you, I believe that my love for you will never stop; it will never end. Perhaps it has always been there; maybe we've been together for many lifetimes. When I time traveled that first time back to 1885 and found you, I felt that love had been waiting for us, patiently, just waiting once again to reawaken a timeless love."

"A romantic you are, Eve, and a wee bit head-in-the-stars for me."

Patrick was brought back to the present when rain tapped his hat. He looked skyward into rolling gray clouds, squinting, feeling the cool pricks of rain on his face. He ducked into a doorway and blew into his fists to warm them. He'd forgotten to buy gloves. Eve had often criticized him for not wearing gloves.

"Gloves are cheap, Patrick. You can buy them from a street vendor for five dollars. You should buy six pairs and keep them in various winter pockets. Even better, I'll buy two pairs and keep them in my pockets."

Patrick smiled at the memory. He missed her with a pain so acute it nearly doubled him over.

The rain passed quickly, and Patrick started walking again, glancing about into the crowds that flowed around him; glancing at passengers in cars and people that emerged from their apartments.

She was out there somewhere—the woman he'd seen in the taxi—the woman who looked like Eve.

He struggled to solve the problem of how to find her. In his day, when he'd been a detective in the 1880s, he'd known the cabbies who frequented his neighborhood and the Fifteenth Precinct where he worked.

In those days, he would have asked a driver if a pretty blonde had climbed into his cab. They all recalled the pretty girls. They would have told him where they'd picked her up and where they had dropped her.

But in this world of 1925, the blonde in the taxi was a needle in the City haystack. Patrick continued on, his eyes searching, his shoulders slumped against the chilly wind.

Later that afternoon, in a light autumn mist, Patrick returned to Central Park and made his way to Sarah Finn's bench. He carried a paper sack holding a wrapped roast beef sandwich, a pickle, and a box of Cracker Jack.

The bench was empty and Sarah wasn't in sight. He decided to ignore the mist and the fog rolling in. He sat and waited for her, losing time and place. He was tired of thinking and hurting, so he shut off his mind.

There was quiet all around him, with just the occasional birdsong, the wheezing of wind, and the far-off sound of a siren. When a woman's ragged cough hit his ears, he sat up alert.

Patrick snapped a look toward the coughing sound and saw Sarah waddling toward him, breaking out of the fog, cradling her bundle, as if it were a baby. Sarah was no Madonna and child, but in that bizarre moment that's the image that slid into his mind.

Sarah didn't see him at first. Then he stood. She stopped, her eyes round and fearful as she calculated the threat.

"Hello, Sarah Finn," Patrick said.

She cocked a wide, startled eye at him, struggling to focus. "Hey, who's there? Who's calling my name? Who knows Sarah Finn?"

Patrick smiled. "Me."

"Me who? Who's me?"

"Patrick."

"I don't know no Patrick. Get away from my bench, you no-good, prodigal-son-of-a-wastrel. That's my bench now. After dark, that's *my* bench."

"I'm Patrick, Sarah. Patrick Gantly. Remember?"

She took a couple of careful steps toward him, her eyes straining to peer through the stringy mist and fog. She scratched her chin, staring, wheezy and nervous.

"I've got my knife with me and I'll use it if I have to. Make no mistake about that."

Patrick lowered his voice. "Sarah, I shared the bench with you the other night. Remember? I'm Patrick."

All at once she straightened, lighting up with recognition. "Buster Boy! It's Buster Boy, come back to share my bench with me."

Patrick gave a little shake of his head. "Patrick, Sarah. My name's Patrick."

Sarah cackled, her mouth open, showing ugly teeth. "Well, what do you know? I don't recognize you, you wearing that hat. Did the old lady toss you out on your tuchus again?"

Patrick removed his hat. "No, Sarah, she didn't." He held up the paper bag. "Look, I brought you supper."

She blinked in the dim lamplight. "Hey, you is all cleaned up. Look at you, with the full, long coat. And, Jesus, Mary and Joseph, you're wearing a tie. What happened to you? Did your rich uncle kick off and give you all his bank money?"

"No. Come and sit down, Sarah. I brought food."

The hacking cough returned, deep and raspy. It was worse than before.

"Have you seen a doctor about that cough, Sarah?"

She coughed on, shaking her head no. When the fit ended, she held up a hand, croaking out the words. "There ain't a doctor in this City I'd go to. All of them is heartless quacks. They'll take your good money, all right, and then shove you off into the arms of the Grim Reaper. I've got the right stuff for my cough. Don't you worry about me none. We'll share a little right now. It's good for what ails you, and it's a mighty fine bracer against the cold and the mist."

Sarah shambled over to the bench and dropped down heavily, blowing out a sigh. "Lord have mercy, I'm a tired, old woman."

Patrick sat next to her, still holding the bag. "Are you hungry?"

She glanced at the bag suspiciously. "What's in that bag?"

"A roast beef sandwich, on rye, with a big pickle."

Her eyebrows lifted in approval. "A pickle? I love pickles. Gimme that pickle. I'll wash it down with some good old whiskey. That'll fix my cough."

"Eat the sandwich, too, Sarah. It'll do you good."

She nodded as she tugged a half-drunk whiskey bottle from her bundle. "All right, Buster Boy, I'll eat it, but first, you and me is gonna drink a toast to my family."

Patrick sat down next to her, interested. "Do you have a family?"

"Well, of course I've got me a family. Everybody comes from somebody, and has somebody, don't they? What do you think I am, a lonely Lucy?"

"Where are they?" Patrick asked, thinking he would contact them.

With her gnarly, stubby fingers, she twisted off the stopper and raised the whiskey bottle, jabbing the neck up into the sky. "Up there, Buster Boy. They're all up there in Beulah Land, sitting with the good Lord. Now, you and me is gonna have us a good swig from this bottle in their honor. Okay?"

Patrick nodded. "Sure, Sarah. Sure we will."

She tipped the bottle back and took a long pull on the whiskey. She winced, coughed, and handed the bottle to Patrick. "Drink up, Buster Boy."

Patrick took the bottle and held it up in the lamplight so he could read the label.

"Allman's Pot Still Irish Whiskey." Patrick glanced at her. "It's from Nuns Island in Galway. Where did you get it?"

Sarah laughed, slapping a knee. "Wouldn't you like to know? Don't you fret yourself about it. Go on, drink to my family."

Patrick set the paper bag down on the bench. He raised the bottle in a toast. "To your family, Sarah."

He grimaced and lifted the bottle, not allowing his mouth to touch the lip. A stream of the whiskey splashed on his tongue. He swallowed, feeling the stinging heat slide down his throat and warm his chest.

"Go ahead," Sarah coaxed. "Drink another. It will hit the spot and then remove it."

She laughed at her joke and slapped her knee again.

Patrick watched with pleasure as Sarah ate, using her jagged teeth to pull off pieces of the sandwich and chew on one side, where some strong teeth remained.

"It's good beef," she said, chomping with her mouth open. "Yes, sir, there ain't nothing wrong with this meat, nor the butcher who cut it. I owe you one, Buster Boy."

"You don't owe me anything. It's rent for sharing your bench."

Still chewing, she gave him another once over. "So are you staying here again tonight?"

"No, I have a place."

"Do you, now?"

"As I was walking around today, I think I may have found you a place to stay. It's safe and warm."

She narrowed her eyes on him. "Huh? What did you say? A place for me?"

"Yes... It's not so far from here. It's a kind of boarding house, not the best and not the worst."

She shook her head. "It ain't for me, Buster Boy, but I thank you for your trouble. I like my bench just fine."

Patrick faced her squarely. "Sarah, you're sick. You need to be sleeping where it's warm."

"I've got me own good whiskey for that."

Frustrated, Patrick glanced away.

"Hey, why are you worrying about an old woman like me? As handsome a man as you are, you should be out with a lady with some class."

Patrick looked at her. "Will you try staying in the place for one night? Just tonight. Please? I'll walk you over there. It's on the West Side. You can check it out. If you don't like it, then you don't stay. What do you say?"

She reached into the Cracker Jack box, grabbed a handful and tossed the treats into her mouth. "No, Buster Boy, thanks all the same. I wouldn't sleep, knowing someone might steal into my room and slit my throat."

"Nobody is going to slit your throat, Sarah."

She looked at him and her wild eyes melted into warmth. "You should have a gal, you know. You should be with her, and not with an old hag like me. Come on, now, tell me. Where is she?"

Patrick stood up. He arched his back into the black sky, feeling the coolness on his face. "I wish I knew, Sarah. God in heaven, I wish I knew."

CHAPTER 14

Early Thursday morning, October 29, Patrick was lying on his bed, fully clothed, staring at the ceiling, his hands laced behind his head. His bedroom was sunny and surprisingly quiet. He could hear his heartbeat in his ears; hear his breath moving in and out. He'd spent the last six mornings standing on the sidewalk where he'd first seen the Eve look-a-like in the taxi.

As a former detective, Patrick knew from experience that people often return to a place they've been seen before. Perhaps the place was on a route to work, or to the home of a family member, or to a weekly doctor's appointment.

It was a long shot for sure, but it was the only chance he had, so he spent his mornings hanging out on the corner of Lexington Avenue and 66th Street, being especially alert around 11 a.m., when he'd first seen the cab stop at the light, the blonde passenger inside.

In the afternoons, he wandered the City like a pilgrim, turning off Lexington onto 67th Street and strolling, hopeful that a cab might deliver her to one of the brownstones or doctor's offices operating there.

He'd also returned to Central Park to see Sarah. She'd shown some signs of improvement, but she'd obstinately refused to see a doctor. Patrick continued to bring her food and, at least, she'd eaten with aggressive satisfaction.

But no matter how he pleaded, she wouldn't leave her park bench for the boarding house, and it saddened him. Despite her improved health, she couldn't last long living on the streets, drinking heavily and sleeping on a park bench.

At 10 a.m., Patrick stood on the corner of 66th Street and Lexington, stamping his feet to stay warm. It was sunny but cold. He'd bought a small RCA table radio and the announcer on an early morning show had said it was going to be a blustery day, with a high of thirty-six degrees.

The City was alive with action, pedestrians hurrying by, traffic moving in fits and starts, and horns tooting for the right of way. A newsboy down the street shouted out the headlines. "**Murder on Wall Street**! Read all about it. Mistress kills for love and money. Early edition!"

A one-legged man on crutches stuttered by, pain on his face. A woman wrapped in a racoon coat and cloche hat sashayed past, tossing Patrick a flirtatious glance. She was pretty, slim and curvy, with an aggressive walk, but she wasn't Eve.

Two talkative women left a soda shop with a younger man. Patrick had learned that since prohibition, the ice cream salons and soda shops were immensely popular. Without bars, at least legal bars to meet and greet in, the ice cream shop had become the place to socialize, date, and mingle. But at this early hour?

When a policeman came into view, Patrick ducked his head and glanced away, aware that he was the same policeman he'd met a week before, when he'd raced out into traffic, chasing the taxi.

The policeman ambled along the sidewalk, down the street and out of view. Traffic motored and rattled; a cursing beggar searched the waste baskets and turned to impassive faces as they hurried past him, his dirty hand outstretched, eyes glassy. A kid zipped by on roller skates, the wheels growling along the sidewalk. Polished businessmen leaned in close as they walked, the smell of deals and profit all about them.

Patrick glanced at his watch. It was twenty minutes after twelve. There was no taxi and no blonde. Crestfallen, he left the corner, his feet tired, his ears and face pink from the cold, his spirit beaten.

He returned to his room with a jar of corn whiskey he'd bought on the sly, from a pharmacist at the drugstore. He toasted Sarah, and whispered Eve's name as if uttering a prayer. He splashed some moonshine into a glass and tossed it back, feeling lonely, puzzled and lost. A pleasurable burn slid down his throat, and he knew he'd be sampling the jar for many minutes, until the loneliness was gone; until Eve's lovely face blurred and faded away.

After dark, Patrick found himself downtown in Greenwich Village. He wasn't entirely sure how he'd traveled there, or why he'd come. He wasn't drunk on the whiskey, having swallowed only a quarter of the stuff, but he was drunk in a sense—feeling as though he were sleepwalking, wandering the streets in a haze of grief and confusion.

Under the glare of streetlights, he walked past the flare and flicker of shop lights and the running yellow lights of a Vaudeville theater marquee. He heard the razzle-dazzle of jazz music drifting out from some doorway nearby, the trumpets brash, the trombones hectic, sliding up a rowdy scale.

He was nudged and pushed by a streaming crowd of young people, a happy-go-lucky carelessness about them; a devil-may-care attitude of celebration that he hadn't seen since the 1880s in the Tenderloin District. Their laughter was shrill and indulgent; their dress gaudy; their bodies loose and free, disturbing the air around them. They seemed intent on living every single moment as if it were their last.

Was this the "Lost Generation" that Patrick had read about in the twenty-first century?

When he saw the woman, he blinked, as if peering through a haze. And then he saw her—really saw her— and it was as if someone had snapped fingers in front of his face, waking him from a trance.

It was she. Impossible. It was the blonde he'd seen in the taxi! Eve! She was alone, walking purposefully on the far side of the street. Recognition fired his blood.

In a desperate reflex, Patrick whirled about and started after her, blundering out into the street. A car horn blared, and Patrick jumped back. The car jolted to an abrupt stop, tires squealing, just missing him. Angry, the driver raised a fist, yelling.

"Are you crazy? Get out of the street, you stupid idiot!"

Patrick ignored the man. He sidestepped left and circled around the rear of the car, his neck craned, eyes sharp. He saw the woman, a flash of a forest green coat and hat, enter through the black door of a nondescript building. Patrick darted off, determined that, this time, she wouldn't get away.

He drew up to the black door and gave it a shove. He was met by a man about his own size, wearing a dark suit, jazzy tie, and slicked-back brown hair. It was an ugly, aggressive face, all angles and sharp lines. He was the perfect candidate for a mugshot.

He blocked Patrick's way, his flat nose and cold eyes dominant. "You a member, pal?" he asked, with menace, in a low Brooklyn accent.

Patrick's mind was a blank. "A what? Member?"

"Yeah, pal, a member. If you ain't a member or don't know a member, you ain't going in, see?"

Patrick removed his hat and ran a hand through his hair, desperate to plead his case. "Look, I just need to take a quick look. I won't be long."

The bouncer repeated his patter, with a little more of a threat. "Like I said, in case you didn't hear me right the first time, if you ain't a member, and don't know a member, you don't go in. Got it?"

Patrick huffed out a frustrated sigh. It wouldn't do any good for him to punch the guy and step over him. No doubt there were more like him inside.

"Go away nice," the bouncer said, gruffly. "Don't be that guy that gets the good knuckles of my right fist."

Patrick stepped outside, turning in a nervous circle. He had to get in. She was in there. Whoever she was, she was in there and he had to talk to her.

Two men came swaying down the street, voices loud with boozy celebration, laughter pitched high after a bawdy joke. They were well-dressed, tanked up, silly, sloppy and ready for more of what they'd had at the last speakeasy. They clumsily pointed themselves toward the black door, then stopped, their attentions captured by a beautiful girl who swayed by.

"Hello there, girlie," one man said, swinging around gracelessly, removing his hat and offering a little courtly bow.

She ignored him and kept going, nose upturned with insult and attitude.

The men fell into merry laughter, one with a high tenor guffaw, the other with "ho-ho-ho-ing" bass baritone joy.

An idea struck, and Patrick made his move. He stepped up to the men, a wide smile on his face. "Gentlemen, are you going inside?" he asked jovially.

One glassy-eyed man looked Patrick over, one eye wandering. "If you mean, sir, are we about to present ourselves to Gadfly's Speakeasy, an unholy and infamous establishment, then you are correct."

"Then you are members?"

The other, a portly man with a florid face, lowered his head and his voice. He held a vertical forefinger to his lips to shush Patrick, and then glanced around dramatically. "We are not only members, sir, we are also on the board of directors."

Both men howled at the joke, and Patrick waited, summoning patience, and forcing an ingratiating smile. When he spoke, he laid his Irish accent on thickly.

"Gentlemen, I'll be a wonderin' if you would be so kind as to allow me to accompany you. It seems you have the advantage on me, having already raised a glass or two to the lads and the lasses. Please grant me the opportunity and the good pleasure of joining you inside, and the first round will be on me."

The portly man came to life. "My dear sir, who can resist such an Irish plea? You speak our language, as it were, and sing in our perfect key. By all means. Yes, you will enter as our guest."

Patrick grinned. "Thank you, gentlemen. My dear old Da, who was from the great Isle of Ireland, used to say, 'One drink is too many for me and a thousand not enough.'"

Both men laughed in agreement. They slapped Patrick on the shoulder, and a friendship was born.

The portly man, wearing a greatcoat and a bowler hat, extended his hand. "I'm Mike Borland, and this poor excuse for a man is the honorable Judge Thomas T. Chappie."

"My name is Patrick," he said, as he pumped first Mike Borland's hand, then turned to Judge Chappie and shook his.

The Judge's white mustache was impressive, his voice deep, loud and filled with authority. "Don't listen to that old duffer, Patrick. He's the most corrupt cop down at 240 Centre Street."

"That's Detective Sergeant Borland to you, Judge. And I'll thank you to keep your compliments to yourself."

They had another good laugh, and Judge Chappie gave Patrick another hearty slap on the shoulder.

"Come on, Patrick, let's go in and have that drink and find us a girlie or two."

With the goodwill of old friends, they advanced through the black door and into Gadfly's Speakeasy.

CHAPTER 15

Patrick entered Gadfly's with the sharp eye of a detective. He quickly scanned the room. The speakeasy was a jolly, glitzy club, featuring a loud, crowded mahogany bar with brass railings, amber overhead lamps and an unexpected cigar store Indian on display on the far end, against the wall.

There was a stage and a small dance floor, with round tables and red padded chairs surrounding it. There were private booths along the back walls, where dim lighting was arranged shrewdly to cast those comfy booths in romantic shadows. All the windows were covered by black cloth. Two exit doors were covered by beefy bouncers wearing black suits and granite-hard expressions.

At the bar stood polished men in tuxedos, and bankers and stockbrokers in expensive pinstripe suits. All shouldered in close to the flappers, who had bobbed hair, flashed shiny grins, and gripped long cigarette holders. One wore a beaded, silver fringe skull cap; another, a navy-blue pillbox hat with a large gray bow and flowers;

another, a chatty blonde, wore a blue turban flapper hat with sparkles.

Many ladies wore tight sequined dresses in black, emerald green and red; dangling earrings; and plenty of eye makeup and rouge. They sipped gin from champagne glasses held in elegant hands, and they leaned and posed and blew feathers of smoke toward the ceiling, their sexy eyes half-hooded, their lips moist and pursed.

A black piano player in a plug hat and white suit was on the stage, thumping out a bouncy tune, accompanied by a piercing trumpet and a belching trombone. In the humid atmosphere, cigar and cigarette smoke hovered like a cloud, and waiters circled the room with trays of balanced cocktails held aloft. Cigarette girls, in skimpy skirts, weaved through the tables, their smiles fixed, eyes watchful as they hovered and flirted and engaged in smooth commerce.

"Come on, Patrick," Judge Chappie said. "Let's get over to that bar before I die of thirst."

Patrick followed the two men to the bar, and they edged in, waving the bartender over.

"What'll it be, Patrick?" Detective Borland asked. "How about a whiskey?"

Patrick nodded as he cast his keen eyes about the room.

Borland ordered while Judge Chappie wrapped a friendly arm around Patrick's shoulder. "How about a good ole Irish joke, Patrick? I heard it from one of the Irish lads I sent to jail just the other day."

Patrick nodded, distracted. "Yes. Fine."

"Okay, here goes. Come over here, Borland, you've got to hear this. It's the best one I've heard in a while."

Detective Borland shouldered in.

Judge Chappie became animated. He chuckled, anxious to begin. "All right, then, Mrs. Donovan is walking down O'Connell Street in Dublin when she meets up with Father Flaherty.

"The Father says, 'Top o' the mornin' to ye! Aren't ye Mrs. Donovan and didn't I marry ye and yer hoosband two years ago?'

"She says, 'Aye, that ye did, Father.'

"The Father asks, 'And be there any wee little ones yet?'

"She says, somewhat downcast, 'No, not yet, Father. We've not had the blessing.'

"So the Father, being sympathetic to her plight, says, 'Well now, I'm off to Rome next week and I'll light a fertility candle for ye, and yer hoosband. Now, how will that be?'

"Mrs. Donovan grows with excitement and she replies, 'Oh, bless ye, Father.'"

Suddenly, Patrick saw her. He froze. He couldn't pull his eyes from her. She was a dead ringer for Eve.

The Judge continued, but Patrick wasn't listening; his full attention was fixed on the blonde.

"So then, Mrs. Donovan and the Father part ways. Well, some years later they meet again.

"The Father asks, 'Well now, Mrs. Donovan, how are ye these days?'

"She says, 'Oh, a little weary, Father. Yes, a little bit weary.'

"The Father asks, 'And tell me, have ye any wee ones yet?'

"She replies, 'Oh yes, Father... We got two sets of twins and six singles. Ten in all!'

"The Father lights up like the sun and says, 'That's wonderful! And how is yer loving hoosband doing?'

"Mrs. Donovan's eyes narrow darkly on the good Father and she says, 'E's gone to Rome to blow out yer fookin' candle!'"

The Judge and Borland exploded into laughter, Borland slapping his knee.

As if in a trance, Patrick stared, not laughing, not seeing anything or anyone except the woman. Was she Eve? How could she be?

Detective Borland followed Patrick's eyes. "Ah, yes, Patrick, that one is lovely, and she's alone. She must be waiting for someone, don't you think?"

Patrick kept his eyes on her. "Maybe."

"You'll want to be careful with that one, Patrick."

Patrick didn't hear Borland's warning. He left the bar, starting toward her, as if being propelled by unseen hands. He crossed the dance floor, dodging couples dancing the Charleston, and edged between the tables, drawing close to the woman.

She sat alone, lovely and eye-catching, with tight blonde curls and cool, icy blue eyes. Her tulip-red dress was a long sleeve, lace cocktail dress with a lace hem. It fit her to perfection. She wore a silver art deco headpiece, crystal rhinestone earrings, and a matching bracelet that caught the light and sparkled. Her red lips were small but full, her cheekbones high, and her face impassive.

Patrick felt a stirring of unease, of being lost in a daydream. The woman looked exactly like Eve; from the tilt of her head and her thoughtful manner, to the elegant way she held her glass.

When Patrick was only a few feet away, a man approached her table. Patrick stopped, confusion darkening his eyes. Who was this man?

He was a broad, attractive man, about forty years old, with chestnut hair and eyes shining with confidence. His dark, woolen suit and golden silk tie were of the latest style.

"Hey, baby. How about a dance?"

The woman's eyes were still, her expression aloof. She looked up from over her coupe glass of champagne. "No… thank you."

Undaunted, the man didn't move. He adjusted his tie. "Are you waiting for somebody?"

"Maybe. Maybe not."

"Okay, baby, I'll tell you this. There isn't another man in this room who'll have the guts to come over."

"I dare say you're right," she said coldly. "Bravo, you won your bet. Congratulations. Now leave me alone."

He turned surly. "Why do you come into a place like this alone, if you don't want some action? And a doll like you could get some action, couldn't you? Lots of guys would put big money up for you."

The woman didn't take the bait and show anger. She reacted with boredom. "Go back to the bar and collect your winnings."

Some of the self-confidence drained from his eyes. "You're gonna get yours someday, girlie. Count on it."

He whirled around, picked his way through the throng, and returned to the bar.

Patrick observed that the woman's hands trembled, but her expression was calm. He also noticed that the man's buddies at the bar had swiveled around and were glaring at her, one with a sneering, threatening grin.

The woman looked away, avoiding their eyes. That's when she saw Patrick, standing only a few feet away, gazing at her. He removed his hat, and his pulse jumped as he gave her a little nod. She had a haunting charisma that unnerved him, just as Eve had, and there was a familiarity in her eyes, in her bearing, in her, whatever it was called, her spirit, her soul.

She looked up at him with long lashes, seeing thick, curly black hair, steady blue eyes, a prominent nose, and a solid, determined jaw. He had good shoulders, and his long legs were solid beneath him.

Patrick couldn't pull his eyes from her, seeing another place and another time, remembering old conversations he'd had with Eve; remembering her laughter and her soft kisses.

He stepped toward the woman, uncertain. He blinked and swallowed. Gradually the past melted from his eyes and he focused on the seated woman, seeing only her.

Her irritated eyes narrowed on him. "Are you with them?" she asked, jerking her head toward the bar.

Patrick didn't speak for a moment, keeping his eyes on her. "... No, I'm not."

"What do you want?" she asked, pointedly.

Patrick tried to speak, but faltered.

"Well?" she repeated.

He lifted a hand, then let it drop.

She was puzzled by his manner and his silence. If this was a come-on, she'd never seen the approach before. And there was no denying that he was handsome, very handsome, a tall, earthy man with focused, mysterious eyes. He had an unusual quality that set him apart from the other men in the room. Other women had noticed his desirability as well. Their eyes had followed him as he'd entered the place, as hers had done.

"I just wanted to say…" Patrick said, his voice barely audible over the raucous band.

She cut him off. "I'm not interested. I just want to be alone."

"It's not that… I mean, it's not what you think."

Her eyes widened on him with suspicion. "Not what I think? How do you know what I think?" she countered, brusquely.

"Forgive me, it's just that…" Patrick struggled to find words.

"What then?" the woman asked.

Patrick lifted a hand again, trying to shape his stalled thoughts. "Forgive me for my words, but it's just that you have the face and look of someone who is dear to me."

She tried to read him. "Someone who is dear to you? Okay, that's a new one. I've never heard that line before."

"It's not a line."

"Fine, where is this person?"

"Was… I mean. What I mean to say is that she *was* dear to me."

The blonde was skeptical. "Girlfriend? Wife?"

"She was my wife."

The woman blinked her long lashes. "If you're trying to pick me up, sir, this is not the best way to accomplish it. You're probably lying, but even if you're not, you should know that women—all women—like to feel special, as if they are the only one… One of a kind. They don't want the, as you put it, 'face and look' of someone else."

Her voice echoed through Patrick's mind. It was so like Eve's voice, possessing the same quality and cadence; the same rise and fall of a sentence. And it was exactly what Eve would have said.

"Well then, madam, you misunderstand me. You *are* one-of-a-kind. Make no mistake about it. That's why I've been looking for you."

Patrick saw sudden alarm in her eyes.

"Looking for me?" Her voice sharpened. "Do you work for my husband?"

"Your husband? No. I don't work for anybody. I don't know your husband. It is you I was looking for."

"Then I'll ask you again. What do you want?"

"Well, now, there you have me. Right now, all I want is to talk to you."

Her chin jerked up. "Talk? Just talk?"

"Yes... I've come a long way... Yes, just talk. Frankly, I could use a friend."

Her eyes went flat and hard. "A friend? Now, that's a line I've heard before."

Dismay tightened his ribs. He was losing her.

She stared into his eyes, noticing that her words had sharpened his sorrow. His handsome face and strange manner intrigued her. Why not talk to him? What harm would it do?

Her face warmed as she studied him. Needed a friend? Was it a line? If it was, it was an old one, overused and pathetic, but despite all that, she began to waiver. Was he in earnest? Was he flirting? After a few moments of deliberation, she decided she liked the flirtation, if that's what it was.

"What is that? Is that an Irish accent?"

Patrick grew hopeful. "A bit of one, yes. My parents were from Ireland."

She gave him a clear, direct look, and she was gently startled by the power of his eyes. They seemed to bore into her; into the depths of her. But there was more; something about the man aroused and attracted her. His eyes held storms and distances, and those eyes seemed bizarrely familiar, as if she'd seen them before, perhaps passing on the street, or in a long-forgotten dream.

"Where is this woman who is dear to you?"

Patrick hesitated, pondering how to respond. "She died."

The woman saw the pain in his eyes. Raw, immediate pain. She turned away. "I'm sorry, but I can't help you. I wish to be alone now."

Patrick saw a bouncer glaring at him. Since the woman had turned away, the bouncer, experienced with female body language, would probably approach him soon.

"Please, madam. May I just speak with you, if only for a few minutes? Please. I won't make a nuisance of myself."

She looked at him, unsure. "Perhaps you've already made a nuisance of yourself."

Patrick gripped the brim of his hat, turning it in his hands. "Then I'll ask your pardon... and I will leave you in peace."

Her eyes swung back to him and she felt a catch in her chest, and a little thrill; a little thrill of desire for the possibility of an adventure; a little thrill of desire to escape from her lonely, troubled life and talk to him, and to be his friend, his "stand in," and maybe more.

As he turned to leave, she said, "Not here."

He faced her.

She spoke conspiratorially, in a loud whisper. "I don't want to be seen leaving with you. I'll meet you later at Lispenard and Canal Street, on the east side of Broadway, where the two streets converge. There's an all-night café called Pan and Spoon. The place sits just below a sign that says Nehemiah Gitelson & Sons, converters of cotton goods. The café's a greasy hole-in-the-wall, but it's open all night and I know the owner."

Patrick swallowed. "When?"

"It's almost ten. I'll be there at eleven-thirty. If I'm not there at eleven-thirty, I'm not coming. All right?"

"Fair enough. My name is Patrick Gantly."

She looked directly into his eyes. "I'm Evelyn. Evelyn Stratford."

Patrick was struck dumb. "Evelyn? Eve?"

"My friends call me Eve. My mother, who is a strict Presbyterian, calls me Evelyn."

Patrick grew cold, heart thudding, his wide eyes seeking answers.

Evelyn noticed his face had gone white. "Are you all right?"

Patrick took a step back, recovering. "Yes... That's a grand name, Eve. I will be there at eleven-thirty. Yes, I will."

Dazed, he meandered back to the bar where Judge Chappie and Detective Borland were locked in animated conversation.

As Patrick drew up, Judge Chappie laid a friendly hand on his shoulder and nodded toward Evelyn.

"Don't you get yourself upset over that girlie sending you on your way, Patrick. She's all danger, that one."

Patrick shot him a look. "What do you mean, danger?"

Judge Chappie leaned in toward Patrick's ear. "She's the wife of a well-known attorney, Vernon P. Scott, who heads one of the best law firms in the City. His clients are the old Victorian wealthy class. Anyway, there are a lot of rumors circulating about those two."

Detective Borland shoved a straight whiskey into Patrick's hand.

"Don't you worry about it, Patrick," Borland said. "There are many more fishies in the sea and, by God, we'll have us a fishie or two before this night is through. Right, Chappie?"

Patrick stared ahead, blankly. He was shaken after seeing Evelyn, and excited that he was going to see her again. He didn't care about who her husband was or what the rumors were. He just wanted to see her again.

After swallowing down his drink, he turned back toward the table where Evelyn was sitting. It was empty; a waiter was swiping the tabletop with a bar rag. She was gone.

Her husband's last name was Scott. She'd told him her name was Evelyn Stratford. Would she meet him, or had she expertly given him the brush-off?

CHAPTER 16

Patrick took a cab to the Pan and Spoon, arriving at 11:15 p.m. He exited the cab on the far corner and, keeping to the shadows, he strolled, casting his eyes about for anything that looked suspicious. It was the former detective in him, and it had something to do with the fact that Evelyn was married, and that, according to Detective Borland, rumors about her marriage to a well-known attorney were circulating.

Patrick tugged up the collar of his greatcoat and adjusted his fedora, cocked smartly above his left eye. A streetcar rumbled by, bell clanging, its yellow interior light spilling out onto the cobblestones.

Patrick saw what must have been another speakeasy on the far corner, its discolored Café sign blinking fitfully, hunched men coming and going. Many of the windows of the dark row houses nearby had no blinds. In one window, the blind hung open, and the sound of a baby crying was mostly swallowed by the humming rhythm of the city.

Patrick shifted his gaze to see a slow horse trotting by, hauling a cart filled with rags and paper, a white-bearded man bent at the reins, his brown, applejack cap pulled low to his ears. The horse edged toward the curb as a model-T Ford chugged past, the lone driver in silhouette.

Patrick unwrapped a piece of spearmint chewing gum and shoved it into his mouth. It was a cold thirty-eight degrees, and it was humid. The forecast was for rain.

Keeping alert, Patrick ambled to the opposite corner on Canal Street. Two cars were parked on the north side of the street, away from the three streetlights, no drivers at the wheels. No passengers. A lighted billboard sign, perched on an apartment roof across the street, read Drink Grape Cola. Patrick nodded at it, suddenly feeling thirsty. Maybe he'd order one at the Pan and Spoon.

Would she show up? He had the feeling she would. There had been a flicker of interest in her eyes, and he knew those eyes well. As disconcerting as it was, he'd seen Eve in those eyes.

He ducked into the dark doorway of a closed tailor shop and waited, seeing nothing out of the ordinary; nothing suspicious.

While he waited in confusion, struggling to manage nervous excitement and a boyish anticipation, he kicked at the ground. Seeing the woman, the Eve woman, had been a shock. It had also been a dubious and suspicious incident. If he were in the real world, that is, his world in the 1880s before he'd become aware of the time travel lantern, he'd have known for certain that there was a swindle in the works. He'd know he was being set up. It was all too opportune and obvious, and nothing hung together in any practical or predictable way. But then, the time lantern was not practical or predictable either, was it?

Patrick cursed the lantern, that erratic trickster that tossed the dice of time travel chance like some drunken gambler throwing the dice, or a mad scientist who didn't give a damn what happened once the lantern's wick was set aflame. In effect, wasn't Nikola Tesla that mad scientist who had programmed the thing?

Patrick heaved out a sigh. *So who is this woman, this Evelyn Stratford?* he thought.

Patrick chewed the gum vigorously, his hands restless in his pockets. At 11:33, a taxi came into view. Quick-stepping it, he left the doorway and hurried across the street and into the glaring light from the Pan and Spoon. He wanted to make sure Evelyn saw him so she wouldn't drive away.

The taxi drew up to the curb and stopped. Sitting inside, Evelyn sat still and erect, feeling fragile. Why was she meeting this man? This tall, brooding and strange man. It was not like her. But then, after everything that had happened to her in the last few months, she hardly recognized herself. She was different. She was changed, and she was still in the process of changing, a chaotic and frightening change that had put her in a small, sad place.

She wanted to escape from that sad place. Was that why she'd come? And there was something wonderfully mysterious about Patrick that stirred things up in her, and made her feel girlish, and made her feel like a woman, and made her want to take a chance. When she'd looked into his marvelous blue eyes, there had been an unsettling sense of recognition that reached down and touched her very aching soul.

Evelyn paid the driver and emerged, tall and willowy, wearing her forest green raincoat and felt cloche hat. When she recognized Patrick, she hesitated, staring at him, unsure, blinking.

As Patrick started for her, she threw glances up and down the street.

"Hello," Patrick said, feeling the magnetic draw of her. "Are you expecting anyone else?"

"Expecting? No. But never underestimate the unexpected."

Patrick let that drop.

"Let's get inside," she said.

They walked toward the Pan and Spoon, and Patrick paused at the plate-glass window to look inside.

"Changing your mind?" Evelyn asked. "Like I said, it's a greasy spoon."

He nudged the single glass door open, and she entered, Patrick following. The Pan and Spoon had the dull yellow light of a tired restaurant; a dull, wooden, scratched and cigarette-burned counter of the last century, and a dull-looking, white-haired man standing behind it. With bored eyes, he grudgingly refilled the coffee cups of two dull-looking patrons, who sat huddled on two of the six counter stools. The Pan and Spoon smelled of grease, cigarette smoke, and coffee.

Evelyn lifted a hand of "hello" to the man behind the counter. "How are you, Mike?" she asked.

He responded with a grunt and a nod.

There were four wooden booths along the window and one in the rear, more private, away from the windows and near the kitchen entrance/exit swinging door. Evelyn chose that one. As she removed her coat, Patrick assisted. She thanked him, and he took it to a wooden hat stand, dropping it on a hook, along with his own coat and hat.

They sat opposite each other, hands resting on the tabletop, waiting, eyes moving, ignoring any direct gaze. Mike shuffled over, wearing a long white apron that hid some of his sagging belly. Mike had a white doughy face; drooping, red eyes; and a I-don't-give-a-damn expression.

Evelyn had not removed her hat. She was all nerves, and Patrick sensed that she was second-guessing her decision to meet him.

"What'll it be?" Mike asked.

Patrick looked to Evelyn. "Since you know the place, do you have any recommendations?"

"Grilled cheese sandwich with tomato. It's the only thing in this joint that won't kill you. Right, Mike?"

Mike's grin was a grimace. "Yeah, you said it."

"Just coffee," Evelyn said.

"Bring her a grilled cheese too," Patrick said. "It's on me. Oh, and I'll have a grape soda, like the one advertised on the billboard outside."

After Mike left, Evelyn avoided Patrick's eyes. "I shouldn't be here. I shouldn't have asked you to meet me."

"I believe it was I who asked you, Evelyn, and you were kind enough to accept. I'm grateful."

She looked at him with restless eyes, then looked away.

Patrick grabbed a paper napkin and removed his chewing gum. He crumbled it in the napkin and lay it aside.

After another awkward silence, Eve finally faced him. "You said you wanted to talk. So let's talk."

Patrick settled his uneasy eyes on her. "I would like to… well, get to know you. Learn who you are, where you came from and what you do."

Evelyn regarded him warily. "Why? Look… what did you say your last name is?"

"Gantly. Patrick Gantly."

"Mr. Gantly… I want to…"

He interrupted. "Patrick."

"Mr. Gantly," Evelyn insisted. "Tell me the truth now, once and for all. Have you been hired by my husband to follow me?"

Patrick leaned back, appraising her. "And what is it you have done to provoke your husband to have you followed?"

She tried to unlock him, his thoughts, and his motivation. She didn't answer.

"Evelyn, I don't know your husband and I'm not following you."

"Back at Gadfly's you said you were 'looking for me.' Doesn't that mean you were following me?"

Patrick waited. She waited. "You can trust me, Evelyn. I told you why I was, shall we say, following you."

"Because I look like your wife, you said."

Patrick was getting himself into a trap. He'd already determined that Evelyn's mind worked similarly to Eve's mind, or exactly like Eve's mind. So if Eve were sitting across from him, what would he say to assure her and not scare her off?

Patrick sat up, twisting his hands. When he spoke, he stared directly into her lovely eyes. "If this is uncomfortable for you, then I'll leave, and you will never see me again."

He saw the swift disappointment in her eyes, and she didn't say a word. That was his cue to continue. "I wanted to talk to you because… since my wife's death, I've been lost. I feel like I've been living a nightmare. Simply put, when I saw you, I felt hope. That's all of it, nothing more."

The conversation stopped when Mike dropped off their sandwiches, poured Evelyn's coffee cup full, and soon returned with Patrick's bottle of chilled grape cola and a chipped glass.

After he'd gone, Evelyn leveled her eyes on Patrick. "Hope can mean many things."

"I just want to talk to you, Evelyn. I won't complicate your life, if that's what you're worried about."

"Okay, so then after we talk, will you walk away?"

Patrick's jaw tightened. She watched him pour the grape soda into the glass and watched it fizz.

"Yes, if that's what you want."

They heard the rattle of dishes and the low murmur of conversation as three people entered the diner and sat at a booth near the windows.

Evelyn reached for her cup and held it to her lips, blowing off the steam. "What was your wife like?"

"She was a lovely woman in all respects, with a good, quick mind and a tongue like a whip when she was angry. She wasn't a saint, but she had a good heart and she went out of her way to help others."

Evelyn sipped the coffee. "My, my, she sounds like a saint to me."

"She was a woman to be loved and admired, and I loved her deeply."

Evelyn softened. "What a beautiful thing to say."

She replaced her cup to the saucer and turned melancholy.

"Did I say something wrong?" Patrick asked.

"No. I suppose I'm envious. And maybe I'm feeling sorry for myself. I've never known that kind of love. Well, how many women have ever known a love like that? Your wife was very lucky."

"You're young, Evelyn. Perhaps you will find it."

She looked at him boldly. "Do you know why I'm here, Patrick? Do you know why I was sitting alone in that speakeasy, dressed like a high-priced harlot?"

Patrick held his eyes on her, curious to know the answer.

She laughed, but there was no mirth in it. "I was rebelling against life. It was my first night out in months. I'm a nurse who helps to run a clinic across town. I haven't taken a day off in weeks and, frankly, I'm exhausted. And at the risk of sending you running off into the night streets, I'll tell you that my husband left me for another woman six months ago and he refuses to give me a divorce."

Patrick's mind stopped and reran what she'd just said. She was a nurse? Like Eve, this woman was also a nurse? It was too fantastic, too much of a coincidence, or, as they would say in the twenty-first century, it was synchronistic. He stared, not interrupting the flow of her words.

"I see your questioning eyes, Mr. Gantly. You're thinking, why don't *I* divorce him? To accomplish that, I have to present my case to the court and provide evidence of his infidelity. Even if I wanted to hire some flatfoot detective to track my husband down and snap photos of him and his mistress, he is a very shrewd and well-connected attorney, who knows many cops and most of the judges in this City."

Patrick nodded. It was the familiar story in any time or place: those with money and connections could buy whatever they wanted.

"But if your husband is in love with another woman, then why doesn't *he* want the divorce?" he asked.

Evelyn snatched her coffee cup and took a drink. When she replaced it, she smiled darkly. "Because he is a highly successful attorney, and surely you must know that divorce carries a heavy stigma. Most of his clients are quite conservative. Also, being older and wealthy and holding fast to their Victorian ways and attitudes, they would not be pleased to be associated with an attorney who is divorced. Once they learned about it and about his young tootsie, they would drop him, flat."

Eve sat back, suddenly uncomfortable with her own sarcasm. Why was she opening up to this man? Because she sensed a kindred spirit? Could she trust him?

Patrick picked up his sandwich and took a bite. Eve couldn't help but study his hands. They were strong, masculine hands, but there was gentleness in the way he moved them. It had been so long since she'd been touched by a gentle man. So long since she'd talked to an understanding and kind man. Patrick seemed to be both.

"There's more," she said softly, allowing herself to continue. "We also have a sixteen-year-old daughter. In case of a divorce, I would have to prove that I am of sound mind if I wished to gain custody of Virginia. My husband has threatened to prove that I am not of sound mind, citing my occasional visits to the psychologist Milton Grange, who studied with William James. Some

time ago, my husband took Virginia to live with him...
and," Evelyn paused, shutting her eyes to stop the flow
of sudden, unwanted tears.

Patrick watched those tears spill from her eyes and
roll down her cheeks. She swiped them away with
irritation. Her eyes stayed closed as she spoke in a
strained, emotional voice. "Virginia has run away, and
we have no idea where she is. We haven't heard
anything from her, and I'm terrified that she might be in
a lot of danger."

CHAPTER 17

In a taxi traveling across town, Evelyn Stratford and Patrick were quiet, each processing the conversation they'd shared in the Pan and Spoon. Outside, a light rain fell, and the windshield wipers scraped across the glass, making a squeaking sound. Patrick broke the silence.

"How long have you been at the clinic?"

"Since the end of the war. I was promoted to director a little over a year ago, which means I spend a lot of time pursuing generous donors so we can keep the place open. I didn't want the job; I much prefer nursing to administration and fundraising, but I suppose I thought I could help save the place."

"And are you saving it?"

She shrugged. "Lately, it's not going so well. The clinic opened in 1914 with solid financial support from wealthy donors, and there was a lot of enthusiasm for it during the war and the influenza outbreak. The clinic saw its share of the twelve thousand New Yorkers who died from the flu. After the war, I was also working part-time at Riverside Hospital, with recently returned World War I veterans. Unfortunately, many of the wounded soldiers had been distributed free narcotics, and they got addicted. It was a difficult time, and when the worst of it was over, I suppose I grew depressed. That's when I sought help and found Milton Grange."

"And what about the clinic now?"

"We've had our hands busy with the recent diphtheria outbreak. And we admit patients with mental problems. We only have twenty beds now, but we also provide outpatient services."

"Do you still have good financial support?"

"The money and donors are, for lack of a better phrase, drying up. We now cater largely to the poor and the destitute, and most can't pay. As you know, the world has changed dramatically since the end of the war, and there's not as much support these days. Without continuing financial support, the clinic will have to close. The real estate is valuable, and our lease is up this year. The owner and a couple real estate agents have already been buzzing around. I have a meeting with several donors in the next two weeks, and I'm searching for more, but time is running out. I truly want to save the place. We have a dedicated staff and we make a difference in the lives of many poor and frightened people."

"Maybe you can find another location for the clinic, in a cheaper neighborhood?"

"We've looked and are continuing to look but, so far, we've found nothing. These are boom times. The stock market is up and so are real estate prices."

With a little lift of her hand, Evelyn sighed and glanced over. "Well, you said you wanted to talk. It seems I've been doing all the talking. Now it's your turn."

"May I ask a personal question?" Patrick asked.

"Why not? I've been personal with you."

"Why don't you use your husband's name, Scott, instead of Stratford?"

Her expression hardened. "Because, in my heart, I have already divorced him. I don't need the court's sanction and a piece of paper. Stratford is my maiden name."

Patrick nodded. "How did you meet your husband?"

Evelyn spoke slowly, reluctantly. "In 1908, I was a silly girl who arrived in New York from Ohio."

Patrick's interest sharpened. Again, there was a connection between Evelyn and Eve. Eve Sharland Gantly was also from Ohio.

"I was only eighteen years old," Evelyn continued. "I met Vernon soon after I moved here. He was brash, ambitious and smart, and I was dazzled by him and the big city. He was studying law at Columbia, his parents were wealthy, and I was impressed. I was born and raised on the poor side of town. So, yes, I was impressed, and I was silly, believing we'd live happily ever after. Our love affair was hot and rushed, and when he asked me to marry him, I didn't hesitate. His family hated me for marrying him, a poor girl from Nowhere, Ohio, and they still hate me. I never see them."

"So you married in 1909?"

Evelyn grew reflective. "Yes... We had some good years before I realized he wasn't the man of my dreams. But it wasn't all Vernon's fault, was it? It takes two people to fail a marriage. He must have sensed that I had changed and grown away from him. Anyway, we had only one child… and now both our lives are a mess, and our little beauty, Virginia, is missing. God forgive me for what I've done."

"Don't blame yourself for living, Evelyn. Life is a game of trial and error and tossing the dice. We do the best we can with what we've got, and hope we do more good than bad."

Evelyn looked at him with gratitude, her lower chin quivering as she fought emotion. "So, you're a philosopher, too?"

"Just go easy on yourself. And, anyway, look what you've done for that clinic. It's a very good thing, and you've helped a lot of people who had nowhere else to go."

"That's a nice thing to say. I guess I needed to hear that right now."

Patrick angled his body to face her. "Have you hired detectives to find Virginia?"

Her face fell into anguish. "He hired a detective… I mean Vernon hired one. I call him every day to find out if he's learned anything, and every day he says the same thing. 'I'll call you when I receive any information.'"

Evelyn opened her purse, removed a lace hankie and blotted her misty eyes. "I don't know who the detective is or where he's searching. Vernon won't discuss it with me."

The taxi pulled to the curb of East 19th and 5th Avenue, where the St. Mary Mercy Clinic stood, a four-story brick building with few adornments. A tall, formidable bank flanked it on one side, and the Atlantic Department Store stood on the other.

Patrick insisted on paying the driver, and the couple emerged in a light rain and hurried to the entrance through a glass door. Inside, they wiped their feet on a brown welcome mat and Evelyn pointed to the lobby desk.

"This won't take long," she said. "I'm just going to check in and see if everything is all right."

Patrick sat in a comfortable wooden chair while Evelyn chatted with the young night nurse. He removed his hat and crossed a leg over the other, glancing about, smelling soap, lemon and rose. The tiled floor was newly waxed and the white walls held oil paintings of seascapes and flowers.

His mind was stuffed with vague questions, ideas, and plans, but his thoughts flitted about like butterflies. He couldn't pin any one of them down. Being with Evelyn had short-circuited his usual clear thinking.

She moved, walked and talked like Eve; she thought like Eve, and she was a nurse, just like Eve. As he watched her lean to speak to the night nurse, he thought again, she *was* Eve. When she smiled and nodded her head, Eve. When she turned and smiled at him, he melted. That smile was Eve's smile. Patrick felt a singing joy, and a bewildering misery. She was Eve, and yet she was not Eve, and she was married to another man.

Minutes later, Evelyn approached, and he rose. "Can you believe it? Everything is fine. They don't need me."

"I don't believe it," Patrick said.

Her expression changed. It relaxed as she studied his face. "Who are you really, Patrick Gantly? I haven't talked this much in years. Why do you seem familiar to me somehow?"

Patrick wanted to tell her, but how could he? He wasn't even sure himself.

When he looked away from her, she stepped back, afraid she'd said too much. "It's late. I should get home."

The taxi drew up to a four-story brownstone just off West End Avenue and 78th Street. Patrick told the driver to wait, and he escorted Evelyn through a wrought iron gate to the front entrance. They paused at the base of the stairs that led up to the front door. Both stared shyly at the other.

Evelyn extended her hand. "Well, I guess this is goodbye. I enjoyed our talk more than you will ever know."

Patrick took her hand and held it, and she didn't pull it away. "Evelyn... I used to be a detective."

Evelyn retracted her hand, the fear returning. She stared with a focused intensity. "So you *are* working for Vernon?"

"No, I'm not. Please believe me. I'm not working for your husband in any way, shape or form. I only mention that I was a detective because, with your permission, and if you'll supply me with all the information you have, I will see if I can find Virginia."

Evelyn searched his face. "You're a detective?"

"I was, some time ago."

"Where?"

"Here, in New York."

"Why aren't you still a detective?"

"Now, that is a long story and one I'll save for another time, that is, if there will be another time. Do you want me to search for your daughter? If you don't, I'll understand and I'll walk away. But if I walk away, Evelyn, it won't be easy. I don't want to walk away."

Evelyn began to tremble. She looked down and away. Mist gathered on her hat and glistened in the lamplight. "I just don't know. This has been such a strange and confusing night."

She looked at him. "I just don't know, Patrick."

"Then think about it. I can call you in a couple of days if you like. Or you can call me."

"Yes, I've got to think."

"How long has Virginia been missing?"

"A week... a little over a week."

"I was a good detective, Evelyn. You can trust me."

Their eyes locked. Evelyn saw warmth in his. Patrick saw an opening, and a flicker of desire in hers.

The taxi waited, and the mist was replaced by a sudden, hard rain that tapped their hats. A cat darted out from behind a metal garbage can and skittered off into the night.

Evelyn's eyes filled with conviction. "Okay... I don't need more time. Can you meet me tomorrow at a cafeteria near the clinic called Ralston's? It's a block away. I don't want anyone from the clinic to see us together. They might get the wrong impression."

"Okay. What time?"

"About one o'clock?"

"I'll be there."

"I'll collect some papers and photographs tonight that might be helpful and put them in an envelope."

Evelyn started to reach for his hand, but then stopped. "Do you think you can find Virginia, Patrick?"

"No promises, but I'll do my best. I won't give up."

Evelyn wanted to reach for him. She wanted to kiss him and thank him. She wanted him to embrace her, to hold her and to tell her everything was going to be all right. It had been so long since she'd been touched by a man; held by a man.

An inner voice told her she could trust him, and she also knew, despite having only just met him, that she could easily fall in love with Patrick. She blocked the feeling. It was childish and irrational. She was being impulsive, and she wasn't an impulsive woman, regardless of what she'd done tonight.

"Oh, wait a minute," Evelyn said. "How much do you charge? I have no idea about these kinds of things or how they work."

"No charge."

"No, no, I insist on paying you."

"No charge. Now, let's get out of this rain before we catch pneumonia and end up in one of your beds in that clinic."

Patrick turned about and started for the taxi, calling back over his shoulder. "Tomorrow at one o'clock. See you then."

After the taxi was gone, Evelyn stood in the rain, pulsing with hope and swelling with emotion.

As she bounded up the stairs, she smiled. "Yes, Patrick, tomorrow at one."

CHAPTER 18

Evelyn entered her two-bedroom apartment, shed her coat, removed her hat and strode into the living room. She stared, not moving, feeling a tangle of thoughts and emotions. She walked to the mantel, braced her hands against it and bowed her head, standing there for minutes.

What was she doing? Had she lost her mind? She left the living room for the kitchen, put a kettle on the stove and reached for a cup. While the water heated, she leaned back against the sink, hanging her head.

"Do you really want Patrick to search for Virginia?" she said aloud. "You don't even know him."

After she'd brewed the tea, she took a full cup to her bedroom. Standing, and not moving except to sip the hot tea, she realized she was lost in a mental fog. Seeing Patrick had disturbed and excited her. He'd ignited something inside that she didn't understand.

After a shower, she slipped into a gown, downed the rest of the tea, sat on the edge of the bed, and tried to reason with herself. Finally, she switched off the lamp and climbed into bed, pulling the comforter up to her chin. In the darkness, she heard the rush of wind outside her window, and it made her lonely.

"No, Eve. Don't do this," she said into the darkness. "If Vernon finds out Patrick is looking for Virginia, he'll think the worst. He'll make your life a living hell."

Eve rolled over onto her side. "Stop talking to yourself and go to sleep."

Deep into the night, rain rapping against the windows awoke her in the middle of a dream. Sitting up, she recalled it: Patrick was standing at the foot of her bed, looking at her longingly. Dressed in a green and black checked flannel shirt and jeans, he was bathed in a kind of bluish light.

"I've missed you, Eve," he'd said. "I've traveled a long way to find you again."

Evelyn shook the dream away, tossed back the comforter and left the bed, padding into the living room. The clock said it was after four in the morning. Sitting on the couch, she covered her legs and feet with a brown and white crocheted blanket and tried to shake the dream. It had seemed so real. She had wanted to reach out for Patrick, and she had called to him. "Come be with me, Patrick," she'd said, but he had faded away.

Evelyn folded her arms across her chest and searched the darkness for answers. She was tired, there was no doubt about that. Working so many hours was having an impact on her; it was making her obsessive and impulsive.

"No... I won't go through with this," she said. "I'll send him away."

At one o'clock the next day, Friday, October 30, Evelyn left the clinic, turned east and started for

Ralston's Cafeteria. The day was bright, the traffic heavy, and her nerves frayed. She'd finished out the night sleeping on the couch, awakening with a stiff neck and a backache. Her stomach was upset, so she'd eaten little, and she felt light-headed.

Evelyn approached Ralston's with trepidation, and she halted several times, wishing she hadn't agreed to meet Patrick. But if she didn't meet him, he would come to the clinic, so she had to go.

Inside, Ralston's was chrome and glass, with formica tabletops and wooden chairs with red cushions. There was a wide collection of inexpensive entrees, side dishes and desserts, all kept warm on steam tables. The bustling lunch crowd swarmed the place.

Evelyn searched for Patrick, spotting him at a small table by the side windows, his hand raised, waving at her. With her heart in her throat, she started over.

"Hello, Patrick," she said, feeling on edge.

"Is everything all right? You look nervous."

"Yes, I'm fine."

"It's good to see you again, Evelyn."

Evelyn ducked her head. "You can call me Eve... I mean, you might as well."

"All right."

They stood, uneasy.

"I got coffee and a roll," Patrick said. He pointed toward the steam tables. "I would have gotten you something, but I didn't know what you might want."

"Of course. I'll just dash over. I'm hungry. Do you want anything else?"

"No, I had a late breakfast."

Patrick sat and waited while Eve grabbed a metal tray and moved quickly through the line. She returned to the table with a tray carrying a cup of coffee and a plate of meatloaf, mashed potatoes, and green beans.

After she sat and began to eat, not looking at him, Patrick examined her. Her face told him nothing, but something had changed. She was guarded, her eyes not meeting his.

"How are things at the clinic?" Patrick asked, making conversation.

"Busy... We took in two more patients this morning, one, a man, who seems quite disturbed. I left him with a doctor and an orderly. He was a soldier in the war. We still get them sometimes. They suffer from bad dreams, tremors and panic attacks."

"Where I come from, they have a fancy term for it. They call it post-traumatic stress disorder."

Eve lifted her eyes. "I've never heard of it. It seems an apt description. Incidentally, I think I did all the talking last night. Where *do* you come from?"

"I was born here in New York."

"Do you have family here?"

"No, not anymore."

"So you're alone?"

"Yes. Quite alone."

"But you have friends?"

"I have at least one, maybe two, but they're in Europe and won't be back for some time."

Eve returned to her food, cutting the meatloaf into small pieces. Being with him again, and under his soft gaze and hearing his sonorous, masculine voice, she began having second thoughts about declining his offer. What was it about him that seemed so comfortable and so familiar?

She turned her eyes on him. "You are somewhat of a mystery, I think, Mr. Gantly. There is something about you that seems, I don't know, elusive."

"And you, Eve, seem uneasy. Is everything all right? Has something happened since I last saw you?"

Eve didn't respond right away. After she'd eaten half her dinner, she reached for her coffee and then looked at Patrick. "Patrick… I've changed my mind. I don't think it's a good idea for you to go searching for Virginia."

Patrick slid his empty coffee cup aside. "And what has changed your mind?"

"I don't know… It just doesn't seem right, somehow. And if my husband finds out, he could make it difficult for both of us."

"I'm not worried about the difficulty for me, but I understand if you're concerned for yourself. If he is an aggressive and controlling man, then, yes, I understand."

Eve kept her eyes low. "I do appreciate the offer. It is very kind and thoughtful."

Patrick stared, determined. "Eve, has it occurred to you that your husband may know where Virginia is?"

She snapped him a look. "What? Why? I mean, if he knows, then why doesn't he tell me? It doesn't make any sense."

"I'm suspicious that a professional detective has not been able to find your sixteen-year-old daughter in over a week. Virginia is not a seasoned professional who is skilled at eluding detection. She must have left an easy trail. Have you contacted the police?"

"No… I wanted to but, again, Vernon said he didn't want the publicity. That's why he hired a private detective."

Patrick was carefully choosing his words. "Eve, if, as you said, you believe it is possible that she is... that Virginia might be in danger, then again, by now, a true professional should have been able to learn where she is or, at least, what has happened to her."

Eve pushed her plate away, feeling nauseous. "I can't think about that. I can't."

"All right, but if Virginia is in distress, then time is crucial. As I said last night, I can be discreet."

Eve placed her elbows on the table and pressed the heels of her hands into her forehead. "Oh, God, I don't know what to do about anything. I'm so damned confused."

Just then, Patrick saw a young woman, dressed in a white nursing uniform, enter the cafeteria. She whipped her head about, searching, her expression tense.

"Eve... I believe one of your nurses is looking for you."

Eve sat up and turned. Seeing the nurse, she shot up, waved, and hurried over.

Patrick rose, seeing the sudden alarm on Eve's face. He followed her, waiting until the nurse spoke in a rapid loud whisper, over the hum of conversation that was all around them.

"What's happened?" Patrick asked.

Eve was absorbed and worried. "It's about the former soldier I told you about. His name is Warren Carver. He was featured in the New York papers after the war, publicized as a war hero. He saved ten men's lives, but he was badly wounded. Anyway, he came in this morning, disoriented, but able to communicate. Just now, during an examination, he broke away, grabbed a knife and stabbed the doctor. The orderly tried to fight him off, but Warren wounded him too. Both men managed to get outside and lock the door. Warren is still in the room, and they say he's gone crazy, yelling and screaming as if he's on a battlefield. The doctor and orderly are being treated, and they're going to be all right."

"Has somebody called the police?" Patrick asked.

"No… not yet. If this gets in the newspapers… I know it sounds selfish, but the negative news will finish off the clinic. Vernon will make sure of it. Some of our donors already think we're understaffed, and that we're treating the wrong kind of people. Vernon will make sure we lose those donors."

Patrick gave her a mystified look.

"Yes, Patrick, Vernon is that spiteful. He has turned into a real bastard."

"Do you have security?" Patrick asked.

"Yes, but he refuses to go into the room."

"All right. I can try to subdue him but, if I fail, you'll have to call the police."

Eve looked at him with surprise and apprehension. "I can't ask you to do this."

"I have some experience with knife fights. Let's go."

Inside the clinic, Patrick found frightened nurses and concerned doctors standing around on the first floor, the security guard threatening to call the police and two nurses trying to calm him down.

As Patrick and Eve mounted the wrought iron stairs to the second floor, Patrick heard Warren's loud terror rant.

"I'll kill you. I'll kill you all! Don't you see them coming? For God's sake, don't you hear the machine guns? You bastards! Kill them! Shoot! Fight!"

Patrick and Eve exchanged worried glances. As Patrick approached the second floor, he turned to Eve. "Stay back. Is there another exit on the other side of the hall?"

"Yes."

"Can you block it off with something? A table, chairs?"

"Yes."

"Is there anybody else up here? Anyone else in those rooms?"

"Two patients, but they're locked in, nurses standing by."

"Okay. Tell everyone to stay off the floor. I'll need a volunteer to stand by with a hypodermic needle with a sedative. Do you have hypodermic needles in nineteen twen… in this clinic?" Patrick asked, unsure.

"Of course," Eve said.

"Good, then have a doctor standing by. When I get Warren restrained, he'll have to rush in and administer the shot."

"I'll do it," Eve said firmly.

"No, a man must do it."

"No. I'll do it," Eve repeated with force.

Patrick lifted an eyebrow, sizing her up anew. "Yes, Miss Stratford… Eve. I should have known."

She stared, puzzled.

"All right… And have someone bring me a chair and a couple of towels."

"Okay. I'll be right back."

Patrick surveyed the space. The corridor ran about fifty feet. There were seven doors, including the room Warren occupied. They were all closed. At the end of the hall was a window, but it was boarded up and secured by steel bars. The walls were bare, and the five ceiling lights, about eight feet apart, were covered with wire mesh.

The man's frantic, terrified voice screamed out from the third door.

"They killed Johnny. For God's sake, they killed Johnny. I'll kill them. Kill them all! Oh, no! No! Gas! Put on your masks, men. It's gas! Oh, my heaven! Oh, my precious Jesus! Run, men!"

Eve had given Patrick the key to the locked door. He stared at it while Warren howled and hammered on the door with his fists. "Run for it, men! Run! I'll stay behind and fight them off. Run... Run for your lives!"

An orderly appeared, toting the chair and the white towels. He approached gingerly, his eyes spooked. Patrick told him to leave the chair and towels and go, and he did so gladly, bounding off down the stairs.

Minutes later, Eve arrived with the hypodermic, pausing on the step below him. She gave him a firm nod. "The stairs on the other side are blocked off."

Patrick removed his hat and shouldered out of his overcoat. He removed his black suit coat, rolled up his sleeves and inhaled a breath, placing his clothes on the floor to his right, out of the way.

This was not what he'd imagined when he'd awakened that morning. He'd hope for some quiet time with Eve, so they could get more acquainted; so he could ask her more pointed questions. He'd thought she might hold a clue as to why the lantern had dropped him in this time.

Patrick never liked knife fights. They were unpredictable and ugly. His first such fight had occurred when he was fourteen years old. Sean Hughes had been older and taller, and he was the block bully. Sean had taunted Patrick for weeks; threatening him, and Patrick's smaller friend, Dicky, a nervous, shy kid.

One hot summer day, Patrick had brought his knife with him and, when Sean taunted him, they fought.

In the end, Patrick had been slashed across his arms and torso, bleeding through his shirt. But he, being lightning quick and thin from lack of food, managed to slice Sean across the face, hand and hip. When Patrick caught Sean off-balance, he slashed him across the chest, and then punched him hard in the face.

Stunned and bleeding, Sean staggered, and Patrick took the moment. He darted in, knife glistening in the sun. He seized a clump of Sean's curly hair, yanked him in close and jabbed the knife's point into Sean's neck, applying enough pressure near a throbbing vein to draw a drop of blood. In that angry, violent silence, a red stream trickled down Sean's sweaty neck. Feeling it, his eyes bulged in terror and he screamed for mercy.

Patrick pressed the knife point, his eyes burning. "Promise me you'll never go after Dicky again, Sean. Promise!"

Sean did so, his chest heaving, eyes wild. Patrick lowered the knife, spun Sean around and kicked him square in the ass. He sprinted off like a scared squirrel.

Thankfully, the adrenaline rush had kept Patrick from fainting from the heat, the exhaustion, and his injuries until after he'd arrived back home. Nobody was there when he dropped to the floor, spent and wounded. He awoke a half hour later, his sister standing over him, crying. It was a memory he would never forget.

Patrick had been a little crazy in those days. Maybe he was still a little crazy. He was certainly crazy for getting himself mixed up with poor Warren Carver, the damaged war hero.

And the name Carver hadn't been lost on Patrick. Carver, knife. Why did the universe do things like that? Were the gods laughing?

Patrick almost smiled. Almost.

CHAPTER 19

Patrick stood at the door, a towel wrapped around his right arm, securely tied. The chair was at the ready. Chairs were the best protection in a knife fight. You could push, jab and cage your opponent. And then you could attack.

As Patrick was preparing himself, Warren stopped shouting. Patrick waited, listening, calculating. He quietly approached the door, raised his fist and lightly knocked.

"Who is there?" Warren yelled. "I'll kill you! You lousy bastard Hun! I'll kill you!"

Patrick got an inspiration. It might work, it might not. He decided to try. He gathered in a breath and lowered his voice. "Warren, it's Patrick. It's okay. The battle's over now. The guns have stopped. It's all quiet."

"What did you say? Over! Did you say it's over?" Warren yelled.

"Yes, Warren. The battle's over. The Huns have fled back to their trenches. We scared them off. It's all right. We're fine."

"They killed Johnny. Those dirty Germans killed Johnny."

"No, Warren, he was wounded, but he's going to be fine. He's behind the lines at the base hospital. He's with the pretty nurses right now."

"I saw him. I saw the machine guns rip into him."

"No, Warren, I tell you he's fine. Johnny's getting the best of care right now at the base hospital. Okay, I'm going to open the door now and you and me are going to take a rest. There's a nurse here, a real pretty nurse, and she's going to help us both. Okay, Warren?"

Silence. Then, in a low, suspicious voice, Warren said, "Who did you say you are?"

"You know me, Warren. It's Patrick. Corporal Patrick Gantly. We've shared many a trench together. Come on, now. Let's get back to our lines."

Silence.

"Warren... listen. All is quiet. I tell you, the battle is over. Just relax. I'm going to open the door now."

Patrick shot Eve a nervous glance and shrugged a shoulder. He mouthed the words, "Wish me luck."

Eve nodded, her face tight with stress.

"Okay, Warren, I'm putting the key in the lock now. I'm opening the door. Stand back."

Warren didn't answer.

Patrick turned the key and, with a gentle nudge, the door opened, Patrick taut and ready for an attack. The chair was beside him, an easy reach.

Patrick sucked in a quick breath, forced a friendly smile, and opened the door fully.

Warren Carver stood before him, his bold eyes stormy, lost in another time and place.

Patrick's eyes lowered on the knife that Warren held at his side, in his right, shaking hand. It had a three-inch blade; some kind of surgical knife, Patrick thought. Warren wore a blue shirt that was sweat-soaked and flecked with blood. He was shoeless, his trousers wrinkled.

Patrick stared into Warren's tragic face, packed with terror. "Hello, Warren," Patrick said, softly, with a hint of a disarming smile.

Then, for dramatic effect, he let out a long, exaggerated sigh. "Well, we made it through another one, didn't we? That was a close one. They nearly overran us, but we stopped them, didn't we, Warren?"

Warren's eyes twitched. His mouth twitched. "I don't know you."

Not missing a beat, Patrick said, "Yeah, well I don't know you either. You look like you've been through hell." Patrick laughed. "And we've both been through hell."

The two men stood staring at each other. Warren was slight of build, with a boyishly handsome face, a constellation of freckles and tousled, light red hair.

Warren licked his lips, still confused. "I forget things, you know. Sometimes I forget... well, names and things."

"Don't we all, Warren. I forgot where I put my penknife, and I've had that knife with me ever since... Well, since my father gave it to me."

Warren blinked, and with the back of his free hand, he wiped sweat from his forehead.

"I forget names and faces. So many men have died... And I want to forget, and yet I can't forget. I can't forget their names and faces. I mean... somebody has to remember them, don't they? I can't forget."

"I know, Warren," Patrick consoled. "I know. We won't forget them. We'll always remember them."

Patrick glanced back over his shoulder. "But now, there's a nurse right outside, and she's real pretty. She just gave me a shot to help me sleep. I'm feeling better now. Maybe you should have one too. We both need sleep, Warren. We have to sleep. We'll just sleep and forget the war for a while. Can I bring her in?"

Warren ran a hand along his jawline. "Sleep? Oh, God, if I could sleep."

"We'll both sleep now, Warren. Now that the battle's over. Oh, and I put my rifle outside. I don't need the thing now. Why don't you give me the knife? There aren't any Huns around. We scared them off. Did you see them running for their trenches?"

Warren turned, staring at the walls. "Yes... I saw them running off when our artillery trapped them in no-man's-land. That was a sight to see, wasn't it?"

"You said it, Warren. It was a beautiful sight."

"What did you say your name was?"

"Corporal Patrick Gantly."

"You sound like Quinn with that accent. Did you know Quinn?"

"No, Warren, I didn't know him."

Warren lowered his head. "He's dead... You sound like him, Patrick."

"So let's get some sleep now, Warren, while we can. Give me the knife now, let's get the pretty nurse in here, and let's forget about the world and its mountains of worries for a while."

Warren looked at his knife, and he seemed surprised he was holding it. He held it up. "That's right. I remember now. We were fighting hand-to-hand with those German bastards."

"Yes, but it's over, Warren. We've got to take our rest. Let's find us a beer or two, have some laughs and then sleep for a week. What do you say? Let me have the knife now, Warren."

Warren's eyes fluttered, and his face fell into exhaustion.

Patrick felt sweat on his forehead and upper lip; he felt it wet on his back. His heart thudded so hard, he had to swallow away the fear. "Sleep, Warren. That's what we need now. Good and blessed sleep."

Warren nodded. He started toward Patrick, the knife still gripped tightly in his hand. Patrick stood as still as a statue, ready to spring into defensive action if he had to.

Standing only three feet away, Warren raised the knife. "Thanks for being here with me, Corporal. I thought they were all dead. I thought I was alone. I'm glad you made it."

Warren hung his head and dropped the knife. It hit the floor, loud and hard in the quiet room. To Patrick's utter surprise, the weary soldier lifted his arms, fell into Patrick's arms and wept. "Oh, God, Corporal, when will this war ever end? When?"

Patrick held the man as he sobbed. "The war's over now, Warren. You did your duty. You are the best of soldiers."

When the emotion had finally run itself out, Warren stood back and lifted his wet, anguished eyes on Patrick.

"Don't let them kill you, Corporal. Don't let them," he said, his voice breaking from grief.

Patrick felt Eve's presence behind him. "They won't get me, Warren, and they sure as hell aren't going to get you either."

And then, with a quick change of pace, Patrick brightened. "Hey, Warren, here's our pretty nurse, Eve. She'll give you a shot and we'll both sleep for a week. Now, how does that sound?"

Warren nodded, the energy drained from him. "Yes... sleep."

Eve slowly slipped by Patrick and stepped into the room. She made her voice sound casual and breezy. "All right, you soldiers, let the nurses take over. Warren Carver, let's give you that shot now."

Warren lowered his head, obediently, and was listless when Eve slowly rolled up his sleeve and inserted the needle into his arm, administering the sedative.

Meanwhile, Patrick had positioned himself so that his left foot was clamped down firmly on the knife where Warren had dropped it.

Within minutes, the drug had taken effect and Patrick helped Eve escort a drowsy, harmless Warren out of the room and down the hallway. Eve unlocked a door, and they led Warren inside and over to a single bed. They eased him down, and he fell back, his head dropping onto a pillow, his eyes closed, already asleep. Eve covered him with a warm blanket and they left the room, locking it behind them.

Outside, she and Patrick leaned back against the wall, drained, their heads down.

"I'm exhausted," Eve said. "How are you?"

"Grateful I didn't have to fight Warren, and sorry for his damaged mind. I sense a good man there. A fine man."

"Thank you, Patrick," Eve said, softly.

"We got lucky."

"Lucky or not, I don't know what I would have done without you. Most likely, the police would have kicked down the door and shot poor Warren."

"Maybe, but cops aren't always so heartless."

She pushed away from the wall, crossed her arms and faced him. "There's something about you, Patrick, that I don't understand. No, understand is not the right word. There's something about you that," she searched for the right word, "... something that seems familiar. I hope that doesn't sound too flirtatious, but then again, maybe I don't care if it does."

Patrick kept his eyes on her. He knew that what he was about to say would make no sense to her, but he didn't care. "Eve, I believe that we, you and me, have been familiar in many various times."

His words trembled through her body. "I don't know what you mean."

Patrick straightened, resettling his tense shoulders. "No, I don't suppose you do." He changed the subject. "What will you do with Warren?"

Eve readjusted her mood with effort. "Oh... Well, we'll send him to Tower Sanitarium in upstate New York. They have doctors who know how to treat Mr. Carver's symptoms."

"Does Warren have any family?"

"Yes, his wife came with him when he was admitted. It was difficult to watch her as she stood waiting, looking careworn and defeated. I sent her away and told her I'd be in touch. Now… I'll have to contact her. I dread that."

"In your experience, can Warren improve? Will he heal and be able to live a normal life?"

Her eyes traveled to the ceiling and then down to the floor. "I don't know. I hope so, but I don't know."

There was sadness in her voice, but also a hint of hope. "I want to return to school to study psychology. I'd like to be able to help men like Warren. It interests me. There is an Austrian neurologist named Sigmund Freud. Have you heard of him?"

"Yes. You would be a good psychologist, Eve. You should pursue it."

Eve looked up and down the corridor. "It's not so easy for women. Despite the nineteenth Amendment, it's still very much a man's world, as I'm sure you know."

"That won't stop you."

She was going to speak, but she stopped, thinking better of it.

"We should go downstairs and let everyone know it's all over."

Minutes later, Eve accompanied Patrick out of the clinic, down the stairs, and onto the sidewalk.

"Thanks again. I don't know how I'll ever thank you."

"There is a way, Eve."

Eve waited. The sun was on her face and she squinted away from it. "And what would that be?"

"Allow me to search for your daughter. I think it will help put your mind at ease."

Eve regarded him with a hopeful lift of her eyebrows. "I was going to say that I'd changed my mind. I was going to ask you to do just that, but after all that business inside… I thought…" Her voice faded.

"When can I see you again?" Patrick asked, directly.

His question warmed her to her bones. "Well… I…"

He jumped in. "So you can tell me about Virginia, of course. I'll need to know everything you know about her; where she might have gone; the people she knows, friends, family… all the details."

Eve's spirits lifted. She could feel his confidence and, for the first time since Virginia had disappeared, Eve felt optimism.

She fumbled with her thoughts, searching for the right words. "I'm grateful," she said, crossing her arms. "Why don't you come for dinner tomorrow night? I'm not the best cook, but I'm not the worst either. I can make my mother's pot roast."

"I love a good pot roast. What time?"

"Six-thirty?"

"I'll be there… And I know where you live," he said, with a playful wink.

Patrick placed his hat squarely on his head and gave her a little head bow. "Until tomorrow night then, Eve."

Eve watched him stride away, and her breath came a little faster. Patrick Gantly was the most attractive and desirable man she'd ever known.

Eve had not thought about having a man in her bed for a very long time. A lousy marriage and a cold, vindictive husband had driven desire and the possibility of a new love relationship completely out of her.

But then Patrick had come along. Last night she'd had a sexy dream about him. All day she'd spun fantasies about him, like a school girl, and now she was aroused just looking at him. Where had he come from?

149

And who was he, really? Their meeting at Gadfly's had seemed, at the least, peculiar. His mystery added to an already powerful attraction, and the near miracle with Warren Carver was remarkable. His hands had been steady and his eyes calm; he had never wavered. How many men in the world had Patrick's courage?

After Patrick turned the corner and moved out of sight, Eve let out a long, slow breath. Yes, she wanted Patrick Gantly in her bed. She smiled at the thought of kissing him, of exploring his body with her hands and mouth.

Patrick Gantly had completely changed her life.

CHAPTER 20

Eve awoke to a driving rain that lashed the bedroom windows, as thunder rolled across the sky. Glancing at the clock, she saw it was nearly 4 a.m., and she felt the familiar panic that often came in the night.

Where was her lovely daughter, her Virginia? Was she lost or hurt, wandering alone out in this awful storm? Why hadn't she tried to make contact? Had she been kidnapped? Is that why Vernon wasn't sharing any information? Had Virginia been killed and was Vernon keeping it quiet to save his career?

Eve rested her head into the pillow, staring into the darkness. If she didn't find Virginia soon, she would go out of her mind. She'd been masking the fear and dread in public and around colleagues and friends, but she couldn't keep it up much longer.

Shutting her eyes, the fragment of a dream still clung to them. She sat up in the flashlight of lightning, straining to remember it and draw the complete dream back from unseen depths. Little by little, the dream surfaced, revealing images, faces and words.

Patrick was in a park, tossing a ball to a barking, brown and white spotted dog, who sprinted off after it. Snow was falling and there was a sense of celebration in the air, as if it were Christmas.

She had seen herself in the dream, holding a strange looking flat, rectangular pad with a lighted window. She'd stared into it, reading something, as moving pictures danced across a screen.

Patrick called to her. "Come on, Eve... Come play with me and..." What had he called the dog?

Evelyn squeezed her eyes together, trying to remember. "Georgy Boy!" Yes, that was the dog's name.

Still in the dream, Eve ran to Patrick, and he gathered her up into his arms, swinging her about, kissing her full on the mouth. That kiss had seemed so real, so wet and warm, so filled with love, a love she'd never experienced in waking life.

After he'd eased her down, they stepped apart, and Patrick gaze lovingly into her eyes and said, "I love you, Eve, and I always will, in any time and in any place."

Evelyn made a cup of tea and went shuffling off to the living room couch. Sometime around 5 a.m., she fell back to sleep, curled up, the tea half consumed.

Later that morning, she applied light makeup, fussed with her hair and dressed in a form-fitting, gray tweed suit with black patent leather low heels. She stepped to the full-length mirror and appraised herself. Her eyes were small and tired, and the makeup did little to hide her fatigue. No matter.

She'd made up her mind to pay Vernon a visit—to confront him—and demand that he share the detective's report on Virginia. Why had she waited until now? Fear of his wrath? Fear of what he might tell her about Virginia? Witnessing Patrick's courage with Warren Carver had changed her. Now it was time she showed some backbone, some courage.

Even though it was Saturday, Eve knew Vernon would be at his office. He always worked half a day on Saturday. She had a headache and dreaded the meeting, but there was no stopping her. She'd been a fool to wait this long.

With a firm determination, Eve left the house and caught the downtown subway, exiting at Chambers Street. With her head up and her shoulders back, she walked briskly, allowing the keen morning air and abundant morning sunshine to bolster her courage and strengthen her conviction.

Vernon was a strong-willed, combative man who hated to lose, and he seldom did lose. He took only those cases he was sure he could win, and if it appeared he had miscalculated and might lose, he schemed, cheated, lied or cut some deal so that it appeared as though he had won.

Five years into their marriage, she'd lost her admiration for him, although she still believed she loved him, in some indefinable way. After all, wasn't a wife supposed to love her husband and do all she could to make him happy?

Long before he told her he was going to move out to be with another, younger woman, Eve sensed he was cheating on her, and she knew he had done so in the past. Still, she'd believed in her vow, "till death us do part."

Once, when she was a teenager, Eve overheard her mother and father arguing. Eve noticed that her mother backed down, even though it was obvious her mother was right and presented more logical points. Later on, Eve asked her mother why she hadn't challenged her father. Her mother had looked her squarely in the eyes and said, "Evelyn, women are smarter than men, and they are stronger than men, but it is our duty not to let them know that. Our duty is to be there for them and give them whatever they want, in the kitchen and in the bedroom."

Evelyn now scowled at the thought. *In other words, be a doormat.* In a whisper to herself she said, "This is 1925, Mom, and I'm not going to be a doormat any longer."

Vernon Scott's law firm was on the twelfth floor of a stately, twelve-story building called The Belair. It was located on lower Broadway, not far from the historic Trinity Church. It was designed in the Beaux-Arts style, fronted with classical columns and terracotta designs.

The firm was one of the first tenants to move into the newly constructed building, and shortly after they moved in, women discovered that the designers had failed to include any ladies' restrooms. Until ladies' bathrooms were constructed, management had to designate bathrooms for men and women on alternating floors.

Evelyn believed that the oversight revealed much about the way women were ignored, disregarded or relegated to the home, their roles being to clean, bake, nurture children and take care of men. Thank God the 1920s had finally arrived, allowing women to break free from Victorian attitudes, fashion, manners, and strict social structures.

The Belair lobby was spacious, with gleaming brown marble floors and oil paintings on the walls. There was a bank of shining gold elevators and, standing by, were elevator operators dressed in royal blue and gold uniforms and pill box hats.

Eve stepped into the elevator with others, a man coughing, a man smoking, a perky woman wearing a flowery hat, and a tall man sporting spectacles, his small, anxious eyes darting about, his forehead beaded with perspiration.

She exited the stuffy elevator with relief, turned left and started down the long, carpeted hallway to her husband's law offices. At the door, she paused, sucked in a breath, and straightened her shoulders. "Give me moxie," she said in a prayerful whisper.

The cool, gold doorknob turned easily. Evelyn entered the office, and her nose was immediately assaulted by the scent of rose perfume.

The receptionist glanced up from behind a typewriter. She and Evelyn had never met. Evelyn had been to Vernon's office only twice before, and the receptionist she'd met then had since departed.

The young, pixy-faced brunette receptionist had a classic 1920s bob hairstyle, slightly waved, with plenty of bangs. Her puckered lips were bright red, and she chewed gum with vigor. The blue dress she wore was fashionable, her pearl choker fake, and her doll's eyes round with wonder.

"Hello and good morning," she said, in a high, nasal voice, presenting a wide, toothy smile. "Can I help you?"

Eve's hands were clammy, her throat tight with tension. "Yes, I am Mrs. Scott. Mrs. Evelyn Scott. I'd like to see my husband."

The girl's smile vanished, and her eyes shifted left and right, like those of a trapped animal. Obviously, she'd been instructed as to what she must do if the notorious Mrs. Evelyn Scott dared make an appearance.

The receptionist cleared her voice, and then she lowered it, hoping to sound official. "Well, you see, Mr. Scott does not work on Saturday and…"

Eve cut her off. "… Yes, he does," Eve said, curtly. "I know he's in his office because he always works a half day on Saturday."

The receptionist was a doe caught in headlights. Eve took the opportunity to bypass the woman. She angled left and walked aggressively down the richly carpeted hallway. The receptionist boosted herself up and, in seconds, she was on Evelyn's heels.

"You can't go in there, Mrs. Scott. Mr. Scott is… He's…"

Evelyn finished the young woman's sentence. "He's in there, and I'm going in."

With renewed courage, Evelyn grabbed the doorknob, turned it, and pushed the door open.

Vernon Scott was speaking assertively into the telephone. "I don't care what you have to…"

His eyes lifted on Evelyn, and he stopped mid-sentence, his face frozen in surprise. The receptionist burst in behind Eve, fearful and apologetic.

"I'm sorry, Mr. Scott. She… well, she just… I mean, I tried to stop her but…"

Vernon cupped his hand over the receiver and shouted, "Be quiet, Ruby! Get out and close the door behind you."

Ruby, flushed in embarrassment, dropped her chin and scurried out, closing the door.

Vernon's burning eyes landed on his wife. He let out his breath in annoyance. "What are you doing here, Evelyn?"

Eve was trembling and, when she spoke, her voice quavered. "We need to talk."

"That's impossible. Can't you see I'm at work?"

"I'm not leaving until we talk," Evelyn said, firmly.

"Dammit, Evelyn. This is not the time nor the place."

Evelyn stood resolute, chin set. "Then make it the time and place. I'm not leaving."

Vernon removed his hand from the receiver and spoke curtly into the phone. "I can't talk now. I'll call you later."

He slammed down the receiver and shot up, anger coloring his face pink. Evelyn took in Vernon's immaculate, dark, pinstriped suit, white shirt and patterned tie. He was a fastidious man and a pompous one. When she was younger, she'd taken his pomposity to be sophistication.

At forty-one years old, Vernon was still an attractive man, with a square face, wide-set, penetrating dark eyes, a dimple in the center of his chin and an aristocratic, sharp nose. His glossy, patent leather-looking hair was still mostly black, with hints of gray at the sideburns. At six feet, he was still trim and fit, and he worked hard to keep himself that way, by keeping to a strict diet and a regular routine of calisthenics.

"You have no right, and no business, coming here like this," Vernon said, tersely. "It is entirely inappropriate."

Evelyn had never confronted Vernon before on his own turf. They stood staring, him prickly and Eve determined. For the first time, Evelyn noticed crow's feet near his eyes and wrinkles around his mouth. He was pale, and he didn't look happy.

"Was that your girlfriend you hung up on? Is there trouble in paradise, Vernon?"

"That's not funny, and it is none of your business."

"Oh, no, of course it isn't," Evelyn said sarcastically. "Now, wait a minute, am I the other woman, and Miss What's-her-name the wife, or am I still the wife and she's the other woman? Help me out, Vernon. I'm confused."

"I have no time for your adolescent jealousy. You're a big girl now, Evelyn. You know how things are, and you know that it is entirely your fault that things are the way they are. Now, what do you want?"

Evelyn's face flamed. She moved toward the comfy, burgundy leather armchair and sat. Vernon came from around his desk in protest, as Evelyn folded her arms.

"You can't stay, Evelyn." He glanced at his watch. "I have an appointment in five minutes. A very important client."

Evelyn eased back in the chair, glaring at him. "Where's Virginia?"

"I've told you. I have told you everything that the private detective has reported to me."

"I don't believe you."

"Well, believe it or not, that is the way it is."

Eve shook her head, her hand outstretched. "Okay, fine, then I want to see the reports. All of them."

Vernon started to speak, then stopped. "No," he said, whirling around, returning to stand behind his desk. He took a cigarette from a silver case and placed it between his lips. He didn't light it.

"And why not, Vernon? Virginia has been missing for over a week. You were supposed to look after her when you took her from me. When you kidnapped her, while I was at work."

"And she went with me willingly, Evelyn. Yes, willingly. She couldn't wait to get away from you. You smothered her and controlled her. She went with me gladly. She was happy to leave you. She told me she never wanted to live with you again."

His words stung, but Evelyn controlled herself. "Virginia is a rebellious, high-strung girl and you know it. Of course she went with you because you are never around, and she could do whatever she wanted, and go out with anyone she wanted. Vernon, you need to call the police."

He jerked the cigarette from his mouth. "No, I will not call the police. They are bungling fools, and all that would happen is that my face would wind up in the newspapers. I would lose my best clients. My clients would never tolerate seeing their lawyer, the man who represents their financial interests, scandalized in the newspapers."

Evelyn pushed up. "Scandalized? What does that mean, Vernon? Tell me what is going on!"

"I won't have it, Evelyn. Take it from me, I'm doing all I can, and I will not destroy a career that has taken me years to build."

"Do you hear yourself, Vernon? Who gives a damn about your career, when your sixteen-year-old daughter is out there somewhere—God only knows—and for all you know, she could be dead!"

"She's not dead!"

"And how do you know?"

Vernon tossed the cigarette down, turned and walked to the windows that looked down on the street below. He clasped his hands behind his back. "Take it from me, Virginia is not dead."

Evelyn could barely control her frustration and rage. "Take it from you? No, I will not take it from you, Vernon. If you insist on shutting me out of what you have learned, then I will find out for myself."

Vernon swung around, pointing a threatening finger at her. "I'm warning you, Evelyn. If you don't stay out of this and let me handle it, you will regret it. I will cut you off without a penny, and I will hire reputable doctors who will testify that you are mentally unbalanced and an unfit mother. I will have them contact all the donors who throw their money away on your pitiful clinic, and I'll have it closed down so fast it will make your head swim."

Eve's eyes flashed with fury. "When did you become the selfish, disgusting bastard that you are, Vernon, and why did it take me so long to see you for what you are?"

Evelyn pivoted, walked to the door and yanked it open.

"I'm warning you, Evelyn," Vernon called after her. "Stay out of it."

She glanced back at him. "Oh, shut up!"

She left, slamming the door.

CHAPTER 21

"The pot roast is delicious," Patrick said, sitting across the dining room table from Eve.

She was pleased by the compliment, and she gave him a transient, distracted smile as she reached for her glass of wine. "Thank you."

Patrick continued, "I took a trolley ride down Forty-Second Street and watched a Rudolph Valentino movie, *Cobra*. Have you seen it?"

"No…"

Patrick cut into the meat, noticing Eve's restless eyes. "You seem preoccupied. How are things at the clinic?"

"Fine."

"How's Warren?"

"He left by ambulance this afternoon, heavily sedated. Poor man, I hope he can recover his broken mind."

"Is that what's weighing on your mind? You seem despondent."

"I'm sorry. I'm afraid I'm not very good company tonight. I went to see my husband this morning, and it wasn't very pleasant."

Patrick sat back, letting her words hang in the air.

She looked at him, frankly. "You gave me the courage to do it."

"I did?"

"Yes, and I'm grateful. I confronted him, and I never had before. I asked where Virginia was, and I demanded to see the detective's report."

Patrick waited.

Eve sipped at her glass of red wine, staring down at it. "Of course, he refused. I know there's something else going on, but I have no idea what that is. And he threatened me again, as before. He said he'd find doctors who would testify that I was mentally unbalanced... and then have them contact the clinic donors. He said he'd cut me off without a cent. It was his usual threats."

There was a gap of silence as Patrick processed her words. "Have you changed your mind, then? Would you prefer I not look for Virginia?"

"No," Eve said forcefully, her eyes filled with conviction. "No. I don't give a damn what Vernon does. I want you to find Virginia. I have to know where she is. I'm going crazy. Maybe crazy is a bad choice of word, given what Vernon said about me being mentally unbalanced."

Eve took another drink of wine, her mind burning with anger and confusion. "I don't care what he does to me, but I'm concerned about you."

"Me?"

"Yes. Vernon is a vindictive man, and he knows a lot of, how do I say it gracefully? He knows some unsavory types: gangsters, bootleggers. Through a friend, I've learned that his girlfriend, or mistress, or whatever you want to call her, is the daughter of Joe McGuire. Have you heard of him?"

"No."

"Simply put, he's a high-brow bootlegger, and a very connected one, to lawyers, judges and the police. As they say, he has a lot of them in his pocket and I suspect that includes Vernon."

"What do you mean, a high-brow bootlegger?" Patrick asked.

"It means his liquor is never diluted. It's high quality, and it's expensive. I hear many people say that the gin or whiskey they get is so bad they have to dilute it with ginger ale or Coca-Cola to mask the awful taste. Not so with Joe McGuire's hooch."

"How do you know all this? Who told you?"

Evelyn stared down at the table, and then up again. Her eyes said something grave. "A man at the clinic who was a small-time bootlegger. He had a run-in with some of McGuire's men, and they nearly beat him to death. They blinded him in one eye and broke an arm and a leg."

Patrick kept his eyes on her. "Have you met your husband's girlfriend?"

"I saw a photo of her in a newspaper article. She was attending a pool party at her father's sprawling house on Long Island. She's in her mid-twenties and very pretty. Her name is Louise McGuire. I don't know anything else about her, and maybe I don't want to."

Eve stood up, turning her face aside. "Patrick, Vernon can be a dangerous man, and he knows dangerous men, as I've said. I've heard things about him since he left me. Even when we were still together, he was surrounding himself with low characters that put my teeth on edge. Yes, I want you to find Virginia, but I also don't want you to get involved with these dregs of society. You could get hurt."

She started to walk away, then stopped and glanced back at Patrick. "I need some music. Do you mind? I'll crank the Victrola and play *Rhapsody in Blue*. Will that be all right?"

"Yes. Fine."

Patrick smiled. It was yet one more connection between this Eve, and his wife in the twenty-first century. Eve loved to play music during dinner, everything from light classical to jazz to pop. She had even played *Rhapsody in Blue* during dinner on occasion, once telling him that it was one of her favorite light classical pieces.

Patrick heard the opening clarinet. It drifted in from the living room—the half-octave glissando that makes *Rhapsody in Blue* as instantly recognizable as Beethoven's *Fifth Symphony*. A twist of longing washed over him and he sat still, his eyes closed, listening to the rather thin, scratchy sound of the 78 RPM record.

"Do you know this piece?" Evelyn asked, returning to the table.

Patrick's eyes fluttered open, and Evelyn saw the loneliness and longing in them.

"Yes, I know it."

"I was there," Evelyn said, a bit proudly, as she sat down.

"You mean that you were at the first performance?"

"Yes, at the Aeolian Hall, in February of last year. It was billed as an educational event, the 'Experiment in Modern Music.' The concert was organized by Paul

Whiteman and I received a ticket from one of our clinic donors, who had no interest in going."

"And hearing it for the first time, did you like it?"

Eve reached for her glass of wine, her eyes turning dreamy. "Yes, I loved it from the start, and I even met George Gershwin backstage after the performance. I told him how wonderful I thought it was. He was rather shy at first. I asked him how he managed to create something so original and inspiring. He said, 'When I'm in my normal mood, music drips from my fingers.'"

"You're smiling," Patrick said. "... And it's a coy sort of smile."

"Yes, I suppose it is. He looked into my eyes, some of his shyness melting away, and he said, 'Life is a lot like jazz... it's best when you improvise.' We talked for a while and then, to my surprise, he asked for my telephone number. I gave it to him."

"And?"

She laughed a little. "And he never called. Well, I was an older woman, wasn't I? He was only twenty-six."

They ate, listening to the music. After the first side ended, Eve left for the living room to crank the Victrola and flip the record.

When she returned, Patrick noticed that her mood had shifted.

"All right," Eve said. "Now that I have managed to distract us from the business at hand, and now that you know about Vernon and Joe McGuire, do you still want to…"

Patrick interrupted. "… Search for Virginia? Yes. It won't be the first time I've dealt with, as you put it, the dregs of society. I hope I can be a quiet shadow, and no one will even know that I'm sniffing around."

Evelyn swallowed the last of her food and drained the last of the wine. "If you're wondering where I commandeered the wine, I'll just say that I got it from a reliable source. Prohibition is silly and unenforceable. All it has accomplished is to create a subculture of gangsters, bootleggers, and thugs. It's still hard for me to believe that the amendment was ratified by three-quarters of the states. It will never last."

Patrick wanted to tell her that it would last until late 1933, but he didn't. "So, tell me about Virginia."

Evelyn's face filled with tension, and her eyes shifted as she searched for the right words to describe her daughter.

"Virginia was always a willful and difficult child, and yet she is also a loving child. She is a contradiction and a surprise, highly volatile and emotional. She ran off twice, once when she was thirteen and again when she was fifteen. She's been hard to keep in school. I would often tell her how difficult my own schooling was compared to hers, hoping that would help. I told her stories about my teachers at Miss Peebles and Thompson's School for Girls, and how hard they were on us. But, of course, that didn't work. Virginia hated school and the discipline of learning. So she'd run away."

"Where did she go?"

"The first time, she tried to hide at a friend's house on Staten Island. Fortunately, her friend's mother called to tell us where she was. The second time, she ran off with a boy, a very low-class criminal-type from Hell's Kitchen, and she has never told me how they met. She refuses to give me any details. As I'm sure you know, there are warehouses in that area that are ideal locations for bootleg distilleries and for the rumrunners who control the liquor. The boy, Pike Morgan, was nineteen, and he worked for one of the bosses, a man named Harry Owen. Both Harry Owen and Pike are dead. Not so long ago, they were found shot to death in a back alley on West 51st Street."

Evelyn paused, looking down at her twisting hands. "I'm afraid it's not a pretty story. Our daughter was... well, Virginia was compromised at that time, if you know what I mean. I wanted her to see my psychologist, Milton Grange, but she refused. Vernon agreed with her, saying I was taking things too far. He took the opportunity to add, as he often did, that women should have never been given the right to vote, especially me, because my head is always stuck in the fog."

Eve made a face of contempt. "Vernon blamed me for everything, and he still does. He says I was too strict with Virginia and too controlling. He says I should have never insisted on sending her to a private school and that I should never have continued working as a nurse, and then as an administrator. He says that's why he finally took Virginia from me, because I wasn't being a true mother."

The music stopped, and all was quiet. Patrick saw the anxiety and guilt on Eve's face. After all, it was a face he knew well; a face he'd seen in three centuries, the nineteenth, twentieth and twenty-first.

Evelyn continued. "We are not, and never were, I'm sorry to say, a happy family. But then life never goes quite the way you want it to, does it?"

Her eyes slid away from any direct stare. "But there were moments when Virginia and I were as close as a mother and daughter can be. After the boy, Pike, was killed, Virginia slept with me for weeks, trembling, crying, begging me to forgive her. I took time off from work; we went to museums and vaudeville shows. And she loved the circus. We talked for hours and I truly felt we had grown close and trusting. She said she wanted to finish school, and she even volunteered at the clinic for a few days…" Eve chuckled. "She told me she wanted to be a doctor and help people."

Patrick pushed his chair back from the table. "Why did your husband take her recently? Did something happen?"

Eve's face clouded over. "Virginia has a dark side… Well, I guess we all do to some degree, or so I'm learning from my sessions with Dr. Grange. Virginia left the house one night after I'd gone to bed. She got drunk on gin at some flapper party, as it's called. The police raided the place, and she was found…" Eve's eyes welled up and she struggled to continue. "… She was found in bed with an older man, a man old enough to be her father. Vernon managed to get her released from jail before there was a scandal and his precious reputation was soiled. Soon after, he took her away from me."

"And how long ago was that?"

"About a month ago."

"And when exactly did she run away from your husband's care?"

"I don't know for sure. According to Vernon, it was Wednesday, October 21."

"And who was watching her or chaperoning her at the time?"

"According to Vernon, a very tough, matronly woman who once worked at a women's prison somewhere near Boston."

Patrick lifted an eyebrow. "Prison?"

"Yes."

"Do you know the woman's name?"

"No. Vernon won't tell me."

"Do you know what the name of the prison was?"

"I'm afraid not. I'm sorry. I'm completely in the dark."

Patrick got up and stood behind his chair, his mind working. "Do you have that information on Virginia that you were going to give me?"

"Yes. I'll go get it."

She soon returned with a stuffed manila envelope and handed it to Patrick. "There are photos and school records, with a list of teachers and friends. I also enclosed confidential medical records and a newspaper article about Pike's and Harry's murders."

"What about your parents and your husband's parents? Would she go to them?"

"They would have called. And, anyway, Virginia is not fond of Granny Scott, who has said of Virginia, 'I've got no use for that wild and wanton girl.' My father is dead and my mother is a pious, religious woman. Virginia would never travel to Ohio to visit her. She loves New York and, if at all possible, she would never leave. My mother loves Virginia, but my daughter calls her a Mrs. Grundy."

"A Mrs. Grundy? I don't know the phrase."

"It's slang for an uptight or very strait-laced individual. My mother is a pious woman who attends church often."

Patrick sat down, opened the envelope, and reached inside. He drew out a black and-white photograph of Virginia and held it up, studying it.

Virginia was a young beauty, who had the alluring magic to make any man swoon on one quick look. She was sixteen going on twenty, with sultry eyes, a flirty, puckered mouth and lush dark hair, styled in smooth, sculpted waves. Her chin had a proud angle and, for all her electric charm and flashy jewelry, Virginia seemed coldly ornamental.

She had inherited her mother's cheekbones and nose, but her eyes were her own, or they were from her father. As Patrick focused more deeply on those eyes, he saw that behind the forced, sexy gaze was an aloof self-confidence, devoid of innocence.

"It's not a photograph I admire," Evelyn said, her voice low with sorrow, "but Virginia loves it. She said she wants to be famous like Clara Bow."

"Who is Clara Bow?"

"I'm surprised you don't know her. She's a famous movie actress. She's on the cover of nearly every magazine."

"Virginia is a very pretty young woman," Patrick said, leaving it at that.

"And very mature for her age, I hate to say. Much more worldly wise and confident than I was at her age. But, then, this is 1925, and down is up and up is down. Do you think you can find her?"

Patrick slipped the photo back into the envelope. "I'll study everything tomorrow and then form a plan."

"I wish I weren't so afraid," Evelyn said.

Patrick wanted to take her hand, pull her into him and reassure her, but he didn't.

"I have dessert," Evelyn said. "Chocolate cake."

"My favorite," Patrick said, with a smile.

When Eve left for the kitchen, Patrick set the envelope down, closed his eyes and massaged his forehead. He didn't have a good feeling about Virginia. No, not at all.

CHAPTER 22

Patrick stared down at a generous slice of chocolate cake, displayed on a yellow dessert plate. As Evelyn had served him, she'd leaned in close, and he'd inhaled the scent of her entrancing perfume. He smiled inwardly, certain she'd darted into the bathroom to spray some on, before stepping into the kitchen to cut the cake.

She poured freshly brewed coffee from a floral enamel coffee pot. It caught Patrick's eye, and she noticed. "It's from France," she said. "I've never been to France. Virginia ordered it from a catalogue, and it cost a fortune. She likes unusual and expensive things, just like her father."

Evelyn poured herself a cup and sat. They ate quietly, as the music of a Strauss waltz on the Victrola drifted in from the living room.

Patrick had said little since their conversation about Virginia, and Evelyn interpreted his silence as disappointment. It wasn't a pretty story, and she'd dreaded sharing it, but there was no way to soften it if he was going to search for Virginia.

No doubt he thought her a terrible mother, and she'd often thought so herself. No doubt he thought she had been a failure as a wife, and perhaps she was guilty of that too. Perhaps he even wanted to back out of his offer to find Virginia, but he was too much of a gentleman to say so.

"The cake is very good," Patrick finally said, after swallowing two bites.

"Thank you. It's one of Mother's recipes. I hate to admit it, but I think it tastes better when she makes it. She grew up on a farm in Ohio and had to cook and clean for four brothers."

"I haven't had cake this good since eighteen eight..." Patrick stopped, realizing his mistake. He had almost said, "since eighteen eighty-four."

"Since eighteen eight?" Evelyn asked.

"Since I was a boy. It's good."

After they'd eaten their cake and their coffee cups were empty, they stared at each other for a long moment from across the table. "More coffee?" Evelyn asked.

"No, thanks."

The music had stopped, but Eve did not get up. The phonograph arm moved back and forth, making a sker-ratchety, sker-ratchety, sker-ratchety sound, like a whispering cricket.

Evelyn studied Patrick with a sober attentiveness, not hiding her attraction to him.

The intimate excitement Patrick felt was tempered by confused emotions—feelings and a passion he couldn't catalogue or identify. Who was the woman sitting across from him? He had no idea, and no vocabulary to interpret and explain why he had come to this time, or why he had met Evelyn Stratford, who seemed to embody Eve Gantly's essence; her very heart and soul.

Evelyn was, from all appearances, the woman he'd loved and married, and yet she was mysterious and unique. She was Eve, and yet she was not Eve.

Patrick heard the phonograph needle in the living room scratch a hypnotic rhythm, making him uneasy and wanting; wanting the woman who sat opposite him.

Eve saw the conflict in his eyes, and she felt her own emotional battle of want and fear.

Patrick was confronting something raw, strange and frightening. Old, buried feelings were being dredged up from hidden depths, from beneath the river of his consciousness. They rose fierce and naked, and the woman who sat across from him was the source of it. That he knew.

He felt scattered, as if his atoms had been dispersed into the air and had landed in the soil of three different centuries. He felt the pull of nineteenth century morality, twentieth century transformation, and twenty-first century innovation and disruption.

He didn't know who the woman was who sat across from him, and suddenly he didn't know himself either. The only thing he did know was that, in the depths of his very soul, he was clinging to Eve Sharland Gantly, and he could not, and would not, let her go.

"You seem a thousand miles away, Patrick," Evelyn said, feeling as though the words and events of the evening had drained away all their spontaneous attraction.

"I'm sorry if I spoiled the evening with the ugly truth of my life," she said.

Patrick started to speak, but the words died on his tongue.

"You can back out if you want to, Patrick. Truly."

"Evelyn... Eve... I want to help you. I'll find your Virginia."

He slid his chair back and rose to his feet. "Now, shall I help with the dishes?"

She let out a little laugh. "The dishes? Good gracious, where did you drop in from? I have never before heard a man offer to help with the dishes."

"I'm a good dishwasher. My wife and I didn't have a dishwasher for a time and..." Patrick stopped, again realizing his mistake. He was certain there were no electric dishwashers in 1925.

But Eve didn't respond as he'd expected. "Well, of course, I used to have a housekeeper who did the dishes, but when I moved here five months ago, I decided I didn't need one, and that I could do the dishes myself. Thank you for your offer, but no thanks. I'm not sure what I'd do with a man in my kitchen."

"Well then, it's getting late and I should go."

Eve lowered her head, sorry that he was leaving. "Yes..."

"Would you like to walk with me for a bit? The cold air might do us good."

He'd made the suggestion for his, and for her protection. He wanted to embrace and kiss her and make love to her. It's what he'd wanted ever since he'd first seen her sitting alone in Gadfly's.

Eve brightened, getting to her feet. "Yes, I would like that. The cake was a little heavy."

They walked west, toward Riverside Drive. The night air was crisp, with a light breeze, and the crescent moon seemed to be chasing the clouds. The amber streetlamps cast pools of light on the sidewalk as they walked in and out of shadow.

They spoke of lighter subjects: the weather, Eve's new coat and hat. She asked him why he didn't wear gloves.

"I bought some the other day, but I forget to put them on. If I remember, then I lose them."

Evelyn chuckled softly, feeling relaxed and comfortable with Patrick, a man she hardly knew, and yet a man who made her feel extravagantly sexy and desirable.

"Eve... I'll only contact you when I find something important, and I'll do so at the clinic by correspondence or messenger."

Evelyn halted, surprised. "But why?"

Patrick stopped and faced her, noticing her face was lovely in the soft glow of the streetlight. "To protect you. It's better if we're not seen together."

Her lips tightened. "I suppose."

"Has Vernon ever struck you?"

"What does that matter?"

"It matters. Has he?"

Eve turned her face away, and a car approached, its headlights washing over them as it passed.

"All right, it's none of my business," Patrick said. "Look, Eve, it's best this way. I need to work in the shadows. I don't want you hurt, losing money or losing your clinic. Let me do this my way. If things change, then I'll rethink my approach. For now, it's best if we don't see each other."

Evelyn spoke in a tense, whispery voice. "I despise what Vernon has done to Virginia and me."

Patrick reached and touched her shoulder. He felt the thrill of it, just as he always did whenever he touched Eve, his Eve. "Let's walk."

They strolled, leisurely, in the quiet, cold night.

"If anything happens to you, I'll never forgive myself," Eve said, an edge of anxiety in her voice.

"Stop worrying. I'm a big boy. By the way, I may have a potential new donor for the clinic."

She turned. "Who?"

"Her name is Lavinia Joan Foster Vanderbilt. She's married to Benedict Vanderbilt. Have you ever heard of him?"

"Of course I've heard of him. He's one of the richest men in the country. You're constantly surprising me. How do you know his wife?"

"Through an old friend. I did some research on Mrs. Vanderbilt in the library the other morning, and I learned that she's involved with several charitable organizations, and she gives generously to others. I took the liberty of calling a number listed for all charitable inquiries, and I spoke with a secretary. I hope you don't mind. I mentioned your clinic. She said you could present her with a proposal, including the financials, the current status, the history, goals, etc., and she will look them over. If she feels it is worth Mrs. Vanderbilt's time and attention, she will forward the proposal. The secretary was helpful and friendly."

Patrick reached into his pocket and took out a folded piece of paper. "That's the name and address where you should send the proposal."

Evelyn stopped walking again, her bright gaze tilted up at him. She took the paper, opened it and held it up to the lamplight. "I don't believe it. Are you my knight in shining armor?"

Patrick moved toward her, his hands stuffed into his greatcoat pockets. "The woman could offer no guarantees and, by the way, if you do get to meet Mrs. Vanderbilt, don't mention my name to her."

"And why is that?"

"Let's just say that it wouldn't be helpful."

"You are a mystery man, aren't you, Patrick?"

He shrugged a shoulder.

Eve trained her eyes on him and, again, she felt an unexpected swell of desire.

Patrick felt the drum of his heart, and the passion of a man in love. Her lips were gently parted and her head slightly upturned, as if she were waiting for his kiss.

He longed to feel the animal closeness of Eve's body, the whisper of her sexy breath in his ear, the play of her hands, and the soft pressure of her lips on his. He hungered for the human joining of two souls, who celebrated the intimacy and the mystery of life and love.

Patrick fought the urge to kiss Evelyn. He didn't move.

Finally, Eve said, "I have enjoyed tonight. I will miss you, Patrick. I had hoped I could see you again soon."

He slowly released a breath, touched the brim of his hat with two fingers and bowed. "I will be around, Evelyn. You may not see me, but I will be around. And when I have any important information to share with you, I'll be in touch by way of the clinic."

Eve pulled the collar of her coat up, trying not to show disappointment. Then she thought, *Patrick is wise not to kiss me. I would never let him go. I would take him to my bed and love him through the night, and I would never let him go.*

Patrick said, "I should walk you back. It's getting late."

As they approached her house, Evelyn said, "Do you have a number or address where I can reach you, in case of an emergency?"

CHAPTER 23

Patrick spent Sunday, November 1, studying the materials and photographs Evelyn had provided. The black-and-white photograph of Vernon Scott was of special interest to him. Patrick paced his rooms thinking about it, pausing occasionally to lift his back bedroom window and present his face to the cold wind to keep his mind sharp.

Back in the 1880s, Patrick had acquired the skill of analyzing the mugshots of criminals from various levels of society: the low-class pickpockets, the bank robbers, the swindlers and the shiny, upper-class con men with their shark-teeth smiles.

He'd learned to read people through their mugshot photos and, later, by interrogating them. He recalled a conversation he'd had with Eve in 1885, shortly after they had met. She had asked him what he'd been up to.

"A few detectives have been told to explore the relationship between appearance and criminal behavior," he'd said. "We have sorted mugshots by crime in order to see if all forgers look alike, or if all murderers look alike, or if all burglars have the same facial features."

"And what have you found?" Eve had asked.

He'd smiled. "I find it particularly fascinating, Miss Kennedy," (Kennedy had been her pretend name at the time) "that you find this conversation both proper and interesting."

"I do," Eve had said. "I find it very proper and very interesting."

He had countered, "Frankly, I am skeptical about the whole thing, but some of my superiors are excited by the research, as are members of the press and many Americans. You have probably read about it in the newspapers."

"No, I haven't, but I would think that criminals are much too clever to get themselves categorized by appearance or by face and head type."

Patrick had smiled again, delighted by her intelligence and lovely lips. "And you would be right, Miss Kennedy, at least according to my experience."

The haunting moan of a boat whistle on the East River brought Patrick back to the present.

From the two-year-old photo, Patrick deduced that Vernon Scott was smart and ambitious. He had a strong, broad face and clever, dark eyes. His thin mustache made him look a bit sinister, or calculating. His black, shiny hair was combed back to tight perfection, and his smile was contrived to project friendly trust and competency.

Patrick's impression was of a smooth, fiercely ambitious man, who could keep a secret and caress corruption like a lover, if the deal was right and the money was securely in his hand.

Toward evening, Patrick was in Central Park, lingering near Sarah Finn's park bench, a paper bag in hand holding an egg salad sandwich, two pickles, a piece of apple pie and hot coffee.

Once again, she wasn't there. Though he'd been by several times in the last few days, she'd never appeared. He'd given his bag of food to other homeless souls, "tramps" and "hobos" as they were called in 1925.

Patrick was worried about Sarah. Two days back, he'd asked a cop making the rounds if he'd seen her. The policeman had been a bored-looking flatfoot with heavy jowls, a stubby ball for a nose and a grouchy manner.

"Which tramp? They all look alike, don't they?"

"Not exactly, sir. Sarah is probably sixty years old, about five-feet three-inches tall, a bit stocky and hunched over. She always carries a bundle, and she might talk to herself."

The cop rested his indifferent eyes on Patrick. "What do you care? Is she your mother? Are you out looking for her or something?"

"No, sir, she is not my mother."

Patrick saw it was useless. He wanted to curse the man and his cynical attitude, but what would have been the use? The cop would have clubbed him on the head and dragged him off to jail.

Just as in every other profession, there were dedicated, conscientious workers; there were also the apathetic and jaded. Who knew what this cop had been through in his career, or what he'd seen: political liars, wealthy cheats, hopeless thieves, brutal murderers, harlots with hearts of tarnish gold, battered wives and kids, and maybe even a female saint who was found dead in a back alley, murdered by the man she'd hope to console and change with her unselfish love.

Yes, Patrick had seen all those things, and more, when he was a detective in the 1880s, so he wasn't going to judge this cop harshly. After all, from the looks of him, the poor soul hadn't had the good fortune to have his life altered and blessed by an Eve Sharland or a little lass named Colleen.

"You daft romantic fool," Patrick muttered to himself as he moved on. "Thank you for your time, officer."

The cop called after him. "She probably dropped dead someplace, and the wagon picked her up. She's the better for it."

Patrick wandered a path, staring into the west. The sunset was a banked fire, smoldering, with cobalt-colored clouds hovering.

After dark, he strolled back through Central Park, along a paved walkway between a grove of trees. He stopped short when he saw a figure sitting hunched on Sarah's park bench. He hurried over.

"Sarah!"

Sarah jumped, reaching for her knife. When she saw Patrick approach, she relaxed, made an ugly face and cursed. "May the good Lord bless me for not dropping over dead from fright. What do you mean, sneaking up on an old woman like that and scaring the life out of her?"

"I'm sorry, Sarah, but I've been looking all over for you."

She cocked a suspicious eye. "What for, Buster Boy? Why would you be looking for me?"

And then she coughed, a deep, hacking cough, filled with crackling phlegm that doubled her over.

Patrick looked on with concern. "Sarah, it sounds worse than before."

The cough gagged her; pinched her face with pain. It was minutes before she recovered. "Don't... you... worry none, Buster Boy," she forced out. "Old Sarah... She's still got a jig or two in her yet... by the will of the good Lord above."

"The good Lord above can't help you if you don't help yourself, Sarah."

She patted the bench. "Sit down, Buster Boy. Sit down and have a good and much-needed drink of whiskey with a broken-down sack of an old woman."

With a shake of his head, he obeyed and sat. She reached inside her bundle and tugged out a paper bag. With a shaky hand, she withdrew the half-drunk pint of whiskey and smiled with broad, delicious pleasure.

"Look at that beauty, Buster Boy. Ain't that a picture?"

"Go easy with that, Sarah."

"Are you preachin' to me?"

"No... Just take it easy, that's all."

She popped the cork and took a swallow, then winced and coughed. "God bless me, that's as good as the nectar from the Gods. I hope you didn't bring me another roast beef sandwich. It's hard to chew with these old jagged choppers of mine."

"I brought you an egg salad sandwich and a piece of pie. Also, some hot coffee, but I'm sure it's not so hot now."

She smiled, showing her jagged teeth. "Coffee? Well, Lord love you, Buster Boy, let's put some good ole Irish in that coffee and drink to my health. Now, tell me what's wrong with that? Who's going to say we ain't living the life of the Rockefellers and Vanderbilts, huh?"

Patrick pulled the coffee from the bag, pried off the lid and held it so Sarah could tip in some whiskey. She poured too much, it overflowed, and coffee spilled to the ground.

Sarah laughed. "Better the coffee than the whiskey, eh, Buster Boy?"

Patrick sipped on one side of the paper coffee cup, while Sarah gobbled down the sandwich as if she hadn't eaten in days.

It pleased him to watch her eat. After all, Sarah was the first person he'd met in 1925; his first friend.

After she stuffed the last of the pie into her mouth and was chewing vigorously, Patrick said, "Sarah, I want to take you to a clinic for an examination."

Shocked, she spit pieces of the pie as she spoke in protest. "I ain't going to any kind of clinic."

Patrick faced her sternly. "Do you see how determined I am, and how big I am?"

Sarah swallowed the last of the pie, narrowing her threatening eyes on him. "Yeah, and I've got me a knife, Buster Boy, and that says I'm staying put."

"No, you don't, Sarah Finn."

Her eyes widened. "What do you mean?" she said, snaking her hand inside her bundle to produce the knife. Her face registered alarm as she patted and felt and shook her bundle. "What the hell?" she barked.

Patrick stood up and whipped her knife out from behind his back.

Sarah leapt up, but Patrick easily raised his arm and blocked her. She darted left and right, but Patrick kept her at arm's length. Finally, he gave her a little shove, and she dropped heavily back onto the bench, confounded.

"Give me my knife!"

"Only if you agree to go with me tonight to the clinic and let somebody take care of that cough. Then I'll return it to you."

"You bastard... I thought I could trust you."

"You can trust me. The clinic is not that far away. We'll leave the park at Fifth Avenue, catch a cab, and be there in no time. Now, what do you say?"

She shook her head in sorrow. "That's my knife, Buster Boy. That's my favorite knife that my son gave me. How did you steal it from me?"

"You dropped your pickle, Sarah, and when you stood up, your bundle fell. Being the gentleman I am, I retrieved it for you, quickly taking the knife."

She lowered her eyebrows. "You've been blessed with fast hands, you have, but I ain't sayin' that's a good thing, or something to be proud of. You hoodwinked an old woman, and that's a sad bit of business."

"I'll give it back to you, after the examination. Shall we go?"

Her eyes looked at him like two black, angry barrels of a gun. "I'll get you back for this, Buster Boy. Make no mistake about it."

Patrick dropped the knife into his front coat pocket and stretched out his hand. "Come on, Sarah. Tonight, you'll be sleeping in a real soft and warm bed. No hard, cold park bench for you."

Sarah tilted her head back and raised her arms toward the heavens. "May the good Lord help me. Treachery, that's what it is. Treachery."

CHAPTER 24

Monday morning, November 2, was a sunny day with a brisk, chilly breeze. Patrick decided to begin his search for Virginia by shadowing Vernon Scott. Perhaps he would split his time between Vernon and his mistress, Louise McGuire, or perhaps he wouldn't have to. It would all become clear once he put his surveillance into motion and began to put all the pieces together.

But Patrick's first order of business concerned purchasing a pistol, a passport, and a driver's license. He had no idea where the trail would lead, but being able to drive a car might be a necessity.

After breakfast, he took the trolley and the subway downtown to Mercer Street. He once knew a man named Clay Weaver, who worked in a tailor shop back in the 1880s. He'd been an expert forger, specializing in passports and identity cards. Clay also had a good collection of revolvers that he kept hidden in a back bedroom under a floorboard and sold for a decent price.

Of course, a lot of time had passed since 1885, but it was a good place to start. Maybe Clay had a son or cousin who had kept the business going.

Patrick turned onto Mercer, walked twenty feet and stopped. The tailor shop was gone, replaced by an Italian restaurant, Pasquale's. Patrick wasn't surprised. He walked the street for a time, observing a milk wagon rattle by, a Model T Ford bump along the cobbles, and two matronly women in their sixties drift by, shopping bags in hand. They were dressed more in Victorian fashion than in the 1920s fashion, with lavish hats and long dresses, obviously corseted.

In contrast, a young woman across the street was walking briskly, head held high and smoking a cigarette. She wore a smart-looking modern coat, showing her lower legs and heeled shoes. Her close-fitting, orange cloche hat added an air of sexy confidence.

Patrick marveled at the overlapping of history and the contrast between the women's fashions. He decided he preferred the 1920s look to twenty-first century fashion, and he certainly liked both more than the covered, laced and corseted fashion of the Victorians.

Nearby, Patrick saw a florist shop, a two-story automobile repair shop and, of all things, a carriage house. They still had those in the 1920s?

Patrick strolled to the corner newsstand and pretended to peruse the impressive assortment of newspapers, and movie and finance magazines.

The gray-haired proprietor stood enclosed behind a counter, a half-smoked stogie stuck between his teeth, a pair of eyeglasses perched on the end of his nose and a racing track form held up close to his eyes.

Patrick cleared his throat, and the man grudgingly lowered the page. "What'll it be?"

Patrick pulled a dollar bill from his wallet and held it up between two fingers. He'd learned that a dollar went a long way in 1925. "I need to purchase a revolver and obtain a passport and a driver's license, not necessarily in that order."

"Do you mean an operator's license to drive a car?"

"Yes, an operator's license. Do you know of anyone around who can help me?"

The newsman looked at Patrick, then at the dollar bill, and then back at Patrick. It was a wrinkled, implacable face, with a right twitching eye.

The man said, "Do you play the horses?"

Patrick was confused by the question. "No…"

"I've got a tip for you, if you do."

"I don't play the horses, or the dogs, or the automobiles, and certainly not the lottery. I've never been good at it. I always lose. So, being fond of my money, I don't bet."

Newsman didn't seem to hear. He leaned a little closer. "Belmont Park. I love Belmont. It has a straightaway of just under seven furlongs. Good, fast racing. Anyway, tomorrow afternoon at four-thirty, third race, place your bet on Queen Vick to win. I know a guy. He don't miss. I make money from his tips. He's good and quiet and he has contacts, you know what I mean? I'm saying he has good, dependable contacts. That's what I'm saying, and you can believe it."

"I told you, I don't play the horses," Patrick said.

Newsman pulled the stogie from his mouth and shrugged with indifference. "I'm doin' you a favor Bub, okay? You don't want my tip, then don't take it. It ain't no scuff on my shiny boots."

In one swift, sweeping motion, Newsman snatched the one-dollar bill from Patrick's fingers. Patrick was about to leap over the counter and deck the guy, when Newsman held up a hand. "Easy, Bub. Go easy." His right eye twitched. "Thanks for the Washington. Business is slow. I'll buy some good cigars and take in a Clara Bow picture. Okay, so here's your guy who can set you up. The mug's name is Horn. Casey Horn. He lives just down the street next to the florist shop, second floor, room 2C."

"Is he good?" Patrick asked.

"He's got contacts. The best you'll get this side of Flatbush. He'll sell you a pistol. He's got a good selection, and you know how it works. He knows a guy who knows a guy, who'll fix you up with a passport and an operator's license. Just tell Casey that Bill Stripe sent you. And, if you change your mind about Queen Vick, there's a barbershop down the next corner on the right. Can't miss it. Ask for Lugo. He's the best barber and the best bookie around."

Casey Horn did indeed sell Patrick a Colt Police Positive .32 Smith & Wesson Revolver. He also sent him to Christopher Street, where he met a crickety, nervous man who had a crickety, nervous wife. Casey Horn had given Patrick the password: *Baseball.*

They wanted payment up front and Patrick complied. The wife took Patrick's photo with a box camera, and her husband did the print work and finishing. They said little to each other, or to Patrick, as they worked with assiduous care and precision.

Patrick returned the following morning and took possession of the passport and a 1925 Operators License, without a photograph, as none was needed. The license expired on June 30, 1927. During the course of business, no one spoke a single word, not even "Hello" or "Goodbye."

Late Tuesday morning, Patrick was standing outside the impressive building that housed Vernon Scott's law firm. He studied the people going in and coming out. He strolled the neighborhood, chewing two sticks of spearmint gum. At noon, workers streamed out from the building and Patrick tucked himself unobtrusively behind a column to see if Vernon would emerge.

At ten minutes after one, he did, and he was alone. Patrick's feet were already sore in his new boots, and he was chilled to the bone. He was grateful to follow Vernon two blocks uptown, into the warmth of Stanley's Restaurant. Patrick hung back until, through the front window, he saw the ruler erect maître d' tuck two menus under his arm and lead Vernon away into the dining room.

Patrick ducked inside, grateful for the warm breath of heat, and made his way to the bar, sitting on a tall wooden stool, near a fresh vase of flowers. The place was nearly full, filled with lively conversation, clouds of cigar and cigarette smoke and hustling waiters in white shirts, ties and black aprons. Shouldering trays, they carried broiled steak, grilled fish and pasta entrees.

Vernon was seated at a private table in the rear of the restaurant beside a single window, partially covered by a red velvet curtain.

Patrick's stool offered only a partial view of Vernon, but it was good enough to watch him.

The balding bartender looked sad in his black vest, black tie and white shirt. Since the restaurant couldn't serve liquor, Patrick ordered a fountain Coca-Cola with cherry syrup. It came in a tall Coca-Cola glass with a straw and appeared quite delicious. But the bartender frowned at it, and then glared at it, as if it were an enemy.

"Good lunch crowd," Patrick said, after a quick sip of the Coke.

The bartender's heavy, hooded eyes reminded Patrick of a weary hound dog after a hunt.

"It doesn't matter how busy we are. We're closing in a few weeks. We ain't been busy much since they killed the booze. These are regulars, come to give us last rites."

"You're closing the place because of the no booze law?"

"Yep, of course. Those do-gooder, Sunday Psalm singers, and those no-good, over-paid bastards in Washington are killing the restaurant business. Now everyone goes to the cafeterias or to the soda fountain lunch counters."

"It will change."

"It won't help this place if it does change, unless it changes in a week. This place is done for. It's sad. This restaurant has been in business since 1890."

"Are you working anywhere else?" Patrick asked.

"Yeah, at a speakeasy over on the Lower East side. I'm ready to get out of here."

During his conversation with the bartender, Patrick had kept his eyes on the entrance door. When he saw her enter, he straightened. There she was, Vernon's mistress, Miss Louise McGuire. He recognized her from the newspaper photo Evelyn had included in the envelope.

Louise wore a chic mink coat, a white fur hat and what appeared to be dangling diamond earrings. Patrick assumed they were real. She sashayed into the restaurant like she owned the place. Her face was round, her eyes large and dreamy, her nose upturned. Her button of a mouth was red; her cheeks rosy and a little pudgy. Patrick had the impression that, for all her dazzle and attraction, she was not so comfortable in her skin.

The maître d' made quick steps to greet her. He gushed, gave a little bow, and sucked in his belly. With a dramatic flair, he escorted Miss McGuire to Vernon's table. As she approached, Vernon stood, standing stiffly.

"Do you know her?" the bartender asked.

"No…"

"She's a hotsy-totsy, ain't she?"

"Yes, I suppose she is."

The bartender inclined forward, keeping his hound dog eyes on her. "Her papa is one of the big bootleggers in the City. His name is Joe McGuire. The place I work on the East side, called Big Baby, used to be a blacksmith shop. Anyway, Joe McGuire supplies all the booze for the place, and it's good. The best. Anyway, that girl is his daughter, and don't she know she's the cat's meow."

Louise shed her coat and hat, and when Vernon offered to kiss her cheek, she jerked her face away in an obvious snub, and sat, her back to Patrick. She lit her own cigarette and turned her face aside, as Vernon used his hands and an apologetic expression to explain and placate Louise. She refused to look at him.

Patrick ordered the cod fish cakes in tomato sauce, while keeping a sharp eye on Vernon and Louise.

Ten minutes later, she shot up, yelling something at Vernon, but Patrick couldn't hear what she said. She grabbed a glass of water, slung it into his face, then pivoted and marched toward the entrance. The distressed maître d' snapped his fingers for the waiter to bring her coat and hat.

It was obvious that Vernon didn't want to draw further attention to himself, so he sat in a frown of irritation while the waiter blotted water from his face and shoulders.

Adorned again in her coat and fur hat, Louise made a grand exit, as if she were an opera star having just finished the high note in an aria.

Patrick looked at the bartender, who was polishing a glass. "That cat's meow can scratch," Patrick said.

"That ain't the first time those two have fought. Why he stays with her, I don't know."

Then he laughed, a man's knowing laugh. "Like we don't know why he stays with her, huh?" And then his eyes went vague and lusty. "She probably scratches in bed, too, and he probably likes it. Yeah, well, with that one purring all over you, who wouldn't like it?"

CHAPTER 25

Early Tuesday morning, Patrick strolled by the impressive Broadmoor Hotel at Park Avenue and Fifty-Fourth Street. Only recently completed, it boasted of twenty-one stories and four-hundred and ninety-five rooms. It was innovative for 1925, with automatic refrigeration and closets large enough for "a queen's wardrobe." It also boasted of spacious rooms, suites, and maid service.

Suite 1008 was the residence of Vernon Scott and Louise McGuire, and for the next two days, Patrick spent his mornings following Vernon from the Broadmoor to his office downtown and shadowing him as he ate lunch at Stanley's. During those two days, Louise didn't meet him for lunch. He ate either alone or with one of his partners, and Patrick had identified all of them.

After work, to Patrick's frustration, Vernon went straight home and stayed there, most likely to placate Louise for some infraction that Patrick had yet to learn about. From vast experience, Patrick knew it would take time to gather pertinent information, and learn the patterns of Vernon's everyday life.

Late Thursday night, November 5, one of the pretty maids in the hotel told Patrick that Louise had come down with a cold, and that's why she hadn't left the apartment.

On Friday morning, after Vernon emerged from the hotel, caught his usual cab, and motored off toward his office, Patrick decided not to follow him, lingering outside the Broadmoor instead.

About an hour later, he got a break. Louise swept out, dressed in her furs. The doorman skipped a step to hold the door, then he hustled outside and whistled for a taxi.

Patrick left the cover of the adjacent awning next door, waved down a taxi and slid in, slamming it shut. "Follow that cab."

The driver, wearing a brown uniform complete with a taxi hat, yanked down the metal arm on the fare meter and gunned the accelerator. The car jumped away from the curb and entered the flow of traffic.

While Patrick eased back into his seat, his mind rambled with thoughts of Evelyn and Sarah. Sarah had left the clinic after only one night's stay. He'd stopped by the clinic on Tuesday night to check on her, and the nurse told him that Sarah had left the clinic earlier that day.

Although she'd slept soundly the night he'd admitted her, snoring like a bear, by morning she was raring to go, and no one was going to stop her. She'd cursed, fought and complained until she was released.

The knife Patrick had taken from her was reluctantly returned to her by a security guard, on Patrick's instructions, since he'd promised Sarah she would get it back.

"The woman is ill and needs prolonged care," the nurse had said, with a professional air of wisdom. "She has a terrible cough, and she fought a nurse and a doctor to keep her whiskey bottle. A doctor bluntly warned her that she would die if she didn't receive medical attention, but she refused, even after she was told that her bills had been paid and would continue to be paid."

Patrick had gone looking for the stubborn old woman on Thursday night, but she wasn't at her usual park bench, and he'd waited over an hour before leaving. It saddened him to think that Sarah would die alone, cold and sick, her body carted off and buried in a potter's field on Hart Island in the Bronx.

Patrick wasn't entirely sure why the crazy old woman had touched him so. Maybe it was because she was the first person he'd met in this time. Maybe it was because she'd lost a son in World War 1, a son she'd deeply loved. Maybe it was because he had a soft spot for the lost souls of the world. Eve had often said he was a contradiction.

"You can be so practical, so hard and, seemingly, so cold sometimes, Patrick," Eve had said. "And then you give five dollars to some homeless guy on the subway. Why?"

He didn't know why. Maybe because he'd had to kill people when he was a detective in the 1880s. They had been criminals; many, downright evil, but in retrospect, maybe he didn't feel so good about it. Maybe one or two might have been innocent but, like most cops in the 1880s, when his life was threatened, he fired first and asked questions later.

But maybe it all had to do with his father. Patrick had never told Eve the entire truth about his father. He'd never told her that his father had lost his way in life and had taken to drink. Many a night, Patrick had had to haul him from a saloon, drunk and feisty, or drag him off the street where he'd stumbled and was begging for money so he could buy more whiskey.

No, Patrick had never shared that with Eve. He'd always painted a shiny image of his old Da. He'd purposefully portrayed his father as a fine Irish gentleman, who had wit and charm, and a bit of the kindly philosopher about him. Yes, Patrick supposed that was it—his soft spot for the lost of the world, born of an old, dark memory of his father.

Evelyn Stratford had been on Patrick's mind constantly, and it had been an agony not to see her. And since he had nothing to report, he had not left her a message at the clinic. No doubt, she was anxious and on edge, checking every hour for some word from him.

He wondered if Evelyn had contacted Lavinia Vanderbilt, Joni's daughter. He had a good feeling about Lavinia. If she was anything like her mother, she would have a generous heart. He hoped that Lavinia had not become like her brother, the coldly suspicious William Foster.

The taxi driver's voice snapped Patrick back to the present. "Sir, the car ahead is drawing up to the curb. How far do you want me to stay back?"

"Stop here. I want to see where she goes."

Patrick quickly reoriented himself. Where was he? What neighborhood? He should have been paying attention, focused and alert, not distracted.

"Where are we?"

"West One-Hundred and Forty-Sixth Street."

Patrick saw five row houses, all four-story redbrick apartment buildings with zig-zag fire escapes in front. He saw a billboard sign on the roof nearby advertising **Squibbs Dental Cream**. A smoke shop was on the corner, next to a candy store. A school and playground were close by, with kids chasing, screaming, playing tag.

It wasn't a fashionable part of town, not a neighborhood he'd expect Louise to visit.

Patrick ducked his head and watched Louise exit the cab. She glanced about nervously, readjusted her shoulders, then climbed the four cement stairs to the apartment building on the far left. Her taxi performed a U-turn and retreated downtown, as delicate snow flurries began to drift.

Patrick's driver had placed his hands on the top of the steering wheel. "What do you want me to do?"

"Keep the meter running. I'll be back."

The driver shook his head. "No, Buddy, if you leave my cab, you gotta pay me what you owe now. Then I'll start a new meter."

Patrick fumbled into his pants pocket, drew out his wallet and handed the driver a large bill. "Keep the change and wait."

The driver was pleased by the bill. He jerked a nod. "Whatever you say, Buddy."

After Louise disappeared inside the building, Patrick left the cab, relaxed his shoulders and strolled casually toward the building Louise had entered.

He waited a couple of minutes, then climbed the stairs. At the door, he paused, reached and turned the doorknob. The hallway was square, thinly carpeted in brown, with wooden mailboxes on the left side of the wall. A winding staircase led up into gloomy heights. Above, Patrick stood listening to a baby cry and a radio playing jumpy music. He smelled freshly baked bread that made him hungry, and then he heard the yap, yap of a dog coming from somewhere high above. And then a "Shut up, you stupid dog!"

He turned his attention to the mailboxes and searched the names. Maybe one would be familiar. None were.

So where had Louise gone, and why?

Just then, he heard a frantic scream that tore into the silence like a bomb. He tensed, every muscle on alert. Another scream sent him bounding up the stairs to the second level, where he thought it came from.

In the shadowy hallway, a door burst open and Louise came boiling out, staggering, her pretty face ugly with terror. An apartment door opened a couple of inches and a woman's frightened voice called out. "What's going on? What is it?"

Another door flew open and a bushy-headed man poked his head out. "Stop the noise! Stop it, I say, or I'll call the police!"

Patrick hurried over to Louise. She had braced her hands on the flat banister railing, her head down, mouth breathing, her face as white as snow.

"What is it?" Patrick asked, glancing right through the open door.

"Oh, my God. Oh, my good gracious God, they've murdered him!"

Patrick stared hard. He left her, stepped toward the apartment, and gingerly entered. Looking right, he saw a man lying on the floor, sprawled on his back, his flat, wide eyes open, his white shirt soaked in blood. He was young, probably in his late twenties or early thirties. His mouth was partially open in a kind of loopy, weird smile, and blood had pooled around his head.

He was very dead, and he'd been dead for some time, by the look of the dried blood. Instinctively, Patrick glanced about, spotting a saxophone on the couch next to an open instrument case, and a bottle of milk on the floor nearby, half drunk.

Patrick didn't want any part of this. It had bad news written all over it. He turned and left the room, returning to Louise, who was still at the banister, panting for breath.

"You'd better leave, now, unless you want to explain this to the police."

"I'm going to be sick."

"Not now you're not. Hold it until you're away from here."

When she lifted her head to see who was speaking to her, her shocked eyes were packed with tears, her eye makeup smudged, her expression holding dazed disbelief.

She offered him her shaking hand. "Please… Take me away from here."

With reluctance, Patrick took her hand, led her along the hallway and down the stairs. She moved mechanically, as if guided by remote control, making little gulping sobs.

Outside, she wept, as snow fell, as sirens wailed, approaching. Patrick managed to hurry her along the sidewalk and get her inside the taxi, sliding in behind her.

The driver stared at them in his rearview mirror, a smirk on his disapproving face.

"Drive downtown," Patrick commanded.

"Where downtown?" he asked, trying to be irritating.

"I don't give a damn where downtown, just drive," Patrick snapped.

The taxi lurched away from the curb and advanced north, before turning right. Two police cars raced by and Patrick lowered his head.

Louise buried her face in her hands and bawled like a baby.

Patrick leaned forward, toward the driver. "Drop me two blocks down and take the lady anywhere she wants to go."

Louise dropped her hands and clamped a hand on his arm, squeezing, her eyes wet and pleading. "No, don't go. Please don't leave me. Please... don't leave me alone."

Patrick gazed straight ahead, seeing the snowfall thicken, falling in a frenzy, and he thought to himself, *Well, Gantly, what kind of mess have you gotten yourself into?*

CHAPTER 26

On Friday afternoon, Evelyn exited her taxi at Fifth Avenue and 77th Street. She paused, as her awed eyes took in the massive mansion that rose up before her, constructed in the style of a French Château. This was the Benedict Vanderbilt mansion, where Lavinia Vanderbilt resided. The nine-story house contained 110 rooms, thirty-one bathrooms, four art galleries, a swimming pool and Turkish baths. High-tech for its time, with electricity and central air-conditioning, it required seven tons of coal per day, brought in by a private subway line.

Benedict Vanderbilt's wealth came from inherited family money as well as from his own business interests in copper, radio technology and railroads.

The previous Tuesday morning, via messenger, Evelyn had sent Lavinia the clinic's portfolio, including its history, positive press clippings and financials. She had been cheered by Patrick's positive intervention on the clinic's behalf, and further encouraged by Mrs.

Vanderbilt's secretary's receptiveness to forwarding the information to Lavinia for her consideration.

Evelyn had been stunned when, on Thursday evening, she'd received a hand-written note from Lavinia Vanderbilt herself, inviting her to tea the following afternoon. Evelyn hadn't expected to hear from Mrs. Vanderbilt for weeks, or even months, or maybe never.

As snow flurries drifted in an easy wind, Evelyn adjusted her hat, feeling the proverbial butterflies in her stomach as she passed under the impressive cathedral arch and stepped up to the tall, oak door. She lifted the gold knocker and gently tapped twice.

Moments later, the door swung open and a tall, middle-aged butler, dressed in a black tie and tails, stared back at her with cool, appraising eyes. "Yes, Madam?"

Evelyn cleared her throat, nerves shaking her voice. "I am Evelyn Stratford. I'm here to see Mrs. Lavinia Vanderbilt."

Feeling like a beggar, she half expected to be shoved backwards by this tall, stone-faced man, who stared at her as if she were an up-start imposter.

So Evelyn was surprised when the butler's face became pleasant. He offered a little bow and the hint of a smile. "Yes, Mrs. Stratford. Mrs. Vanderbilt is expecting you. Please come in."

Evelyn did so, entering a spacious lobby with white marble floors, a large chandelier and a wide, sweeping, red-carpeted staircase that led to upper floors.

Eve followed the long strides of the butler through a rotunda and into a marble-paneled main picture gallery that was ninety-five feet long and two stories high. Evelyn saw an organ loft that housed an impressive chamber organ and a small, two-tiered choir loft.

They branched off left, and the butler escorted Evelyn under an archway into an elegant library, with high ceilings, a stone fireplace with a roaring fire, and many gilded-framed landscaped oil paintings and portraits.

Floor-to-ceiling cherry wood bookshelves had a winding staircase and balcony level, where one could roam and browse. Rare and leather bound hardback books could also be accessed by two rolling ladders on either side of the vast, soaring room. Tall windows looked out on a dormant fountain and footpaths that meandered through manicured hedges and a distant garden, and Evelyn imagined that garden bursting with color in spring and summer.

Smiling graciously, Mrs. Lavinia Joan Foster Vanderbilt stood by a small, ornate table that was covered by a white linen tablecloth. The table was set for tea and refreshments, with gold-rimmed cups and a silver tray displaying tea sandwiches and cakes.

An extravagance of fresh flowers bloomed from rose-colored vases on tables nearby, scenting the room with their subtle fragrance.

Evelyn nervously slipped out of her coat and removed her hat, handing them to the awaiting butler. With some ceremony, he draped her coat over an arm and silently withdrew, closing the door behind, leaving Evelyn and Lavinia in an opulent peace.

Evelyn had agonized over what to wear, sampling five dresses and four pairs of shoes, finally deciding on a brown patterned dress with a beaded neckline. She hoped it showed fashion, but was still conservative enough not to offend.

"And so there you are, at last," Lavinia said, her eyes eager, her smile warm.

Mrs. Vanderbilt appeared to be in her early-to-middle 30s. She wore a magnificent burgundy gown, a choker of expensive pearls and matching earrings. With lush, auburn hair piled on top of her head and styled in waves and curls, Evelyn thought the woman a novel beauty and a fortunate catch for any wealthy man.

Lavinia looked at Evelyn with enchanting, brown eyes that held a faraway, dreamy quality and, yet, there was also a brightness of curiosity and intelligence in them.

Lavinia left the table and approached Evelyn with her hands outstretched and a melting smile, as if they were old friends.

Lavinia tilted her head left and took Evelyn in fully. "Ever since I received your letter, I have been forcing back nerves and excitement."

Evelyn was surprised and bewildered by the greeting. Evelyn took Lavinia's hands with a little swallow, and a heart flutter.

"Forgive me, Eve, may I call you, Eve? I feel as though I've known you for many years."

Evelyn struggled, momentarily lost for words. "... Yes, of course, Mrs. Vanderbilt. Yes, Eve is perfectly fine."

Lavinia gently squeezed Eve's hands, her smile holding. "I have to admit that I am still having difficulty believing that you are here, in the flesh."

Evelyn was certain that Lavinia had mistaken her for someone else. "Mrs. Vanderbilt, my name is Evelyn Stratford."

Lavinia nodded, still holding Eve's hands as if she would never let them go. "Yes... Yes, of course you are, Eve. Please, let us go sit down and have our tea."

Lavinia led Eve to the table. "I trust you like smoked ham and turkey? The cakes are divine, raspberry, my favorite, and chocolate, again my favorite."

A man dressed in a smart, royal blue uniform with gold buttons promptly appeared, and held the chair first for Eve, and then for Lavinia. Lavinia nodded to the servant and said, "You may pour our tea now, Charles, and thank you."

Charles moved to a side table, removed a cozy from a silver teapot and returned to the table, first pouring Eve's cup and then Lavinia's.

"Thank you, Charles. You may leave us now."

He bowed. "Very good, Mrs. Vanderbilt."

After Charles had exited through a side door, Lavinia held a hand over her heart, as if she were breathless. "I have so many questions for you, Eve. I'm sure you can imagine."

Evelyn sat rigid with growing anxiety.

"And you look just as my mother described you."

"Your... Mother?"

"Yes. As soon as my brother called me to say Patrick was in town, I immediately sent a telegram to my mother in Europe. Last night, I received her response and another this morning. You can imagine that she is simply gushing with excitement to see you again. She is catching the next ship back to New York. Of course, my father is against it, but that won't stop her. As you know, my mother has always had a mind and a will of her own, and I love her for it. She was an independent woman long before the Nineteenth Amendment passed, wasn't she?" Lavinia said, adding a knowing wink.

Eve opened her mouth to speak, but nothing came out. She couldn't find the words to form a question.

"I had hoped that Patrick would be with you. I so want to meet him. When I was a girl, my mother told me stories about you two. Of course, she told me not to tell my father. And then when I was a teenager, my father told me that if either you, Eve, or Patrick Gantly, ever appeared, I was to ignore you both and send you away with no questions asked."

Evelyn's pulse was soaring. *Patrick? Her mother and father? Her brother had told her about Patrick? What on earth was this woman talking about?*

Lavinia continued. "I knew if Patrick had returned, then you had returned as well, Eve. And when I received your letter, I was thrilled beyond imagination. Oh, and don't either of you have a single care about my brother, William. When he called, he demanded that I not see either of you. He is a stiff, stuffed shirt, just like Daddy, only more so. When he called and told me that Patrick had gone to see him, I grew faint with excitement. Of course, he told me to never, ever invite him in, and William demanded that I not even speak to Patrick. Well, can you imagine?"

Lavinia stopped talking to reach for the creamery. She tipped some into her tea and then, with silver tongs, she gripped a lump of sugar and dropped it into her cup. After a stir and two sips, she replaced the cup on the saucer and inclined her neck forward, excited and ready for more conversation.

"Now, Eve, if you would, please tell me why you have returned. Is it just to see my mother again, or has something drastic happened that has brought you back? Mother always said that if you and Patrick ever did appear, it would be because something drastic had happened that forced you to light that lantern again and return."

Confused and perspiring, Evelyn's mind was a muddle. "Mrs. Vanderbilt..."

"Oh, Eve, please call me Lavinia. After all, you and my mother are old friends. And you are my best new friend. My very best."

Evelyn's breathing quickened as she stared down into her untouched teacup. She squirmed and grasped for words, any words.

"Is the tea to your liking, Eve?"

"Yes. Yes, very nice... Lavinia... I'm here because of the clinic. I sent you the proposal, as your secretary had instructed. You see, I thought that perhaps you would..."

Lavinia cut in. "Of course, Eve, I will assist you in any way possible to keep your clinic open and operating. Don't you have a care about it. I don't know how it figures in with your, shall we say, travel plans, but I do not have to know that at this time. I trust Patrick Gantly is helping you with the clinic?"

Evelyn was drowning in bewilderment. She stuttered out the words. "... How... How do you know about... Mr. Gantly?"

Lavinia reached for a square cut of the chocolate cake with smooth vanilla icing, placing it carefully on her plate. She smiled, sheepishly. "I told you, Eve. My brother called and told me about him. Mr. Gantly had visited him at his bank. I knew that it was just a matter of time before you or Mr. Gantly would contact me. William said that he'd told Patrick that my parents were away, so I knew one or both of you would come and seek me out. And here you are, and I couldn't be more delighted."

Lavinia's eyes warmed. "My mother has missed you terribly, Eve. From her last telegram, I could tell she is bursting with anticipation. When I was in my twenties, Mother finally shared mad and ridiculous tales about the two of you living in the future, in the twenty-first century."

Eve sat in a taut silence, her usual fleet-acting mind short-circuited by Lavinia's incomprehensible words. "… Future?"

Lavinia ate the teacake with eloquence, chewing slowly, watching Eve sit uneasily. She'd taken but one sip of tea and not tasted a single finger sandwich.

It suddenly occurred to Lavinia that Eve was troubled. But of course she would be troubled if she had had to time travel again. Her mother had said, more than once, that Eve would only time travel if things were grave and they couldn't be solved any other way.

Lavinia turned sympathetic. She took in a little breath, folding her hands, resting them in her lap. "I am sorry, Eve. Here I am chattering on and you must have come to me because you need my help."

Evelyn found her voice, a small, tentative voice. "Yes… Mrs. Vander… Lavinia. I came because of the clinic."

"Well, don't give that another worried thought, Eve. As I said, we'll work it out and make certain that the clinic remains vital and successful."

Lavinia cast her eyes about the room to ensure they were alone, and they were. Lavinia spoke in a soft, confidential tone. "Now… well, I have to tell you something that I'm sure you are just burning to know.

My mother never told me where she hid the time travel lantern, and she was adamant that she never would. Of course, she never told William either. She was sure he would destroy it, and that terrified Mother. My father never spoke about it, not once, when he warned us against you and Patrick."

As she sat there with perspiration forming on her forehead, her heart thumping, Evelyn was certain that Lavinia was completely out of her mind. Eve shifted her weight and decided she would have to play along with the mad woman. What else could she do? She needed the money for the clinic, and Lavinia had already said that Evelyn could have it.

"Yes… well… Of course, the lantern."

Lavinia's eyes enlarged as she leaned forward. "You need the time lantern so you and Patrick can return to your own time, don't you, Eve?"

Evelyn's smile came and went. Then she forced another, a patient, strained smile. "Yes… the lantern."

"Do not worry, Eve. Mother will be on the next ship from Southampton and return home to New York within six days, or sooner, if she can arrange it. Now, aren't you excited?"

Evelyn nodded, completely mystified. "… Why, yes. Yes, of course."

"It will be like old times again. You, Patrick and Mother together. And don't you worry, Eve, Mother will give you the lantern so you can return home to the twenty-first century."

Evelyn's stomach twisted in panic. Lavinia Vanderbilt was respected and renowned, married to one of the wealthiest and most powerful men in the country.

Why was she left alone? Shouldn't she be in the care of a physician? She was as mad as a hatter. Completely and utterly mad.

What should she do? Could she recommend Milton Grange to her?

CHAPTER 27

In a taxi heading downtown, Patrick used his most soothing voice to calm Louise McGuire.

"Take some deep breaths and try to relax."

She did so, her eyes wet, her mouth a trembling frown.

"Feel better?"

"I've got the shakes real bad," Louise said. "I'm coming apart... Shaking to pieces. Look at my hands, shaking and red."

Patrick watched curiously as she hitched up a long, sexy leg and tugged a silver flask from her red garter belt. She screwed off the cap, tossed her head back and took a generous drink. After a long, gulping swallow, she offered the flask to Patrick, but he declined.

After another pull from the flask, she replaced the cap, twisted it firmly, and slipped the flask back into her garter belt.

She extended her hands, staring down at them. "Look at my hands. I tell you I'm shaking all over. I'm shaking inside and out. Shaking like a leaf in a storm. Dammit,

213

but I'm all whirled out like a crazy dancer. I need to hold up somewhere and settle. I've got to pace. I've got to think."

Patrick saw a light go on in her misty eyes. She faced him and said, "Let's go to your place. You've got a place, right? Wait a minute, do you live in that building back there? Did you know Frankie?"

"No. I don't live there. No, I didn't know Frankie."

"Good. That's good. Then let's go to your place."

Patrick was certainly not going to take her to his apartment. He'd be subjecting himself to every kind of danger. "Can't."

"Can't? What do you mean, can't? I tell you I'm shaking apart here. Can't you help a girl who's going to pieces? Who's all busted up inside? I've got the heebie-jeebies all right. So what does 'can't' mean?"

Louise had a Brooklyn accent that didn't fit her put-on-airs face and her overall presentation. He'd expected slower speech, less slang, more measured words.

"I mean, I live with my mother," Patrick said, a quick, convenient lie.

"Your mother?" She sniffed, her eyes searching his face. "You still live with your mother? What is that? You don't look the type."

"The type to have a mother?"

"No, the type who lives with his mother. I don't figure that. Now, that's all crazy."

"Well, figure it or not, I do, and she wouldn't like it if we barged in on her."

The flow of tears took a pause as Louise thought about it. "She must be a right broad then, huh?"

"Yeah, I guess you could say that."

"Does she read the Bible and such? Does she go to church and maybe she sings in the choir?" she asked, pronouncing church as "choych."

"Now and then, yeah. She sings in the choir and she likes singing in the choir," Patrick added, not sure why he did.

"I've got to respect that. I should do more of that. You know, go to church and such."

Louise thought about that for half a second, then turned frantic again. She glanced over her shoulder. "Are we being followed?"

Patrick turned, but all he saw was blurring snow. "Who would be following us?"

"I don't know. Frankie's dead, ain't he? You saw him, didn't you? Frankie's dead and somebody shot him. Shot him in the head and chest. Just killed him with his saxophone close by. What kind of thing is that to do, huh?"

"Who was Frankie?"

The tears welled up again. "He was my guy, okay?"

"What was his last name? Frankie, what?"

"Frankie Fox. Jazzy Frankie Fox," she cried.

"Do you know who killed him?"

Louise went to pieces again, sobbing into her hands. "No, no, no... He was my guy... My guy... My guy... Oh, my good Lord in heaven, he was my guy."

She wailed and rocked, and Patrick noticed the cab driver was watching the drama in his rearview mirror.

Patrick glared at him. "Drive, okay? This isn't what you think."

"So who's thinking?" the driver said.

"Keep not thinking... and stop watching us and watch the road."

The driver shrugged.

Patrick knew the driver would call the police just as soon as they left the cab. He had to act fast.

Louise yanked her hands from her red, splotchy face. "I tell you I've got to land someplace. I've got to hide or run or something."

Patrick leaned forward toward the driver. "Pull over and let us out."

Water poured from Louise's bulging eyes. "Where are we? Why are we stopping? I'm coming apart here. I'm a bad train wreck. Why are we stopping here?"

"Stop here?" the driver asked, surprised.

"Yes!" Patrick demanded. "Just pull over to the curb. We're getting out."

The driver mumbled a curse and whipped the car right, narrowly missing a pedestrian who had jutted out from between parked cars.

Patrick retrieved a bill from his wallet and handed it to the driver, while Louise blabbered on in protest.

"Keep the change," Patrick said, not wanting to wait, and hoping another generous tip might be a good enough bribe to keep the driver's mouth shut.

Ignoring Louise's motor-mouth, he grabbed her arm, shoved his door open and got out, dragging her outside into the attacking snow. She shielded her face as Patrick tugged her onto the sidewalk and over to the protective green awning of a shoe repair shop.

"What the hell's the matter with you?" Louise yelled. "Are you crazy? It's snowing in a fit out here. And it's cold as hell," she whined, yanking up the collar of her fur coat.

Patrick waited until the taxi left the curb, returning to the snarling traffic.

"Who the hell are you, anyway?" Louise cried.

Still ignoring her, Patrick searched for another taxi. There were none, not in this weather. He glanced about, squinting through the snow, spotting the Galatzer & Botoshamer Tea & Coffee House, across the street. With Louise in tow, he led her, complaining, across the street, up the four stairs and into the narrow café.

Inside were five round tables, and a wall that held several wooden shelves stacked with tea jars and coffee jars. Two of those tables were pushed together and occupied by three smoking men and one heavy, old woman. They were stooped over ceramic coffee cups and plates of sliced bread or cake. A potbelly stove heated the place, and three overhead gas globes cast an eerie light.

Patrick led a miserable and dazed Louise past a glass display case filled with pastries and cakes, to a table in the back. Every suspicious eye was stuck to them, and Patrick felt like an intruder who had no business in this private neighborhood club.

"Sit," Patrick ordered and Louise, surprisingly, obeyed, keeping her back to the room. Patrick sat opposite her, keeping his eye on the waiter, who was studying them. He was bald and heavy-jowled, with a sad white mustache, white shaggy eyebrows and wire spectacles. Keeping his eyes on them, he removed his spectacles, cleaned them with a napkin and slipped them back on.

"What are we doing here?" Louise asked.

"Keep your voice down," Patrick said.

She scowled at him, wiping old tears from her eyes, and then glanced about in distaste. "This ain't no class joint, I'll tell you that, and I'm not drinkin' any noodle-juice."

"And noodle-juice would be?"

"This stuff here. Tea and stuff."

"You can put some of your flask booze in it."

Her eyes widened. "Good idea. You bet I will."

"Just keep your voice down," Patrick said. "We have to talk."

"Talkin' is okay by me. At least it's warm in here. I'm cold and wet from that snow, and I'm not taking my hat or coat off. That old stove gives off stinky smoke."

The waiter waddled over. He lifted his spectacles and lowered his eyes on Louise. When he spoke, it was in a thick European accent. "What can I bring you, young lady?"

Louise looked him over. "You look a little like my gramps, except he had a little more hair."

He smiled and gave a little bow of his head. "Thank you for that. I'm sure your gramps is a nice man."

"He was. He kicked it about a year ago. We buried him in Brooklyn at the Green-Wood Cemetery. But we gave him a swell send off with one of them gothic-style gravestones with an angel on top. It looked real nice, and everybody said so."

Patrick rolled his eyes. "Sir, can you bring the lady a coffee and cake, and me a coffee?"

Louise shot him a look. "How do you know I like coffee?"

"Because you said you didn't like noodle juice," Patrick said.

"Yeah, well, coffee and cake's okay by me. But I don't like cake with no frosting on it." She looked up at the waiter. "Can you make sure there's lots of frosting on it?"

"Yes, I will make sure of it," the waiter said, patiently. "Extra frosting."

She smiled at him. "Yeah, okay, coffee and cake, gramps. Thanks."

"Have you been crying, young lady?" he asked.

"Yeah, sure, I've been crying. Ain't everybody cryin' about somethin' most days? I bet you this coat that my eyes look like two coal piles, don't they? Well, I got some bad news today, and it was a real shocker."

"I'm sorry to hear that," the waiter said. "I hope my coffee and cake will cheer you up. My wife bakes the pastries and they're all the best of the best."

When the waiter was gone, Patrick leaned toward her, lowering his voice. "Why did you go see Frankie?"

"I told you. Because he's my guy."

"Do you have any other guy?"

She was insulted. "What do you mean by that?"

"I mean, you're an attractive young woman. You must have more than one guy."

She calculated Patrick's compliment. "You think I'm a dumb Dora, don't you? And now you're laying the apple sauce on me."

"I don't know what you're saying. I'm not up on your slang. Who is a dumb Dora?"

"Who? *Me* is who. *Who* is me. You think I'm a dumb broad. I see it in your eyes and then you start with the flattery, the apple sauce."

"Just keep your voice down. These people are already staring at us."

She folded her arms, defiant. "And where did *you* come from with the big boy handsome face, and the

219

hang-me-on thick neck and heavy shoulders? You must have a couple of flapper girls in your back closet where your mother never cleans. And what's with that accent? It's Irish, ain't it?"

"A bit of Irish, yes, and maybe I'll add a wee bit more if I think I'll be needing it."

"Yeah, well the Irish are okay with me since my grandfather was from Ireland. Are you from there?"

"No. Here."

"Here? Hey, wait a minute. Come to think of it, you just popped in from nowhere, didn't you? You just dropped in to save the damsel in distress. Who are you, anyway?"

He ignored her. "Who would want to kill Frankie?"

The sound of Frankie's name did her in, and the grief returned, and so did the tears dripping from her eyes.

"Poor Frankie. Poor saxophone Jazzy Frankie. I called him Jazzy Frankie, you know. He could play jazz sax like nobody else. And he could dance, and kiss, and play me just like he played that sax. He made me feel like I was floating up in one of them dirigibles that sometimes fly out over the Hudson River. Poor Frankie. Poor Jazzy Frankie."

She cried into her napkin and blew her nose, making a honking sound. Patrick sighed, waiting patiently for the tears to run out. He couldn't tell if they were real or pretend tears. He had the feeling that Louise McGuire was a spoiled drama princess, and that made her dangerous, especially if she was "Daddy's Girl."

Was Daddy involved in Frankie's killing? Was Vernon Scott?

Patrick would have to tread carefully while he gently probed to learn the whereabouts of Virginia Scott.

CHAPTER 28

Patrick watched, amused, as Louise used a spoon to scoop the chocolate frosting off the slice of vanilla cake and shove it into her mouth. Her lips pursed with satisfaction, her tongue worked, her eyes went vague with pleasure.

Patrick sipped his coffee, trying to come up with the questions that would help him learn more about Virginia. "Do you like the cake?"

She nodded, her mouth full, still savoring the sweetness. "Really good…"

"Do you know if Frankie was in some kind of trouble?"

Louise's attention was on the cake. She swallowed, cut a piece and slid it into her mouth, chewing with relish. "He gambled," she said, with her mouth full.

"What kind of gambling?"

"Horses… Craps. Cards."

"Did he win or lose?"

She shrugged, leaned left, pulled the silver flask from her garter belt and twisted off the cap. "Like every gambler, he won some and he lost some," she said, tipping the booze into her coffee. "So maybe he lost more than he won, but his luck could have changed. Frankie was smart."

"Is that gin?" Patrick asked, pointing at the flask.

"Yeah, and it's good gin."

"Can I have some?"

Without a word, she reached and poured a good dollop into Patrick's coffee.

"That was a generous pour. Thanks."

After replacing the flask, she went back to the cake.

"Where do you live?" Patrick asked.

Her eyes grew suspicious. "What's it to you? Are you going to bring your mother over for a visit?"

"No, I was going to make sure you got home safely."

"Well, don't take me home. I ain't going home, all right? Is that all right with you?" she snapped.

"Sure."

"So maybe I'll go home with you and spend some time with your mother, and maybe I'll go to church with her. Yeah, maybe some church time would do me good."

Patrick took a good drink of his coffee, wincing at the strong juniper overtones in the gin. He thought, *This girl is a loose cannon. Why did Vernon leave Evelyn for Louise? Yes, Louise is young and pretty, but she's also emotional, spoiled and volatile.*

Patrick recalled the weary look of resignation on Vernon's face that day in Stanly's Restaurant, after Louise had tossed the water in his face. And the bartender had said that it wasn't the first time they'd argued.

Patrick decided on another strategy. "Louise, did Frankie know your parents?"

"My parents? My mother's dead. Daddy has the biggest ears you'll ever see, and he sees all, hears all, and knows all."

Louise looked at Patrick with an air of arrogant challenge. "What the hell do you want to know, anyway?"

Patrick shrugged. "It's not every day I see a dead man, Louise. Did your father ever meet Frankie?"

She shook her head. "No... and I wanted to keep it that way."

"But do you think he knew about Frankie?"

Louise unbuttoned her coat. "It's getting hot in here." She blinked with anxiety. "Yeah, he knew. Of course the old man knew. I told you, he's got the ears of a rabbit in heat."

"Where did you and Frankie meet?"

"In some gin joint, up in Harlem. He saw me, and then I saw him up on that bandstand, and that was it. Pow, bang and wham! His eyes struck me in the heart. I knew he was for me."

"How long ago did you meet?"

"Only two months ago. Ain't that sad? I mean, you meet that perfect guy, and things are going hot and fast like a speeding train to dreamland, and the next thing you know, bang, he's stone, cold dead on the floor, shot through the head. It makes you ask the big questions, don't it? I mean, what kind of world are we living in?"

Patrick calculated his next question, but before he could ask it, Louise spoke up. "Hey, wait a minute. What's your name? I don't even know your name."

"Sean," Patrick lied.

"Sean." She thought about it. "You don't look like a Sean."

Patrick shrugged. "I didn't have a choice, did I?"

"Yeah, well, it's okay. I like it."

Patrick asked, "What's your name?"

She replaced the spoon with a fork and chopped the rest of her cake up into little pieces. "I'm Louise."

Patrick reached out a hand. "Nice to meet you, Louise."

She looked at his hand and blinked; then lifted her chin and met his eyes. She laid her fork down, staring, as if seeing him for the first time. "Hey, Sean. You've got some nice eyes. They're all deep and stormy in there, and it makes a girl want to go inside and open an umbrella or something."

Patrick scratched his head and looked away. "Louise, were you alone when you met Frankie?"

She snapped out of her flirtation. "Alone? No... No, I wasn't alone. I was with a man. And you know what that man says to me? He says, 'Louise, you're the type of girl that always has to be with a man.' And do you know what I told him? I said, 'Yeah, and why not?' Well, you know what? He didn't like it that I was batting my long lashes at Frankie. And then Frankie sent me a note, by way of the waiter, and my man didn't notice."

Louise held a hand over her heart and swooned. "And those were some of the prettiest words I've ever seen. I could taste those words. Those words kissed me, didn't they?"

Patrick thought, *The girl might be a little crazy, but she's poetic.* "What did the note say?"

"It had a phone number. It said, 'Call me.' It said, 'I love you, pretty princess.' It said, 'Every note I'm playing is a note for you, flapper girl.' Aren't those pretty words?"

"Yes. So what happened to the man you were with?"

She screwed up her lips in disgust. "I'm leaving him. He's so nothing, and he's older than I thought. He lied to me and said he was younger. And he does business with my father. He's married, too, and that can't be right, right? So I told him to go back to his wife. Then he slaps me around. He slapped me around a lot. He said I'm spoiled and stupid and he doesn't want to be seen with me anymore. So I said, 'That's just fine with me, old man.' Then he comes at me like an animal and his hands are on me, pawing me like a wolf. Then he takes me, huffing and puffing like a freight train."

Patrick surmised the gin was helping to loosen her tongue. He pressed on.

"Does he have any children?"

She took a long drink of the coffee. Her eyes were glassy, her mouth sagging. She rested an elbow on the table and propped her chin in her palm. "Yeah, he's got a kid. He's got a girl, and you know what? She ain't that much younger than me. I think she's about sixteen. Anyway, it don't seem quite right, right?"

"Where is his daughter?"

"Don't get me started with that. Don't get me flapping my gums about her."

Patrick was so close to discovering where Virginia was, he could feel it. "Have you met his daughter?"

"Are you kidding? Me meet his darling girl who, by the way, ain't so much of a darlin', so I've heard."

"And who have you heard from?"

She laughed. "Do you know what, Sean? You're a gossip, ain't you? You with the one-hundred questions and those take-me-in-your-arms eyes looking right at me, like you want something from me." She batted her eyes. "Do you want something from me, Sean?"

Patrick leaned back, deciding to flatter to keep her talking. "Louise, I'm a man, and I'm a curious one. Can't a guy be curious?"

Louise turned serious. "Hey, no kidding now, can I go home with you and meet your mother? I don't feel so good. One man's been slapping me around and the other's dead. What kind of life am I living, huh? When did I hit the skids? Where did I go wrong? I could use a mother who reads the Bible and sings in the choir."

Patrick wished he'd kept his big mouth shut. "Didn't your mother read the Bible to you?"

The tears started again. "No, never. Do you know what? She drowned in our pool. Yeah, just one morning, Daddy found her there, floating so peaceful and dead."

Louise drained her coffee. "Daddy thinks she did it on purpose."

"Why would she do that?"

"Because Daddy's no good, that's why. He was always runnin' with women."

Louise sniffed and Patrick handed her his handkerchief. She took it with a look of gratitude. "Thanks. I think you're one of the good boys, Sean."

"Where's your Daddy now?"

"Don't get me wrong about Daddy. He's always been right with me."

"You said he does business with your man, right?"

"Oh, yeah. Daddy thought it was a good match-up, you know. He says to me, 'An older man will settle your dancin' shoes down.'"

"Who is he? I mean, what's your man's name?"

Louise stared with suspicion and reluctance. "Vernon Scott. There. I said it. Vernon Snot is what I call him."

"What kind of business is your father in?"

"Bootleggin.' My Daddy's one of the biggest bootleggers around."

"And Vernon? What does he do?"

"He handles Daddy's legal things, so he gets a piece of the business. That's how I met Vernon, at one of Daddy's big bashes. At first, I thought he was distinguished. You know, he had some gray around his temples and his clothes were spiffy sharp. And he had manners, and he was educated. I mean, he's a big-time lawyer and highfalutin, and all that. Well, I swarmed him like bees on honey. I had him in the upstairs bedroom before he knew what hit him. But maybe I'm not so proud of that now. Maybe I need to meet your praying mother."

Patrick lowered his voice, hoping not to spook Louise. "And Vernon's daughter… Is she around?"

"Around? No. She's upstate with a guy. One of Daddy's men."

"Do you know his name?"

"What do you care?"

"I don't care, but do you know his name?"

Louise probed Patrick's face, her eyes going dreamy. "Hey, there are those eyes again, Sean, all moody and looking back at me. I like them."

"I like your eyes too, Louise. What's the guy's name?"

Louise thought about it, the booze slowing her down. "He's one of Daddy's men. He handles things. He's a manager and a fighter. He likes to pick fights with his fists and his gun, and that's why Daddy likes him. His name is Sam Keller."

"Did he pick a fight with you?"

"No, he didn't look at me. He wanted Virginia, and he took her."

Louise suddenly had a thought. "Hey, why don't you have a girl? A guy who looks like you, with 'man' written on you like a tattoo on a sailor's chest. You've gotta have a girl somewhere."

Patrick had a way out and he took it. If he said he had a girl, Louise would drop her demand to see his mother. "Yes, I have a girl."

Louise's eyes flashed with sudden anger. "Damn you, Sean. You led me on."

"No, I didn't, Louise."

"Well, why didn't you tell me you had a girl when I said I wanted to meet your mother?"

"Okay, I'm sorry. Maybe I wasn't thinking so good. I mean, this has been a strange and tipsy day, hasn't it?"

Louise dropped her voice. "You said it. Anyway, has your girl met your mother?"

Patrick thought fast. "Yes."

Louise's face fell into disappointment. "Do you love her? The girl?"

"Yes, very much."

"Yeah, you would. I see that in your eyes. I just saw it when you said, 'Yes, very much.' Well, ain't that something?"

That surprised Patrick. It even touched him a little, but he needed to steer the conversation back to Virginia.

"If you don't go back to Vernon, maybe you could go upstate and stay with Vernon's daughter. What's her name?"

Louise heaved out a sigh. "Virginia. Her name's Virginia, and, hell no, I ain't going up there. It's too damn cold."

"Where is there?"

"Rochester, New York."

"What's in Rochester?"

Louise didn't answer the question. She fell into a hazy, booze-weary state. "Jazzy Frankie... God help me, but I'm going to miss Frankie's kisses. Some men just have those warm, caressing lips, and Frankie had them."

Abruptly, Louise rose. "I'm leaving."

"Where?"

"Long Island. I'm going home. Daddy will take me back. He's got a great big mansion of a house and nobody to fill it but his girlies. Yeah, I'm going home."

Patrick stood up. "Okay, I'll find you a cab."

Patrick paid the bill and escorted her outside. The snow had faded into flurries, but the wind was sharp, blowing in gusts.

They crossed the street and Patrick flagged down a cab. As it pulled to the curb, Louise lifted her gloomy eyes to take in Patrick's face. "What's your girl's name?"

"Eve."

"Hey, like Eve in the Bible. I like that name. Yeah, Eve. Well, if she runs off with a saxophone player, give me a call, Sean. You could do a lot worse than me. I ain't so bad in a pinch."

Patrick opened the cab door for her. "Take it easy on the gin, Louise."

Louise shrugged. "I hope you don't think I'm always on the make, but hell, I like your eyes, Sean. Goodbye and say hello to your mother. Tell her to say a prayer for me in church."

Louise stood on tip toes and kissed Patrick on the mouth, and then drew back with a sassy grin. "Hey, Sean, that was for nothing."

She ducked inside the cab and sat, her fingers wiggling a final farewell as he closed the door.

While he watched the cab move away, he let out a deep sigh of relief. He had the feeling that it wasn't the last time he'd see Louise.

He turned and shouldered into the wind, searching for the nearest subway stop. At last, he had something to report to Eve, even if the news was troubling.

Would she want him to travel to Rochester to find Virginia? Sam Keller didn't sound like the friendly type.

CHAPTER 29

Late afternoon of the same day, Patrick returned to his apartment. He wearily climbed the four flights of stairs, stepped onto the fourth-floor landing and paused to catch his breath.

"Look for another room," he said to himself, panting.

He inserted his key into the lock and shoved open the door. After he'd closed and locked it, he removed his coat, hat and gloves, tossed them on the sofa and dropped down next to them, tilting his head back, shutting his eyes.

After he'd left Louise, he'd traveled to the clinic. Eve wasn't there, so he left a note at the front desk, asking her to contact him ASAP.

The bizarre and exhausting incident with Louise had taken a toll on him. He loosened his tie, inhaled some deep breaths to calm his nerves and fell into a deep, welcomed sleep.

A light tap on the door snapped him awake. He sat up, reaching into his left greatcoat pocket for his revolver. He pulled it, stood and crept to the door, waiting. There was another shy knock.

"Who is it?" he asked, revolver poised.

"It's Evelyn."

Patrick sighed, lowered the gun and reached to turn the lock. Opening the door, he saw Evelyn standing there, stiff and uneasy, her perfume scenting the air.

Her worried eyes flicked up to meet his. "I hope you don't mind. I had to see you."

Patrick glanced beyond her toward the staircase. "Are you sure you weren't followed?"

"I don't think so. I did what you told me."

He reached for her hand and led her inside, closing the door and locking it. She looked at him with anxious tension.

"I took two cabs, like you told me to do; one uptown for ten blocks, then exited. I walked two blocks and didn't see a car or anyone following me, so I caught a downtown cab and got out two blocks away. Again, I didn't see anyone."

"Good," Patrick said, pocketing his gun. "Here, let me help you with your coat."

She took a step back, away from him, as if she were frightened of him. "I'll keep it on, if you don't mind."

"No, I don't mind."

"I can't stay."

"Is everything all right?"

She didn't meet his eyes. "It's just that…" Her voice trailed off.

"Did you get my note?"

Her eyes jumped to his. "No… I haven't been to the clinic since I visited Mrs. Vanderbilt. I walked… Stopped and had a light lunch."

Patrick saw she was trembling; saw the tension lines around her mouth and eyes.

"Are you sure you're all right?"

She nodded, her eyes traveling the room, taking it in, the walls, the furniture, the snug kitchen.

Patrick said, "Yeah, I know it's not much to look at. It's only temporary until I find something better."

"Well… It's quiet, and it's warm." And then she tried for a little joke. "Those stairs seem to get steeper the higher you get."

"I wasn't feeling so good when I took this place. It was one of the first I looked at, and then I got busy."

And then Evelyn blurted it out, her eyes boring into his. "Who are you?"

Patrick considered her question, sure that something dramatic had occurred, especially since she hadn't been to the clinic and read his note. She'd come on another matter.

"How did the meeting with Mrs. Vanderbilt go?" he asked, deflecting her question.

Her half-grin was tired. "I guess I could say it went well. She offered her support. She said she'll help any way she can."

Patrick smiled. "That's great news, Eve. Fantastic news. You must be relieved."

Eve's gaze lowered. "Forgive me, but do you have any alcoholic spirits? I'm not feeling myself."

"Sit down and rest," Patrick said. "The sofa's reasonably comfortable."

She eased down, folding her hands tightly on her purse, staring straight ahead.

"I have some whiskey I got from a man at the barbershop. It's not the best, but I've had worse."

"Just a little with some water, please," Evelyn said, fingering the buttons of her winter coat.

"Don't you want to take that coat off?"

"No… No, I'm not staying."

Patrick stepped into the narrow kitchen, opened a cupboard door above the sink and reached for a half-filled mason jar of light brown whiskey. He found two glasses and splashed a shot into Evelyn's, and a little more into his own. From the faucet he added a stream of water into Eve's glass. He'd drink his straight, and he could see he was going to need it.

Back in the living room, he handed her the glass. Holding his, he tapped hers. "Cheers."

Eve stared at the whiskey, and then swirled it absently, as if stalling. Her lips were careful when she sampled the booze, wincing from the bite of it.

Patrick swallowed half of the whiskey in a gulp, observing her vague, troubled eyes.

He sat in a heavy, Victorian clawfoot armchair opposite her, cradling his glass in both hands, and leaned forward. "What happened, Evelyn? What happened at your meeting with Lavinia Vanderbilt?"

Evelyn swirled the booze again, staring into it as if it held secrets. "I believe the woman is mad."

"Mad?"

"She is out of her mind. She said the most outrageous things. She's unbalanced and, I don't know, a little frightening to be around."

Patrick sat up. "Why do you think she's unbalanced?"

"She said she knew me, and she talked about you and about some… Some time travel lantern. It was so unsettling to sit there and listen to her go on about such fantasies… And she believed them. Truly believed them. At first, I didn't think so, but she just went on and on until..." Evelyn stopped talking, the words trailing off into the silence.

Patrick took another sip, not responding.

Evelyn continued, her voice filled with stress. "She said her mother and I were old friends. She said she'd wished you'd have come with me. She said, when she was a girl, her mother told her stories about you... and Eve, and she thought I was some other Eve. Her father had told her that if Eve or Patrick Gantly ever appeared, she was to ignore them both and send them away without a word. The deluded woman thinks I'm some other woman named Eve who came from the twenty-first century. I... I just didn't know what to think or what to say."

Patrick sat back, thinking.

Eve said, "I didn't mention your name like you asked, but she knows who you are. She called you Patrick."

Patrick gave her an awkward glance before looking away.

Eve's voice was small and breathy. "Mrs. Vanderbilt said her mother is boarding a ship in Southampton and she will be in New York in about six days."

"Six days?" Patrick asked, suddenly alert.

Evelyn looked at him, pointedly. "Patrick, what is going on? Why did you send me to that woman? I can tell you now that, whatever it is, I want no part of it. Yes, I need money, but... I don't understand what is going on. The woman is insane, filled with delusions, and yet she knows you."

Patrick downed the rest of his drink, set the glass on a side table, and got up. He strolled to the front window and looked down on the busy street, his hands locked behind his back.

"You should take the money, Evelyn. The clinic is a labor of love for you, and you need money. Many poor souls depend on that clinic, and they have nowhere else to turn."

"Do you truly know Mrs. Vanderbilt's parents, as she says?"

Patrick pondered his answer. "Yes, I know them."

Neither spoke for a time.

"Then I don't understand. Is it true that Mrs. Vanderbilt's mother is coming from Europe to see you?"

"Yes..."

"Why? How do you know these wealthy and influential people, and why did you seek me out, putting me in this awkward and disturbing situation? I have enough problems without adding more."

Patrick slowly turned. "Evelyn, I'm sorry, but none of this is what you think."

She twisted around to look at him. "And how do you know what I think? I don't even know what I think."

"Because I have been in the same situation you're in now."

Eve searched his face and then took the whiskey down in two swallows. "I'm lost, Patrick. I'm just lost."

Patrick took a few steps toward her. "Eve... Evelyn, let's not discuss this now."

She turned, showing him her back. "Oh, believe me, I'm never going to discuss this again. It's madness, and I'm not about to get mixed up in it, money, or no money. And I don't ever want to see you again. You have put me in a very uncomfortable and impossible situation."

She shot to her feet, gripping her purse tightly in her right hand. She entered the kitchen and set her empty glass in the sink. Patrick started toward her, but her raised hand and strident voice stopped him. "I'm not going to see you again, and I won't see Mrs. Vanderbilt, or take her money. I'm finished with this, whatever it is. Now, I'm leaving and that's the end of it. If you have…"

Patrick cut her off. "I have found Virginia."

Evelyn felt faint, and the air left her lungs. Her legs gave out, and she collapsed.

Patrick darted over and caught her before she hit the floor.

CHAPTER 30

Evelyn awakened in the dark and made a little cry of fear. A moment later, Patrick was in the bedroom, a few feet away. "Eve, it's okay. It's Patrick."

Evelyn sat up in Patrick's bed, searching the room, light spilling in from the living room. "Oh... What happened?"

She glanced down to see that she was fully clothed, shoeless and partially covered by a blanket. "What time is it?"

"About seven-thirty."

She sat, breathing, remembering.

"Feeling better?"

"I don't know. Did I faint?"

"Yes."

"I don't think I've ever fainted in my life. It must have been that whiskey."

"I think you've had a difficult day," Patrick said. "Are you hungry? Shall I take you to dinner? There's a little Italian restaurant about a block from here. It has checkered tablecloths, candles, and an accordion player. Unfortunately, it doesn't have Chianti."

Eve sat in silhouette, touching her head. "I have a little headache. Maybe I'm hungry or hungover. What was in that liquor?"

"Mostly corn. Maybe some old shoes and socks thrown in for flavor," Patrick said, hoping for humor.

Evelyn sighed, audibly. "Now I remember... I guess we have to talk about Virginia. You did say you have found her, didn't you?"

"I haven't found her, but I believe I know where she is."

"Is she all right? I mean... well..." her voice faltered, unable to say the awful words *Is she dead?*

"I don't know for sure, but I believe she's all right."

Evelyn shut her eyes in relief.

"I'll tell you all I know over dinner. I'll leave now, so you can freshen up. I'll be in the living room when you're ready."

Tony's Di Napoli was doing a good Friday night business. Tony, himself, found Eve and Patrick at a small table near the front window away from the lively crowded bar, where only sodas and juice were being served.

After they were seated, Patrick looked up at Tony. "I suppose you don't have wine?"

Tony's bushy, black mustache frowned, and when he spoke, his hands went to work, and his accent was authentic. "Iffa I servea you any wine, the cops come for me and they shutta Tony down, okay?"

Patrick nodded, sadly. "Yes, Tony, I understand."

"It'sa shame of shames, you know. Tony no like dis, but it'sa dah law."

Evelyn ordered the baked rigatoni and Patrick the spaghetti with extra meatballs.

After the waiter withdrew, Tony returned with two silver cups, placing one before Evelyn, the other before Patrick. He gestured grandly, his big eyes narrowing, his smile extravagant. "Now that'sa the besta wata that you gonna get anywhere inna New Yorka, or Tony gets on the nexza boat and floats home to Napoli."

They tasted the water while Tony waited. They smiled up at him, knowingly, Patrick with a wink and a nod. Tony beamed.

"Thank you, Tony," Evelyn said. "It's very good water."

"Now, you wanna song from Vito? He canna play anything."

Evelyn smiled. "I'd love to hear *Surriento*."

Tony clasped his hands together in delight. "*Torna a Surriento*! I love you for that, Signora. It's a greata Neapolitan song. You got it," Tony said.

The wine was dry, with a bite, but Eve and Patrick were grateful for it, and for the light buzz that came after a few sips. Thanks to the accordion player, Surriento softened the mood and the conversation, making the room relaxed and romantic.

But Eve couldn't push Virginia from her thoughts. She had to know what Patrick knew. "Please, tell me about Virginia," she said, firmly.

"I will, Eve. I'll tell you everything, but can it wait, just a few more minutes?"

"It's just that... Well, I've waited so..."

Patrick interrupted. "I know, Eve, but can we escape from the world for a time while we eat? There's nothing we can do right now, anyway, and I'm still trying to work things out in my head."

She nodded in weary acceptance. "But you must promise to tell me everything."

"Yes, of course I will."

"And as far as you know, she's alive and well?"

"Yes, as far as I know."

Just then, Vito drifted over to their table with his accordion. He lingered near Eve, smiling down at her, finessing the song with his gifted fingers.

Eve's lovely face, parted red lips and golden hair were lit by the soft glow of the center candle. In that entrancing light, Patrick watched with a new pleasure as her eyes closed, and she gently swayed to the music, humming along. In that moment, time dissolved, and he fell in love with Eve all over again.

When the song finished and Vito had drifted away, their dinners arrived. They ate, mostly in silence, occasionally discussing the music, or the weather, or their childhood Christmases. Neither uttered weighty words or raised heavy subjects, not wanting to break the dreamy spell of music, wine and tentative, growing attraction.

After their dinner plates were removed, they sipped coffee and shared a cannoli. As the dinner high was melting away, and the candle was a meek, flickering flame, Eve's mood gradually changed, and she grew remote and somber.

"Where is Virginia, Patrick?"

"Rochester, New York."

Evelyn fought alarm. "Oh, my God... Why is she so far away?"

"I'm not sure."

"How did you learn this?"

"From Louise McGuire."

Evelyn's vivid eyes opened wide. "Louise?"

"Let me explain," Patrick said. And then he started from the beginning, telling her everything that had happened.

At first, her face was waxen, her blinking eyes moving, seeking escape from the sordid details of her husband and the young woman. Slowly, in degrees, she lowered her head, only lifting it again when Patrick told her where Virginia might be, and who she was with.

When he finished, Evelyn was enraged. "I'm going to get her. I'll call the police. I'll call the FBI. I'll call anybody and everybody."

Patrick spoke softly. "It may not be that easy."

"I'll make it that easy. I can't leave her up there with that criminal. Who knows what he's doing to her. It makes me sick. The whole thing makes me sick, and to think that my husband has done nothing. He knows she's up there and he's done absolutely nothing. Why has he lied to me? Why hasn't he done anything? It's his daughter, for God's sake. What kind of man is he?"

Patrick kept his voice low. "I'll go to Rochester. They don't know who I am. I can look around and get the lay of the land; find out where Virginia is. When I get more information, then we'll know how to proceed."

"I'm going to call the police."

"And say what?"

"Tell them that Virginia is a minor who is being held against her will."

"What if she isn't being held against her will? What then?"

"Well, of course she is."

"Are you certain?"

"Of course I'm certain!"

"And what if these people have, shall we say, friends in all the right places? The police, politicians, lawyers, judges. From what I've learned, Joe McGuire is connected, and he has a lot of money to grease lots of palms; to handsomely pay the dregs of society and generously pay off the high and the mighty."

Evelyn's distraught eyes looked away. She was lost in a thicket of emotion, her mind burning. She put her face in her hands. "This is a nightmare... My little girl. My poor, lost, little girl. What am I going to do?"

Patrick leaned in, his voice low, but firm. "I can leave tomorrow morning. As soon as I learn anything, I'll contact you."

Evelyn dropped her hands, her eyes hard, jaw fixed. Tears ran down her cheeks. "I'm going with you."

"No, Evelyn. I don't think that's a good idea."

"Then I'll go alone. I'm not going to sit here and wait while my little girl is being held captive by some dirty, twisted bootlegger. No, I'm going, and when I find her, I will call the police and have them all arrested."

Patrick felt the force of her words. "Like I said, Eve, what if the bootleggers have paid off the cops? What if you spook the bad guys, and Virginia, and they run off into the unknown where we'll never find them? Please, let's keep our heads. We don't know for certain if Virginia is even there. Louise may have old news, or she could be lying. Let me go and look around, explore. As I said, when I learn anything, I'll contact you."

Evelyn's eyes remained hard. "All right, but I'm going with you. I'll stay out of your way—I'll stay hidden out of sight—but I'm going with you."

Patrick heaved out a sigh. "Yes, Eve, I should have known. I should have known who you truly are in your soul, and in your heart of hearts."

She stared at him, not comprehending his meaning.

CHAPTER 31

O n Saturday morning, it was pouring rain, large drops exploding off the streets, blurring the city in gray and silver. Patrick was at the cavernous Pennsylvania Station a half hour early, his canvass suitcase next to him. He was waiting for Evelyn at their agreed-upon spot near a kiosk at the New York Central ticket window.

Promptly at 9 a.m., she arrived, shaking out her umbrella, wearing a dark blue raincoat and tan rain hat, a brown leather suitcase in hand.

She drew up to him, breathless and spotted with rain. Setting her suitcase down, she closed her umbrella and leaned it against a wall.

"What a day for a journey," she said. "It's really coming down out there. You look dry."

"I've been here a while. Shall we purchase the tickets?" Patrick asked, glancing at his watch. "The train leaves in twenty-five minutes."

"I'm going to pay," Eve insisted. "I'm funding the entire trip, and please, don't argue with me about it."

Twenty minutes later, they sat next to each other on the Lake Shore Limited. It would make eleven stops and take seven hours and twenty minutes to arrive in Rochester, New York.

They said little as the train lurched ahead, rumbling through a dark tunnel, gathering speed, soon emerging into the rain-drenched day.

Patrick's socks were damp, and Evelyn's shoes soaked through. She left for the bathroom with her suitcase to change into dry ones, while Patrick snapped out *The Sun* and searched for an article on Jazzy Frankie Fox's murder.

Patrick had read *The Sun* when he was growing up in the 1860s and 1870s, and it was one of the papers he read most when he was a New York City detective in the 1880s. He was aware that *The Sun* was the first newspaper to report crimes and personal events such as suicides, deaths, and divorces. He also knew that one of its famous City editors, John Bogart, made what is perhaps the most frequently quoted definition of the journalistic endeavor: "When a dog bites a man, that is not news, because it happens so often. But if a man bites a dog, that is news."

Patrick searched the first and second pages and found nothing. On page four, he found what he was looking for. The headline read,

MUSICIAN FOUND SHOT DEAD IN WASHINGTON HEIGHTS

Frankie Fox, a musician who played the saxophone in jazz clubs about town, was found shot dead in his Washington Heights apartment. Detectives are searching for two people for questioning—an attractive

woman in her middle 20s, described as wearing a mink coat and fur hat, and a tall man in his early or mid-30s, who led her from the crime scene.

Lieutenant Shanahan stated that the woman might be Mr. Fox's girlfriend. At this time, the police believe the motive could have been a lover's quarrel, or a payback hit by gangsters over Mr. Fox's outstanding gambling debts.

Patrick folded the paper and stuffed it in the forward seat pocket. When Evelyn returned, he slid out and swung her suitcase up on the overhead luggage rack. After they were both seated, Evelyn saw Patrick's worried and absorbed expression.

"Is everything all right?"

Patrick looked at her. "Remember the story I told you about yesterday; Louise's murdered boyfriend?"

"Yes…"

"It's in the paper. The police will easily find her, if they haven't found her already."

Evelyn processed that. "Then Vernon will find out that Louise was two-timing him. He won't like that."

"Maybe he already knew."

"What do you mean?"

"Is your husband a jealous man? A violent man?"

"I don't know. I never knew much about his business. Later on, when things were going bad for us, I didn't want to know. I don't think he could kill a man, no."

"Could he have someone else do it?"

"I hope not. I just don't know."

She twisted her hands. "But Louise will tell the police who you are, won't she?"

"I told her my name was Sean, and she doesn't know where I live. But I do have one concern."

"And that is?"

"Your safety. When Vernon and the police question Louise about me, she'll probably tell them I asked questions about Virginia. Vernon might suspect that you hired me to find Virginia."

"Why? How would he know that?"

"You told him you were going to find out for yourself, didn't you? He won't know for sure, but if he's the smart man I think he is, he won't take any chances. He'll probably come looking for you for answers. I also suspect he will contact both Louise's father, Joe McGuire, and Sam Keller in Rochester."

Evelyn shut her eyes and pinched the bridge of her nose. "It's a horrible dream, and I can't wake up."

A minute later, she opened her eyes and faced him. "Are you sure you want to go through with this, Patrick?"

"I'm sure, or I wouldn't be here. But I'll need time in Rochester to check things out. First off, we have to find Sam Keller, and find the house where Virginia is most likely being kept. If we find her, it may not be so easy to free her, especially if she doesn't want to be freed."

Evelyn was on overload, and her face showed it. There was a wildness in her eyes and tight worry around her mouth.

Patrick was thankful she hadn't brought up her meeting with Lavinia Vanderbilt, peppering him with more questions about Joni and the time lantern. He figured she didn't have the strength for it; that she was saving her energy to focus on finding Virginia and facing the risks that were to come.

The train thundered on through the rain, passing the Hudson River-side communities of Rhinecliff, Croton-Harmon and Yonkers.

For his part, Patrick was burning with anticipation at seeing Joni again. At last, he would have an old friend who knew him, understood the situation, and would help him any way she could. But more importantly, when Joni met Evelyn, would she see Eve Gantly in Evelyn Stratford's eyes, as he did?

Joni also had the time travel lantern. But that presented questions he had no answers for. If he lighted the lantern and returned to the twenty-first century, would he return before Eve and Colleen were killed, or after? If after, then what? He couldn't stay in 2020 without them. He'd light the lantern again, and God only knew where he'd end up.

If he stayed with Evelyn, in 1925, and their love deepened, shouldn't he remain in 1925, and live out the rest of his life with her? At least he'd have a sure thing, a certain thing. He would have a version of Eve; a near exact replica.

He shut his eyes, hoping to still his endless, rambling thoughts, and soon, he dozed off.

The train threaded its way through farmland, woodland, and small towns, rolling past whistle stops and the cloud-shrouded cities of Rome, Utica, and Amsterdam.

They arrived in Rochester, New York, a little after five o'clock and, as they left the train depot, they saw a conspicuous sign announcing

ROCHESTER, NEW YORK
THE FRIENDLY CITY

Inside a taxi, they motored off toward the center of town, both in a somber mood, dreading what was to come. The taxi turned onto Clinton Street and drove past theaters, a drugstore, and a department store, finally pulling up in front of the Seneca Hotel. A uniformed bellhop approached as Evelyn climbed out. After Patrick paid the driver, he joined her at the entrance.

Glancing about, Patrick saw a Planter's Peanuts store, spreading its aroma of fresh-roasted peanuts all over the area. Across the street, there was an old novelty shop, a florist, and a busy, upscale café.

The Seneca Hotel was a Renaissance-style building, the largest hotel in the city, or so the desk clerk told them. Each room came equipped with a private bath, an impressive feature at the time.

Due to the social norms and appearances of 1925, Patrick had made a reservation for two rooms on opposite ends of the seventh floor. At the lobby desk, he signed them in under assumed names, Evelyn as Anne Stratford, and himself as Charles Bendix.

As they left the elevator to go their separate ways, it was agreed they'd meet in the lobby at seven-thirty to have dinner and discuss the next course of action.

After Evelyn tipped the bellhop and closed and locked her door, she stood frozen, unable to move. She'd never felt so vulnerable and so frightened in her life.

The thought of being alone, in a strange room and in a strange city, knowing her daughter was out there somewhere, possibly being abused, nearly sent her into a mad panic. She removed her gloves, hat and coat and dropped them on the bed, before wandering aimlessly to the windows.

Without another thought, she reversed, crossed the room and opened the door. She stepped into the hallway, braced her courage with a breath, and closed and locked her door. With anxious, moving eyes, she started walking down the plush carpeted hallway toward Patrick's room.

She did not want to be alone. She could not be alone. She wanted someone close. Someone she could trust. It had been so long since she'd been with a man. There had been so many lonely days and nights.

On the train, Eve had fought desire, having Patrick's shoulder and arm and leg so close to hers; and when she'd awakened from her nap, he had been asleep, leaning ever so slightly against her. She'd felt the weight of him against her upper arm. She'd inhaled his scent and studied his body as he slept, his breathing chest, his large hands resting on his thighs. He was so very handsome, and he was so very sexy, and he had been so very kind.

She wanted Patrick to hold her. She wanted to feel the press of his hands against her back. She wanted him to kiss her and make love to her.

CHAPTER 32

The room was dark and quiet, with only the hum of traffic outside the windows, and the rattle of a room service food cart being rolled past Patrick's hotel room door.

Evelyn lay in the double bed asleep, a blanket pulled up to her chin. Patrick stood by the window, gazing out at the twinkling lights of the city, his thoughts, unlike the room, noisy and unruly.

He pushed his hands into his pockets and turned his head to look at Evelyn, a quiet, shadowy figure under the blanket. An hour before, she'd stood at his open door, projecting a sweet bewilderment.

"I can't be alone right now," she'd said.

He'd invited her in, then closed and locked the door behind her. A bedside lamp was the only light illuminating the room.

They stood looking at each other, his wounded, stricken heart beating all the faster as he read her wanting expression and open body language.

Patrick had turned away, but she had touched his hand to bring him back. The moment had felt odd, mystical and deeply disturbing, and he recalled Eve's words on Christmas Eve in 2019—a lifetime ago it seemed.

Eve had held up her champagne glass and touched his. She'd said, *"I fell head-over-heels in love with you—and it scared me how fast and how much I fell in love with you. But that love seemed timeless, didn't it? As if it had been waiting for us? As if I'd known you before and you'd known me before. As if we were soulmates just waiting to come together again, to merge again. Didn't you feel that, Patrick?"*

"What are you thinking?" Evelyn had asked. "You look a thousand miles away."

He didn't tell her what he was truly feeling—that he felt psychologically cross-wired and psychically stranded, two expressions that would have never occurred to him in 1885. They were twenty-first century phrases he'd learned in his psych classes at John Jay College.

He didn't say anything for a while, and she'd grown increasingly uncomfortable. And then they had forced their way into a stumbling conversation, with Evelyn finally asking him if he found her attractive.

He'd said, "I think you know the answer to that."

When he hadn't made a move to kiss her, she'd lowered her head and said, "I've been living in a confused and cloudy atmosphere for the last few months. I hardly know who I am anymore. Here I am, throwing myself at you and you're not interested."

"It's not that, Evelyn. It's not what you think."

She'd turned moody, slightly irritable. "I guess I wasn't thinking. For once in my life, I didn't let myself think, I just walked out of my hotel room and walked to yours, and it seemed the natural and the right thing to do."

"And so it is."

He'd placed his hands gently on her shoulders. "Evelyn, there is no common vocabulary that allows me to explain who I am and where I came from."

Her eyes had lifted. "I'm afraid to ask if it has something to do with the lantern Lavinia Vanderbilt spoke about."

"Yes, it does."

That had been the mood breaker. Evelyn had pulled away and started for the door.

"Don't go."

At the door, she'd paused, keeping her back to him. "I'm so tired, Patrick. I'm so very weary, and so very tired."

He'd gone to her and stood close. "Why don't you slip under the blankets and go to sleep? Forget about everything for a while and rest. It will do you good."

She'd turned. "And what will you do?"

"I'll watch you sleep."

Her eyes had hardened a little. "You're a bastard, do you know that? You seduce me with your eyes and your words, and yet you won't make love to me."

Patrick had opened his mouth to speak, but Evelyn shut her eyes, frowned, and held up a hand to stop him. "Don't... I shouldn't have said that. I sound like a scorned woman. I sound pathetic."

"You're not pathetic, Evelyn. If I could only explain... Explain how it is."

They'd stood in the lengthening quiet, their eyes not meeting. After she'd kicked off her shoes, she wandered to the bed, yanked back the comforter and climbed in, covering herself.

Patrick felt the silent call of her, but he resisted. If she hardly knew who she was, then he was lost as well, lost in a riddle of time and place, tossed into 1925 by a random force, whose intent seemed sinister and ambiguous.

"You're right, Patrick. This feels good. Safe and warm. Perhaps I *will* lie here for a while."

Within minutes, she was asleep.

Now, an hour later, Patrick left the window and lowered himself down into the chair. He, too, was exhausted, more emotionally than physically. He closed his eyes, visualizing Eve and Colleen in Riverside Park, Colleen in her stroller, pointing at Colin, who romped about, barking, leaping and catching a rubber ball that Patrick had tossed him.

He'd had a perfect life—a storybook life—and the loss was savage and cruel.

Was that Eve sleeping in his bed? How could he know? He laced his hands behind his head and tried to sleep, but he couldn't. He had to find Virginia and then come up with a successful escape plan that wouldn't get them caught or killed.

Patrick heard Evelyn's sleepy voice. "Patrick... are you there?"

He opened his eyes. "Yes, I'm here."

"How long do you think it will take to find Virginia?"

"I thought you were sleeping."

"I was... but I had a dream, a dream about Virginia when she was just a little girl."

Patrick thought of Colleen.

"So how long do you think it will take?"

"I don't know. Maybe days. We have to assume Virginia is with Sam Keller, so I'll have to find his house, or wherever it is he's living. Then I'll snoop around and see what's going on."

"So, it won't be fast?"

"Not unless we're lucky. You'll have to stay in your room and out of sight until I know what we're dealing with."

"I won't get in your way, but I keep thinking, what if Virginia is in love with this man and she refuses to go with us? I know you're thinking that, too."

"Let's not speculate. We'll take it one step at a time. Are you hungry?"

"Ravenous."

"Room Service?"

"Yes... I don't want to leave this bed. It's the most comfortable I've been in years."

CHAPTER 33

On Sunday evening, Patrick headed for a local speakeasy. The frisky, young desk clerk had been all too eager to share "the hot spot" with him.

"I'm just looking for a little local fun," Patrick had said. "Do you know of a good place?"

The ready-eyed desk clerk, with a mop of brown hair, black-rimmed glasses and a sharp nose, had leaned in, whispering. "Oh, yeah. Do I ever! I know a great joint, with swell jazz and flappers everywhere, looking for free hooch. Everybody in the know, if you know what I mean, goes there."

Patrick caught a taxi and relayed the directions he'd received from the clerk. It turned out that the driver knew exactly where The Blue Nose Speakeasy was. When Patrick mentioned it, the driver acknowledged with a "Yep, oh, yep." He finished with a sharp jerk of his head.

The taxi crossed the Court Street Bridge and Genesee River, drifting out of town, moving through open land, until they came to a fork in the road. As the moon swam through moody purple clouds, the car angled left, skirted the river for a time and then turned right onto a dirt road. Nestled in a grove of bare trees, they arrived at a lone, demurely lit Victorian house, with a steeply pitched roof, gables, turrets and an impressive wraparound porch.

"Who owns this place?" Patrick asked, as they turned into the winding driveway that led to the full parking lot.

"Don't know for sure. A woman named Bette runs the place. Don't know her last name. She used to have a whore house closer to town back before prohibition."

"Where does the booze come from?"

"You a cop or something?"

Patrick laughed a little, ready with his practiced answer. "No, no. I'm a businessman from Albany. I'm always looking for good investments. Do you know who supplies the place?"

The cab driver nudged the car toward the entrance, his tires popping across the gravel.

"A man by the name of William Hoover used to run a restaurant chain up in these parts. He also ran several breweries. Between you and me, prohibition has made him richer than he ever was before. His operation produces four-hundred gallons of beer a week. Don't tell nobody I told you so, but I've heard from riders who come here that Hoover grosses eight thousand dollars a month. And he's got a business partner from New York City, a man named McGuire. It's a big business."

Patrick let that settle. "How does Hoover get by the prohibition agents?"

The driver stopped the car and swatted up the meter arm. He swiveled around. "You didn't hear this from me, but he gets around them by buying their silence at a weekly rate of about two thousand dollars."

Patrick struck the bill of his hat with two fingers. "Go away with ya! Well, I'll be in the wrong business then."

"You and me both, friend. You'll be all right, though. With that Irish accent of yours, you'll fit right in with this crowd up here. You got the Irish, Germans and the Italians all about, with some mutts like me thrown in. What business did you say you are in?"

"I sell restaurant furniture; you know, tables and chairs, booths, swivel stools and patio furniture."

"Your business must be suffering with the no booze policy. Many of our restaurants up here have closed."

"Tell me about it," Patrick said, with another shake of his head. "I'd sure like to get my meat hooks into some of this business."

The driver lowered his voice. "You would not believe the corruption that's going on around here. Now, I'm a family man, and a God-fearing one at that, but prohibition has been the worst thing that has ever happened to this country, outside the Civil War. It's spawned a pirate industry of alcohol manufacturers here in Rochester, and it's created a pro league of alcohol smugglers as well."

"Smugglers? You don't say?"

"Yes, my friend. It's because of Rochester's lake access and proximity to Canada, where alcohol still flows as freely as you please, thank you very much. It's turned our good city into a major bootlegging hub."

Patrick decided to be bold. "One of my business partners said he knows a man around here named Sam Keller. Have you heard of him?"

The driver turned the name over in his mind. "No... Keller? Sam Keller? No, I don't know that name."

"But you do know the name McGuire?"

The driver's face lit up. "McGuire? Sure. I hear that name a lot, driving this buggy around. Like I said, he's in cahoots with William Hoover."

Patrick removed his wallet and paid the man double the price on the meter. "Thank you, sir. You've made a businessman happy tonight."

The driver was one big beaming smile. "It's always a pleasure to help one's fellow man, and I thank you for your generosity. You have a good time now. I hear the place is really jumpin'."

Patrick climbed the broad stairs to the front door, hearing sassy jazz music: a shrill trumpet, a rowdy piano, belching saxophones, the thump of a bass drum, and the rat-tat-tat of a snare drum.

The tuxedoed bouncer at the front door was oddly cordial, waving Patrick in as soon as the password, SUCKER, had left his lips.

Inside, the place bounced with loose-limbed dancers, swaying musicians and bopping music. The room was wide, the dance floor full, the fashion slim, glittering and chic. There were giddy women with bobbed hairstyles, long cigarette holders and gleaming smiles. There were shiny-faced carousers in tuxedos, extravagant conversation, and flowing booze, everything from beer to champagne.

It was a Sunday night in November and yet, to Patrick, it seemed like he'd stumbled upon a New Year's Eve party, fueled by whiskey, sex and narcotics.

He checked his overcoat, hat and gloves at the coat check, turned and took another look at the place. If he cared, which he didn't, he noticed that he was one of the few men in the room who wasn't wearing a tuxedo. Patrick had never worn a tuxedo in his entire life, a life that spanned from the 1860s to the twenty-first century. What did that say about him? Not the formal type, for sure. He adjusted his blue-patterned tie and made his way toward the hectic bar.

It took a good five minutes before he got the attention of the bloated, thin-mustached, black-vested bartender and ordered a whiskey. As he waited for it, he saw a tall, willowy woman, about twenty-five, looking him over. She wore a sleek, bottle-green sequined dress, had jet-black glossy hair crowned with a dazzling, golden headband, with a hanging black tassel that added a touch of the naughty.

Patrick nodded at her, and she flashed him a comely smile, her lush, red lips moist and inviting. She had large, glassy, black eyes and curving, overhanging brows. It was obvious she was high on something, or possibly more than one thing. Moving closer, she tapped the toe of her foot.

"Hey there, big man, with those wonderful eyes that reach out and capture me. Where are you from?"

"Albany."

"Ooohh, baby, that town is all politics and policemen. I had a husband there once," she said, giggling. "I had to take bicarbonate of soda every day with that guy. He said I talked too much. He'd say, 'What are you gassing about now?'"

"What happened to the husband?"

She shrugged a thin shoulder. "Who knows? Who cares? I left him in Albany." Her face awakened to a sudden idea. "Hey, I like that. I left him in Albany. That's a jazzy title for a song, isn't it?"

"Yeah, I guess so."

"Hey big man, wanna dance?"

The bartender's arm jutted out between two people seated at the bar, his hand gripping Patrick's drink. Patrick took the crystal whiskey glass, found a ready dollar bill in his pocket and paid the man, telling him to keep the change.

Patrick pointed to the gyrating dance floor. "I can't do that. I'd hurt somebody, probably you."

"So hurt me, it won't be the first time."

Patrick changed the subject. "Where are you from?"

"Nowhere and everywhere."

"I've been to both, and I didn't like either one."

She laughed from the depths of her flat belly. "Hey, you're funny." She reached into her glittering purse, removed a silver cigarette case, snapped it open and plucked out an unfiltered cigarette. "Want one?"

"Not tonight. It's Sunday. I'm starving my vices."

She laughed again, liking the joke, closing the case and dropping it back into her purse. She placed the cigarette between her very red lips, leaned toward him, and waited for a light.

Patrick lifted an empty hand, presenting a face of apology. "I don't have a light. I'm not really a proper gentleman."

After another laugh, she turned to a man at the bar, begged a light and got one. She blew a feather of smoke toward the ceiling, appraising him anew, up and down. "Yeah, you're funny, and you ain't so bad on the bloodshot eyes either, are you? I betcha you've got a girl around here somewhere, probably off powdering her nose, right?"

Patrick considered that. He thought it best if he didn't have a girl. This one was a talker, and she might know some things. "She powdered her nose this morning, then she ran off with the preacher. Now I'm stuck with the twins and a mortgage. So, here's the deal. You and me, we could set up house. Do you like kids?"

She laughed again, slapping her side. "Buy me a new raccoon coat, big man, and I'll go home with you in a heartbeat. What's your name?"

"Charlie Bendix."

She drew back in surprise. "Charlie? You don't look like a Charlie and you don't sound like a Charlie. With that accent, you sound like my big brother's best friend, Patrick O'Toole."

"Well, well, we can't all be Patricks," Patrick said, grinning, enjoying his own joke. "What's your name?"

"I have the best name in the whole wide world, and I gave it to myself. It's Willow Hart. Isn't that a nice name?"

"Yes, it's a lovely name. A grand name."

She made a sour face, glancing about to make sure no one was listening. "I'll tell you in confidence, but don't tell anybody else in this dump. My real name's Bertha Symanski. My father was Polish, my mother an Italian. Imagine naming your kid Bertha. Do I look like a Bertha? Do I look like a Symanski?"

"Willow Hart suits you. It gives you class."

Under the spell of his compliment, Willow melted, making a sexy, purring sound. "Hey, I like that, handsome man. I like that a lot."

"And what do you do, Willow Hart?"

"I'm a dancer and I sing, but I dance better than I sing and I don't really dance all that good either, except when I'm alone with a guy. Then I dance pretty good, Charlie."

Patrick sipped his whiskey, and it was good quality, smooth with good heat. "Where do you dance when you're not with a guy?"

"Here, for one. I'll be dancing in the show in about ten minutes."

"Good. I'll look forward to watching you. By the way, Willow, do you know where I can find Bette?"

Willow's face turned ugly. She took a drag on her cigarette, blowing the smoke sideways. "Bette? Ooohh, Charlie. Do you go for her type?"

"I don't know, what type is she?"

"Big mouth, big pocket-book and a big ass."

"I've never met her. Is she around?"

"Yeah, sure. She's always around. She runs the joint."

"Do you know where I can find her?"

"Hey, what's with you, Charlie? There's something about you, you know?"

"And what do you think that something is?"

She tilted her head left. "I dunno, but if you stick around till after my dance, I'll try to find out. I like you, Charlie, but don't start talkin' about Bette. I don't like any talk with Bette in it. It spoils a good time."

"All right, so we won't talk about Bette. Do you know a guy named Sam Keller?"

Her faced darkened and her flirty expression vanished, replaced by acid suspicion. "Do you know Sam Keller?"

"No… If he's around, a friend asked me to say hello."

She turned frosty. "Oh, he's around all right. He'll be sitting at that back table over there, with Bette."

Without turning around, she pointed a long, red fingernail. "The very back table."

"So, you do know him."

She turned to stone. "Let me put it this way. It will be a happy day when Sam Keller is tossed into hell. There won't be anybody in this whole, wide world who will give a good holy damn, or who will cry at his funeral. Now, are you going to tell me you know him?"

"No. A friend asked me to drop in and say hello."

"Then I'll just say good luck, pal."

"Why good luck?"

"Because if Sam don't like the way you talk, or dance, or sing or pour gin, or if you look at him the wrong way, he'll slap you around, maybe throw a punch or two until he brings the blood. I ought to know, he's slapped me around enough, and he likes it. He takes what he wants, and I should know that too, shouldn't I, Charlie? Hell, he might even shoot you. I've heard he does that, too, when it suits him, and the bodies are never found, big surprise. If he's even your friend's friend, Charlie, then all I've got to say is goodbye, Charlie."

She turned on a heel and marched away, hips swinging. Patrick called after her, but she departed through a door that must have led to back rooms.

Patrick eased away from the bar and worked his way toward the back table. He wanted to get a look at the infamous Sam Keller.

Patrick asked a passing waiter for directions to the men's room.

"Straight back, turn right."

As Patrick started off, he saw two back tables, both round. One was empty. The other was occupied by two people. A debauched-looking, heavyset woman, with a flaming red pompadour hairdo and a frigid stare, nursed a half-drunk mug of beer. That would be Bette. Seated next to her, facing the room, was a 30s something man, surely Sam Keller.

Approaching the men's room, Patrick slowed his stride to glimpse the man. His eyes were black coals, his face broad, his mouth bent into a sneer. His dark hair was ice smooth, pasted back with no part and, if he were handsome, and Patrick supposed most women would think so, it was a corrupted good looks, calculating and rakish. It was the face of a dissatisfied hedonist who had it all, but all still wasn't enough, and it never would be.

Patrick could almost hear Sam Keller say, "What I want is all of it, all I can buy and take, and then a whole lot more."

When Patrick left the bathroom and returned to the bar, he planted himself in a spot where he could keep a watchful eye on Sam. A little after 11 p.m., Sam finally left the table and exited the club to his car. Patrick flagged down one of the waiting taxis and followed him.

He had been lucky—at least up to now. That was good and bad. In Patrick's experience, good luck in the beginning often meant bad luck at the finish, or, at the very least, a long, hard slog.

Patrick's taxi followed Sam's forest green roadster, hanging back enough so Sam wouldn't suspect he was being followed. About four miles from the speakeasy, they came to a secluded area near a grove of trees and a pond. From a safe distance, Patrick saw Sam's car turn onto a dirt road and travel toward a lighted, two-story house.

Patrick told the driver to kill the headlights and pull to the side of the road. Outside, he crept toward the cover of trees where he had a good view of the house. He watched Sam leave his car, climb the porch stairs, and enter.

The air was filled with the smells and sounds of farm country, damp earth, hay, and fertilizer. He heard thunder and the mournful call of a night bird. On the distant horizon, he saw a flash of lightning, and it made him feel cold and edgy.

He'd start the surveillance tomorrow, Monday, and hope that Virginia was in the house, and that she was healthy, and willing to travel.

CHAPTER 34

Early Monday morning, while Eve remained sequestered in her hotel room, Patrick left the hotel, took a taxi to the one car rental agency in town, and rented a Model T Ford. Having never driven a Model-T, Patrick asked the agent for a fast tutorial.

He had no idea what he was getting himself into. The first thing he learned was that there was no gas gauge on the dashboard. The fuel tank was located underneath the backseat, and the only method of measuring the amount of gas was to lift the backseat, open the gas cap and use a dipstick to check the level. There were five gallons in the tank, enough to travel about one hundred miles.

The Model T had three pedals: the right pedal for the brake, the center pedal for reverse, and the left pedal to shift the gears from low to high speed. There was also a lever on the floor that worked the brakes and the clutch.

Patrick was scratching his head when his instructor had him stand in front of the car. The agent primed the engine by adjusting the choke with his left hand and turning the crank with his right, three times. After adjusting the inside brake and throttle, he had Patrick turn the crank one-half turn with his left hand. Finally, the car kicked to life, rattling and rumbling, a plume of white smoke bursting from the back tailpipe.

There were many other, endless instructions, and Patrick spent the next hour practicing the startup procedures. At last, he climbed aboard and drove the car around the lot, and out on a private dirt road until he gained a measure of confidence.

As he puttered away from the car rental lot, struggling with the gears, he wished Eve were sitting beside him. They would have had a good laugh.

An hour later, Patrick parked the Model T about a half mile from Keller's house under a cluster of trees, near some shrubs. He left the car and crept toward the house, pausing often to listen and study the terrain.

When the house was in sight, he crouched, hiding in a line of trees, his binoculars focused on the house and the land beyond.

To his dismay, a man appeared from around the back of the house, cradling a shotgun, obviously on patrol. Was that normal or had Sam been tipped off that Evelyn had hired a detective to find Virginia? Either way, it was problematic. Was there another man inside, watching Virginia?

Thankfully, it was warm for December; the temperature hadn't fallen below freezing and he'd worn three layers of clothes and two pairs of socks.

In mid-morning, Sam left the house and drove away. No doubt he was off to supervise his various bootleg and club businesses.

Patrick didn't see Virginia the entire first day, and that was worrisome. Had he been taken on a wild goose chase? Were they on to him?

On Monday night, when he debriefed Evelyn, she was distraught and anxious, pacing her room. He stayed with her until she'd dried her tears and dozed off to sleep on her couch.

On Tuesday afternoon, as thin gray clouds shifted through the trees, Patrick was positioned for a good view of the rear of the house. Within an hour, he saw a matronly woman and a young woman emerge from the back door and step down onto the lawn. The young woman wandered for a time before ambling toward the pond. Patrick lowered to a knee and refocused the binoculars.

It was Virginia! No doubt. She was hatless, her hair askew, wearing a long, black flapping coat. The woman hurried to Virginia's side and grabbed her arm, leading her toward the pond where a few nervous ducks noticed they weren't alone. They drifted along the flat, gray surface, communicating in quacking talk. The man with the shotgun was close by, alert.

Patrick held his position, his eyes sharp. Virginia walked unsteadily, as if she were sleepy or drugged. Patrick believed it was the latter, and the thought of it sickened him.

Virginia and the matron circled the pond once, disturbing the anxious ducks, who paddled to the other side. Finally, two had had enough. They flapped wildly, complaining in spirited quacks, beating across the surface of the water, lifting skyward into the slant of wind, gliding away over the trees where Patrick lay crouched. Shotgun Man turned to watch the ducks' retreat, and Patrick flattened himself on the ground, dead still.

When it was safe, he lifted on elbows and peered through the binoculars, keeping low to the ground. Virginia was pointing at the remaining ducks, imitating their quacking speech, her free arm flapping. With irritation, the matron snatched the girl away and hauled her back toward the house. Virginia protested and fought, but the woman slapped her across the face and yanked her ahead.

When they were back inside, Patrick lowered the binoculars, his blood boiling. What if that were his daughter, Colleen? He vowed to get Virginia out of there as fast as he could. But he would have to come up with a plan that didn't endanger her, and that would not be easy.

That night in the hotel restaurant, Evelyn listened to Patrick's description of what he'd witnessed.

"It's not pretty, and I didn't want to tell you."

Evelyn pushed her half-eaten roasted chicken away. "Thank you for telling me. It's not anything I haven't already imagined. What truly sickens me is to think that Vernon let this happen; his own daughter, and he's done nothing to stop it."

Patrick stared down at his steak. "From what I've heard about Sam Keller, Vernon may not have had much of a choice. Vernon is in way over his head. Joe McGuire and Sam Keller are thugs and killers. They take what they want."

Patrick glanced about the room, wishing he didn't have to tell her what else he'd seen. "There's more, Evelyn. Late in the afternoon, I saw a car drive up to the house. A man got out, and he was carrying what looked to me like a medical bag."

Evelyn closed her eyes, bracing herself. "How long was he there?"

"About forty-five minutes."

Evelyn shut her eyes and massaged her forehead, fighting fear and anger. When she opened them, she looked at Patrick gloomily. "So what are we going to do? We have to do something, and fast. Virginia might be seriously ill."

Patrick made a pyramid of his fingers, looking at her over the top of them. "It's not the best plan in the world, but it's all I've got. Give me one more day to study the place and make plans Meanwhile, I want you to go to the nearest department store and buy a frumpy coat and hat, and a plain dress. Make sure the dress has a high collar and long sleeves."

"And why am I doing this?"

"Because on Thursday, you'll be wearing that outfit, and no makeup. You'll be the perfect image of a demure, pious woman. You and I are going to visit Sam Keller's house late in the afternoon, posing as Reverend John and his wife, Sister Mary."

Evelyn examined his face. "Why?"

"To invite them to attend our church, of course."

"Won't the man with the shotgun threaten to shoot us?"

"Not if we play our humble roles just right. He will, I imagine, try to prevent me from approaching the front door, but most likely, he will have his guard down. He's the only lookout, other than the woman inside. Anyway, with his guard down, I'll punch him in the face, take his big gun and club him with it, without killing him. Then

I'll rush the house, and before the matron has time to attack, I'll tie her up, grab Virginia and run for our hired car."

"And then we'll run for the train station?" Evelyn asked.

"Yes... Hopefully, we'll catch the 6:10 back to New York. Keep your bags packed and ready. We'll have to move fast."

"And what happens if they come after us?"

"One thing at a time, Evelyn."

"But won't that man come after Virginia, if he's the kind of animal you say he is?"

"Let me worry about Sam Keller. I've dealt with his type before."

"What will I do with Virginia when I get her back to New York? Vernon will surely come to my apartment, demanding I give her to him."

"Take Virginia to the clinic and put two of your best security men at the door. Don't let anyone in or out. Have the doctor say she's deathly ill and can't have visitors. Tell anyone who asks that she has some, I don't know, disease."

Evelyn jumped in. "... Yes, diphtheria. That will scare them all off, especially my coward of a husband. Yes, that will do the trick."

"Look at my hands," Evelyn said. "They've been shaking like this for days."

She stared deeply into his eyes, seeking reassurance. "It sounds easy. Will it work?"

"In my experience, you make your best plan and you try to execute it, and then you improvise when that plan falls apart."

"That's not very encouraging."

"No, but it's honest. It's a simple plan, and simple usually works best, but there is a risk, because there are always risks. I'd prefer doing this on my own and keeping you out of it, but…"

"I'm not staying out of it."

"That's the point I was about to make. If we stay calm and play humble, I think we have a good chance of pulling it off."

"Mr. Gantly…"

Patrick arched an eyebrow. "Mr. Gantly?

"Yes, Patrick… forgive me for saying so, but you are a large man and, if I may also say so, you are handsomely formed. What I'm trying to say is, do you think you can appear non-threatening? These men are professionals, are they not? Aren't they used to threats and threatening situations? Can you play a convincing role as a minister?"

"Well, I've played a priest once or twice and gotten away with it. I'll keep my head and my hat very low. I will slouch and I will limp. Those tricks have paid off in the past."

Evelyn's smile was nervous and brief. "I don't know what I would have done if you hadn't come into my life, Patrick. I am grateful for what you're doing. You're risking your life for Virginia and me, and I'm grateful."

Patrick nodded.

"I don't know why you're doing it and that's what puzzles me. There's so much about you that I don't know and don't understand."

Patrick looked at her, tenderly. "Evelyn… When the right time shows itself, I will tell you as much as I can, but this is not the time."

Evelyn ran a hand through her hair, looking away toward the windows. "You're still in love with your wife, aren't you? You can't forget her."

"I'd be lying if I said I wasn't in love with Eve."

The pleasant, white-mustached waiter drifted over. "Is everything to your liking?" he asked.

Patrick and Evelyn exchanged a welcomed, humorous glance. Patrick said, "No, sir, it is not to our liking, but there is precious little you can do about it."

CHAPTER 35

The following day, Evelyn left the hotel at a little after eleven and walked briskly toward Getz's Department Store, three blocks away. It was overcast; the temperature had dropped below freezing, and she pulled up the collar of her dark winter coat and lowered her snug-fitting, midnight blue cloche hat. The friendly front desk clerk had told her the store was popular and had the latest styles at the best prices.

Patrick had knocked on her door at 7 a.m. to tell her he was leaving for Sam Keller's house, expecting to return to the hotel by early afternoon. That night, they'd planned to have a room service dinner Afterwards, they would try on their minister and his wife's costumes, practice their mannerisms, and go over the last-minute details. Thursday afternoon, they would appear at Sam Keller's house and, if all went well, they'd rescue Virginia.

When Evelyn was only a block from Getz's Department Store, it began to snow. She was momentarily distracted by a mother and two children; the kids jumping with glee, pointing skyward, their faces stretched in joy.

Evelyn saw two women emerge from a black, four-door sedan that had double-parked at the entrance to Getz's. Evelyn's eyes squinted, her face twisted, and then went vacant with shock. Her stride wobbled, then slowed.

Ice swept through her blood. It was Virginia! It was her daughter, her baby. Her pallid face was slack; her footsteps unsteady as she stepped onto the sidewalk. And the mink coat, matching hat, and satin gloves gave her a cheap, false maturity, as if she were a girl playing dress up.

The middle-aged woman with her was stout and broad, with a tight hat pulled over her forehead, her manner gruff. She gripped Virginia by the upper arm and aggressively led her inside the department store.

Eve stopped, feeling as though a fist had punched her in the heart. Struggling not to fall apart, she leaned a shoulder against a brick wall, bracing herself to keep from fainting. She gulped in three deep breaths, her chest heaving. By the time she regained some strength and composure, the black sedan had driven away up the street. She watched it back into an empty spot and park. The driver didn't emerge.

Were these the same people Patrick had been observing at Sam Keller's house? The woman certainly fit the description. Evelyn stood still, facing doubt and speculation. It took straining minutes before she gathered her thoughts. She couldn't just stand there and do nothing. That was her daughter in there and Virginia, for all her expensive furs, didn't look physically well or happy. Feeling desperate and shaken, Evelyn started forward, as snow circled her.

She entered the department store with a jolt of fear and renewed determination. Inside, her feet hesitated as she glanced about. There was a rawness in her throat and she swallowed it away.

When she spotted Virginia and the matron picking through clothes in the women's wear department, oddly, a sudden calm washed over her. The determined, protective mother in her took over. Her thinking cleared, her pulse steadied. The matron was a heavy-faced woman with an expression of disdain and superiority, as if the rest of the world were fools she had to endure.

It was that nasty face that lent Evelyn the idea. On impulse, without considering the consequences, Evelyn searched for a security guard. There had to be one some place.

She knew what she was going to do and, if it didn't work, then she'd come up with something else. One way or the other, she was going to get her daughter and make a run for it, or she'd die trying.

It was in the women's lingerie department that Evelyn spotted him. The burly, uniformed guard was standing near a row of elevators, staring out the far windows at the gathering snowfall. Evelyn calculated her next move and stiffened her spine.

She drew up to a store clerk, a woman of about thirty years old, who was tidying up a row of bras and panties.

"Excuse me," Evelyn said. "Is there a back door to the store?"

The young, red-headed clerk, with freckles on her pretty face, turned, a bit startled. "A back door?"

Evelyn flashed an easy, friendly smile. "Yes. My car is out back and, with the snow, I was hoping I could leave by a back entrance."

"Oh, yes," and then she pointed. "Walk through the women's wear department, through housewares, and then turn right to the furniture showroom. You'll see two glass doors that exit into the parking lot."

"Thank you," Evelyn said, rallying her resolve.

With firm steps, she walked toward the security guard, casting backward glances at Virginia and her sour jailer.

Evelyn lifted her chin, narrowed her eyes and projected an air of indignation. She came upon the guard abruptly, her voice low, but firm. "Excuse me, sir, but do you know there is a thief in this store?"

The burly man snapped to attention, his gaze suddenly acute and sharp. "I beg your pardon, madam. A thief? Where?"

"I'm not going to turn around, but the rather stout woman in the women's wear department, standing near that young woman wearing furs, is shoplifting. I saw her take two items and stuff them into her purse."

His face tightened in offense as his eyes searched. "Are you sure?"

"Of course I'm sure. I told you, I watched her do it and, by now, I'm sure she has taken other things. I just feel it is my duty as a good citizen to come forward to report this immoral deed."

He squared his shoulders. "Yes, yes. Thank you, madam. Rest assured that I will look into it."

Her head low, Evelyn watched the guard march over with a swaggering authority. Meanwhile, she crept forward, ready to seize Virginia's arm when the time was right.

"Excuse me, madam," the guard asked, standing tall before the matron.

Resistance was in her face. "Yes, what do you want?" she asked, tartly.

"I will ask you politely to please let me examine the items in your purse, or you can return the items that you placed there."

"What!?" she exclaimed, her face turning red with anger.

"Yes, madam, please remove the articles you have placed in your rather large purse."

"I beg your pardon," she snapped, her eyes flaring.

"I'm asking in all politeness, madam. It has been reported that you have taken items from the shelf and put them in your purse. If you will kindly replace the items that you took, I can assure you that there will be no further issue. You can walk away, as long as you promise never to return to Getz's Department Store."

She looked him up and down, with stiff-necked insult. "You big oaf, get away from me before I call the real police on you. You are insulting and you are stupid."

The guard folded his meaty arms, offended, his big eyes burning. "I'm only doing my duty, madam. This is my last warning. Either let me examine your purse or replace the items you took from the shelf."

"My purse!? You insufferable idiot. Where is your boss? This is outrageous. I'll have you fired!"

The guard reached for her purse and, in a swift attack, she stepped back and swung it at him, slamming the purse into the side of his head. The security guard staggered left, stunned, but for only a moment. The matron pressed her attack, ready to hit him again. But the guard blocked her assault easily with his big hand.

Virginia threw a shocked hand to her face and did not see Evelyn close the distance between them.

Curious shoppers crowded in and gawked while a second security guard appeared, much younger and thinner. Within minutes, they had the matron face down on the floor, her hands pulled behind her back and handcuffed at the wrists.

While the big-mouthed woman kicked her feet and screamed out curses, twisting and fighting, Evelyn darted in and grabbed Virginia's right arm and yanked her away from the scene.

"Hey!" Virginia called, not seeing her mother's face, her attention still on the chaotic scene and her chaperone.

Evelyn hustled them through housewares. They were approaching the showroom and double glass exit doors when Virginia finally fought to jerk her arm free. Evelyn tugged on, but Virginia resisted.

Then she saw her mother. The shock came in a gasp, a cry, and then tears.

"Mommy…"

"Yes, Virginia. We have to go. Now."

Evelyn took her arm again and led her to the doors. She put a shoulder to them and pushed. Outside in the fast wind and scattering snow, the cold air revived Virginia, and she called out to her mother.

"Mommy, wait!"

"We can't wait. We have to get out of here."

And then, to Evelyn's shock, Virginia threw herself into her mother's startled arms.

"Oh, God, Mommy... Oh, God, I'm so sorry. I'm so sorry. I want to go home, Mommy. Please take me home."

The tears flowed, her voice high and frantic. Evelyn allowed only a moment of reunion, and she held her daughter close, kissing her cheek. Then, holding Virginia at arm's length, she said, "All right, now. We have to run. Are you up for it?"

"Yes, Mommy. Yes. Let's run from here and that bastard of a man. Sam is a monster, Mommy. He beat me and tied me up. I hate him."

Now close to her, Evelyn saw a fading bruise near Virginia's left eye. It took all her strength to keep the rage controlled. She saw her daughter was about to shatter into pieces and become hysterical. She'd seen it before, and she knew the signs.

"Okay, Virginia. Pull yourself together. Do it, now! We have to run, so stay focused and calm."

"Yes, Mommy. Let's run. I can't go back there," she wailed, her voice thick, tears flowing. "I'll never go back there. I'll die first."

Evelyn glanced about, her breath puffing white vapor. She fought to get her bearings, her mind wild and exploring. "You won't go back. You'll never go back. Over my dead body you'll go back."

Feeling boiling energy in her veins, Evelyn inhaled a bracing breath. "All right. We have to find a taxi and get to the train station," she said, her words blown away into the rush of wind. "Come on!"

As they trudged off into the blurring snow, Evelyn recalled what Patrick had said only the night before.

"You make your best plan and you try to execute it, and then you improvise when that plan falls apart."

CHAPTER 36

By noon, Patrick left the woods near Sam Keller's house in a snow globe world, with circling, blowing wind. There had been no reason to stay any longer, and he was cold to the bone. Earlier, Virginia, her matron keeper and the man with the shotgun had piled into a four-door sedan and driven away. Where? Probably to town. Why? To visit the doctor? He had no idea.

As Patrick bounced along a rutty, dirt road, already covered with a layer of snow, he felt a dread building in his chest. Call it intuition or a gut feeling, but he sensed danger; he smelled danger.

The weather slowed him down, and after he'd dropped off the car at the rental agency, he didn't arrive at the hotel until nearly one o'clock. Inside the hotel lobby, a clerk lifted his hand to get Patrick's attention.

At the desk, Patrick accepted the envelope, his name written on the face, and a time/date stamp of 11:38 a.m.

Worried, he turned and drifted toward the elevators, sliding a finger under the sealed flap and opening the envelope. He removed the folded white page and read.

Patrick:

Forgive me, but I have Virginia and we are catching the next train to New York, the 1:35 p.m. I'll explain later. I know we're being hunted. I didn't tell you, but I have a two-shot derringer and I'll use it if I have to. Must go now. Come if you can. Be careful!

Evelyn

Patrick cursed out loud, slapping the page. He turned to view the hotel clock. It was 1:05 p.m. He didn't have time to dash upstairs and get his luggage. He stuffed the envelope and letter into his pocket and returned to the front desk.

"I need to check out."

The clerk looked puzzled. "Sir, the bill was paid by the lady who was with you when you checked in."

Without another word, Patrick whirled and started for the front doors. Outside, he searched for a taxi, finding one a half block away.

Inside the cab, Patrick leaned forward. "The train station, as fast as you can."

The uniformed driver was on the young side. Patrick's order appealed to his sense of adventure. "Yes, sir! Fast it will be."

The taxi made a U-turn and motored out of town in swirling snow. Patrick sat in tense silence, agonizing over what had happened to Evelyn. How had she managed to free Virginia? Was the man with the shotgun following them?

"Can you drive this thing faster?" Patrick said.

"I'm pushing this girl as fast as she'll go, sir. And the roads are slippery."

Patrick sat back, adjusting his hat, running his hand along his face, feeling every nerve on fire. Did Evelyn know how vicious those men were? Sam Keller would kill her in a heartbeat and have her buried where she'd never be found.

At 1:28 p.m., the taxi swerved right and leaped into the train station parking lot. Patrick paid the driver before the car came to a stop. He darted out of the car, slipping and sliding toward the entrance door of the immense Union Depot train station.

Inside, the warm air didn't relax him. He descended a grand staircase under a tall arch and stepped quickly along the marbled spacious lobby, taut and wary, searching for Evelyn. There was a line of people waiting at Gate 10, but the illumined sign above the gate said BOSTON. More passengers were gathered at a newsstand and sitting on benches, reading newspapers or chatting, while children romped and played tag.

Patrick cast his eyes toward the broad Arrival/ Departure Board and saw that the train to New York was departing at 1:35 p.m. at Gate 8 and the ALL ABOARD sign was flashing. He hurried to the ticket agent window, tugging out his wallet.

"I need one ticket to New York, please."

The ticket agent glanced up from beneath his green visor. "The train's pulling away any minute."

"Then will you please give me a ticket!"

The agent sighed something under his breath and went to work. "Coach, First Class or...

"Coach. Hurry, please."

"That'll be four dollars and eighty-five cents."

Patrick slapped a five-dollar bill onto the metal tray, pushing it under the glass window. The agent took the money, stamped the blue ticket and slid it forward. Patrick snatched it and bolted as the agent called after him.

"Hey, wait for your change!"

Patrick drew up to the gate just as a porter was pulling a chain across the gangway. Patrick held up his ticket, slithered past the startled man and rushed down the pathway out onto the platform, just as the train hissed clouds of steam and the shrill whistle blasted out its departure.

A conductor stood next to the bottom steps leading up into the coach, waving Patrick toward him. "Hurry up, sir, we are departing."

Patrick leapt onto the bottom step and climbed the stairs into the coach, just as the train lurched ahead.

"ALL ABOARD!" the conductor called.

Catching his breath, Patrick had the presence of mind to poke his head out, and glance up and down the length of the train. And then he saw him, two coaches down. Like himself, Sam Keller had just managed to pull himself aboard the train at the last moment.

Another blast of the whistle had children on the platform plugging up their ears and wincing.

Patrick cursed. Still short of breath, he turned right, pulled the coach door open and entered, facing the passengers. He didn't see Evelyn.

His first priority was to get to Sam Keller before he found Eve and Virginia. Patrick started down the narrow aisle, his face set in hard purpose. As he left the coach to the outside, stepping gingerly between compartments, the train began to gather speed and pitch and sway. With his hands braced, he crawled his way across the vestibule and through the flexible gangway connection that led to the doorway of the next car.

Inside, Patrick again scanned the passengers; some reading newspapers, some napping; a mother struggling with two rambunctious kids.

When he saw them at the far end, he froze. Evelyn and Virginia sat together, Virginia's head lulled over onto her mother's shoulder, her eyes closed. Evelyn stared out into the white face of the snowy day, her face wan with despair.

Sensing a presence, her gaze swung away from the window to see Patrick slowly working his way toward her. Her eyes widened, but before she could fully react, Patrick, with a subtle pushing hand, motioned her to stay seated. He shook his head, and she interpreted his urgent expression. *Don't move. There's danger.*

Just then the coach door opened, and Sam Keller entered from the opposite direction and advanced, his busy eyes searching every seat and face. Evelyn turned her head and saw him. His hostile face. He spotted Virginia, and then his reptilian eyes narrowed on Eve. She knew who he was—who he must be. Nausea built in her stomach; Virginia slept, unaware.

Patrick's creed in a fight was always to attack first and keep attacking. He made his move, accelerating toward Sam, who started toward Evelyn and Virginia, three seats away.

Patrick blundered into Sam, stunning him, shoving him so that he went back-stepping, his back bouncing off the entrance/exit door. Enraged, Sam Keller was about to yell out a threat when Patrick grabbed him by the throat, gripping his windpipe, restricting his breathing. Sam's shocked eyes bulged.

A man nearby turned to stare. "Hey, what's going on over there?"

Patrick smiled and said pleasantly to Sam, "Come on brother, dear, you've had a wee bit too much to drink. Some cold air will do you good."

Still clutching Keller's throat, Patrick grabbed the door handle, pulled the door open and sidestepped it just enough to push Sam Keller and himself outside between the cars. The heavy door slammed shut behind them.

Wind and snow whipped at their faces as Patrick shoved Keller hard against an outside wall. The train bounced and thundered down the tracks, and the scream of the whistle echoed through the countryside.

Patrick prayed a conductor wouldn't come along checking tickets. He had no good explanation for what was going on.

Sam Keller's eyes were glassy from the near complete lack of oxygen. Although he was not as tall as Patrick, he was a strong and experienced fighter. In a surprise move, he jammed his right fist into Patrick's stomach, just enough so that, in reflex, Patrick released the pressure on Keller's neck.

Keller sank another fist into Patrick's gut, sending him staggering, his hand falling from Keller's throat. Keller pressed his attack, fists catching Patrick on the left jaw and right upper rib.

The wind howled through the open space, sounding like a wounded animal. Keller's fighting goal was to get Patrick toward the left open gap, to shove him off the train.

Patrick shook off the hard left to his jaw, coldly aware of what Keller was up to. Patrick quickly recovered, blocking the next barrage of fists that came at him.

In the narrow space, Patrick adroitly spun away, readjusting his stance, ready for the next assault. Keller darted in, his face locked in a violent grimace. He swung, missed, swung, his attack blocked. In frustration, he stumbled back and, in a sudden, swift motion, he whipped out a pistol. Patrick was in grave danger. A sitting duck.

Just then, the train swerved sharply and whooshed into a tunnel. In the darkness, the gun went off, an angry flash of orange flame. Then another, the POP nearly swallowed by the wind and the rumbling roar of the train.

Calculating Sam's last position, Patrick threw a hard fist, feeling the instant, sharp pain of connection to flesh and bone. Another shot went off, and the bullet whispered past Patrick's right ear.

As the train rushed out of the tunnel, back into the shock of daylight, Patrick caught a glimpse of Sam Keller, pistol gripped in his hand, plunging backward toward the open gap, nose bleeding, mouth stretched in horror. Reeling, he tumbled off the platform, sucked into a blur of snow.

Panting for breath and feeling a stinging fist-ache, Patrick leaned back against the wall, huffing out white vapor.

CHAPTER 37

As a precaution, Evelyn, Virginia and Patrick left the train at New Rochelle, New York, in case Vernon, Joe McGuire or the police were waiting for them at Pennsylvania Station. They took a cab into New York City, arriving at Evelyn's clinic before midnight.

During most of the trip to New York, Virginia had slept, awakening only one time to stretch and blink around the train car. Evelyn had introduced her to Patrick, who was sitting across the aisle from them, keeping watch in case any of Sam Keller's men were aboard.

"He's a friend, Virginia," she'd said. "He helped me find you."

Virginia regarded Patrick with bloodshot, sleepy eyes and a droopy, sad mouth.

"Nice to meet you," she'd said lethargically. "I don't feel so good."

And then she'd returned to sleep.

Evelyn looked at Patrick apologetically and mouthed the words, "She has a fever."

At the clinic, Virginia was taken to an upstairs private room, where Evelyn immediately took her temperature. It was 102.3F. Evelyn administered aspirin and then put her daughter to bed. She also called in an extra security guard. Patrick waited at the clinic front door until he arrived, in case Vernon, Joe McGuire or the cops appeared. No one did.

Around 2 a.m., Evelyn and Patrick were standing in the hallway outside Virginia's door. Two security guards were on duty and a sign on Virginia's door read,

QUARANTINE ROOM!
DIPHTHERIA!
DO NOT ENTER!

Evelyn look fatigued, Patrick weary.

"You should go home and get some sleep, Patrick."

"And you as well. It has been, as they say, a very long day."

"I'm staying here tonight. I'm worried about Virginia. Dr. Polk will be here first thing in the morning to give her a thorough examination, and I want to be here."

"Virginia is a lovely girl. I must say, I'm impressed at your snatching her away from those two thugs."

"It was odd, really. I didn't think about it. I just reacted. I knew if I thought about it too much, I'd freeze up."

"It was a clever device."

Evelyn met his gaze. "You never did say what happened to that hoodlum on the train."

"Let's just say that he left the train prematurely."

She lowered her eyes. "I wish it were over. How do you think Vernon will respond?"

"I don't know. I guess it depends on Joe McGuire and the police upstate."

"I'll never be able to thank you enough, Patrick... for everything."

"I would have done the same thing for my daughter."

"But Virginia isn't your daughter."

Patrick crossed his arms and leaned back against the wall. "I've had two daughters. Two lovely daughters. I know how you feel."

Eve didn't know what to say, and she was too exhausted to ask any questions. Patrick pushed away from the wall. "There's a comfortable chair downstairs in your lobby. I'm going to camp out there tonight, just in case."

"You don't need to. We have security and, believe me, Vernon will not venture past Virginia's door."

"But he may confront you."

"I have my derringer."

"You constantly surprise me, Evelyn, but let's hope you don't have to use the thing. Anyway, we both should get some sleep. I have the feeling we're going to need it in the next few days."

The following morning, around 8 a.m., Evelyn found Patrick awake, sitting in a lobby chair, sipping a paper cup of coffee.

Patrick rose as she approached, noticing her troubled expression.

"How did you sleep?" Evelyn asked.

"Fine... I could use a haircut, a bath and a shave, but other than that... How are you? Is everything all right?"

She met his eyes and saw his were red-rimmed from lack of sleep. She also noticed a slight bruise on the side of his face, but decided not to ask him about it.

The receptionist was behind the counter, her typewriter chattering away. Outside the front door, two inches of fresh snow covered the ground. Evelyn led Patrick away from the desk toward the public bathrooms and floor plants.

"I can see from your expression that Dr. Polk has completed Virginia's examination," Patrick said.

Evelyn's gaze was direct for a moment, and then it drifted away. "Virginia believes she's pregnant. She also has a mild case of pneumonia, which I suspected last night."

Unwanted tears sprang from her eyes. Her face sagged, lost in heaviness.

"Did the doctor confirm it... the pregnancy?"

"Not conclusively, but Virginia is positive she's pregnant, and she's deeply depressed, and that's not helpful. She just keeps saying how much she hates that man... the man on the train."

"Did you tell her..." Patrick stopped. "Did you tell her that he's dead?"

"No... But I told her he'd never harm her again. I didn't elaborate. She fell asleep, and I want her to sleep. It's the best thing for her now. She must build up her strength."

"What can you do for the pneumonia?"

"Keep her fever down. Keep her warm. Rest. During the war, I treated many influenza patients. Most of them died from bacterial pneumonia after they had the virus infection." Evelyn struggled with her emotions. "I just don't know..."

Patrick spoke in a calming voice. "Virginia is young and strong. Isn't that in her favor?"

Evelyn nodded. "Yes... Dr. Polk is not completely sure what we're dealing with. We're going to perform more tests... send for a specialist."

Eve felt an inner darkness, and a suffocating remorse and guilt for what had happened to Virginia.

Patrick saw it written on her face. "Virginia's safe now, Evelyn, and she's with you, and she knows you'll love her and protect her. Surely that will help her recover."

Evelyn blotted her tears with an embroidered hankie she'd balled in her hand. "Thank you for that, Patrick. Again, thank you for your help."

She reached into her gray suit side pocket and removed a letter-sized blue envelope. She handed it to Patrick. "This came yesterday to the clinic. I didn't read it until this morning. As you can see, it's from Mrs. Lavinia Vanderbilt."

Patrick accepted the envelope and read the gold leaf embossed name on the top left,

Mrs. Lavinia Joan Foster Vanderbilt

On the face of the envelope was written Evelyn's name, in a flowing, artistic script, along with hand-stamped instructions.

Miss Evelyn Stratford
HAND DELIVER
PERSONAL AND CONFIDENTIAL!

Patrick removed the folded note, opened it and read,

Dear Miss Stratford:

It is with the greatest of pleasure that I can inform you that my mother, Joan Katherine Kosarin Foster (Joni, to you, of course) has arrived in New York and she is most anxious to see you and Mr. Gantly, Patrick.

Accordingly, at your earliest convenience, please contact me so that we can arrange a mutually suitable day and time for such a meeting.

As you can imagine, my mother is bursting with excitement to see and speak with you both.

At that time, we can also discuss further plans for my financial assistance of your most worthy medical clinic. In that regard, I have contacted my attorneys and financial officer and they await my further instructions.

I look forward to hearing from you soon!

Sincerely yours,
Mrs. Lavinia Joan Foster Vanderbilt
(Lavinia)

Patrick folded the letter and replaced it in the envelope. He felt a surge of exhilaration knowing that he'd soon see Joni again, an old, familiar friend who knew his past, who knew Eve, and who possessed the time travel lantern.

An eager restlessness grew in him as he thought about seeing, touching, and possibly lighting the lantern once more.

While he listened to traffic sounds, car horns, and pedestrian conversations passing outside the window, fear and apprehension returned. Would he have the courage to light that lantern? Would it take him home to 2020? And if it did, would he wind up returning to the same day and time he left? Would Eve and Colleen be dead or alive?

Patrick lifted his eyes on Evelyn and handed the letter back to her. She took it, replacing it in her pocket.

Evelyn searched his eyes. "Perhaps it's time you explained who Eve is and why Lavinia and her mother think I am Eve, her old friend?"

Patrick sighed. "It's not an easy thing to explain."

"After what we've been through the last few days, I think I can handle the truth."

"It needs a longer conversation than we have time for right now. And maybe because of what's going on with Virginia, this isn't the best time."

"Please, Patrick. I have to respond to Mrs. Vanderbilt's letter. I need the money she's offering. And how can I meet a woman who is supposed to be my old best friend, when I've never even met the woman? I have to know what's going on. It can't wait."

Patrick looked around. "Is there someplace we can talk in private?"

"There's a meeting room just down the hallway. We can go there."

CHAPTER 38

They sat across from each other at a round table in a square room with two windows, both covered by cheerful, blue-patterned curtains. The radiator heat had never successfully warmed the space, and even though Evelyn wore a brown woolen suit and a white sweater, items she'd kept in a closet upstairs, the chill was invasive.

She tried to settle the thoughts that swarmed in her head as she listened to Patrick's story, his eyes filled with a direct, sad honesty. His hands were restless, his voice low and soft, with a personal tone that often faltered as he described Eve and Colleen, as he struggled to explain the lantern, time travel, and his and Eve's lives in the twenty-first century.

Patrick's eyes often came to Evelyn's, to measure her reaction, to interpret her expression and to probe her eyes. He heard his words—words that groped and strained to clarify, to defend and to describe an experience that was simply beyond the grasp of anyone who had never experienced it. He knew that from his own past.

Still, he pressed on, his story sounding more fantasy than reality. The harder he searched for the right word, the more Evelyn's anxious attention wavered. She often turned her head aside toward the windows, as if she wished to be somewhere else. When he finished, she was gazing sightlessly at him.

In the long, deep silence that followed, Patrick waited for Evelyn's response—any response—but she sat stoically still, thinking, processing, laboring to match his words with reality.

With a look and a gesture, she said, "How can you expect me to believe any of this? A lantern that somehow allows you to time travel? And Mrs. Vanderbilt's mother, who just happens to be a friend of your wife's, who lived in the twenty-first century? And your wife just happens to look like me?"

Patrick gave her an uncomfortable look. "I know how it sounds, Evelyn... That's why I didn't want to tell you. That's why..."

She broke in. "... How can I look like your wife, Eve, and speak like her, and do and say the things she did? It's not rational, realistic or believable. It's just... just... Well, it just sounds insane, Patrick. It's mad and ludicrous. Who can believe it?"

She swallowed a breath, pushed her chair back and rose, standing in a bewildering silence. Her eyes captured, then released his. With a shake of her head, she stepped to the windows, drawing back the curtain and staring out.

"I could fall in love with you, Patrick. Perhaps I'm already in love with you, I don't know. But this... this story, just upends me. It scares me. It unnerves me."

She pivoted back to him, staring, straining to understand. "For God's sake, Patrick, how can you expect me to believe such a thing? I can't and I won't. It's absurd and ridiculous. Why do you want me to believe this?"

"Because it is the truth, Evelyn. All of it, whether you want to believe it, or can believe it. Lavinia Vanderbilt is not mad. Joni is not insane. They are intelligent, rational people."

Evelyn's lips firmed up.

"Joni has the time travel lantern hidden away. When we meet, I'm going to ask her for it."

Evelyn slowly eased back down into her chair.

Patrick continued. "I must decide whether to use the lantern to try to return to 2020. It's a risk. There is no guarantee I'll return or, if I do, if I'll return to find Eve and Colleen alive."

His words wounded her. She stared into the depths of his eyes, desperately searching for the truth and, against her will, and against every reasonable atom in her body, she saw that he believed it. She saw an authentic belief in the hard steel of his determination.

Evelyn absorbed a wave of despair and fatigue, and she lowered her head, closing her eyes, putting her face in her hands.

Patrick got up and went to her. He longed to touch her, to comfort her. He hated living between worlds, between emotions, not fully occupying either, trapped in both and being in love with a woman who lived in both, or who had lived in both.

He reached to touch Evelyn's hair, but stopped.

A knock on the door startled them both. Evelyn lifted her head. "Yes?"

"Miss Stratford, your husband is at the front desk, demanding to see you. A security guard is blocking him from going upstairs to Virginia's room."

Evelyn and Patrick exchanged worried glances.

"Alright, Denise, I'll be right out."

Evelyn pushed up, straightened her posture and avoided Patrick's eyes. "I'll take care of this."

"I'll go with you."

"No, I'll do this alone. If he sees you... it might provoke him. I'll be all right. Please just stay in here."

After Evelyn left the room, Patrick paced, regretting his decision to tell her the truth. Instead of helping or clearing the air, he sensed it had only made things worse.

He stopped pacing when he heard a man's shouting voice echoing down the hallway. Patrick opened the door, left the room and went striding toward the front entrance.

He saw Vernon confronting Evelyn, a warning finger pointed at her face.

"Now, I'm only going to ask once more, Evelyn. Let me see my daughter this instant, or so help me God, I'll have the police here so fast you won't know what hit you."

Evelyn had taken two steps back. A nervous security guard stood by, but his resolve was fading with Vernon's threats.

Patrick approached Evelyn, and she turned, her face registering relief.

"Is everything all right, Miss Stratford?" Patrick asked.

Vernon snapped his attention to Patrick, his eyes flat and hard as stone. "And who the deuce are you, and who asked you to butt in?" Vernon barked.

Patrick stared at him with a cool threat. "I'm the man who's going to ask you to lower your voice and speak respectfully to Miss Stratford, or leave the clinic."

Vernon held his condescending stare, but Patrick's size and dangerous look of warning blunted some of Vernon's belligerence. He appraised Patrick, and then he studied his wife.

"Oh, so now you're Miss Stratford," he said, with a sneer.

"Yes, Vernon, that's who I am," Evelyn said.

Seconds later, Vernon had evaluated the scene perfectly, reading the warmth and trust in Evelyn's eyes that rested on Patrick, as well as Patrick's swift appearance.

"So this is the man you've bedded down with," Vernon said, biting into the words. "Oh, yes, it all makes sense now. So this is the man who took Virginia away from me."

Evelyn's anger ignited. "Took Virginia away from you!? You insufferable coward. Virginia was being held captive by a sick, bootlegging thug and you did nothing to stop him, you poor excuse for a father."

"Virginia is still my daughter," Vernon thundered. "And I will take her away from here."

Evelyn moved in, her red face close to his. "You will not see her, and you will not take her away."

"Well, the courts might have something to say about that, Evelyn."

Evelyn's rage sharpened. "If you ever try to take Virginia away from me again, so help me, I'll kill you."

Vernon took a step back and managed a laugh, but it was a shaky one. He turned his wary attention to Patrick. "And you're in a lot of trouble, whoever you are. Sam Keller was found dead early this morning. He fell from a train down a fifty-foot cliff. A witness on the train described two brothers having an argument, and he identified one of the men as Sam Keller. I'm sure the police will love to have a little talk with you. And Sam had a lot of friends. They'll want to talk to you, too."

Patrick took a sure step toward Vernon. "I don't know what you're talking about, and I don't give a damn. You're leaving now, and you will not be seeing your daughter."

Vernon worked not to look intimidated. "And who's going to stop me? You and my whore of a wife?" he said, with clipped darts for words.

It took all of Patrick's strength not to punch the man, but he didn't. It would only make things worse for Evelyn.

"I'll give you two minutes to leave, Mr. Scott. If you linger past that, I will toss you out into the street, and it will be a great pleasure."

Vernon's mouth tightened, but he saw the harsh truth in Patrick's eyes. "Okay... Okay, I'll leave, but I'll be back. I'll be back with the police and a warrant to shut this pathetic clinic down. I will get Virginia, Evelyn. Make no mistake about it."

"I hope Virginia is alive when you return," Evelyn said. "She is very ill with pneumonia."

That cut him, and Evelyn was glad of it. "Pneumonia?"

"Yes. Where were you when she needed your protection?"

His mouth twitched, but he didn't speak.

"Your time is up," Patrick said, taking a step toward Vernon.

Vernon back-stepped toward the door. "I'll be back, you can bet on it. And you'll both pay for this. I swear it. You'll pay. Nobody makes a fool out of Vernon Scott and gets away with it."

"You made a fool of yourself a long time ago, Vernon," Evelyn said. "It's you who are pathetic. You sold your only daughter for money and to protect your career. What does that make you?"

"You haven't heard the last from me," Vernon shouted, yanking open the door and storming out, walking to the curb, and climbing into his waiting car.

When the car had driven away, Evelyn couldn't look Patrick in the eye. "I'm so sorry I got you into this. Your life's in danger."

"We'll fight him," Patrick said.

"How? He knows a lot of powerful people in this City, and he *will* shut down the clinic."

"It's time you answered Mrs. Vanderbilt's letter. I have a good feeling that she'll do whatever she can to help you, and she knows powerful people in this City, too."

Evelyn met his gaze. "When I meet her again, do I have to pretend to be someone I'm not?"

"No, Evelyn. But we do need to set up that meeting, and the sooner the better."

Evelyn tried to avoid looking at his handsome face, but she failed. She spoke in a low whisper, so no one but Patrick could hear. "This may be one helluva time to say it, but I'm in love with you, Patrick. Now, what are we going to do about that?"

CHAPTER 39

O n Saturday morning, Evelyn and Patrick stood waiting for Lavinia and Joni in the grand parlor of the Vanderbilt mansion. It was a tasteful, soaring room in every aspect, with tall windows, woodcuts, prints and original art in gilded frames. On the far wall hung family portraits of lantern-jawed nineteenth-century gentlemen and lavishly dressed ladies in elegant poses.

There were heavy oak tables and rich, brown leather chairs, royal blue draperies and built-in bookcases holding leather-bound volumes that were just for show; they were never for reading.

Patrick glanced about, impressed. "Lavinia certainly married well," he said, rubbing the bald-headed bust of Benjamin Franklin.

A deck of cards sat on a green, baize-covered card table under muted electric light. Patrick went over and lifted the top card. It was the jack of spades. He replaced it with a little sigh.

"I'm so nervous," Evelyn said, staring into the gleaming fire that helped to warm the room. "I feel like a country bumkin in this place."

Patrick turned to her. "I can't wait to get Joni's take on all this wealth. Her one-bedroom apartment in the twenty-first century was modest, to say the least, filled with paperback books, movie magazines, plants begging for water, and photos of Marlon Brando and Brad Pitt hanging on the walls."

"Who are those men, Marlon Brando and Brad Pitt?"

"Actors in the future."

Evelyn shook her head. "You *will* tell Mrs. Foster that I'm not Eve, her old friend, won't you?"

"Yes. I may not be able to tell her right away, but I will in time. I'll steer her away from you and Lavinia while you talk business, and then I'll tell her."

Evelyn rambled on nervously. "Wait until you see Mrs. Vanderbilt's jewelry. It must be worth hundreds of thousands of dollars."

"As I recall from my past, nothing spoke to romance with the elites like expensive jewelry," Patrick said. "As a detective, I worked Fifth Avenue balls, where women sought wealthy men who could drape them in magnificent gems."

Evelyn nodded, staring at the servant who stood by the door where Lavinia was soon to enter. He was dressed in burgundy livery.

"As I'm sure you know, Patrick, a woman's jewelry serves a double purpose for these people. It advertises her husband's wealth and symbolizes his appreciation for her."

Patrick rocked on his heels. "Well, I suppose we've used up our small talk, although we haven't yet discussed the stoic bust of the good Benjamin Franklin."

"I wonder why she's keeping us waiting?" Evelyn asked. "Do you think something has happened?"

At that moment, the far door opened and Lavinia Vanderbilt entered, dressed in a stunning, emerald gown trimmed in black velvet. She wore an amethyst, diamond, and demantoid garnet necklace with matching earrings. As before, her opulent auburn hair was styled in fashionable waves and curls, her makeup, light.

She smiled warmly, with her hands outstretched, as she moved dreamily across the thick, burgundy and tan-patterned carpet.

Patrick was taken by the young woman's grace and poise, having inherited the best qualities of Darius and Joni.

"Hello, my dear friends," Lavinia said, drawing up, her eyes bright with friendliness.

She took both of Eve's hands and turned her curious gaze toward Patrick.

She tilted her head, wistfully, nearly breathless, lost in romance. "And you must be Patrick Gantly, the man my mother has talked about ever since I was a little girl. I am so happy to see you both."

She held them both in her eyes and didn't speak for moments, seemingly overcome by emotion. "First, let me apologize for my tardiness. My son Alexander, who is three years old, has a tummy ache, and he wanted his mommy. I fear the time got away from me. But now, we must sit and have tea and wait for my mother, who, I'm sure you know, Mr. Gantly, is always late."

"Mrs. Vanderbilt, please call me Patrick. Mr. Gantly was my father, and I'm afraid that title never suited the man's lifestyle nor his manner. It suits me even less."

Lavinia laughed a little. "Then perhaps I should call you Detective Sergeant Patrick Gantly, as Eve used to call you."

Evelyn gave him a side glance, a forced smile pasted on her face.

"And may I say, Patrick, that you look and sound exactly as my mother described you, very manly and wildly handsome."

Patrick offered a modest half grin. "Joni was always fond of dramatic exaggeration, being the actress she was."

Lavinia smiled up at him. "She will be hysterically happy to see you, Patrick."

"And you, Eve," Lavinia said, still holding Eve's hands, as she took her fully in. "I must tell you that my mother is so excited to see you again. It is why she is late. She must have tried on twenty dresses by now and arranged her hair in various styles, hoping to melt the years away. You, of course, haven't aged, so don't be surprised if Mother is insanely jealous when she sees you. She is seventy-one years old, but a very youthful seventy-one. She still uses twenty-first century slang sometimes, words like 'cool' and 'awesome', and Daddy hates it."

Patrick smiled. "That sounds like Joni."

They sat at an elegant table with four chairs and place settings, and a fine porcelain gold-leaf tea set, crystal glasses and an opulent bouquet of fresh flowers.

A tuxedoed butler delivered a silver, two-tiered tray of finger sandwiches and tea cakes, and then poured the tea before returning to a side table to stand attentively.

Lavinia said, "I apologize that my husband, Benedict, cannot join us. He sent his regards to you all. He is all about business, you know, and he takes time off only in the summer when we reside in Newport."

Evelyn portrayed a calm demeanor as she sipped her tea. "Did your mother enjoy her trip to Europe?"

"You can call her Joni, Eve," Lavinia said. "She will insist on it. Now that we are having a reunion, all formalities are off. But yes, Eve, Mother enjoyed herself immensely. She and Father had traveled to Paris and Rome, and they were on their way to London when she received the news that you two had suddenly appeared. Well, she was off to Southampton as fast as you can say Jack Robinson."

Patrick did not care for tea. He was strictly a coffee drinker, with a splash of whiskey whenever possible, but he pretended a pleasant smile while he sipped at it.

"Mrs. Vanderbilt," Patrick said, "you seem quite comfortable with the idea of time travel. You seem to accept it without question. Was Joni so convincing?"

Evelyn stiffened. She'd still not made her peace with the idea of time travel. It made her queasy. She didn't believe in it, despite Patrick's story and explanation, and she would never believe in it.

Lavinia laughed. "It wasn't Mother who entirely convinced me. It was Father, dear apprehensive and stern Father, who warned my brother, William, and me about the impossibility of it, while stressing that if either of you ever appeared on our doorstep, we were to slam the door in your faces and promptly call the police."

Lavinia chuckled, holding a hand to her mouth. "Now, that convinced me and, of course, it added another area of interest to my already fervent belief in occultism."

Lavinia leaned in, and in a feathery-soft voice, she said, "I have attended several seances, but I have never told my husband nor my father. Of course, my mother accompanied me because my mother, as you know, Patrick, is a bold adventuress. In any event, do you know what my brother, William, once told me? He said he could not ever, ever, believe in anything he couldn't touch or count, in other words, money. He used to say, 'Lavinia, your ship cannot sail the practical waters of this Earth, yet it can easily sail the airy waters of irrational imagination.'"

Lavinia turned her full attention onto Eve. "To that I say, balderdash! You two are living proof of the supernatural and the unexplained world we live in every single day. Now, Eve, tell me why you have come back in time, and tell me all about the twenty-first century. I so longed to use that lantern and time travel myself, but Mother wouldn't hear of it. She refused my many pleadings, always warning me of its many perils and uncertainties. She has that lantern locked away in some hidden vault and she will not tell me, nor anyone else, where it is."

Lavinia's eyes opened wide with expectation. "So tell me, Eve, what has the clinic to do with your traveling back in time?"

Evelyn's throat tightened, as if something were stuck in it. She could not force out any words.

Patrick jumped in. "It is rather complicated, Mrs. Vanderbilt. Unfortunately, at this time, we must keep our mission a secret, for reasons we hope to explain to you at a later date. However, the clinic's survival is extremely important, which is why we are humbly asking you for your support."

Lavinia reflected on Patrick's words with some disappointment, and she rested back with a gentle sigh.

"Of course, I understand, but I do hope that you will trust me with your secret in the near future. I can be discreet and intrepid. My husband knows nothing about my mother's past, or, to be more accurate, my mother's future, and I have never, not once, ever mentioned to him the time travel lantern."

"Mrs. Vanderbilt," Patrick said, "We will tell you everything, as soon as possible."

That pleased Lavinia as she faced Evelyn again. "So, Eve, please tell me about your life in the twenty-first century. I have lain awake through most of the night anticipating a conversation with you."

Evelyn looked to Patrick for help.

At that moment, the library door opened, and Joni swept in.

CHAPTER 40

Patrick's eyes flickered up to meet Joni's as she came toward them, her stride sure and steady, her face filled with excitement, her eyes damp from happy tears, her chin quivering with expectation. She had turned gray and put on more than twenty pounds, but it was the same unmistakable Joni, dressed in a fashionable blue dress with a discrete diamond necklace and matching earrings.

Patrick rose to meet her. Evelyn slowly got to her feet, tense and conflicted.

Without a word, Joni opened her arms and wrapped Evelyn, her stiff arms at her sides, hugging her supposed friend tightly against her. The tears rolled down Joni's cheeks as she held the embrace, rocking Evelyn back and forth, while Patrick looked on apprehensively, and Lavinia watched the reunion with a gentle pleasure.

When Joni finally broke the embrace and stepped back, taking Evelyn in, she smiled with tender affection. "Don't look at me too closely, Eve. I'm an old woman, with a whole gang of wrinkles I thought I'd never have. Can you believe it? And look at you! You haven't aged a day... Okay, well, maybe a few months. I can see the beginnings of crow's feet around your eyes, but you look awesome as ever. God, how I've waited for this moment. I stayed up half the night remembering the time you and I time traveled to 1884. It seems like lifetimes ago."

Evelyn stood frozen, chilled on the inside and hot on the outside. Joni grabbed and hugged her again. A moment later, she stepped back, taking Evelyn by the shoulders, holding her at arm's length. "I thought I'd never see you again. How nice. How wonderful. How crazy this big old world is."

She turned to Patrick. "And there you are, Patrick Gantly, as handsome as ever, just as you looked back in 1884. My God, has it really been that long?"

He gave her a little bow. "You're a sight for happy eyes, Joni. As my old father used to say, 'The best looking glass is the eyes of an old friend.'"

His words delighted Joni's ears and brought an emotional tickle in her chest. She released Evelyn and went to Patrick, stepping into his raised arms. They embraced, her eyes tightly shut, leaking tears.

"I have missed you two for so long, for so many years. Sometimes I think I can't bear being apart from you."

Joni leaned back, her damp eyes searching Patrick's face. "Okay, so I can't wait to hear why you came back, and why back to 1925, of all years."

Patrick released her and Joni went to Evelyn. "We've got to talk, Eve. Oh, and guess what? I'm wearing a damned corset, can you tell?"

Evelyn stared dumbly. "Oh... Well... Yes."

Joni saw the confusion in Eve's eyes. "A corset, Eve. Remember? Remember how I always hated corsets? Remember how you nearly sucked the life out of me with that corset back in 1884, when I wanted to impress Darius?"

Evelyn stammered. "Yes... Well, yes, of course. I mean..."

Joni saw something pass across Eve's eyes. It was fear and uncertainty, and Joni saw something else as well, but she couldn't define it. "Is everything all right, Eve?"

She looked to Patrick. "Patrick, what's happened?"

Joni swung her gaze back to Evelyn, who turned her head aside.

"What is it, Eve? You look so stressed out. Tell me what's happened and how we can help you."

Neither Patrick nor Eve said anything. Patrick needed to get Joni alone, to tell her what was going on.

Joni nodded. "I'm so sorry. Here you are, probably in some kind of trouble, and I've been shooting my mouth off like I always do, without thinking."

Patrick said, "It's okay, Joni. I need to talk to you. Can we go somewhere private?"

Lavinia and Joni directed their gazes toward Evelyn, trying to make a connection, but Evelyn stared down into the carpet.

Patrick stepped to Joni. "Perhaps Mrs. Vanderbilt and Eve can talk business about the clinic, while you and I have our conversation."

Joni reached a gentle hand toward Evelyn, touching her arm. "It's okay, Eve. I can see you're under a lot of stress. Don't you worry. We'll work it out, whatever it is, won't we, Lavinia?"

"Yes, Mother, of course. Do not worry, Eve. We are your friends and we'll do everything we can for you and Patrick."

Evelyn felt faint with fatigue, worry and anxiety. She steadied herself with an effort. "I'm sorry. I guess I'm not quite myself today."

Patrick took Evelyn by the elbow and led her to a leather chair. She eased down. Lavinia instructed the butler to bring Evelyn a glass of water, and he did so.

Lavinia clasped her hands together. "All right, Mother and Patrick. You two go into the drawing room and have your little talk. Eve and I will discuss the business of the clinic and what needs to be done."

Joni touched Eve's shoulder affectionately, and then she led Patrick across the spacious carpet and through a far door that led down a long, marble hallway. They entered through French doors and into the grand and airy drawing room, decorated with burgundy tufted furniture, a three-tiered chandelier, a fieldstone fireplace and a mahogany-paneled library with a coffered ceiling.

Joni sat on the sofa and patted the space next to her for Patrick to sit. She looked deeply earnest when she said, "All right, Patrick, sit down and tell me what's going on. Eve is pale, tired and freaked out."

Patrick considered his words. Joni had always been a straight-shooter, so he decided to be direct.

"All right, Joni, brace up. Evelyn is not the Eve you think she is."

Joni kept her questioning eyes on him, trying to interpret his meaning. "Okay... I guess I don't understand what you just said."

Patrick folded his hands and looked down at them. "Joni... The woman in the other room is not Eve Sharland Gantly. Her name is Evelyn Stratford."

"What are you saying? Of course she's Eve."

Patrick narrowed his eyes on his old friend. "Joni, I have a rather long story to tell you, and it is going to sound like a fiction dreamed up by some madman with a dark sense of humor. When I'm finished, I think you'll understand, or at least you'll understand as much as I do."

Patrick looked toward the ceiling and began speaking carefully, concisely and, at times, haltingly, especially when he described the events that led to Eve's and Colleen's deaths.

When he finished, Joni stared at him with tearful, startled eyes. He met her eyes, noticing the deep lines in her forehead and around her mouth; her wrinkling neck and sagging skin. But there was still a youthful quality about her, and he knew that the same exuberant and sassy thirty-year-old he'd known still lived in her body.

The silence lengthened as Joni grappled with Patrick's story. She nibbled her lower lip as her watery gaze wandered the room, and blotted her eyes with a hankie she'd pulled from her purse.

"Patrick... I don't understand how that woman in the library can look so much like Eve, and yet not be Eve. How is that possible? It's the same face, the same walk, the same expressions... the same eyes. I do see Eve in those eyes."

Patrick held her stare. "I know, Joni. I know. Neither of us believed in time travel either, did we, until we experienced it? And now, this. Whatever this is."

Joni's face twisted, then went vacant. "What the hell...? What are you going to do?"

"I don't know. I was hoping you'd give me some advice. I'm at a loss. You know the power of the lantern. You also know how unpredictable it is. If I try to return home to 2020, what will I find? If I stay here... Well, is that Eve in the next room, or some duplicate of Eve? If I'm in love with Eve, then am I in love with Evelyn Stratford? Perhaps she *is* Eve. Perhaps then I should ask her to marry me and stay here in 1925 and live out my life with her."

With a calculating eye, Joni studied him. "Do you want the lantern? I have it. It's safe, and I'm the only one who knows where it is. I'll give it to you."

"I don't know if I want it. What would *you* do, Joni, if you were in my shoes?"

Joni thought about it for a moment. "Do you know what Eve would do? She'd find Nikola Tesla and ask him."

"Tesla? Why Tesla?"

"Because he might have some answers. I know that's what Eve would do if she were in your place. I just know it."

"She told me the last time she talked to him, he wasn't all that helpful. She said he was vague and evasive."

"That was over forty years ago, Patrick. He might be different now. It wouldn't hurt to try. Maybe he has invented a new way of time traveling—a better and more exacting way. A safer way. Anyway, why not contact him and see what happens? At least he'd know what you're talking about and you wouldn't feel so alone."

Patrick stood up and shoved his hands into his pockets. "I do feel alone. I feel lost, Joni. I feel lost in time, and I feel lost in my mind. Sometimes I think I'm *losing* my mind. The biggest curse in my life has been that damned lantern and yet, without it, I would never have met Eve."

He turned his sorrowful eyes on Joni. "And who is that woman in there? Is she Eve? Is she Eve in a past life? I don't know. Why did that cursed lantern bring me here to 1925? I don't know what to think and it's absolutely driving me crazy."

"You look tired, Patrick. Have you been sleeping?"

"No, I haven't. How can I? My dreams are about Eve and Colleen, and past worlds and future worlds. My dreams are about birth and death, and time travel, and past lives. What the hell is this world, anyway, Joni? Is it real, or is it a dream within a dream, or a story within a story? Maybe sometimes those stories get all mixed up, and that's what has happened. I don't know. I don't know anything anymore."

Joni lowered her voice to a soothing whisper. "Sit down, Patrick. Please sit down and try to relax."

Patrick breathed out a jet of a sigh and sat.

"Okay, I'll go see Tesla. Maybe he can help in some way. Maybe he'll have some solution. Who knows, maybe he can guarantee that when I light the lantern and return to 2020, I'll do so in time to save Eve's and Colleen's lives."

CHAPTER 41

O n Tuesday afternoon, Patrick traveled downtown
to see Nikola Tesla at his office in the Borden
Building at 350 Madison Avenue. Tesla had become a
famous man, and he did not agree to see people he didn't
know or respect. Mrs. Lavinia Vanderbilt had
forwarded Tesla a personal request for an audience, on
Patrick's behalf, and Tesla granted a half-hour interview.

Lavinia was part of the social circle of Tesla's good
friends, Robert Underwood Johnson and his wife,
Katharine. Katharine, who had recently died, had been
a special friend of Tesla's. Tesla and Katharine were
known to have exchanged flirtatious letters at one time,
but their relationship had always remained platonic.
Katharine McMahon Johnson was, according to some
accounts, the only woman Tesla ever loved.

While Patrick sat in a small reception area, waiting
for Tesla to emerge from his office, he thought back to
the last few days. He'd spent much of the weekend with
Evelyn at the clinic, when he'd learned that Virginia had

taken a turn for the worse. Two doctors were doing all they could for her, and Evelyn seldom left her daughter's bedside. She'd slept on a cot near Virginia's bed, monitoring her every hour. Thankfully, Vernon had not returned to the clinic, and the police hadn't appeared looking for Patrick.

Patrick had also spent time with Joni, eating out in Delmonico's and reminiscing about the old days. Joni told him that Darius had completed his medical conference and was sailing back to New York. When Joni mentioned Darius, she didn't look Patrick in the eye.

"He doesn't want to see you, I'm sorry to say. He's just so scared of the lantern. We had a terrible argument before I left for Southampton. He said he was sure I'd light the thing, leave him, and return to the twenty-first century."

"And would you like to?"

Joni's face was younger in the candlelight, especially when she smiled. "No, Patrick. My life is here with Darius and my kids. I've told him that a hundred times, but he's so stubborn."

Joni grew reflective. "I have to tell you that when I see Evelyn Stratford, I do see Eve. I want to see more of her. I think we can become good friends."

"Yes, I think so, too. Evelyn will need your friendship, especially if her daughter dies, God forbid."

Joni nodded. "Yes, God forbid."

Having no receptionist, it was Nikola Tesla himself who emerged from a doorway, tall, thin and watchful. Patrick rose and approached the man, who was at least two inches taller than Patrick. At sixty-eight years old, his short hair was gray and his skin a bit pale, but his eyes were as penetrating and alive as ever.

He was dressed impeccably but, to Patrick's eye, the man's suit of clothes looked old-fashioned, more like late nineteenth century or early twentieth century style.

When Mr. Tesla spoke, his voice was a thin tenor, but precise and measured.

He extended his hand, with a meager smile that wasn't warm but also, not unfriendly. "I did not get your name," he said.

"Patrick Gantly. I believe you are acquainted with Mrs. Lavinia Vanderbilt."

He nodded, thoughtfully. "Of course, I remember Mrs. Vanderbilt. Yes, I do. She accompanied my friend, Mrs. Katharine Johnson, to various charitable events, and I had the pleasure of dining with Mr. and Mrs. Vanderbilt at Delmonico's on two occasions."

Patrick noted that Mr. Tesla's English was vastly improved from when Eve had first met him in 1884, forty years before, when he'd first arrived in the United States.

"Do you wish to speak of science?" he asked.

"In a manner of speaking, yes, Mr. Tesla."

His gaze was enigmatic, as if he were trying to read Patrick's thoughts. He indicated toward the door from which he appeared. "Let us enter my office and speak, Mr. Gantly."

They entered a small room that held a desk and accompanying chair, another high-backed wooden chair standing against a wall, three wooden file cabinets, and a window covered by cheerful, yellow curtains with a tasteful blue floral design. They seemed out of place in the otherwise Spartan room.

Tesla followed Patrick's eyes.

"Those curtains... They were put there by Katharine Johnson. She died not long ago. I will keep them there in her memory. Please sit down, Mr. Gantly."

Patrick did so, noticing an adjoining room, its door partially opened, revealing a sliver of the laboratory where Tesla conducted his experiments.

"Nikola is a dear, but he's a strange man," Lavinia had told Patrick. "He manages to make a living by working as a consulting engineer, but more often than not, he delivers plans that his clients deem impractical. At our last dinner party, he told Benedict and me that he is working on a flying machine that resembles both a helicopter and an airplane. He said it would be able to rise from a garage or a roof, or even out a window, whatever location was desired. He said it would sell for one thousand dollars and could be used by both the military and the ordinary citizen."

Tesla sat down, sitting very erect, arranging his desk chair so he could face Patrick. He folded his hands, his long fingers still, and he looked at Patrick with a thin and peering face. "Now, what is it that brings you here to me?" he asked.

Patrick rearranged himself in the chair, ready to ask the questions he'd been practicing in his mind.

"Mr. Tesla, in 1884, you met my wife, Evelyn Sharland, although she was known by the name Eve Kennedy. You may recall that she and another woman appeared in your laboratory at the Edison Machine Works."

Tesla didn't stir or speak.

Patrick continued. "They arrived from the twenty-first century by way of a time travel lantern that you had invented. Do you remember the time lanterns?"

There was a smile of recognition, with a hint of sadness underneath. "So long ago that was, Mr. Gantly. Yes, those lanterns were my Christmas toy lanterns. I sent those lanterns out into the world as an experiment to learn what those Christmas gifts of light might do. My passion is light and invention, you know. I am a lover of the wonders of light and the movement of light, and light through time itself. Those little toys came into my mind just before Christmas Eve in 1883 because of the candles, the lamps and the lanterns at Christmas. In 1884, equations came shouting into my head. Oh, yes, Mr. Gantly, I remember the time lanterns."

"Do you recall Evelyn Kennedy?"

The skin around Tesla's eyes tightened as he seemed to go into a kind of trance. There was a long silence before he said, "Yes, there were two young women. A blonde woman was interested in science. Yes, we talked some about science and the lanterns. I remember her. I have recollections of some violence that happened to her."

Patrick sat up. "Yes, that was Eve. We used one of your time lanterns to return to the twenty-first century."

Tesla nodded. "Is she with you now, Mr. Gantly?"

"No. That's why I'm here… it's why I wanted to speak to you."

Patrick explained the airplane crash and how he'd used the lantern again, hoping to time travel back only a few days so he could stop Eve from boarding that airplane with Colleen.

Tesla listened intently, occasionally making little grunting sounds of understanding. When Patrick finished, Tesla nodded, his mind working. "Mr. Gantly, you have traveled here to 1925," he said, brightly. "How fine and how interesting that is, is it not? Time has played with you, and you have played with time. The game of time is bewildering, isn't it? Perhaps one could say time is always playing at its jokes. Yes, time is a jokester. An hour is fast to one person, but slow to another. Time ages one person fast, and another slow. A year is both long and short at the same time. Do you see how time plays?"

Patrick understood now why Eve had been so frustrated with the man when she'd tried to discuss the time lanterns. Tesla saw time, and probably the world, very differently from the way other scientists and most ordinary people did.

"Mr. Tesla, I am not a scientist. My reason for being here is simple: I want to return to the twenty-first century a few days—or even a few hours—before that airplane crashes. When I lighted the lantern in the future, that's what I'd wished for. Instead, I landed here, in 1925, and I don't know why."

Patrick went on to describe how Evelyn Stratford was a near double of his wife, Eve.

"So you see, Mr. Tesla, I'm feeling a bit lost and confused as to why the lantern brought me here."

Tesla remained impassive, his stare fixed, his body still.

Patrick leaned forward. "Mr. Tesla, I have access to one of your time travel lanterns. What I'd like to know from you is…. Is there a way to program the lantern with a guarantee that I can return to 2020 to stop my wife and daughter from getting on that airplane? Can you help me?"

Tesla sat in a motionless trance, as if staring into secret, mysterious worlds.

Patrick waited, hearing the flapping wings of a pigeon landing on the outside windowsill. "I'm a practical man, Mr. Tesla," Patrick said, looking down at the brown and white tiled floor. "I know nothing of the occult or reincarnation, or even time travel and how it works. I just want my wife and my child back."

Patrick raised his gaze and their eyes connected.

Tesla half-hooded his eyes. "Mr. Gantly, the day science begins to study non-physical phenomena, it will make more progress in one decade than in all the previous centuries of its existence. I am telling you this because you have experienced time travel with my toy lantern. Now you know the power of non-physical phenomena. It cannot be explained in the head. It must be apprehended. It must be approached by intuition. Do you see?"

"I'm afraid I don't see, Mr. Tesla. Why did your lantern bring me to 1925, and why is Evelyn Stratford a near duplicate of my wife, Eve?"

Tesla offered a stony stare. "Every living being is an engine geared to the wheelwork of the universe. Though seemingly affected only by its immediate surroundings, the sphere of external influence extends to infinite distance. Do you understand this, Mr. Gantly?"

Patrick strained his mind, willing it to understand. "I'm not sure. Are you saying, Mr. Tesla, that Evelyn Stratford is... or could be... Eve Sharland Gantly in a past life?"

"You saw it in her eyes, did you not? Isn't that so? The eyes are the scouts of the heart."

Patrick thought about it. "Yes... I did see Eve in Evelyn's eyes. That's what caught me and drew me to her."

Tesla directed his gaze toward the floral yellow curtains. "I would know my friend, Katherine Johnson, in any form she might take, just by looking into the eyes. Katherine and I often communicated our thoughts through one look… One simple look."

Patrick pondered that.

"Perhaps, Mr. Gantly, time has taught you something about the universe and about love. Perhaps it has expanded your view of what life is and what people are. Don't you think so, sir, Mr. Gantly? Now you know that your wife has been before, and she has been again. She will never die. She will go on, and your child will as well. Evolution is persistent and it is relentless. It will never stop being and expanding. A flower will wither and die, Mr. Gantly, but we are made of diamond."

Patrick pressed on. "But Mr. Tesla, if I use your time lantern with the wish to return to 2020 to save my wife and child, is there any way I can be sure of returning before the accident occurred?"

"No, Mr. Gantly. There is no way to guarantee you that. Not with my lighted lantern. It is not a precise instrument, like a watch, that can be set by a simple adjustment. Mr. Gantly, in this world, you and I live in the foreground of a wonder. Those lanterns operate in the space of wonder, activated by light and the mystical motors of time."

Frustrated, Patrick shot up, his mind racing, his pulse rising. "I'm sorry, sir, I have no idea what you're talking about. I am not a mystic. I'm not a scientist. I'm a man who breathes, and who lives in the real world, as I see it, and I am a man who loves a woman who was killed in 2020. Now, there must be some way to stop the accident by using the lantern. Can you help me, please?"

Tesla stared at Patrick, blinking. "You can ask her, Mr. Gantly."

Patrick tossed him a look. "Ask her? Ask who? I don't understand."

"Ask the woman in this time. Ask this woman, Evelyn Stratford. But even better than asking her directly... Well, let me see... It is more potent for you to plant the thought in her mind so that in the future she will remember. She will remember and she might, yes, might, make a different choice. She might hear your old voice in her head and choose not to put herself on that airplane. Do you see?"

Patrick eased back down in the chair, perplexed. "How do I do that?"

A silent breath of laughter left Tesla's lips. "It is quite simple. When she sleeps is best."

"When she..." Patrick stopped, certain he wasn't hearing the man correctly. "What do you mean, when she sleeps?"

"When the mind is asleep, the power of suggestion often brings success to intention. Do you understand me? When she sleeps, your suggestion to her is not obstructed by the static of thought that clogs the mind during the waking hours. The true, open, and free mind, devoid of static, can hear and remember and store your suggestion until it is needed. Do you see?"

Patrick sighed audibly, staring at Tesla doubtfully. "What do I say? What suggestion?"

"Simple is best. Say, 'In the future, do not get on that airplane. Death awaits.' Say it softly, with a strong intention. Say it repeatedly."

Patrick straightened his back. He wanted to say, *that's insane*, but he didn't.

Tesla stood up to his full towering height, looking down at Patrick. And then, as if he'd read Patrick's mind, he said, "Mr. Gantly, one must be sane to think clearly, but one can think deeply and be quite insane."

Tesla nodded and folded his hands, looking toward his laboratory. "It has been a good pleasure to speak with you, sir, but now I must work. I have much to do."

Patrick rose and shook Tesla's bony hand. "Thank you, Mr. Tesla, for your time."

"Yes, time, Mr. Gantly. It seems that I have always been ahead of my time. We have so much time and so little time, and yet time surrounds us, always. Isn't that so?"

CHAPTER 42

"Can I help with anything?" Patrick called.

"No," Evelyn said from the kitchen. "I don't want a man in my kitchen. They always break things. I'll be right out."

Patrick smiled. Eve had liked it when he'd helped in the kitchen, chopping vegetables or opening the wine.

He sat on the sofa in Evelyn Stratford's living room, trying to relax. In the kitchen, Evelyn was preparing cheese and crackers, pouring glasses of white wine.

It was Wednesday evening, the day after he'd met with Nikola Tesla. As Patrick waited for Evelyn to return from the kitchen, he thought again about the man. He knew from reading history in the twenty-first century that Tesla wasn't a savvy businessman and, as a result, he suffered financially, despite his achievements.

Poor and reclusive, Tesla would die of a coronary thrombosis at 86 years old, on January 7, 1943, in New York City, where he had lived for nearly sixty years.

In 2020, people couldn't imagine life without a TV remote, neon and fluorescent lights, wireless transmission, computers, smartphones, laser beams, x-rays, robotics and alternating current, the basis of the modern electrical system. All were part of the extraordinary twenty-first century reality, thanks to Nikola Tesla. Yes, he truly had been a man ahead of his time.

Patrick considered issues that he and Tesla had not discussed. By time traveling back to 1925, Patrick had surely changed the past. Of course, he'd faced this question before when he had time traveled with Eve. But the question still remained. In the grand scheme of the world, did it matter if things were altered in the past? Would anyone in the future ever be aware of some small event that had changed? Probably not. That event would simply be part of recorded history; future people would have no knowledge of an alternative history.

So did it matter that Patrick had intervened in 1925? Evelyn had rescued Virginia from her captors, and Sam Keller had tumbled off the train and been killed. Surely none of that would have happened if Patrick hadn't time traveled. The truth was, he was weary of time travel and everything that went with it. He was also sick to death of thinking about it.

Evelyn entered the living room, carrying a tray with an assortment of cheeses, nuts, cut meats, crackers and sliced bread.

"It looks lovely," Patrick said, as Evelyn placed it on the coffee table before him.

"I hope you like it," she said, looking at it with pleasure. "I've always liked to nibble on things, more than I like eating a large meal."

Patrick didn't say, *I know, Evelyn. Eve had said those very same words to him many times.*

"I'll be back with the wine."

When she returned, he stood up. She handed him a glass, and they toasted.

"To Virginia, and her improved health," Patrick said.

"Yes, to my crazy and wonderful darling girl, who I hope has learned her lesson once and for all."

They clinked glasses and sipped.

Evelyn had dressed up, wearing a silver and black fringe flapper dress, with black pumps. Her hair had been styled, waved and topped with a rose gold and rhinestone headband. Her lips were red, eyelashes long, her long golden earrings shining in the light.

They sat next to each other on the couch, plates in their laps, glasses of wine before them on the table. The Victrola played jazz and, outside, snow flurries fell in a calm wind.

"I love walnuts and pecans," Evelyn said, chewing vigorously.

Patrick had never seen Evelyn so happy and animated. Earlier in the day, when she'd heard of Virginia's improvement, her low mood had swiftly changed, and she beamed with new life.

"What are your plans for Thanksgiving?" Evelyn asked.

"Plans? I don't know. When is it? I've lost track of the days."

"November twenty-sixth, a little over a week away."

"I have no plans."

"Would you like to join Virginia and me?"

"Virginia may not want me crashing your Thanksgiving Day celebration."

"She wants you to come. I told her all about you. Even in her foggy state on the train, she remembered you. She said you were very handsome. And she knows that you saved her life."

"Let's be clear, *you* were the one who snatched her away from those... well, let's just call them criminals."

"And you saved her from Sam Keller. She hated the man... but let's not talk about ugly things tonight. Virginia is grateful to you and she wants you to come on Thanksgiving. And by the way, she thinks you're quite the earthy man. Her words."

"Well, as you said, she was in a foggy state and probably couldn't see so good."

"Believe me, Patrick, in any state, delirious or otherwise, Virginia always notices handsome men."

"Then I accept your invitation, but only if you let me bring the turkey."

"No."

"Yes, or I don't come."

"All right, if you insist. You bring the turkey and I'll cook it. Fair enough."

"I don't wish to bring up a nasty subject, but have you heard from your husband?"

"No," Evelyn said flatly.

"Has Virginia asked about him?"

"Yes... She doesn't want to see him. Not ever. I've hired a lawyer. I was going to tell you about it, but not tonight. Tonight I wanted to forget it all. Tonight is reserved for you and me, just the two of us."

After they'd finished eating and Evelyn had cleared the dishes, she poured them each another glass of wine and eased down closer to Patrick, her knees brushing his.

Elyse Douglas

She put a self-conscious hand to her lower neck and looked at him.

"Will you stay the night?"

Patrick looked at her, unsure.

Evelyn continued. "I know I'm being forward, but it is 1925 after all, and women can vote, and drive around the country alone, smoke cigarettes and even go to juice joints alone and order a cocktail. My daughter tells me women have come a long way… And, anyway, I've had two glasses of wine, so yes, I am being bold and maybe I'm being foolish. I don't care."

Patrick stared into her serene, blue eyes; seeing the shining love in them.

"And you know how I feel about you, Patrick. You know I'm in love with you. I don't care that you're still in love with your wife, or if I remind you of your wife. Fine, so be it. I can accept that. I can love enough for the both of us. I know I can make you happy."

When Patrick set his glass down and got up, turning from her, she shrank in dejection, staring down at the carpet. "So I guess I've said too much."

She set her wine glass down, sitting still, knees together, feeling high, aching to be touched and loved.

Patrick was busy making inner adjustments to refocus his mind away from Evelyn's lips and dreamy eyes.

When he spoke, his voice was low, his eyes searching the walls. "How can I be a man, when I don't even know who I am, or where I belong?"

Evelyn pushed up, her face set in a challenge. "She's dead, Patrick, whatever time period you say she lived in. She's dead! I'm alive. Here. I'm here, now, flesh and blood and breathing. How long are you going to grieve? Isn't it time you moved on with your life? Isn't that what your wife would have wanted you to do, if she truly loved you?"

Patrick raked a shaky hand through his hair, faced her, and held her with his eager eyes. He let out a hot breath and took her by the shoulders, pulling her tightly into his chest.

She buried her face into his shoulder, feeling his strength and the masculine power of him, feeling her passion flare, her body ignite with desire. When he kissed her, her heart stopped, then restarted.

Patrick surrendered to the pull of Eve, as he always had. He fell into the tangle of her hair, her scent, her breath, the magic of her soul that seemed to reach out for him. Every cell was alert with delight, as memory and passion collided.

He recalled how their eyes had first met, strong and quiet on that street back in 1885. He recalled their first intimate kiss, and it sparked a fresh, lavish yearning for her.

Evelyn's body awakened with a new passion. Patrick excited her, disturbed her; and when he swept her up into his arms, she thrilled. They kissed as he maneuvered them toward the dark, waiting bedroom.

Inside the room, they touched, probed and kissed, their bodies hungry and ripe for love. Their clothes were pulled and flung, their lips wet and warm. As they turned and danced, delighting in touch, Evelyn tossed her head back, waiting for a kiss, and Patrick found her lips that opened and blossomed.

He had Eve in his arms again and, this time, he'd never let her go. This time, there would be no damned airplanes and death. Eve was here and now, alive and reaching for him, her body warm and wanting.

Eve wanted to pour herself—every cell and atom—into his heart, into his broad hairy chest; melt into his soul and form a nest of safety, peace and love, forever.

Eve awoke from the depths of sleep, rolled onto her side, and in her half-dream state, reached for Patrick, who rested next to her.

"Patrick?"

"I'm here," he said, at a whisper, adjusting his body to face her. Her soft hand explored his lips, tracing them.

In the darkness, with only a faint light spilling in from the hallway, they were two silhouettes.

"What a beautiful sound," Eve said, in a breathy voice. "What beautiful and lovely words. 'I'm here.'"

"You slept," Patrick said.

"How long?"

"Don't know. Maybe an hour."

"Did you?"

"No…"

"Thinking?"

"Not so much. Watching you sleep, mostly."

"That's a sin."

"A sin?"

"Yes, me sleeping with you lying beside me, ready to love me. I should never sleep again."

He kissed her face, her hair. Her heavy eyelids fluttered, then closed. She made a sound of comfort as she snuggled into him, as he stroked her hair.

"Say it again," she said, her voice soft and sleepy.

"What?"

"I'm here. Say, I'm here."

"Yes, Eve. I'm here."

In that perfect intimate moment, she dropped below rolling waves of fatigue and satisfaction into bottomless sleep, feeling Patrick's warm body; feeling calm and safe and surrounded by Patrick's love.

Her breathing deepened and found an easy rhythm. She mumbled his name, but it was a blurring hum, sounding like "Pabreek…"

Patrick watched her sleep for a time before he gently raised up and moved his lips close to her ear. He felt a bit foolish for what he was about to do, but then he reminded himself of the fact that Nikola Tesla was a genius, and it was he who had created the time travel lantern.

Patrick cleared his throat and whispered, "Eve… don't get on that airplane…"

Evelyn stirred, grumbled out gibberish, and fell back to sleep.

Patrick's mouth inched closer to her ear. "Eve… in 2020, don't board your father's airplane with Colleen. Remember these words, Eve. Remember… You must remember."

Patrick repeated the mantra several times until it became a kind of chant.

Some time later, he stared into the uncertain darkness, feeling a shiver of dread come over him. When his eyes returned to Evelyn, she was curves and shadow, resting in peace, far from the turmoil that paced inside him, and kept him from the welcome escape of sleep.

CHAPTER 43

"My mother says she's in love with you," Virginia said, frankly.

Evelyn folded her arms, twisted up her lips and looked away.

Patrick kept his eyes on Virginia as she lay in her hospital bed, her back propped up against two pillows. Bright sun poured in from two windows, and a large bouquet of flowers sat on a side table, a gift from Patrick.

"Do you always have to be so blunt, Virginia?" Evelyn asked.

"If it's true, then why not say it?" Virginia responded.

Virginia's eyes flashed with new life as they focused on Patrick. "Are you in love with my mother, Mr. Patrick Gantly?"

Patrick didn't answer.

That gave Virginia permission to ramble on. "Well, let me tell you something about my dear mother you probably don't know. She can be quite vain, and very fussy with her hair. When I was young, she used curling tongs. You know, those metal rods you have to put over heat and hope they don't get so hot they damage more hair than they curl. Sometimes I could smell mother's singed hair. I hated those things, but mother seemed to love them." Virginia pointed to her mother's hair. "Now she has one of the new permanent wave machines. That's how she manages to create such tight, curly waves. Do you like those tight, curly waves, Mr. Gantly?" Virginia asked, purposely trying to provoke him and her mother.

"Yes, I do. They are lovely," Patrick said.

"You still haven't said whether you love my mother. Do you, Mr. Gantly? Are you in love with my mother?"

Virginia had improved, that was clear. Patrick observed that she was a dramatic, high-strung and precocious young woman. He saw no fear in her, and he sensed a rebellious impulsiveness, which surely suited her in the 1920s. She'd already demonstrated that dangerous impulsiveness and, unfortunately, he was sure she'd do it again. There was also abundant sexual energy stored behind those coquettish eyes, which seemed in search of the next impetuous, romantic adventure.

"Does your silence mean, 'no', you're not in love with my mother, Mr. Gantly?" Virginia asked.

Patrick leveled his eyes on her. "Well, Miss Scott, as my father used to say, 'A curious, pretty girl should learn a good lesson from a sleek, curious cat.'"

"And what would that be?" Virginia asked, with a flirtatious smile.

"A cat knows when to purr, and when not to, and her survival can depend on it."

Virginia grinned. "Oh? And are you saying that I'm purring right now?"

Elyse Douglas

"I suspect, Miss Scott, that your purr is much worse than your bite, but twice as dangerous, especially as it concerns the Sam Kellers of this world."

Evelyn turned from her daughter, impressed by Patrick's comment.

Virginia's face fell, unsure as to Patrick's meaning. "Is that an insult?"

"Take it as you like."

Virginia crossed her arms, pulling her offended eyes from him, pouting. "I don't think I like you very much, Mr. Gantly. You can both go now. I want to be alone."

Evelyn and Patrick were descending the stairs to the clinic lobby when they heard loud voices. Evelyn immediately recognized Vernon's voice, and she stopped. They had one curving set of steps to go before they would be seen. She and Patrick traded worried glances.

At a whisper, Eve said, "It's Vernon."

"We might as well face it," Patrick said.

When she and Patrick descended the last step, it was already plain to see what was going on. Three policemen stood by the lobby desk, one plainclothes and two uniformed.

Vernon spotted Evelyn, and his eyes expanded in triumph. He held up a piece of paper and started toward her. "This is for you," he said, thrusting the paper at her. "It's an injunction. You have thirty days to vacate this building, including furniture, equipment and patients. If you don't leave by then, you will be thrown out and all your property seized."

Eve slapped the paper away, looking beyond him, her face hard. "What are these policemen doing here?"

"Ah, yes. Well now, they are here, firstly, to witness that I have served you with this injunction and secondly, to arrest your lover, Patrick Gantly."

Patrick recognized the plainclothes policeman. He was the portly cop with the florid face and bowler hat Patrick had met at Gadfly's Speakeasy, Detective Sergeant Mike Borland.

It was Evelyn who aggressively nudged Vernon away and marched boldly to Detective Borland. He removed his hat when she approached.

"What are you arresting Mr. Gantly for?" she demanded.

Detective Borland turned his attention to Patrick, offering a smile of apology. "Hello there, Patrick. Wish our reunion could be under better circumstances."

Patrick nodded. "Detective Borland. It's good to see you again. What can I do for you?"

Borland's face turned grim and serious. He turned his attention to one of the uniformed cops and nodded. The cop left the clinic for the outside. While everyone waited in a tense silence, he soon returned with a young woman.

Louise McGuire entered the lobby reluctantly, with downcast eyes, a petulant mouth and slumping shoulders. She wore an expensive fur coat and hat, and a dazzling pair of diamond earrings that flashed under the lights.

Vernon looked on smugly, a gleam of victorious satisfaction in his eyes.

Detective Borland let out a heavy sigh. "Patrick, do you know this woman?"

Patrick smiled at Louise. He wasn't all that surprised to see her. "Hello, Louise. How are you?"

She refused to look at him or speak to him.

Elyse Douglas

"Do you know Louise McGuire, Patrick?"

"Yes, Detective Borland, I do."

Borland looked at Louise, his stare cold. "Louise, is this the man you say shot Frankie Fox?"

Louise's chin trembled. She shifted her weight from her right foot to her left, not answering.

"Miss McGuire, look at Patrick Gantly and tell me if he's the man you say shot and killed Frankie Fox."

Vernon took an anxious step forward. "Tell the detective, Louise."

Louise jerked erect, her flaming eyes fixed on Vernon. "Shut up, Vernon, okay? Just shut your mouth. You don't talk to me. You don't ever talk to me again!"

Borland's voice took on an edge. "Louise, for the last time, is Patrick Gantly, the man standing before you, the man you saw shoot and kill Frankie Fox?"

Evelyn swung her obstinate eyes to Patrick, to Louise, and then to Detective Borland. "This is wrong," she said. "This is a travesty. Of course Patrick didn't kill anyone."

Borland shouted at Louise and she flinched. "Now, Louise! Is that the man, Patrick Gantly, the man you saw murder Frankie Fox!?"

"Yes!" Louise shouted. "That's the man who killed Frankie Fox, okay?! Are you happy now?!"

She whirled and reached for the door handle. Patrick called after her and she stopped, her hand gripping the steel handle, ready to yank the door open.

"Louise... It's okay. I understand."

She turned to him, tears glistening in her eyes. "I bet you don't even have a mother, do you? I betcha she never went to church or sang in the choir, either. What a sucker I am for a good set of peepers, Sean," she said, using his alias.

Patrick held his smile, but said nothing.

When she was gone, Detective Borland moved toward Patrick. "Patrick Gantly, I arrest you for the murder of Frankie Fox."

Evelyn's eyes were hard. "He didn't do it. He didn't kill anyone."

"This is none of your affair, Evelyn," Vernon said, shaking the injunction. "This injunction is your affair. Now, I demand to see my daughter."

Evelyn stormed over to him. "You low, filthy coward," she said, forcing the words out between rigid teeth. "I will shoot you if you ever set foot in this clinic or in my apartment again. Do you hear me? Now get out!"

Vernon stepped back, startled by the force of her words and burning eyes. He stammered out. "Well... We'll just see about that... I mean..."

She cut him off, her face jammed in next to his. "Get out, Vernon, or so help me God, I'll kill you, right now!"

He staggered back, tried to recover some dignity, but failed. He went to the desk, slapping the injunction down, then raising a threatening finger. "I'll be back, Evelyn. I'll be back for Virginia. These policemen have heard your threats. They've heard you, so if anything happens to me, you'll go to prison for the rest of your life! Do you hear me? Everyone heard your threats. These are my witnesses."

Vernon pointed at Patrick. "Now arrest that man and let's get out of this crazy place, run by a crazy woman. I'll be back with a doctor's order, Evelyn. Don't you think I won't."

Vernon jerked around and exited.

The two uniformed cops lowered their heads as Patrick and Borland started for the door.

"I wish we could have a pint or two before you toss me into that box," Patrick said.

Detective Borland lifted his eyes and winked, lowering his voice. "Two is impossible, Patrick. But I think one can be arranged. We'll drink to the lasses."

After Patrick was handcuffed, standing by the door, Evelyn rushed over. "Patrick...," she said, her voice breaking with emotion. "Patrick, I'm so sorry."

Patrick smiled, reassuringly. "It's okay, Evelyn."

Patrick looked at Borland. "I'd say, Detective Borland, that Louise's father, Joe McGuire, has something to do with this. Am I right?"

"If I were a betting man, Patrick, I'd say you're as right as rain."

Evelyn looked at Detective Borland. "Where are you taking him?"

Borland tipped his bowler. "To the jail, at 240 Centre Street."

"I'll get help," Evelyn said. "Don't worry, Patrick, I'll get help."

Borland looked at her sympathetically. "He'll need that help, madam. McGuire has lots of high friends in high places, and his money pours easy, like a good old Irish ale."

CHAPTER 44

A s jails went, it wasn't the worst Patrick had ever seen or occupied. Detective Borland had arranged for Patrick to share a cell with a quiet, elderly man named Carlton, who'd been charged with killing his wife and son.

Carlton spoke little, spending most of his time reading or praying, sometimes until late into the night.

On Thanksgiving Day, Patrick and Carlton were escorted to the large, gray and yellow dining hall and given a meager turkey dinner, along with the other prisoners.

The gaunt, tall, and somber-faced warden read a "Prayer of Thanksgiving," and a white-haired minister with a small, trembling voice said a prayer.

The day after Thanksgiving, Evelyn visited him again, one of the many times she'd come by.

They met in a dark, gloomy, gray common room, with no windows, Patrick seated on one side of a glassed-in wall, with a small speaker hole, and Evelyn on the other.

He wore a gray-striped prison uniform and Evelyn wore black, with a conservative feather hat.

"How are you, Patrick? I wanted to come yesterday and bring you a real Thanksgiving Day dinner, but the authorities wouldn't allow it. I guess they thought I'd put a gun in the turkey or something silly like that."

"Not to worry. I had a proper turkey dinner, complete with runny cranberry sauce, overcooked stuffing and dry turkey. But the company was wonderful. Quite uplifting," he said, with a wry grin.

Evelyn's mouth sagged. "I don't know how you can find any humor at a time like this, Patrick."

"It's the old detective in me. Cops have to find humor where they can, or they'll do themselves in. Anyway, did you hear anything from Lavinia Vanderbilt? Is there any way she can help me?"

Evelyn sighed heavily and looked down. "I've tried twice."

"It doesn't sound promising."

"She said she was sorry, but her husband won't hear of it. He told her, in no uncertain words, that he will not allow the name of Vanderbilt to be, and I quote, 'soiled around in the newspapers by the low and unseemly rabble of society.'"

Patrick nodded. "He certainly doesn't mince words. I admire him for that."

"I have hired a lawyer for you, Patrick. He was recommended by a doctor at the clinic."

"I'll cover his fee," Patrick said, knowing he still had some cash from the second ring he'd hocked. "I hope he's good. From what Detective Borland told me, Joe McGuire has stacked a solid case against me."

"But Louise is his daughter, Patrick, and she's lying. And you said they don't have the gun that you supposedly shot that man with. They have no real proof."

"They have an eyewitness, and Joe McGuire is a brutal man. Detective Borland stopped by the other day and told me he'd heard rumors that McGuire beat his daughter up pretty bad, when she told him she wouldn't finger me in court."

Evelyn shook her head in despair. "These men are monsters."

"They are that, no doubt. So I will need the best attorney we can find, and then a miracle or two; maybe even the intervening magic of a leprechaun."

"I'm so sorry I got you into this, Patrick."

"Stop it, Evelyn. I got myself into it and, one way or the other, I'll get myself out."

She looked at him firmly, troubled. "And what if you can't get yourself out? Then what?"

"Then I'll either hang for Frankie Fox's murder or be sent to prison for twenty or thirty years."

Evelyn hung her head. "I can't bear this, Patrick. I just don't know what to do."

When she lifted her eyes, they were damp with tears.

"Don't cry. I'll think of something," Patrick said. "So how is the clinic? What's the latest?"

Evelyn blotted her eyes with a handkerchief. "Lavinia was able to help with that. One of her lawyers interceded and stopped the injunction."

Patrick lit up. "That's the best of news, Evelyn. The very best. Thank God for that good woman. And will she help fund it?"

"Yes... Yes, and she is arranging to meet with her friends and solicit their help as well."

Patrick grinned broadly and clapped his hands together. "All that is good, then. A good and happy day it is."

She tried to smile but failed. "I can't be truly happy until you're out of this place, Patrick."

"All in good time. God and Patrick can sometimes work together in mysterious ways."

"I didn't know you were a religious man."

"Evelyn, I've concluded that most men find religion under three conditions: when going into a shootout, when facing a hangman's knot, and the day a lovely daughter is born. When my dear Colleen was born, I was a sad man for a time because my wife passed during the birth. But in time, thanks to... thanks to Eve Kennedy, I found my way. I asked the Good Father to watch over Colleen and to keep her safe always. I'm still holding the Big Man to that."

Evelyn gazed at him, trying to understand. But in that moment, she didn't understand anything: why Patrick had come into her life, and why things had turned out so badly.

A squat, beefy prison guard with a blunted nose stepped over and grunted. "Time's up, madam. Say your goodbyes now, please."

Evelyn flattened her hand against the glass, and Patrick lifted his; through the glass partition, they touched.

"I'll be back tomorrow," Evelyn said.

Patrick rose and watched her leave, and she glanced back over her shoulder with a final wave.

As he turned to leave the room and return to his cell, a prison guard on his end of the glass partition entered the room.

"Sit down, Gantly. You have another visitor."

Patrick said, "On this side of the glass?"

"Yes, that's right, and if there's any funny stuff, I'll pump you full of lead. Got it?"

Patrick nodded.

The guard stood by, his muscled arms crossed as the door opened. A stomach-heavy, medium-built man entered, with a cigar poking from his surly mouth. He was in his late 40s or early 50s, dressed in a brown tweed suit with a white shirt and tight vest; an orange bowtie seemed comical, and a plug hat was pushed back off his forehead. He pulled the cigar from his mouth, and his smile was a slice of fierce confidence.

"Patrick Gantly, I presume?"

Patrick considered the man, quickly sizing him up. He'd seen this type back in the 1880s when he was a New York City detective. Prowling predators had swarmed what was called the Tenderloin District, which ran from 24th Street to 42nd Street and from Fifth Avenue to Seventh Avenue. It was an area packed with smelly saloons, brothels, gambling parlors, dance halls, and clip joints. Shysters roamed freely, and they were everywhere. Every cop knew the neighborhood well, and they knew the cutthroats, the prostitutes and the grifters.

The man coming toward Patrick would have been right at home on that street. Patrick studied him. This was a dangerous, false, affable man, with the dancing, crafty eyes of a card shark or snake oil salesman. He'd delight in the easy con, and the intimidation with hard fists. His type was addicted to the adrenaline rush of violence and creative lies. They lived for the buck-pocketing swindle, and the easy payoff to the corrupt City's power players, who always had a ready hand extended, anxious for a stack of new, dirty greenbacks.

Patrick was certain he was staring into the cool, predatory eyes of Joe McGuire, Louise McGuire's father, and the man who'd set him up for the murder of Frankie Fox.

The guard picked up a chair, brought it toward Joe and set it down.

Joe held Patrick in his stare for a moment, obviously sizing him up as well.

Joe waved for another chair. "Bring another, Guard," Joe said, in a commanding voice.

The guard did so, placing the chair so that it faced Joe McGuire's.

"Sit down, Mr. Gantly, and relax. I want us to talk."

Patrick did so.

McGuire backed into his chair and scooted it closer to Patrick, the chair legs scraping across the gray tiled floor. While he kept his eyes on Patrick, he rolled his head around, cracking his neck.

McGuire puffed the cigar for a time, then withdrew it, finally ready for business. "I'm Joe McGuire, Mr. Gantly."

Patrick nodded.

"Patrick Gantly... Well, now, that's a good old Italian name, isn't it?" McGuire said, grinning at his own joke.

Patrick stayed silent.

Joe continued. "McGuire and Gantly. It has a nice ring to it, don't you think?"

Patrick sat still, not blinking, not responding. He wanted this man to reveal himself through his expressions and words.

McGuire's voice was low and raspy. "I don't have an accent, as you can hear," he continued. "My mother was from good old Massachusetts American stock. My father was the son of an Irish priest, if you can believe it. But old Daddy was no priest. He was a butcher and a brawler. He worked his way out of those filthy tenements and got himself into a good position with the Tammany Hall bunch. He knew Boss Tweed, and they were good pals. Yes, sir. They were good men for their day. Before your time, of course, Patrick. Did you know my old Daddy died in the same jail where Boss Tweed died? Yes, he did. Different year, of course. Old Daddy was in his seventies when he met his maker, right after the First World War. The Spanish Flu got him. Yes, indeed, the Ludlow Street Jail was the City's Federal prison in Boss Tweed's days, and it's still around, located over on Ludlow and Broome Streets. Have you seen it, Patrick?"

"No, I haven't had the pleasure," Patrick said.

"I understand that Detective Borland found you a nice living space here. I think that's fine. Yes, a fine thing."

Patrick decided to be direct. "Why are you here, McGuire?"

McGuire cut him a glance. "You're a good-sized man, Patrick, and I suspect you can take care of yourself in a fight."

McGuire sat back, his stomach straining at the buttons on his vest. "I've got to tell you, Patrick, that Sam Keller was the best fighter I ever knew. I never, not once in our years working together, knew him to lose a fight, fair or otherwise. No, sir, he never lost. Hell, I was even scared of him. That's why I hired him, and he was my best man."

McGuire stuck the cigar back into his mouth and laced his fingers across his ample stomach.

"Tell me, Patrick. How did you take him? It's been eating away at me."

"Can I ask you a question first?" Patrick asked.

McGuire nodded. "Of course. Ask away. Anything. Anything at all."

"Who really killed Frankie Fox?"

McGuire jerked the cigar from his mouth and laughed. "Frankie Fox, Patrick? Who indeed?"

McGuire pointed the tip of his cigar at Patrick. "Do you know what that gassing saxophone player once told me? He said he moved to New York from some dirt water town down south, because he was a no-good bum, and New York was a grand and a great city. He moved here because he hoped some of the greatness of New York would rub off on him. That's what he told me."

"I guess he was wrong," Patrick said.

"Nah, Patrick, the city is grand and great for the bold and the takers, but it ain't so great for no-good saxophone bums who shove morphine, opium, and cocaine down my dumb flapper of a daughter's throat. Hell, Frankie had a direct line to the stuff from some drummer who hailed from New Orleans. There ain't much in the newspapers about this kind of thing, Patrick, but I've got my eyes wide open and my big ears to the ground. Nobody takes old Joe McGuire for a damned fool, when his daughter is being doped up and bedded down by a no-good loser of a bum. Nobody."

Patrick lowered his eyes. He had his answer. Either Joe killed Frankie himself, or he had one of his men do it.

McGuire's eyes flared with sudden rage, his voice a growl. "Frankie Fox thought I was just another dumb-shit bootlegging fool, Patrick. Meanwhile, my scrambled-brained daughter was so hopped up on juice and dope she didn't know who she was, or who she was bedding down with. Hell, the whole female generation is like that today. They've gone cold-crazy wild since the war. They got that damned right to vote, and they got the Model T Ford to drive, and the next thing you know, they go hog wild with those shiny dresses and jerky music, kicking up their legs and rouging their knees like harlots in heat. With all the do-dads and whatnots of today, what the hell is a father to do, Patrick? I ask you. What's a father to do?"

McGuire stuffed the cigar back into his mouth and shook his head. "And look at Vernon Scott's daughter, Virginia. She wants to be Clara Bow, but all she is, is a brat with good tits, hot eyes and a body that loves to sin. Hell, the best thing that ever happened to the girl was Sam Keller. Yes, that's right, Sam Keller kept her in line. Whenever she went into heat, like a cat on the prowl, he took her down a notch or two. Yes, sir, and that's just what she needed."

And then McGuire's eyes changed. He frowned with displeasure. "And then *you* came along, Patrick, and rubbed out good old Sam Keller. Now that I have answered your question, you can answer mine. How did you take him?"

The silence lengthened.

Patrick folded his hands and looked at them. "Sam Keller was quick and clever, no doubt. I was able to fight him off all right, but he pulled a pistol on me. I was flatfooted, nowhere to go. If that train hadn't lurched and entered a tunnel, I wouldn't be here. It was a blind punch in the face, in the dark, that got him."

McGuire shook his head, grinning, enjoying himself. "Well, ain't that something? And ain't that just the way it happens sometimes, Patrick? A blind punch in the dark."

And then there was a swift change of mood as McGuire was suddenly all business. "Patrick, I need a good man to replace Sam. I know you're the man for it."

Patrick opened his mouth to speak, but McGuire threw up a hand like a stop sign. "Hear me out first. I run a good, profitable operation. We pay off the cops, the mayor and the judges, and everybody is happy. You'll oversee my East Coast operation, from Maine to Rochester, including all of Massachusetts and New York City. And we're growing. I'll pay you well, furnish you with a car and all the booze and girlies you could want. Now, I know you've gone sweet on Vernon's wife, and that's okay with me, but you may get tired of her. I'll treat you right, Patrick. If you're loyal to me, I'll be twice as loyal to you. Now, what do you say?"

Patrick ran a hand through his hair and down his face. He hadn't seen it coming. Maybe he should have, but he didn't. He was trapped, and Joe knew it.

"And if I say, no?"

"Then you're a fool, and you'll hang for Frankie Fox's death. Hell, I'll see to it myself, and I pay the judge who'll be trying your case. Don't forget, Patrick, we have an eyewitness, and I guarantee she'll dazzle the jury when she's put on that witness stand. Louise will cry, and rage, and point her pretty little finger right at you. Now, I don't think you're stupid, Patrick. I don't see it in you. I think you're a smart, reasonable and practical man. I'll only ask once, and you must answer now. Right now, or the offer is gone... forever."

Patrick felt the cold swell in him.

"Oh, and your bail is on the high side. Vernon Scott himself saw to that. I also heard that Mrs. Evelyn Scott's attempts at dragging the Vanderbilt money into your defense didn't go so well."

Patrick gave him a long, considering look.

McGuire took a puff on his cigar and blew the smoke toward the ceiling. The lethal edge in his voice said more than the words. "So, Patrick, what's it going to be? It's last call."

CHAPTER 45

Patrick spent the next week in his cell or working in the laundry room. He often thought about Evelyn, hoping for the best for her and Virginia, hoping that mother and daughter would be able to mend their relationship. But most of the time, he thought about Eve and Colleen. He yearned for his life with them in the twenty-first century. Here, he had no anchor in his life. He was a confused, time-travel wanderer, left to the whims of fate and that whimsical time travel lantern.

Sometimes he remembered his first friend in 1925, Sarah Finn. The nights had grown windy, snowy, and cold, and he was sure that, by now, the old woman had died. No doubt, she'd been found lying dead on her favorite park bench by some passerby, her poor and punished body tossed into a pine box and buried in a pauper's grave.

The nights crowded in on him and the days were a blur. His roommate, Carlton, wept many days and prayed many nights, and he never found comfort in either. He wouldn't speak to Patrick except to repeat, in a low, hollow voice, "I don't believe hell is a hot place. No... I believe it is a cold and lonely place, and so very far away from the warm rays of the sun. Lost souls like me will not be burned, nay, I will be a frozen thing, like cold, hard granite, cursed for all time by every living thing. God forgive me for my sins."

Patrick had tried to comfort the man several times, but Carlton wouldn't hear of it. "Save yourself, my lost cellmate. Save yourself and pray that you will not be cast out into a timeless, cold abyss for all eternity."

On Monday, December 7, a sober-face guard marched up to Patrick's cell.

"Pack your things, Gantly, and hurry."

Ten minutes later, Patrick was escorted from his cell through a series of long, winding hallways, into a wood-paneled reception room, warmly lit by amber light and furnished with a wooden bench and chairs.

The guard left Patrick alone in the windowless room, still clutching his tattered suitcase. Minutes later, the far door opened and Patrick was astonished to see a tall, dignified, gray-haired man enter the room, sporting a gold-headed ebony cane. He wore a fine cashmere winter coat and a burgundy scarf, and he was holding a black fedora at his side.

Patrick would have known the man anywhere, from his upright carriage to his tight, determined mouth and steely, focused eyes.

"Well, if it isn't Darius Compton Foster," Patrick said with surprise.

Darius did not make a move to close the distance between them, nor to offer Patrick his hand in a friendly shake.

Darius stood stiffly, frowning. "And there you are, Mr. Gantly, having not aged at all since last I saw you. I, in turn, have become an old man."

Darius sighed through his nose. "Frankly, Mr. Gantly, it was a disagreeable surprise when I learned of your presence here. I truly believed, no, that is not accurate. I truly wished and hoped that I would never see you or Eve Kennedy again."

Patrick nodded, disappointed in Darius' words. "Yes, Darius, I have no doubt about that. By the way, I received the same warm greeting from your son, William, who seems much like you."

Darius took some offense, pursing his lips. "William and I are not so much alike. He worships the God of money, and all the false respect and dubious friends that money seems to offer. I, on the other hand, would..." he stopped, searching for the right words. "I am a doctor, a healer, and I..."

Patrick cut in. "And you, Darius, are a good man, who has come to my aid, and I appreciate it. Or am I misreading all this?"

Darius avoided Patrick's eyes. "My wife and my daughter have pestered me and they have bullied me. Quite honestly, I resisted as long as my conscience would allow."

"Am I free to go, then?" Patrick asked.

"Yes. I have posted your bail."

"Then I thank you, Darius. I've heard it was quite inflated."

"It was that, all right. How you manage to get into mischief so swiftly and so thoroughly, and with the lowest ruffians of society, is beyond my meager imagination. I just hope and pray my name is not dragged through the mud. I could lose all of my best patients."

"If it's of any consequence, Darius, I didn't want to come here to 1925, and I wish I'd never heard of, or ever seen, that damn lantern. Nonetheless, here I am, and I thank you for your help. I will pay you back."

"The only compensation I seek from you is for you to return to… well, to wherever you came from, and I don't want to know where that is."

Darius glanced about. "Now, let us leave this disreputable place immediately. God forbid that I ever have to return to this back-end of Hades."

They sat in the plush leather backseat of Darius' 1924 midnight blue Cadillac Town sedan, driven by a chauffeur in a dark cap, black suit and tie. They moved through light morning traffic, bumping over trolley tracks and edging around pedestrians and push carts.

"I understand from Joan that you have been seeing a married woman?" Darius asked, with obvious scorn.

"Is that all Joni told you?"

"Unfortunately not."

"Did she explain who the married woman is, and who she favors?"

"Again, unfortunately, yes."

"Did she also tell you that Evelyn has been seeking a divorce for some time, and that her husband walked out on her, taking their only daughter? Did Joni tell you that?"

"I am not the judge nor the jury of the world, Mr. Gantly."

"Oh, for God's sake, Darius, call me Patrick. Have you met Evelyn Stratford? Have you seen her?"

"No, and I don't plan to. I am not about to fall into some fantasy world of pixies, fairies and magic. Next, Joan will be trying to drag me off to a seance. I tell you, I won't have any of it. It's balderdash, and I won't be a part of it. I don't care if this Evelyn Stratford looks like the Queen of England or Nellie Bly. I won't be any further part of this ridiculous escapade. Joan gets herself all worked up, and then it takes days for me to calm her down. It is finished, I tell you. Take the damn lantern and sail off to some other time, where I am either unborn or dead."

Patrick let that settle. "All right, Darius. I won't trouble you any further, but I do thank you for your help."

Darius didn't respond. "Where shall I drop you?"

Back in his own apartment, Patrick stripped off his clothes, drew a bath and climbed into his clawfoot bathtub. The water was warm and comforting. He sank further into the tub, resting his long legs on the opposite rim and closing his eyes. As his muscles relaxed, he allowed the smells, the sights, the sounds and the grim reality of that jail to drain out of him.

Even though he was out on bail, he knew his ordeal wasn't over. Joe McGuire surely knew he was out. Would he send men to kill him, as he had with Frankie Fox? And what about Vernon?

During her last visit, the day before, Evelyn had told him that Virginia was once again living with her, refusing to speak to her father on the phone. Not only had he threatened to take Virginia and send her to a high-class reform school, but he had also threatened Evelyn.

"I have two doctors' signatures, confirming that you are mentally unstable and an unfit mother," he'd said.

"A third doctor is reviewing the case now. You have only a few days before I come by and take Virginia away from you."

Patrick pushed the noise and static from his mind and began to focus on his wife, Eve. He played back memories of them cooking together, sledding together, arguing over what movies to watch and which pizza shop had the best pizza in the neighborhood.

He saw them strolling through Central Park with Colleen and Colin on a warm summer day, Patrick clutching a wicker picnic basket packed with sandwiches, cheese, potato salad, chips and a bottle of white wine.

Seated on the red and white checkered blanket, Patrick sampled the wine, and then Eve's waiting lips. Eve held Colleen up, kissed her on the nose and told her frog jokes, even though Colleen didn't understand. Sometimes she laughed, especially if Eve wrinkled up her nose and made a funny face.

"Colleen, what do frogs drink on a hot summer day?" Eve looked at him. "Do you know, Patrick?"

"Nope."

"Ice cold croak-a-cola."

He winced in pain. "That one hurt."

"Okay, see if you can guess this one, Colleen… and Patrick. What do frogs do with paper?"

Patrick shook his head. Colleen fussed as a fly buzzed her head.

"They rip-it!" Eve said, laughing as if it were the funniest joke in the world.

Patrick smiled as he settled deeply into the tub, his thoughts melting away, the stress of the last few weeks fading. He thought to himself, *How close you are and yet how utterly far away you seem, Eve.*

Moments later, he was sound asleep.

CHAPTER 46

At the curb in front of Evelyn's apartment building, Patrick stepped out of the cab and held the door while she climbed in. He slid in next to her and closed the door. They had agreed to take a cab to Central Park for an evening walk. Patrick wanted to search for Sarah Finn, or at least try to find out what had happened to her.

Once they were underway, Evelyn turned to him. "This afternoon, I put Virginia on a train to Vermont to stay with my sister, Edna, for a while."

"Does your husband know where your sister lives?" Patrick asked.

"He knows she lives in Vermont, but he doesn't know where. My sister hates Vernon, and he's scared of her. Edna is the black sheep of the family, and she likes it that way. Her husband works for the railroad and is gone most of the time. She keeps two mean dogs and a shotgun handy at all times."

"Does Virginia get along with her?"

"Surprisingly, yes. It was Virginia's idea to go. She and Edna have always had an easy relationship, the only easy one Virginia has ever had."

They left the taxi at 72nd Street and Fifth Avenue and entered Central Park, strolling a meandering path, just as the sun sank below gray and purple clouds. The amber park lights glowed as night settled in, and the Park was quiet.

"Are you cold?" Patrick asked.

"No, the night air feels good. It's been so long since I've walked in the Park at night. It's good to get away from the clinic and my apartment. I know that Vernon or the police are going to show up sooner or later."

"But the clinic is safe now," Patrick said. "Lavinia Vanderbilt is on your side."

"Yes, that's true, but I've heard through various sources that Vernon is losing some of his wealthy clients, and I believe Lavinia is behind it. She's a much stronger woman than I first believed, and I learned that she worked tirelessly for the woman's suffrage movement both before and after she was married, to her husband's dismay."

Patrick looked at her. "We both know Vernon will want revenge."

"Yes. His good name, if you can call it that, is under siege, and when he's backed into a corner, he'll fight."

She gave Patrick a worried glance. "I'm afraid for you, Patrick. I'm afraid that he or that horrible man, Joe McGuire, will come after you."

"Yes, well, I've been looking over my shoulder for the last couple of days and my neck's getting sore."

Evelyn linked her arm into his. "Oh, Patrick, I wish all this nasty, awful business would go away. I wish we could go off someplace where nobody would ever find us, and we could spend time getting to know each other. Why has our timing been so bad?"

"I don't know… In my life of late, time and timing have been a curse."

"Is there a trial date yet?"

"Yes, Monday, January 11."

"Can you beat this thing, Patrick? Is there any way you can prove you weren't the killer?"

"Only if I can somehow get to Louise McGuire. She's the key to the whole thing. From what I've heard, her father has hidden her away, and my detective friend, Mike Borland, has been trying to find her. If he does, I think I might be able to convince her to make a statement and drop the accusation. Of course, then I'll have to help her leave town to get away from her father."

"What will you do if they can't find her?"

Patrick shrugged. "Go to my backup plan."

"And what is that… your backup plan?"

"I'm working on it. I don't have it yet."

They strolled for a time in silence before Evelyn spoke. "I don't want you to leave, Patrick, but if you have to, I'll understand. If all this time travel business is true, then maybe you should… I don't know, use that lantern and go."

Patrick stopped, facing her. "It's an awful risk, Evelyn. I could lose Eve and Colleen, *and* you, don't you see? I may end up trapped in yet another time. There's no way to know what that time lantern will do. Do you understand?"

She shook her head, despondent. "No, Patrick, I don't see, or maybe I don't want to see."

They walked again, lost in thought.

"It's quiet tonight," Evelyn said. "There's no one around. Maybe we should leave the park."

Patrick stopped again, taking her by the elbow. "We could leave together, Evelyn. I mean, leave the country."

Evelyn brightened. "Where would we go?"

"I don't know. South America. Maybe England or Ireland."

Evelyn had hope in her eyes. "Yes, Patrick. Why don't we? Why not?"

They locked eyes, thinking, speculating. Slowly, Evelyn lowered her eyes.

"What's the matter?" Patrick asked.

"I can't leave Virginia."

"We could take her with us."

"No… It wouldn't work. Virginia is… erratic. She needs stability… and she's going to stay with Edna until she has the baby. I've got to be here for her."

Patrick pocketed his hands. "I wish that life and love were not so untidy, Evelyn."

At that moment, they both heard someone advance toward them. It was the silhouette of a man wearing a long greatcoat and a fedora, with the brim pulled down over his forehead.

Patrick felt the threat and turned, but it was too late. By the time he reached for his revolver, Vernon lifted his head, a pistol pointed at Patrick's chest.

"Don't reach for it, Gantly!" Vernon snapped.

Shock stole Evelyn's breath. "Vernon!"

"That's right, dear wife of mine. It's Vernon." He motioned with the barrel of his pistol. "Both of you move over there, off the path and away from the light."

Patrick took Evelyn's arm, and they moved from a pool of amber light into the shadows, away from the path, stepping down to a secluded, low grove of trees.

Vernon faced them, a dim light from the park lamp lighting their faces.

Vernon stared at Evelyn with soulless eyes. "I followed you from your apartment, Evelyn. I had a car waiting. I knew lover boy would come around."

"What do you want, Vernon?" Evelyn said, her voice trembling.

"Want?" he said, barking out a laugh. "It's too late for that, unfaithful wife of mine. It's way too late for that. I've lost half my clients already, and now that my name's showing up in the newspapers, I'll lose the other half next week."

Evelyn sought to appease him. "You can get new clients, Vernon."

"No, Evelyn, I'm finished here. I'll have to move, maybe to Chicago or California, where I can start again. It won't be easy, but I'll survive. I always survive."

"Your fight is with me, Vernon. Let Patrick go," Evelyn said. "He's done nothing to you."

Vernon laughed again. "He's done nothing? Really?"

Vernon directed his hard eyes on Patrick. "Tell me this, big man, where did you come from? You seem to have just dropped out of thin air. Yeah, tell me that."

"From here and there," Patrick said, softly, measuring distances and a possible attack.

"I had a good life until you showed up. Yeah, I had everything I could want or need. And then you crashed in and ruined everything. Speaking of which."

He returned his gaze to Evelyn. "Where is Virginia? What did you do with her?"

Evelyn lifted a defiant chin, although inside, she was scared to death. "I sent her away to have her baby."

Vernon was surprised by that. "Baby?"

"Yes, Vernon. Virginia is pregnant, and please don't ask me who the father is."

Vernon processed the information, then tightened his grip on the gun. "Oh, don't tell me. You sent her to live with that crazy, violent sister of yours, didn't you? What's her name?"

"Edna."

"Yes, Edna. Well, good riddance to Virginia and good riddance to you, Evelyn. I'm sick of you both and I'm sick of this Patrick Gantly."

"Vernon, stop this and let us go," Evelyn said.

"Let you go? Oh, no. You'll both be found here sometime tomorrow morning, I would guess. By then you'll be long, cold dead."

"You'll be a suspect," Patrick said. "You're taking a big risk."

"Not so big. I've still got some friends around town. Don't you worry about me. They'll swear I was playing poker with them until the very early hours. And anyway, Patrick Gantly, I'm doing you a big favor. You'd lose that trial, you know. There's no doubt about it, and you'd hang for killing Frankie Fox. It's all been fixed. So you can thank me for killing you here and now and saving you a long, tedious agony of a trial."

"Let Evelyn go, Vernon," Patrick said. "She's the mother of your child, for God's sake, and she's still your wife."

He laughed darkly. "Both my daughter and my wife are nothing more than common harlots. They'll both get what they deserve. And let me tell you something. Shooting you both is going to be one of the highlights of my life. Now, if you have any prayers to say, say them now, because I'm finished talking."

Patrick surmised that his only hope was to rush Vernon, take a shot or two in the chest and hope he had the strength to break Vernon's neck before he killed Evelyn.

"Goodbye, Evelyn," Vernon said, aiming the pistol at her. "We had more good times than bad, but everything has to end, doesn't it?"

Patrick was ready to spring forward, every muscle taut, his heart slamming into his chest.

In an instant, everything changed. Vernon's back arched. His face bulged with shock. His pistol arm jerked up, and he fired high, a loud POP. Evelyn screamed. Patrick darted in front of her, to protect her.

With wild eyes, his face upturned, Vernon squeezed off another shot, aimed wildly into the far trees. The pistol crack shattered the night, echoing in the silence.

Patrick stepped forward, confused. What had happened?

Then Vernon staggered, recovered, and turned on unsteady legs. He leveled his gun at something in the dark and fired a single shot. Evelyn shrieked. Patrick was set to attack, then stopped, watchful.

With his back to Patrick, Vernon stumbled, dropped his gun and fell to his knees. He slumped, coughed, then crumpled face down, arms splayed.

Patrick rushed forward with Evelyn behind. When she saw it, she gasped. The light from a lamp on the path above illumined it. The handle of a knife jutted from Vernon's back.

Patrick kicked Vernon's pistol away, frantically searching the darkness. He saw a gray figure sprawled on the ground, a few feet away. He hurried over and dropped to a knee.

Sarah Finn lay on her back, gasping for breath. In the faint light, Patrick saw her wincing with pain.

"Sarah... What in the hell did you do?"

She strained to speak. "I got him with my knife... The bastard shot me..."

Patrick searched for the wound and found the bullet hole near her heart. "We've got to get you to a hospital, Sarah."

"Nah... Too late for that now."

Patrick glanced around. "Take it easy, Sarah. Just take it easy."

Evelyn drew up. "Vernon's dead."

"We've got to get Sarah out of here and to a hospital."

With a weak hand, Sarah touched Patrick's sleeve. "No hospital. No... please."

"I'm not going to let you die, Sarah. I'll go get some help. Just hang on."

Patrick made a move to leave, but she reached for him, coughing, her breath staggered. "Don't leave me... Please, don't leave me alone to die like an old dog. Stay... stay with me till I'm gone."

Patrick stroked her old, wrinkled cheek, cold to the touch, finally yielding to the grim reality. "All right, Sarah. All right. I'll stay."

Sarah's voice turned raspy as her breathing became labored. "Do you think the good Lord will know me... Buster Boy?" she said weakly, her chest heaving.

"Just take it easy." Patrick looked up. "Evelyn, go get some help."

Sarah coughed. "Help? Nah... this old woman is done for. You know it, and I know it. Just stay with old Sarah. Grant this doomed woman her last wish."

Patrick glanced about, helpless.

Sarah's pleading eyes looked into his. "Did I help you? Did I? He was going to plug you, Buster Boy, the bastard. Did I help?"

"Yes, Sarah. You saved my life. Thank you for saving our lives."

Her smile was faint, her voice small. "Good... I thought..." She struggled to get the words out. "... It was the least I could do for my old park bench mate..."

She managed a wink. "Hey... Do you think the Lord will have a little drink of the Irish with me... Buster... Boy?"

"Yes, Sarah, I believe he will. He'll make an exception for you. Just one, though. Don't push your luck with the Big Man."

Her grin was strained, her eyes glassy. "Okay... Then maybe he'll forgive this old woman... for all the things..." Her voice trailed off.

"There's nothing to forgive," Patrick said. "Now don't talk so much. Rest."

She tried to smile. "Okay... Patrick. See, I know your name. I knowed it all along, Buster..." and her voice stopped. She swallowed, then tried again. "I'm going to Beulah Land now, to see my boy... Yes... It's... not so..."

Her breath caught and her eyes went vacant. She sank back, and the life drained from her. Patrick held her head up, caressing her old, weathered head. In a voice choked

369

with emotion, he said, "Okay, Sarah... Okay, good woman. You go see your boy now. You rest now. Just rest."

Evelyn laid a gentle hand on Patrick's shoulder. "We've got to go."

"I can't just leave her like this. She saved our lives."

"You have to, Patrick. She'd want you to. She's gone now. If you're found here with Vernon, they'll put you back in jail and you'll never get out. Please, Patrick. Let's go."

Patrick gently kissed Sarah on the forehead and laid her back gently into the grass. "Goodbye, Sarah Finn. The saints be with you."

CHAPTER 47

At 8:20 p.m., Patrick and Evelyn sat in the back seat of a taxi, parked in front of Mr. and Mrs. Foster's stately Gramercy Park brownstone.

The driver waited patiently, the engine purring, tiny flakes of snow dancing by the windows, beginning to dust the ground. While he smoked a cigarette, he avoided glancing into his rearview mirror, trying to appear uninterested. Christmas wreaths, some with lavish red bows and shiny holly berries, adorned several front doors, reminding the world that the Christmas season had begun.

Patrick held his face in his hands. Evelyn stared ahead, seeing the snow and the Christmas wreaths as a distraction. She thought it would have been more appropriate if black bunting had been draped in the trees and hung from the windows. Vernon was dead. Virginia was gone, and Eve was painfully aware that Patrick would soon be leaving her forever. He had no other choice.

"How long has it been snowing?" she said, feeling floaty and detached, speaking to herself, as if she were already alone.

Patrick lowered his hands and watched the gliding snow for a time before he turned to Evelyn. "I should go in. There isn't much time. Let's get out," Patrick said, with a head nod, indicating toward the driver.

They did so, with Patrick exiting first, then holding the door as she stepped out. They strolled away from the car, then stopped, standing face to face, as snow floated down in utter silence. The brittle, hanging moment possessed a timeless quality, and neither stirred nor spoke, longing to prolong it, preserve it.

A newly arisen wind kicked up, whistling through the trees, and agitating the snow. The timelessness melted away, replaced by a second burst of wind, and a terrible air of inevitability.

Evelyn's voice was reflective and resigned. "I keep wondering, how did my life come to this? After we were married, Vernon and I were happy for a time. I could have never imagined him as he was tonight. I thought I knew him. How did it turn out this way? What happened to him?"

Patrick could find no words of comfort. "It's easy… It happens little by little. Finally, money and power get you by the throat and you say 'yes' too many times, when you should say 'no.'"

She looked at him, exploring his mouth, his eyes, his hair. "I can't watch you go, Patrick. I can't watch whatever it is that you're going to do with that lantern. I don't believe it, and I can't bear it."

"I understand, Eve."

"Will I ever see you again?"

He looked directly into her eyes, his filled with a heavy sadness. "No, Evelyn. No, I don't think so."

"Then I don't understand. Where will you go? How does it work? How can it work? It makes no sense. Nothing makes any sense anymore. The world has just gone crazy."

Patrick took her gloved hands and said, "Look at me. We know each other and we love each other. I don't know anything beyond that. Maybe we are soulmates after all."

"Soulmates?"

"Yes, as my wife once said, maybe we are one soul, split apart for a time. But we always find ourselves back together again, in any era, in any time, and throughout all time, connected by some invisible thread. And if that sounds like some ridiculous fantasy, then so be it. I have no other explanation."

He leaned, kissing her softly on the lips. "Evelyn... Eve, I have loved you and I will always love you."

She touched his cheek. "And I love you, Patrick."

"Go now... Get home as fast as you can. Like we discussed, if the police come by asking about Vernon, tell them you were in your apartment all night."

"What do I tell them when they come looking for you?"

"Tell them I skipped town, off to South America."

With an agonized look, Eve turned and started for the taxi.

Patrick watched the cab drive away. Evelyn didn't turn to wave goodbye, and he wished she had. As snowflakes lighted on his shoulders, he felt like the loneliest man in the universe.

Five minutes later, Patrick stood inside the Fosters' foyer, waiting humbly as the young and nervous night maid hurried up the carpeted stairs to Joni's bedroom.

Minutes later, Joni appeared, hair piled on top of her head and pinned, wearing a velvet burgundy housecoat and matching slippers. She was all whispers and hand-patting as she led Patrick into the front parlor and asked her maid to bring fresh coffee.

They sat on a sofa near a comfortable fire, staring, each keenly aware of why Patrick had come.

He told her what had happened and Joni listened quietly, her face drooping when he was finished.

"What a story. I'll get in touch with Evelyn, Patrick. When you're gone, I'll make sure she's not alone."

Patrick looked toward the stairs. "Is Darius asleep?"

"Not yet. He wouldn't come down. I'm sorry. He's washed his hands of the whole thing. Between you and me, sometimes I wish I hadn't married that man. Sometimes I wish I'd gone back home with you and Eve."

"You can't blame him, Joni. He loves you and he's scared to death of that lantern."

Joni's face softened. "Yeah, I know, and dammit, I love him too, the old pain in the ass."

After the tray of coffee and cookies was delivered, the maid hurried away into a side room.

Patrick sipped the coffee, grateful for its warmth. "Joni, I'm glad you're going to stay in touch with Evelyn. She's been through hell."

"She is so much like Eve that it scares me. She could be her twin sister or doppelganger. In a weird sort of way, it will be like having Eve back. I hope we can become good friends."

Patrick stared down at the coffee. "I wish we could have had more time together, Joni. Thank you for cutting your vacation short and coming back."

"Don't thank me for that. It's been so wonderful seeing you again."

Patrick raised his hopeful eyes. "You do have the lantern, don't you?"

"Yes, I have it. It's here, in the house."

Patrick's eyes widened. "Here?"

"Yes. I got it yesterday from the vault where I've kept it all these years. I've got to tell you, Patrick, this morning when I woke up and looked at the thing, for a few tempting seconds I had the urge to light it. Isn't that wild? I suddenly missed my life in the twenty-first century. There are so many good things about that time. And I longed to see Eve again and have our old life back. God, how I fought with myself not to light that freaking lantern. And then I knew why Darius hated you for coming back. He knew I'd be tempted all over again. Sometimes I think he knows me better than I know myself."

"You would miss it here, Joni, your family, your husband."

She gave him a sheepish smile. "Patrick... I've lived my life here. I've raised my kids and I've loved my husband."

"Joni, time travel won't make you young again."

Joni leaned in toward him. "How do you know? It might. It could."

"Well, I don't know for sure, but it's never worked that way before."

Joni reached for her coffee cup and took a careful sip, blowing off some of the steam. "I won't go, of course. I mean, I didn't light the lantern, did I?"

Patrick steadied his eyes on her. "I don't know what's going to happen to me when I light that thing."

"No, Patrick. There are no guarantees in life, and there are certainly no guarantees with that lantern. Even Tesla told you that."

Patrick arched an eyebrow. "Tesla... What a strange man he is. He lives on another planet."

Joni replaced her cup and saucer on the silver tray. She considered her words carefully. "Patrick, if, when you return home... Well, if things don't go the way you hope they'll go, will you light the lantern again? Will you try to go back in time again to save Eve and Colleen?"

Patrick stared ahead. "Of course, Joni. What else can I do? I'll keep trying until I find them."

He drew in a breath to bolster himself. "But right now, I'm going to light the lantern and get out of here before the police grab me. No doubt, they'll pin Vernon's murder on me as well. Old Joe McGuire will insist on it. And I don't want you or Darius pulled into this mess in any way."

Patrick reached into his pocket, drew out a wad of bills, and handed them to Joni. "Go ahead, take it. Give it to Darius. It won't begin to cover the bail, but it's something. Also, do me a big favor. I told you how Sarah Finn saved our lives."

Joni nodded. "Yes, the poor old woman."

"I want her to have a proper burial and not wind up in a pine box in some nameless pauper's grave. Can you, or Lavinia, find some charity that might accomplish that?"

Joni took the money. "Yes, Patrick, I'll manage something. And don't worry about Darius and his money. He's made plenty, and he inherited piles of it from his father years ago. In short, Darius is loaded. I'm keeping this money for myself," she said, laughing that young, wicked laugh that had always been contagious.

Patrick laughed with her. "I've missed you, Joni. The twenty-first century is not the same since you left."

Joni bored into him with her eyes. "It ain't over yet, Patrick. I may wind up on your doorstep someday."

A half hour later, Joni descended the stairs, dressed in a lovely, full-length coat and lavish feather hat. She carried a new floral canvas bag that held the time travel lantern.

At the base of the stairs, Patrick looked her over and said, "I wish you and I could take a Selfie right now."

Joni laughed again. "I called our chauffeur. He'll be waiting."

In the car, they sat in anxious silence with the canvas bag between them. Traffic was light as they drove uptown, under a light snowfall, toward Central Park. At Fifth and 72nd Street, they left the car and Joni instructed the driver to wait.

Patrick led the way, taking a different path from the one he and Evelyn had taken earlier, veering off to the right toward a line of empty park benches in the distance, dusted by thin snow.

The area was quiet, with the sound of their own footfalls scratching along the path, and the glowing park lights casting an eerie light.

Patrick chose the park bench, recalling the place being similar to an area in 2020. He waited uneasily while Joni tugged the lantern from her bag and sat it on the bench, taking a step back to view it.

"Hello, you old, crazy thing. Take Patrick back home safely."

Patrick stared at it, his pulse kicking through his veins. It was the same lantern, of course. The very same lantern he'd used to time travel from 1884 to 2019. It was twelve inches high, made of iron, with a tarnished green/brown patina. The four glass windowpanes were the same, with wire guards and an anchor design.

Patrick turned to Joni. "Do you have matches?"

She made a distorted face. "Of course I brought matches."

"Sorry, I'm nervous."

From her fat purse, she plucked out a box of long-stem matches. "There are a hundred in here, just in case."

"Let's hope it doesn't take that many."

Joni held up the box, her eyes revealing a spark of mischief. "I still haven't completely decided, Patrick."

"About going?"

"Yep. I even left a letter for Darius on my vanity, explaining everything."

Patrick put hands to hips. "Joni, are you serious?"

"You're damn right I'm serious."

Patrick lowered his arms and massaged the back of his neck. "I have a headache."

"So do I. I always get a headache whenever I'm around that friggin' lantern."

Their eyes met. "Well, then, Joni, step over here, light the thing and let's go."

Joni did so, moving in close to Patrick. She angled him a look. "Snow or no snow, let's sit down and hold hands. I don't want to get lost in some God-forsaken place, with you gone off to some other God-forsaken place."

They sat with the lantern between them. Joni slid the matchbox lid open, removed a match and looked hard at Patrick. "Ready?"

"Yes. Let's hope the saints are with us."

Joni swiped the match head against the striker on the side of the box. The match flared, then burst to life. Patrick had the glass door open, waiting. Joni bent forward, and with one hand protecting the flame, she guided the blazing match toward the wick. It caught, sparked, flicked and bloomed with light.

Patrick stared into it, reaching for Joni's hand. But her hand was gone. She was gone. He looked up. She had left the bench and backed away, waving at him.

"I can't do it, Patrick. Wish I could, but…" She shrugged. "Good luck. I love you. Tell Eve I love her, too. I know you'll find her. I just know it."

Patrick saw the golden light expand and surround him. Joni's form danced and trembled. She began to melt away into sparkles of blue light.

"I'll write to you, Patrick," Joni shouted. "I'll write you and Eve a letter, and I'll keep the lantern, just in case you need it again. You never know."

Joni waved. "Goodbye. Merry Christmas!"

The last thing Patrick saw was a bright flash of blue light. The world fell away beneath him and he sank like a rock into the dark blue ocean of infinity.

CHAPTER 48

The young woman sat slouched on a Central Park bench, smoking a cigarette and texting, with a blue protective mask hanging below her chin. She wore purple lipstick, pink sneakers and an old, too-large-for-her body bomber jacket. Her jeans were tight, with stylish holes in the knees, and her blonde hair was styled in a tailored mohawk, with pink tips.

To her right and from above, a mass of blue sparkling lights descended, whirling like a little twister. In a flash, the light disintegrated, and Patrick appeared, sitting upright, dazed and disoriented. It took a few moments before his blurry vision cleared and the breath in his lungs caught. He gulped in air and held a shaky hand over his eyes to block the morning sunlight. His heart raced, and his mind was scrambled.

Mid-text, the young woman cut him a glance. She'd not seen the whirling light, nor had she seen Patrick pop in from thin air. She'd been lost in her phone.

"Hey… How's it going?" she said, thumbs pausing.

Patrick peered at her, struggling to find his voice.

"I like that hat," the blonde said. "Nice coat too… Real retro look. I'm in fashion. I'm a junior at F. I. T."

Patrick managed to force out. "F. I. T.?"

"Yeah, you know, the Fashion Institute of Technology."

Patrick's brain slowly glued itself back together. He glanced about, squinting. He saw the blonde, her outfit, the cell phone and the people passing, their dress modern and casual. He jerked erect as if touched by a live wire.

"Where am I?"

The girl drew back. "Whoa… Hey, you okay? Where's your mask?"

"What day is it?"

"What day?"

"Yes, what day is it?"

"Saturday…"

"What's the date?"

The young woman's eyes grew suspicious. "Are you sure you're okay?"

"Just tell me the date," Patrick said, with force. "Please."

"Okay, okay. It's December nineteenth."

"Year? What year?"

"Oh, man. Have you like, gone all crazy?"

"Please. What is the year?"

"It's 2020, okay?"

Patrick's eyes had wildness in them. "December nineteenth… It's 2020."

He shot up. The world spun around him, and he dropped back heavily onto the bench, reaching for his sore and swimming head.

Frightened, the young girl sprang up and hurried off, shouldering her backpack, glancing over her shoulder at Patrick, who was bent over, his head in his hands.

It took precious minutes before Patrick recovered enough to connect all the dots. As always, part of his atoms still seemed to be hovering, or left behind in 1925.

He pushed up, searching. "What time was it?" he said to himself. He saw a young couple drift by and he hurried over to them. "What time is it? Please, do you have the time?"

The couple looked him over warily, but the man checked his phone. "It's after nine o'clock. Put a mask on, man."

Panic stabbed Patrick like a hot poker to the chest. Eve's airplane was just taking off!

Patrick snatched for the man's phone, but the man jerked left, his body protecting it.

"Hey, man, get the hell away from me!"

The couple quick-stepped it away.

Desperate, Patrick saw a well-dressed Asian woman wearing a black mask. He ran to her. "Please, Miss, please may I use your phone? It's an emergency. Please. It's a matter of life and death."

The attractive woman appraised him with slow, careful eyes. She reached into her purse, drew out the phone and entered her password. "Give me the number. I'll call."

"Thank you," Patrick said, breathless.

He shook his head to clear it, worked to focus his still blurry eyes, and rattled off Eve's number. His heart kicked as he waited. Each ring was an agony.

"It went into voicemail," the woman said.

Patrick cursed out loud. "Tell her to get off that plane. Tell her to get off that plane now!"

Startled, the Asian woman turned away and hurried off, not looking back.

He had to get to a phone. Had to. Who else could he call? Like a lightning strike, the name Dr. Simon Wallister snapped into Patrick's head. He frantically raced about the area, drawing up to people who had phones. He begged to use one, pleaded, but no one offered. Thinking Patrick was out of his mind, they scurried away from him.

The heavy weight of the moment was suffocating. Patrick fought for air, fought for breath, tossing away his hat, yanking down his tie and unbuttoning his top shirt button. He stood breathing, pulsing, and lost.

He was trapped in a tornado of emotion. If he'd only had a phone, he could have called Eve's cousin and father; he could have called friends. Having no money or credit cards for a taxi, he'd need to run home. Run as fast as he could. Time was dripping away.

CHAPTER 49

In a throb of misery, Patrick sat on his living room couch in utter darkness. He'd been able to get into the apartment thanks to their neighbor Brantley, who sometimes walked Colin and had a spare set of their keys. Brantley had come to the door with a toothbrush in his hand, apologizing that he didn't have time to talk; he was rushing to get to an appointment. Patrick took the keys, mumbled a "thanks" and stumbled toward his apartment door.

Patrick had been home about an hour, and he was filled with sarcasm and dark thoughts. Had the time lantern performed another one of its clever tricks—a worthless trick in this case? A joke? Had it been programmed to reflect Nikola Tesla's dark humor? Would he have thought the situation funny? "Well, look at it this way, Mr. Gantly," he might have said. "You were very close… infinitesimally close. You must admit that the timing, although unfortunately not perfect, was still remarkable."

Patrick had stood in the dark living room, shedding his coat, letting it fall where it landed. He had flopped down on the couch, his spirit killed, his body lethargic.

He had not left the couch since, not to switch on a light or turn on his cell phone. The messages would be the same as before. There would be several calls from a sobbing Denise, Eve's cousin, and there would be more calls from Eve's family telling him about the tragic plane crash.

So Patrick sat in the dark, unable to move or process all that had happened to him and why. Now, as he saw it, he had but two choices: live in this time without Eve and Colleen, or return to the bedroom closet, retrieve the lantern, light the cursed thing and escape to yet another time. Who knows where he'd end up? Would another version of Eve appear, maybe in the 1700s or perhaps even in the future?

At some point, Patrick was overcome by grief and exhaustion, and he teetered over and fell asleep.

Patrick heard a buzzing sound and, in his dream, he saw a hillside of wildflowers, shouting with color, honeybees zooming by his ears. He strolled with a walking stick as a swarm of honeybees descended on the flowers, as the sound of a rushing ocean reached his ears.

With Colin at his heels, he climbed a winding dirt path up a slope until he crested it. Shading his eyes from the sun, he peered down. There she was. Eve! She was roaming the tide as the sea rushed in, glazing the beach and splashing around her ankles.

But those loud, buzzing bees still swarmed him, swooping down in dark clouds, alive with a persistent Morse-code-style buzzing.

Patrick jerked awake when he heard the key in the lock. He sat up, sensing a threat. Where was his revolver? He couldn't remember. What time was it? What century was he in?

When the door swung open, and a square of yellow light spilled into the room in stark illumination, Patrick stared at the mirage before him. He was still dreaming, he was certain of that.

"Patrick?"

He heard his breathing in the quiet air.

"Patrick? Are you in there?"

In that broken, insane and startling moment, Patrick heard himself say, "Eve... Eve!"

And the mirage entered the room and found the light switch. Light crashed into the room, and Patrick blocked the light with the flat of his hand.

It was impossible. There she was. Eve Gantly, cradling Colleen.

She stared at Patrick strangely, reading his stunned surprise.

Patrick was caught in a moment of happy terror. Was Eve real or was she not?

"Patrick? What's the matter? What's happened?"

Patrick could only stare.

"Why didn't you answer the door? I pushed that buzzer for a good minute. I left my suitcase and Colleen's bag out in the hallway. Will you go get them?"

As if still in a trance, Patrick slowly rose to his feet. Afraid that Eve could still be a ghost or a mirage, he went to her, his eyes roaming across her face. He looked at Colleen, all pink from the weather. She reached for him and made a little gurgling sound. He took one of her fingers, holding it tenderly.

"Patrick... Are you all right?"

Patrick reached for Eve, wrapping his wide arms around her and Colleen. Without a word, he held them close, still uncertain if they were real. How could they be real?

He released them and stepped back, examining Eve's face again, her eyes, her nose, her mouth, and her beautiful hair spilling out from beneath her ski cap. He kissed Colleen on the forehead.

With tearing eyes, Patrick said, "Heaven and the saints be praised."

"Patrick, you're acting weird. I've only been gone a few days."

Patrick took in a breath. "How are you here? How can you be here?"

"I texted you a hundred times, and I called you. No answer. You scared the hell out of me. Where have you been?"

"Didn't you get on that airplane?" Patrick asked.

"I texted you."

"I didn't turn on my phone. Did you get on your father's airplane? Just tell me."

Eve squinted at him. "No, Patrick, I didn't."

Patrick waited for more.

"I left you a message... I told you about it."

"What did it say?"

Eve looked over her shoulder. "Maybe you should get the bags."

"No. I can't wait. I've got to know. Please. Why didn't you get on that plane?"

Eve sharpened her eyes on him. "What's happened, Patrick?"

"Tell me. You were supposed to get on that plane. You and Colleen... your parents... were on that plane."

Eve's studied him. "No, we didn't go. With his connections, Dad helped us get a flight to LaGuardia. That's why I'm here."

Patrick's mind boiled with questions and possibilities. "But why? Why didn't you?"

Colleen began to fuss, and Eve gently rocked her. "You're going to think I'm nuts, but I had a dream."

"A dream? What dream?"

"Last night. In my dream, I was with you. It was a strange and vivid dream. So real. We were in some other time... the 1920s, I think. Anyway, you had kissed me, and we had made love. It was such a wonderful dream. I had fallen in love with you all over again. I was crazy in love with you. Anyway, afterwards, just as I was falling asleep, you whispered something in my ear, over and over. You told me not to get on that plane."

Patrick's face turned white. Words failed him.

"When I woke up this morning, I couldn't shake the dream or your warning. So I told Dad we shouldn't go to Florida. It didn't feel right. The dream had been so real, Patrick. I can't explain it, but I actually felt that I was living in that time. I even had a daughter... and, as wacky as it sounds, I was married to some other guy that I hated."

Their eyes held while the seconds passed. Eve watched Patrick's changing expression shift from anxiety to wonder and, finally, to love.

He reached out a hand and brushed her cheek. "Thank God and Tesla for strange dreams."

Eve smiled. "Tesla?"

"I'll tell you all about it, but not now."

Eve went to tiptoes and kissed him. "Alright, Detective Gantly. I'm just so happy to be home with you." Then she glanced down at Colleen and held her up, talking to her. "Good thing we got here before your daddy left to catch that train to Florida," she said. "I'd be pretty upset if we had flown home and he wasn't here."

Patrick took Colleen from Eve and kissed her on the cheek. She snuggled against his chest and made a cooing sound of comfort.

Eve glanced about. "What were you doing here in the dark?" Eve said. "Why didn't you pick up or answer my texts?" She lifted a stern eyebrow. "Were you out with that professor of yours?"

"No, Eve. I was out with you, and we had one devil of a time."

CHAPTER 50

It was well after midnight. Eve and Patrick were sitting up in bed, their backs propped against pillows, their thoughts still turning and wrestling with all they'd shared, past and present, dream and reality. They'd finished the last of the medium pizza, and the empty box lay on the floor, near Colin's dog bed and Colleen's crib.

They were drinking the last of a bottle of red wine and listening to Christmas music.

"I'm telling you, Patrick, that dream seemed so real. Your description of Virginia is exactly how I saw her in my dream. I knew she was my daughter, and I was so worried about her. I despised Vernon. And then you entered my dream. You were the same except... you were different somehow, or I was different. Does that make any sense?"

"Yes, it does, because when I time traveled and met you in 1925, you were the same, and yet you weren't the same, but I couldn't figure it out. Well, anyway, nothing makes sense anymore."

He leaned over and kissed her on the head. "But this time, I'm glad I had that lantern. At least I had the chance of traveling back in time and rescuing you and Colleen."

Eve looked at him. "I don't understand, Patrick. How does the whole thing fit together? Was I Evelyn in a past life? And if I wasn't Evelyn, then why do I remember that dream? Why didn't I get aboard Dad's airplane, and why don't I remember dying in a plane crash, like you said we did?"

Patrick shook his head. "I don't know, Eve. All I know is, once again, the lantern saved us."

Eve thought about that. "Patrick... If I *was* Evelyn in a past life, then were you Patrick in a past life?"

Patrick considered the ceiling. "I haven't a clue in the world."

Eve took a sip of wine. "In that dream, I certainly knew you were Patrick Gantly, and I knew that I was in love with you. Do you know what else I remember? I remember thinking, why did it take you so long before you finally decided to make love to me? I was getting angry at you."

Patrick grew defensive. "Because I didn't know if you were Eve, or Evelyn... or what. I didn't even know who I was or why I was there. Things were pretty chaotic back there. I was completely confused. I didn't know if I'd ever return to 2020. And I was about to face a hangman's noose."

Eve reached for him, wrapped an arm around his neck and drew him down to her lips. She gave him a long kiss, filled with longing. They were nose-to-nose when Eve said, "Patrick, you kept your promise."

"What promise?"

"Don't play dumb with me, Detective Sergeant Patrick Gantly. The Christmas Eve promise. Last year on Christmas Eve I said I wanted both of us to promise that, no matter what happened to us, no matter what time or place we found ourselves in, no matter what obstacles we faced, we would always find each other, help each other and love each other, for all time. Remember?"

"Yes, I remember, but let's not make another promise like that this Christmas. We both barely survived it."

Eve nodded. "I wish I could have seen Joni. I wish she had come back with you. I miss her like crazy."

"She was so close to coming with me. She begged off at the last minute. I asked her to check in on Evelyn now and then. I told her I hoped they could become friends."

Eve's eyes shined with eagerness. "Do you think we'll get a letter from Joni, Patrick?"

"She said she would write."

Eve drained her wine glass. "Mr. Detective, Patrick…

"Oh my, the good saints above protect me. When you say my name like that, I know I'm in for it. What?"

"Have you thought about it?"

"Thought about what?"

"The lantern."

"I don't want to think about the lantern, ever again."

"You always say that."

"And I always mean it. I'd rather think about shopping for a Christmas tree or talking about all the presents you're going to buy me this year."

"Patrick... You were a detective. I know you have thought about this."

Patrick blew out a breath. "All right, Eve, stop beating about the bush and tell me."

"We have a lantern in the closet, don't we? I mean, you opened the safe an hour ago to make sure it's still there, right?"

"Yes. It's still there, right where it should be."

Patrick folded his arms and turned his face from her. "Yes, Eve, I know what you're thinking and, yes, I have thought about it. I thought about it that night back in 1925, when Joni lighted the lantern and then dashed away from me."

Eve folded her arms, pondering. She said, "If Joni contacts us, will she send us her lantern again?"

Patrick drank his glass dry, holding the glass up to his cheek. "Is that even possible? How can there be two identical lanterns existing in the same time and space? Joni sent us a lantern in 2019. This year, I went back in time to 1925, using that lantern. To return here, in 2020, I used the same lantern that she was going to send us in 2019. In 1925, she hadn't sent it yet. But that lantern is in your closet in a safe."

Eve finished the thought. "So here it is: if Joni sends us another lantern, it will be the same identical lantern that we already have in my closet."

They stared ahead, thinking, processing.

Eve finally said, "Okay, my head is about to explode. I can't think about this anymore. Let's get some sleep before Colleen wakes us up at the crack of dawn wanting her breakfast."

An hour later, in the deep quiet and silky darkness, Eve was awake, her mind spinning, but her body relaxed and thankful. It was so good to be home.

She nestled in close to Patrick, feeling the warmth of him, smelling the man of him, feeling his sleeping breath on her. She lifted on an elbow, leaned over and whispered in his ear.

"Hey, Detective Gantly… I will always love you."

EPILOGUE

On Christmas Eve, Eve and Patrick were in the kitchen, hard at work on an eggnog recipe Eve had found on a *YouTube* video. Colin was underfoot, sniffing, and Colleen was close by in her crib on the edge of the bedroom, making smacking sounds.

Their smart speaker was playing a Christmas mix, with Michael Bublé singing *Have Yourself a Merry Little Christmas*.

Eve had already whisked the egg yolk and sugar together in a yellow mixing bowl and was putting cream, milk, salt and nutmeg into a saucepan which Patrick held over medium-high heat.

"After the cream and milk simmer, we have to do something called 'tempering' the eggs," Eve said, her face pinched in concentration.

"Okay, but how do we know when the milk and cream have simmered enough?"

"Instinct, I guess," Eve said. "All I know is that we don't want them to boil."

They studied the saucepan's ingredients like two mad scientists hoping for a miracle. Eve was the first to spot them: bubbles pimpling the surface. "It's simmering! We did it! Okay... Now, are you ready for the next part?"

Patrick nodded. "Yep, bring it on."

Very carefully, Eve took small spoonfuls of the hot mixture and added them to the egg mixture in the yellow bowl. "I'm not sure if I'm doing this right. Things never go as they should the first time you do them."

"Well, we're about to find out. As long as we add a generous bit of Irish whiskey into it, I'm sure it will be okay."

Eve continued adding spoonfuls of the hot liquid into the eggs. When most of it was mixed in, they poured the entire mixture back into the saucepan.

"You have to whisk it now," Eve said, "until it starts to thicken. Then you take it off the heat."

After thirty seconds, Patrick looked up. "What do you think? Has it thickened enough?"

Eve stooped, staring. "I think so. I mean, what do I know? I'm not the best cook in the world, you know. You'd think I *would* be. I got A's in chemistry."

"Well, does it look like the mixture on *YouTube*?"

"I guess so. Yeah, I think so."

"There's nothing like a definite maybe to inspire confidence in your sous-chef," Patrick said.

"Okay, turn off the heat. I'll add the vanilla. It's supposed to continue thickening as it cools," Eve said.

"Then what?"

Eve glanced up, her face flushed and damp with perspiration. "Then we refrigerate the whole thing until it's chilled."

"When do we add the whiskey?" Patrick asked, hands on his hips. "Let's face it, Eve, the whiskey is the most important ingredient, at least it was back in 1885."

Eve winked at him. "If I know you, Patrick, back in 1885, you skipped the eggnog entirely and just went straight for the whiskey."

"Truer words were never spoken, Mrs. Gantly."

"Okay, so why don't you just splash some into a glass right now and let's pretend it's 1885? Get us both started."

Patrick pointed a finger at her. "You, Eve Sharland Kennedy Gantly, are a pretty, sexy genius, especially in those tight jeans, red top and Christmas tree apron."

Eve offered a bob of a bow. "Thank you, kind sir. Now, please wipe my face with that towel over there. I'm sweating like it's the Fourth of July."

Just as Patrick was tipping a bottle of 18-year-old Tullamore Dew into a glass, the front buzzer sounded.

Eve and Patrick traded startled looks.

"Oh, wow," Eve said, glancing up at the kitchen clock. "It's just after five."

"Expecting anyone?" Patrick asked.

Eve screwed up her face. "You know the answer to that one. Okay, you go answer it while I slip the eggnog into the fridge."

At the front door speaker, Patrick pressed the TALK button. "Yes, who is it?"

"Lorna Paulson. I'm looking for Mr. and Mrs. Patrick Gantly."

"I'm Patrick Gantly."

"I'm an attorney, with Austen, Clark and Paulson. May I speak with you and your wife?"

A few minutes later, Patrick opened the door and Lorna Paulson entered, wearing a blue mask, a stylish dark winter coat, and leather gloves.

Eve noticed Ms. Paulson was carrying a black leather attaché case, but no package. Did that mean there was no lantern, as there had been in 2019?

While Patrick shut the door, and Eve and Patrick slipped on their masks, they exchanged introductions and Christmas greetings, and then Eve hung Lorna's coat in the closet.

Lorna was an African-American woman in her 40s, with a curly, relaxed hairstyle, a fitted blue suit, and low heels. She had an open, friendly face, with alert, intelligent eyes and a graceful manner.

She sat in the recliner, six feet away from Patrick, who eased down onto the leather couch. Eve left to retrieve Colleen and soon returned to join Patrick on the couch, bouncing Colleen on her knee.

"What a pretty little baby girl," Lorna said, smiling. "What's her name?"

Eve turned Colleen to face Lorna. "Colleen. Say hello, Colleen."

Colleen made a squealing sound and then stuck a thumb in her mouth.

"Hello, Colleen," Lorna said. "Merry Christmas."

Eve caressed the top of Colleen's head. "She's had her nap, so she's a happy girl."

Lorna looked about. "I love your Christmas tree with that lovely angel on top. And the lights around the mantel make the room so cozy. Are you staying in town for Christmas?"

"Yes," Eve said. "My parents and some friends are coming for dinner tomorrow. How about you? Will you stay in town?"

"Yes. I have a big family and all fifteen of us are cooking different things, so it's going to be a kind of potluck Christmas."

While Patrick stared at Lorna's briefcase in expectation, Colin circled the tall, glistening Christmas tree, finally settling on the hearth before the fireplace.

Lorna lifted her nose. "What wonderful smells."

Patrick said, "Eggnog and a pumpkin pie. It's our first attempt at the homemade eggnog. Would you like some? It hasn't fully chilled, and we haven't added whipped cream, but I stole a little sip earlier. It's good."

"Oh, no, thanks. I've already been eating way too many sweets."

"I'll drop in a bit of Irish whiskey, Ms. Paulson. Guaranteed to satisfy," Patrick said.

Lorna's eyes shined in the firelight. "How can I resist? And you'll both have one, won't you?"

Eve and Patrick nodded.

Patrick went to the kitchen, soon returning with two cups for the ladies. He was back in a minute with his own, and they adjusted their masks while they toasted and then drank to a Merry Christmas.

They sat in silence for a time, while Lorna set her cup of eggnog aside and removed some papers from her case.

"All right, now, let's get down to business, and I hope it will be pleasant business," Lorna said, with a smile. "Our law firm represents Mr. Charles Benedict Vanderbilt."

Eve shot Patrick a look. He kept his eyes on Lorna, all ears.

"Mr. Vanderbilt is the grandson of Benedict and Lavinia Vanderbilt. He is currently in his sixties and is in fragile health. In any event, he has entrusted our law firm to handle his legal business as it concerns his grandmother, Lavinia Vanderbilt, and his great-grandmother, Mrs. Joan Katherine Kosarin Foster. Accordingly, there is a letter in the Vanderbilt file that was willed to Mr. Charles Vanderbilt by his grandmother, Lavinia Vanderbilt. The letter was given to her by her mother, Joan Kosarin Foster."

Lorna held up the letter. "I have that letter here."

Eve and Patrick stared eagerly.

"As you will see, it is hand-addressed to Mr. and Mrs. Patrick Gantly, and it is stamped Personal and Confidential, Not to Be Opened by Any Other Person or Persons. Our instructions were clear: if our firm was unable to locate either of you in 2020, or next year, 2021, or, finally, in 2022, we were to destroy the letter."

Eve swallowed. Patrick remained still.

"So, now that that is out of the way, all I need from you is your signatures on this release form, and then I will notarize it. Do you have any questions?"

Eve and Patrick shook their heads.

After both had signed the release form and
Lorna had notarized it, she ceremoniously
handed the letter to Eve.

"I'm glad I was able to find you this year.
Have a wonderful Christmas and New Year,"
Lorna said, gathering her things, then standing.
"Let's hope next year we won't have to wear
these masks."

Patrick found her coat and led her to the door.

"Thank you for that delicious eggnog," Lorna
said. "I'll have to add some Irish whiskey to my
father's recipe."

Patrick winked and nodded. "And thank you
for toasting a merry Christmas with us, Ms.
Paulson."

When Ms. Paulson was gone, Patrick turned
to see Eve staring at the creamy bond envelope
and Joni's unmistakable handwriting—the
slanted letters, the T's crossed high and long.
Eve couldn't help but feel a pang of longing, and
she thought to herself, *I wish you had come back
with Patrick, Joni.*

Eve passed the envelope to Patrick. "You
read, I'll listen."

Patrick nodded, accepting the letter. He slid a
forefinger under the flap and carefully opened it,
the old glue not giving way easily.

He reached in and took out the heavy bond
pages, which were folded twice. He reached up,
switched on the overhead lamp for more light,

and smoothed out the pages. After taking an anxious breath, he began to read aloud.

Dear Eve and Patrick:

I hope this letter finds you both together again, reading this in your Upper West Side apartment, way out in the future, in 2020.

It has been eighteen years since I last saw you, Patrick. It's Christmas Eve, 1943, and I am eighty-nine years old. When you were here, Patrick, you told me that I had already written you a letter and that you and Eve read it in 2019. But then you returned to my life, and everything must have somehow changed, or been reset. Frankly, I have thought about this and I don't have any idea how all this time travel business works. All I know is, I was grateful you returned, Patrick. It was wonderful to see you again and spend some time together. It felt a little like the old days.

Evelyn Stratford and I became such good friends—the best of friends—just as Eve and I had been, and that would not have been possible if you hadn't time traveled to 1925, Patrick.

There's so much I want to say in this letter, but my strength isn't what it was, even a year ago. The doctor tells me my blood pressure is high and I have hypertension. He prescribed some damn medicine called Pentaquine. They're giving it to soldiers in the war for malaria. I don't take it, of course. How I have missed modern medicine. Anyway, my heart likes to race, I sometimes see spots and I get short of breath. Well, the hell with that! I still do a dance routine or two. I just don't kick as high as I used to.

Anyway, Eve, I hope you did not die in that awful airplane crash. I hope Patrick was able to return and somehow save you and little Colleen from that. After Patrick lighted that lantern and vanished, I prayed myself to sleep every night for years, praying for all of you. Praying that you'd all be reunited, safe, happy and always in love.

Eve, how can I tell you about Evelyn? When I look into her eyes, I see your eyes. When she laughs, it is your laugh. Her generous, good heart is your heart. Before Darius died some years ago, even he finally admitted that Evelyn was your twin, Eve, and it unsettled him. First, time travel unsettled him, lol, and then reincarnation. I couldn't help but laugh, and that really set him off.

Patrick, after you left, my friendship with Evelyn grew and deepened. For a time, she was depressed and sad. But then, believe it or not, about six months later, she met a man. He's older, was fifty-one when they met. They were married about a year later. He's a doctor, a surgeon, and he is so good and kind to Evelyn. I really like him. His name is Fredrick Vanston, and he worked for a time at Evelyn's clinic, for free. He also encouraged Evelyn to study psychology, and she did. They were very compatible, and after Evelyn got her degree, she was so happy working at the clinic as a psychologist. For a few years, she also worked with poor, sick and battered women, gratis, at a clinic in the Bowery.

Evelyn and Fredrick moved from New York about two years ago, when Frederick's health began to fail. They live in a little town outside Philadelphia, where he was originally from. I can't tell you how much I miss Evelyn. I received a letter from her a week ago and she said that she was still working at a local hospital, but that Frederick had retired, and he was feeling stronger.

Unfortunately, Evelyn's daughter, Virginia, lost her child in childbirth in 1926. She went a little crazy after that and, as you know, she was already a little crazy. Sadly, she ran off with another gangster type and, in 1930, she and her man were found shot to death in their hotel room in Chicago. It's not a pretty story, but there it is. Thank God Frederick was there for Evelyn. The news hit her hard, even though she hadn't seen or heard from Virginia in over two years.

After you disappeared, Patrick, the police looked all over hell-and-half-of-Russia for you. They were baffled, and I laughed at them when I read about it in the newspaper. They classified Vernon Scott's death as a failed robbery attempt. They said that your friend, Sarah, tried to rob him and he shot her. The police did visit Evelyn but, fortunately, they did not charge her with any crime.

As to Sarah Finn, I did as you wished. I asked Lavinia if one of her charities could ensure the poor woman got a proper burial. It was done, and Sarah was buried at The Cemetery of the Evergreens in Brooklyn, with a stone marker that simply reads, "Here Lies Sarah Finn." I hope that is what you wanted.

You might be interested in learning what happened to Joe McGuire. I hadn't thought about him in years when, in 1934, I read his obituary. It said he died of a heart attack soon after prohibition ended. His only daughter, Louise, had married a musician some years before and they had moved to Paris. She did not return to New York to attend her father's funeral.

Now we must talk about the time lantern. After you left, Patrick, I didn't want any part of that lantern. Tempted once. Tempted twice. Darius and I had a couple of doozy arguments over the years, and more than once I was tempted to light that thing and go anywhere it took me.

To make a long story short, I took the thing to Nikola Tesla. Do you know what he said? "I don't want it. I was finished with that toy many years ago. Go put it on the street somewhere and let's see what the random numbers do with it."

Well, I didn't put it on the street. I have willed the lantern to Lavinia, with the provision that she never tell anyone about it. She promised and, fifteen years ago, I gave it to her. We have not spoken about it since. What I'm saying is, I have no idea where it is or what she has done with it. I hope this news doesn't upset you. According to what Patrick told me, you already had a lantern, and you didn't want another. And I couldn't wrap my head around the fact that you would have identical lanterns that somehow came from two different times. Is that even possible?

So where is the lantern? No idea. Perhaps Lavinia will use it someday? Perhaps her descendants. Who knows? She was completely blown away when I told her that Evelyn wasn't Eve, but perhaps Eve in a past life. The thing about Lavinia... Well, she actually said, using my slang, "That is awesome!" Lol.

All right, my good friends, it's time for me to sign off. I miss you both and I love you both. I'm not going to say goodbye because, who knows, we might see each other again. Hey, in this crazy world, anything is possible. Right?

Merry Christmas!

My deepest love to you both. A kiss to Colleen, and a pat on the head to the dog. (Sorry, I forgot his name.)

Joni

December 24, 1943

Later that night, Eve, Patrick, Colleen and Colin piled into a cab and headed down to Rockefeller Center to look at the towering, glittering Christmas tree.

When it began to snow, despite social distancing and mask wearing, there was celebration in the air.

Eve felt joyous and silly, turning in a circle, dancing with Colleen. "Feel the snow, baby? See? It's snow. Santa Claus is coming to town, and he's going to be wearing one of those masks over that long white beard. Won't that be something, Daddy?" she giggled, looking up at Patrick.

Patrick shook his head. "Personally, I think he'll take some time off this year."

"No way," Eve exclaimed.

Colleen's eyes searched in wonder, her hands swatting at the snowflakes. When Eve handed her off to Patrick, she made gurgling sounds. It was his turn to dance with her.

Eve held Colin's leash and laughed, enjoying the show. With one hand, she snapped photos of Patrick prancing about with Colleen in front of the tree. A Salvation Army volunteer, wearing a

Santa cap, was ringing a bell, dancing and singing along with a Brenda Lee recording of *Rockin' Around the Christmas Tree.* Patrick joined in.

"Patrick, you're way off key," Eve said, laughing. "I mean, *way* off key."

Grinning, he turned Colleen to face Eve. Colleen giggled. "Colleen doesn't think I'm off key," Patrick said. "She loves it. She's just like her father. Completely, and proudly, tone deaf."

As joyful crowds rambled, pointed and took photos, Eve snapped her own photos. Colin barked and gobbled a treat that she adroitly slipped him. Tugging the dog, Eve hurried to Patrick's side to take a family selfie.

She glanced up at him, angling the cell phone so they were all in the frame. "Hey, there, Patrick and Colleen. You're both beautiful. Smile for the camera. Hold it... Hold it... Lower your chin just a little, Patrick. Lift Colleen's head just a bit. Yep. Perfect."

Thank You!

Thank you for taking the time to read *The Christmas Eve Promise*. If you enjoyed it, please consider telling your friends or posting a short review. Word of mouth is an author's best friend, and it is much appreciated.

Thank you,
Elyse Douglas

The Christmas Diary
Christmas for Juliet
The Christmas Bridge
The Date Before Christmas
The Christmas Women
Christmas Ever After
The Summer Diary
The Summer Letters
The Other Side of Summer
Wanting Rita

Time Travel Novels

The Christmas Eve Letter (A Time Travel Novel) Book 1
The Christmas Eve Daughter (A Time Travel Novel) Book 2

The Christmas Eve Secret (A Time Travel Novel)
Book 3
The Lost Mata Hari Ring (A Time Travel Novel)
The Christmas Town (A Time Travel Novel)
Time Change (A Time Travel Novel)
Time Sensitive (A Time Travel Novel)
Time Shutter (A Time Travel Novel)

Romantic Suspense Novels
Daring Summer
Frantic
Betrayed

www.elysedouglas.com

Editorial Reviews

THE LOST MATA HARI RING – A Time Travel Novel
by Elyse Douglas

"This book is hard to put down! It is pitch-perfect and hits all
the right notes. It is the best book I have read in a while!
5 Stars!"

--Bound4Escape Blog and Reviews

"The characters are well defined, and the scenes easily
visualized. It is a poignant, bitter-sweet emotionally charged
read. 5-Stars!"
--Rockin' Book Reviews

"*The Lost Mata Hari Ring* captivated me to the end!"
--StoryBook Reviews

"A captivating adventure..."
--Community Bookstop

"...Putting *The Lost Mata Hari Ring* down for any length of time proved to be impossible."
--Lisa's Writopia

"I found myself drawn into the story and holding my breath to see what would happen next..."
--Blog: A Room Without Books is Empty

THE CHRISTMAS TOWN – A Time Travel Novel
by Elyse Douglas

"The Christmas Town is a beautifully written story. It draws you in from the first page, and fully engages you up until the very last. The story is funny, happy, and magical. The characters are likable and well-rounded. This is a great book to read during the holiday season, and a delightful read any time of the year."
--Bauman Book Reviews

"I would love to see this book become another one of those beloved Christmas film traditions. Don't miss this novel!"
--A Night's Dream of Books

THE SUMMER LETTERS – A Novel
by Elyse Douglas

"A perfect summer read!"

--Fiction Addiction

"In Elyse Douglas' novel *The Summer Letters*, the characters' emotions, their drives, passions and memories are all so expertly woven; we get a taste of what life was like for veterans, women, small town folk, and all those people we think have lived too long to remember (but they never really forget, do they?).

I couldn't stop reading, not for a moment. Such an amazing read. Flawless."

5 Stars! -

--Anteria Writes Blog - To Dream, To Write, To Live

"A wonderful, beautiful love story that I absolutely enjoyed reading."

5 Stars!

--Books, Dreams, Life - Blog

"The Summer Letters is a fabulous choice for the beach or this year, so you can live and breathe the same feelings and smells as the characters in this wonderful story."

--Reads & Reels Blog

Printed in Great Britain
by Amazon